SILVER

STEVEN SAVILE

VARIANCE
ARKANSAS

Variance Publishing
1610 South Pine St.,
Cabot, AR 72023
(501) 843-BOOK
www.variancepublishing.com

Library of Congress Catalog Number— 2009942288

ISBN: 1-935142-05-4
ISBN-13: 978-1-935142-05-8

Cover Illustration by Larry Rostant
Jacket Design by Stanley Tremblay
Interior Layout by Stanley Tremblay
Interior Dagger design by Daniele Serra
Maps provided by Jackie McDermott

Judas Repentant, Rembrant

Visit Steven Savile on the web at: www.stevensavile.com.

10   9   8   7   6   5   4   3   2   1

The people in my life are worth so much more than this, but this is the best of me and I give it with love to

Mum, Dad, David, Sonia, Sarah, Amy and Marie

Everything I do is either for you or because of you. I guess that means you have a lot to answer for.

ACKNOWLEDGEMENTS

A few good men and women helped make me look a lot smarter than I really am. To those unsung heroes in the trenches a simple thank you is never enough:

Jim Sowter • Deborah J Stevenson • Kurt Criscione
Sonia Helbig • Shane Thomson • Stan Tremblay

And of course Tim Schulte, for deciding to unleash this monster on an unsuspecting world.

Then there are those who help keep us sane while we lock ourselves away in the local café, hammering out our mad plans. So to those people who come bearing coffee and smiles:

Sandi • Milo • Pierre • Siba
Rima • Kim • Jacob

You guys feed my soul. Without you Silver would have taken years to write. It's amazing what caffeine can do!

Silver owes a debt of gratitude to too many great musicians to name, but, to one in particular, James Grant, thank you not only for the decades of good listening but for so graciously providing Noah a soundtrack for his midnight drive through London.

And last but by no means least, friends, Romans, and countrymen:

Stefan Lindblad • Steve Lockley • Kevin J Anderson
Stel Pavlou • Brian M Logan

Life would be pretty dull without you guys.

SILVER

STEVEN SAVILE

PIECES OF HATE
THEN - THE TESTIMONY OF
MENAHEM BEN JAIR

One garden had a serpent, the other had him.

There was a fractured beauty to it; a curious symmetry. The serpent had goaded that first betrayal with honeyed words, the forbidden fruit bitten, and the original sin on the lips of the first weak man. His own betrayal had been acted out from behind a mask of love, again on the lips, and sealed with a kiss. Both betrayals were made all the more ugly by the beauty of their surroundings. That was the agony of the garden.

Iscariot felt the weight of silver in his hand.

It was so much heavier than a few coins ought to be. But then they were more than a few coins now, weren't they? They were a life bought with silver. They were his guilt. He closed his hand around the battered leather pouch, making a fist. How much was a life worth? Really? He had thought about it a lot in the hours since the kiss. Was it the weight of the coins that bought it? The handful of iron nails driven into the wooden cross that ended it? Or the meat left to feed the carrion birds? All of these? None of them? He wanted to believe it was something more spiritual, more honest: the impact that it had on the lives of those around it, the sum of the good and the bad, deeds and thoughts.

"Take them, please," he held out the pouch for the farmer to take. "It's five times what the land's worth. More."

"I don't want your blood money, traitor," the man hawked and spat at the dirt between his feet. "Now go."

"Where can I go? I am alone."

"Anywhere away from this place. Somewhere people don't know you. If I was you, I'd go back to the temple and try to buy my soul back."

The man turned his back on him and walked away, leaving Iscariot alone in the field. "If that doesn't work," he called without turning back, "I'd throw myself on God's mercy."

Iscariot followed the direction of the man's gaze to the field's single blackened tree. Lightning had struck it years ago, cleaving it down the middle. Its wooden guts were rotted through, but a single hangman's branch still reached out, beckoning to him against the dusk sky.

He hurled the pouch at the mocking tree. One of the seams split as it hit the ground, scattering the coins across the parched dirt. A moment later he was on his knees, scrambling after them, tears of loss streaming down his face. Loss, not for the man he had betrayed, but for the man he had been and the man he could have been. He lay there as the sun failed, wishing the sun would sear away his flesh and char his bones, but dawn came and he was still alive.

Under the anvil of the sun, he stumbled back through the gates of Jerusalem, and wandered the streets for hours.

His body's screams were sweated out in the heat. There was no forgiveness in the air. No one would look at him. But he couldn't bear to look at his shadow as it stretched out in front of him, so why should they want to look at him? He deserved their hate. He shielded his eyes and looked up toward Crucifixion Hill. He thought he could see the shadow of the cross, black against the grass. The soldiers had taken the bodies down hours before. The only shadows up there now were ghosts.

At the temple they mocked him as he pleaded with the Pharisees to take back the silver in exchange for his confession and absolution.

"Live with what you have done, Judas, son of Kerioth. With this one deed you have ensured your legacy. Your name will live on: Judas the Betrayer, Judas the Coward. The money is yours, Iscariot, your burden. You cannot buy back the innocence of your soul, and it is not as though you have not killed before. Now go, the sight of you sickens us," the Pharisee said, sweeping his arm out to encompass the entire congregation gathered in prayer.

He hit Iscariot's hand, scattering the silver he clutched across the stone floor. Judas fell to his knees, as though groveling at the feet of the holy man. Head down, he collected the scattered coins. The holy man kicked him away scornfully. "Take your blood money and be gone, traitor."

Iscariot struggled to his feet and stumbled toward the door.

On the road to Gethsemane he saw the familiar figure of Mary seated by the wayside. He wanted to run to her, to fall at her feet and beg her forgiveness. She had lost so much more than the rest of them. She looked up, saw him, and smiled sadly. Her smile stopped him dead. He felt the weight of the coins in his hand. Suddenly they were as heavy as love and twice as cold. She stood and reached out for him. He had never loved her more than he did in that moment. He had gone against so much of his friend's teachings, but never more so than in coveting the woman he loved. He ran into her arms and held her, huge raking sobs shuddering through him. He couldn't cry. After all of the tears he had shed he was empty. "I am sorry. I am so sorry."

She hushed him, gentling her fingers through his hair. "They are looking for you. Matthew has whipped them up into a rage. He hates you. He always has. And now he has an excuse for it. They are out of their minds with grief and loss, Judas. You can't stay here, or they will kill you for what you have done. You have to go."

"There's nowhere left to go, Mary, he's seen to that. This is his revenge," he laughed bitterly at that. "I should never . . . I am sorry. It wasn't meant to end like this. All of this because, fool that I am, I couldn't help but love you."

"Our god is a jealous god," she said. She sounded utterly spent. The emptiness in her voice cut deeper than any words could have. She was crying but there was no strength to her tears. "Please, go."

"I can't," he said, and he knew that it was true. He needed to be found. He needed to feel their stones hit. He needed their anger to break his bones. He was finished with this life. The farmer had been right, there was only God's mercy left to him. But what kind of mercy was that? What mercy did a suicide have with the gates to the Kingdom closed to him?

Judas' mind was plagued with doubts, it had been for days. His friend had known he would not be able to live with this blood on his hands, yet still he had begged for this betrayal. So perhaps this stoning was actually one final mercy?

"Please."

"Let them come. I will face them and die with what little dignity is left to me."

She wiped away the tears. "Please. If not for me, then for our son," she took his hand and placed it flat against the gentle swell of her belly.

"Our son," he repeated, falling to his knees before her. He kissed her hands and then her belly, crushing his face up against the coarse cloth of her dress. The Pharisee's words rang in his head: Judas the Betrayer. What greater betrayal could there be? He pressed the torn leather pouch into her hands. "Please, take the silver, for the boy, for you."

He saw the life he had lost reflected in Mary's eyes. He knew she loved him, and he knew love was not enough. He couldn't tell her how alone he felt at that moment.

She turned her back on him.

He left her to walk the long road to death.

He had time to think, time to remember the promise he had made, and time to regret it. It was a walk filled with last things: He watched the sun sink down below the trees; he felt the wind in his face; he tasted the arid air on his tongue. He pulled off his robe and walked naked into the garden.

They were waiting for him.

He didn't shy away from the hurt and hatred in their eyes. He did not try to justify himself. He stood naked before them.

"You killed him," Matthew said, damning him. They were the last words Judas Iscariot heard. Matthew held a rope in his hands. It was fashioned into a noose.

He welcomed the first stone from James as it struck his temple. He didn't flinch. He didn't feel it. Nor did he feel the second from Luke, or the third cast by John. The stones hit, one after another, each one thrown harder than the last until they drove Iscariot to his knees. All he felt was the agony of the garden.

Matthew came forward with the rope and looped it around Judas' neck.

Judas wept.

Trafalgar Square, Westminster, London

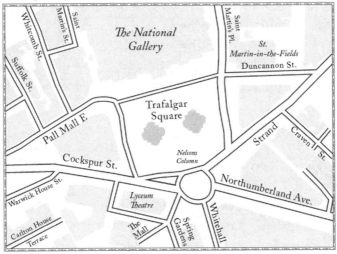

2

BURN WITH ME
Now

It was two minutes to three when the woman walked into Trafalgar Square.

Dressed in jeans and a loose-fitting, yellow tee-shirt she looked like every other summer tourist come to pay homage to Landseer's brooding lions. There was a smiley face plastered across her chest. The grin was stretched out of shape by the teardrop swell of her breasts. Only it wasn't summer. The yellow tee-shirt set her apart from the maddening crowd, because everyone else was wrapped up against the spring chill with scarves and gloves and woolen hats.

She stood still, a single spot of calm amid the hectic hustle of London. She uncapped the plastic bottle she held and emptied it over her head and shoulders, working the syrupy liquid in to her scalp. In less than a minute her long blonde hair was tangled and thick with grease as though it hadn't been washed in months. She smelled like the traffic fumes and fog of pollution that choked the city.

Pigeons landed around the feet of the man beside her as he scattered chunks of bread across the paving stones. He looked up and smiled at her. He had a gentle face. A kind smile. She wondered who loved him. Someone had to. He had the contentment of a loved man.

Around her the tourists divided into groups: those out in search of culture headed toward the National Portrait Gallery; the thirsty ducked into the café on the corner; the royalists crossed over the road and disappeared beneath Admiralty Arch onto Whitehall; the hungry headed for Chandos Place and Covent Garden's trendy eateries; and those starved of entertainment wandered up St Martin's Lane towards Leicester Square or Soho, depending upon their definition of entertainment. Businessmen in their off-the-rack suits marched in step like penguins, umbrella tips and blakeys and segs, those uniquely English metal sole protectors, tapping out the rhythm of the day's enterprise. Red buses crawled down Cockspur Street and around the corner toward The Strand and Charing Cross. The city was alive.

A young girl in a bright red duffel coat ran toward her, giggling and flapping her arms to startle the feeding birds into flight. When she was right in the middle of them the pigeons exploded upwards in a madness of feathers. The girl doubled up in laughter, her delighted shrieks chasing the pigeons up into the sky. Her enjoyment was infectious. The man rummaged in his plastic bag for another slice of white bread to tear up. The woman couldn't help but smile. She had chosen the yellow tee-shirt because it made her smile. It seemed important to her that today of all days she should.

She took the phone from her pocket and made the call.

"News desk." The voice on the other end was too perky for its own good. That would change in less than a minute when the screaming began.

"There is a plague coming," she said calmly. "For forty days and forty nights fear shall savage the streets. Those steeped in sin shall burn. The dying begins now."

"Who is this? Who am I talking to?"

"I don't need to tell you my name. Before the day is through you will know everything there is to know about me apart from one important detail."

"And what's that?"

"Why I did it."

She ruffled the young girl's hair as she scattered another cluster of pigeons and burst into fits of giggles. The girl stopped, turned and looked up at the woman. "You smell funny."

The woman reached into her pocket for her lighter. She thumbed the wheel, grating it against the flint, and touched the naked flame to her hair. She dropped the phone and stumbled forward as the fire engulfed her.

All around her the city screamed.

3

THIRTEEN MARTYRS

Noah Larkin lay on his back, looking up at the cheap hotel room's equally cheap ceiling fan. The blades stuttered as they turned, making a painfully shrill squeal every fourth revolution. The room, in the basement of an old Victorian Town House, set him back twenty quid a night. As the old saying went, you got what you paid for, and what he'd paid for was a mattress riddled with the black smears of crushed bed bugs, a crusty top sheet that hadn't been washed since Victoria herself sat on the throne, and water stains that crept more than halfway up the wall.

The light from the fly windows looking onto the street was almost non-existent.

The room smelled of whiskey-fueled dreams, stale sweat and week-old kebab relish. It was not a pleasant mix.

He closed his eyes.

On the other side of the bed the woman shifted her weight, causing the entire mattress to yaw alarmingly. A coil of bedspring stabbed into Noah's backside. The woman beside him wasn't a beauty, but that really didn't matter to him. It wasn't that Larkin was deep or looked beyond the shallows of beauty; he wasn't and he didn't. There were no hidden depths to him. Like the room, she was cheap, and like the room, he got exactly what he paid for. It wasn't about sex. He hadn't touched the woman. He just wanted someone to sleep beside him. Of course, he couldn't sleep.

Mercifully, his mobile rang. He reached over for the phone on the night stand.

"Larkin," he said, sliding back the handset.

"Where the hell have you been?" Ronan Frost's Derry brogue grew more pronounced when he was angry. That one sentence would have been enough for a linguist to pinpoint what street he was born on.

Noah looked down at the prostitute as she lay beside him. Her red lace bra sagged beneath the weight of the years. She opened her eyes. They were lost, like one of T.S. Elliot's Hollow Men. She smiled up at him. "Preoccupied," he told Frost.

"Well, stop arsing about and get yourself down here, soldier. The brown stuff's exploding all over the fan."

"On my way, boss," he said.

On the other end of the line Frost grunted.

Noah killed the connection and fumbled the phone back onto the nightstand. Beside it, the neon light of the clock tried to convince him it was almost midnight. He didn't believe it for a minute.

He pushed himself out of the bed.

The prostitute leaned forward on her elbow, studying his naked body. He repaid the compliment. He would have said something but he couldn't remember her name. Instead he took his wallet from his pocket, folded a handful of notes in his hand and offered them to her.

"It's too much," she said, looking at the cash. It was. It could have paid for her for a week.

Noah shrugged. "Call it a bonus for not having to do the deep and meaningfuls while we cuddled up."

She rolled the notes and stuffed them into her bra.

"The room's paid for the night. Stay here, sleep. Get yourself a good breakfast in the morning."

He went across to her side of the bed, bent down and kissed her gently on the forehead. It was a surprisingly intimate and tender gesture. She reached up and touched his cheek, her red-painted fingernail lingering on the scar that cut through the midnight shadow of stubble. And for just a moment they might have been lovers. The roll of money in her bra banished the illusion quickly enough.

Noah left her in bed. As he closed the door behind him he remembered her name: Margot.

He stepped out into the street. The North Star was bright in the night sky. Street lights burned sodium yellow on the pavement. A fat-bodied rat scurried out from beneath the mountain of plastic trash bags stacked in the gutter. No matter where you were in London you were never more than ten feet away from a rat, or so they said.

Noah's 1966 racing green Austin Healey was parked up against the curb. It looked like a relic from a better, nobler age, surrounded by the corporate uniformity of the Volvos, Fords, BMWs and Citroëns lining either side of the street. The Austin's side panels were beige, finished off with gold and black piping. The black leather soft top was down. He had fallen in love with the car when it was a wreck up on cinderblocks in a wrecking yard by Clapham Common. There was just something about it. It was like the proverbial bullet with his name on it; they were destined to be together eventually.

The registration papers listed its original date of sale as March 27, 1966. He liked the idea of the car being "born" on the same day Pickles found the old Jules Rimet trophy under a hedge in South London. Noah had spent thousands of pounds and hundreds of hours restoring the car. In truth, the car was the one constant in his life; the one thing he loved. No doubt a shrink would point to a loveless childhood and a lack of hugs when he scraped his knee, either that, or every time he entered the car he was thinking about his mother in some Oedipean way. Sometimes, though, a car was just a car, and that man-love was just man love for the wire rims and the walnut dashboard.

He gunned the engine and peeled away from the curb.

London at night was a strange beast. It was alive with the pheromones of danger, adultery and random acts of senseless violence. Like Sinatra's New York, it was his kind of town. On the corner he passed a three-legged dog trying to piss up against the wall without falling over. Ahead of him two girls walked, arms linked, down the white line in the middle of the road. He honked once, then swept around them, accelerating from a crawl to sixty in a couple of seconds and back to a dead stop at the first set of red lights. Noah loved the illusory freedom the wind in his hair gave him, even if it was short-lived.

This part of London existed on three levels: the underground; street level, with its instant gratifiers of fast food joints, discount clothes shops, electronics stores and florists; and overhead, with its amazing architecture that everyone down below was too preoccupied to notice. Windows were hidden behind steel shutters, the steel shutters hidden beneath inventive graffiti and spray-painted gang tags. He could never get used to the sheer emptiness of the city at night. It wasn't that the city was dead. It wasn't. It was vampiric. Come midnight the only people out were those who for one reason or another were afraid of sunlight.

Bracing the wheel on his thighs, he reached down for the rack of CDs lined up beside the gearstick and picked the one he wanted. Ignoring the lights, he took the left onto Belgrave Road at seventy-five and chased it down through Pimlico, hitting Vauxhall Bridge Road just shy of ninety miles per hour.

As he crossed the Thames, James Grant's melancholic voice wondered who in their right mind would want to live in this city of fear. It was a fair question. Noah loved London almost as much as he loved Grant's voice. Both had that lived-in quality that made them immediately comfortable, familiar but not so much so as to breed contempt. Both of them were so much more than they appeared to be when you scratched away at the surface. The voice and the streets were steeped in hidden subtleties. He couldn't imagine living anywhere else. He was a London boy to the core. He lived and breathed the city. He grinned, knowing full well that no one would be in a rush to accuse him of being in his right mind.

The needle on the speedometer only dipped below ninety twice on the thirty-mile drive out to Ashmoor and Nonesuch Manor. He cranked the volume up louder as the road opened up and lost himself in the music. Noah left the main road a mile short of Ashmoor proper, and took a bridle path up that jounced and juddered along the side of the grazing land toward the trailing avenue of lime trees that marked the way to Nonesuch. Out of the city the night was absolute. There were no stars. The branches trailed low, whispering in the Austin's wake. Up ahead of him rose the towering iron gates of Nonesuch Manor House. Two grotesque gargoyles perched on the gateposts watched him drive up. Their eyes had been hollowed out and replaced with surveillance cameras.

Noah decelerated, tires spitting gravel as he followed the drive up to the house. The drive was spotlighted. All around him the powerful lights conjured shadow demons that bent and bowed with the wind. He pulled up alongside Ronan Frost's Ducati Monster 696. It was the only bike in the courtyard. The rest were cars, and every one of them was something special. There was a Lamborghini Diablo with mud splashes up its sides, a flame-red E-Type Jaguar, a

Bugatti Veyron, a canary-yellow Lotus Elan, Sir Charles' own Daimler, a timeless classic, and pick of the bunch, a silver v12 Aston Martin Vanquish. As Frost liked to say, if you had no life, the very least you could do was drive a nice car.

Noah lifted himself out of the bucket seat. He left the keys in the ignition.

No one was going to steal the Austin from outside of Nonesuch.

He walked toward the house, though calling it a house was a misnomer. In truth it looked more like a castle. The left wing was even crenellated, part of which had crumbled where the climbing plants had undermined the masonry and worked their way deep into the crevices between the bricks. The ring wing appeared to be a huge gemstone, opalescent in the night. It was the old man's atrium with his hundreds of rare plants. The glass turned the night on itself. Lights burned in three of the windows on the ground floor, the rest covered with wooden shutters.

The old man's butler, Max, was waiting for him beneath the portico. "I trust you had a pleasant drive, sir?" Noah nodded. There was no love lost between the two. "Sir Charles is waiting for you with the others in the drawing room. May I take your coat, sir?" Noah shrugged out of his leather jacket and handed it over. "Thank you, sir. Will you be requiring anything else?" And then, almost as an afterthought, the butler added, "Toothpaste, perhaps? Your breath reeks of whoever had the misfortune of sitting on your face tonight."

Noah ignored him and went inside.

Nonesuch was a huge, sprawling old house with narrow passages, mezzanine levels and servants' staircases. The foyer was oak paneled. They showed signs of water damage. The old man's family crest stood above a huge open fire-place. There was no sign that a fire had burned in the grate in the last decade.

On a small table beside the empty fire, an exquisitely carved chess set played out the Saavedra position. It was a beautiful endgame and a wonderful example of how one move could make someone famous well outside their own lifetime. It was a salutary lesson to every man who didn't understand the nature of war. Sometimes subtlety is more important than might.

A granite and iron staircase rose in three tiers to the upstairs. The center of each riser was worn smooth by the scuffing of thousands of footsteps over the three hundred years since the old house had been built. There was a wheelchair stair-lift and wear marks along the wall where the old man's chair had bumped up against it. Somehow he couldn't imagine Sir Charles enduring the humiliation of the stair-lift. He wasn't that kind of man. No, he was more likely to claw his way up on his hands and knees. That was the kind of man that he was.

For all the grandeur of the entrance hall there was an almost tired air to it, like the staircase and the cracked oak shutters covering the windows. There were no priceless works of art on display, no old masters, no precious antiquities. The casual visitor would have been forgiven for thinking the old man was broke. He wasn't; he just invested his money elsewhere.

Noah crossed the foyer. The drawing room was the first door on the right, opposite the library.

He didn't knock.

He pushed the door open and walked inside.

The drawing room was anything but the classic Englishman's retreat. The old man called it the crucible. Noah thought of it in military terms: it was the debriefing room. The vast room was essentially the gloss of glass and the sharp lines of steel juxtaposed against Old World England's conservative charm. Everything in the room was laid out with Sir Charles' disability in mind.

One entire wall comprised twelve huge high-definition plasma displays capable of showing either a single image as a visual mosaic or spliced into a dozen individual ones. On the second wall there were two bookcases: one filled with priceless first editions—Bunyon, Marlowe, Fielding and Goethe on the first shelf, folio editions of Lavater and Glanvil, Maturin and Collins, each annotated with corrections in the author's own hand—and the other with worthless antiqued faux leather books. If Noah didn't already know which was which, he never would have been able to guess.

Behind the fake books was a service elevator down to an area they called the nest. It was the nerve center of Nonesuch. It housed the servers and their zettabytes of stored information, harvested newswires, ran surveillance equipment, monitored satellite signals and maintained emergency power for the manor. It was the beating heart beneath the floorboards. The ruse wouldn't fool a halfway decent intruder—wheelchair tracks in the deep pile of the carpet disappeared beneath the second bookcase—but a halfway decent intruder would never make it as far as the crucible. The fake books were there simply because Sir Charles enjoyed the game.

Recessed spotlights were set into the ceiling. They were dimmed low. The screens showed a powerful single image: a burning woman with her arms spread wide. It was time-stamped 1500 hours Zulu Time. Almost ten hours earlier.

Marble statuettes stood on plinths, each offering an aspect of war personified. There was Babd, the Celtic crow, and her sisters, Macha and Morrigan, the ghosts of the battlefield; Bast, the Egyptian lioness, standing proud and tall, fiercely defiant, while the Greek Ares and the Roman Mars both wore the guise of hunters; one-eyed Odin, with the ravens Hugin and Munin on either shoulder, encapsulated fury and wisdom, wrath and beauty, the Norse god the dichotomy of war itself; and of course, in the center of them all, Kali, the Hindu goddess of death.

The statuettes lent the room a curious air of the occult that the old man liked to foster. They were a reflection of his eclectic tastes and another part of the game. He could have chosen anything to decorate the crucible, for wealth was not an issue. Neither was taste. The old man possessed both in abundance. No, the statuettes were a very deliberate nod to the past, to death, and rather ironically, to glory.

Other than the bookcases, the main concession to traditional taste was what at first glance appeared to be a Georgian mahogany dining table in the center of the room, only instead of the leather inlay the entire table top had been cut away and embedded with a powerful touchscreen computer.

The table was surrounded by five high-backed, green leather chairs.

In four of the five chairs sat a member of Sir Charles Wyndham's brainchild, codename Ogmios. They were bound by Mandate 7266 issued by the Secret Service, their job, to do anything and everything necessary to preserve the sovereignty of the British Isles. What that meant was more difficult to pin down. They weren't spies. Officially they weren't anything but outside of the law, removed from the security of the State. They were deniable. If something went wrong they were on their own. If something went right no one ever said thank you. When things went south, they were there.

The old man might call them the Forge, Noah called them the Lost Cause. It was a slightly different interpretation. Noah didn't know who they reported to, who watched the watchmen, so to speak, but he assumed it was someone in MI6. Someone breathing the rarified air of the "higher ups." The old man only ever referred to him or her as Control.

Noah didn't know how the old man had picked his team. He didn't know very much about them at all, despite the fact that every one of them would put their lives on the line for him. He knew that because they did, every day.

They put themselves into areas of unrest, sometimes to mediate, other times to facilitate, and when necessary, to bring the hammer down.

Good lies were simple lies, so they kept cover stories to a bare minimum. Less detail to remember meant less detail to forget. And of course, being deniable, any background checks run against any of the team would fail to find any links to the Secret Services.

Closest to him was Ronan Frost, the blue-eyed boy, steel-gray hair, steel-gray suit fashionably cut by Ted Baker. Frost didn't look up. He had served with 1 Para in Kosovo in '99 before joining the SAS' Special Projects team—counterterrorists, to the rest of the world. Next to him was Orla Nyrén, every bit the Mediterranean ideal with her flawless olive complexion, rich chocolate eyes and shoulder-length black hair, fine bones and heart-shaped lips. She was actually mixed decent; her father came from a small Italian town down on the Amalfi Coast, her mother from the ice of northern Sweden. And Orla herself was a curious blend of both gene pools. Her Scandinavian heritage was obvious in her build. Coupled with her beauty—and she was beautiful, strikingly so, Noah thought—at half an inch shy of six feet she cut an imposing figure. Her Italian side manifested itself in other ways, most of them skin deep, including one hell of a temper. Noah had been on the receiving end of it once, and once was more than enough. Nyrén was ex-MI6, a Middle East intel specialist, fluent in a dozen languages, two of them dead. She was also the closest thing Noah had ever had to a crush.

On the other side of the table Konstantin Khavin inclined his head in greeting. Konstantin was ex-KGB and the very definition of the spy who came in from the cold: he had come over the wall in '88 with nothing more than the clothes on his back and his id. He was older than the others, but he had lived the kind of life that carved itself into every inch of skin. His mouth was a thin slit like a knife cut above a dimpled chin. Noah had the distinct impression that the Russian only smiled when he wanted to emphasize just how eager he was to take you outside and beat you bloody with fists and feet. Needless to say, Noah was quite happy that Konstantin wasn't smiling. He sat there making a cat's cradle out of his stubby fingers. The tip of the right index finger was missing and his shirt sleeves were rolled back on a cheap plastic digital watch.

They, each of them, had their own stories, their own flaws. None of them were squeaky clean or they wouldn't have been working for the old man, but Konstantin was different. Sometimes it was impossible to tell if his stories were down to his rather dry Russian sense of humor or not. He had done things the rest of them couldn't imagine, but he had a habit of reassigning all of the ills suffered by his people a place in his own story. He'd told Noah a story once of how he had been forced to walk down the street with his mother's entrails draped around his neck to prove his loyalty to the State. Noah wanted to believe it was just one of Konstantin's macabre stories because he couldn't begin to imagine what kind of man could put a kid through something like that. It didn't fit into his philosophy, and trying to claim that by doing it the nine-year-old Konstantin would somehow be proving his loyalty to some invisible government? It went beyond inhuman.

And then there was Jude Lethe, the cuckoo in this nest of soldiers, the team's tech wizard. He was a nerd, but more than that, he was their nerd. He looked painfully serious in his black Joe 90 glasses.

Together they were Ogmios, named after the Celtic hero who himself was fashioned after the legends of Hercules.

What should have been the sixth seat at the head of the table was left open for the old man's wheelchair.

These were his people, and they made an unlikely—and dangerous—group.

"So glad you could join us, Mister Larkin," the old man said from his place at the table.

Noah nodded and took the last seat.

"Now perhaps we can get started?"

"Don't mind me," Noah said.

"Thank you."

The old man adjusted the position of his wheelchair. It was the paraplegic equivalent of arranging his papers. He reached out and tapped his finger on the empty touchscreen, bringing the computer beneath it to life. The image on the wall array brightened immediately. Another tap and it started playing.

"London is one of the most closely watched cities in the world. There isn't a square meter that isn't covered by some sort of CCTV or private surveillance camera. What you are seeing now happened in Trafalgar Square at three p.m. today. There are various angles but they all show the same thing." There was no need for Sir Charles to elaborate; the picture was worth considerably more than a thousand words. Noah watched the woman burn. She held her arms wide and turned and turned, stumbling finally as though she had become dizzy. "A minute before she committed suicide the woman placed a call to the BBC news desk," the old man continued. He stroked the touchscreen, minimizing the freeze-frame of the burning woman on her knees, and brought up the audio recording of her call.

She spoke to them with the voice of the dead: *"There is a plague coming. For forty days and forty nights fear shall savage the streets. Those steeped in sin shall burn. The dying begins now."*

"Who is this? Who am I talking to?" a second voice asked.

"I don't need to tell you my name. Before the day is through you will know everything there is to know about me apart from one important detail."

"And what's that?"

"Why I did it."

Sir Charles played it again.

And again.

Her final sentence hung in the air.

"Do we know who she is?" Orla Nyrén asked. She leaned forward in her chair. The woman had a habit of coming alive when things around her became interesting. Most people did, but it was her definition of interesting that set her apart from "most" people.

"Mister Lethe? Would you care to share your discovery?" Sir Charles inclined his head slightly.

Lethe nodded, and rather self-consciously fiddled with the black rim of his glasses. "We ran facial recognition software, looking for a cross-match for our Jane Doe in various databases. IDENT1 struck out. Likewise there was nothing on the Server in the Sky, so we're not talking FBI's Most Wanted here. That meant we had to look closer to home. We got hits from the DMV down in Swansea along with one from the IRIS system at Heathrow. Those helped us find out all the not-so-nitty-gritty details.

"Our fiery female is one Catherine Meadows, age 39, graduate of Newcastle University, with no romantic entanglements. Ms. Meadows was, at the time of her combustion, a relatively well regarded forensic archeologist. Most recently she had testified at the Radovan Karadzic war crimes tribunal at The Hague. Her résumé reads like a Who's Who—or Where's Where, I guess—of archeology. But that's it. That's her life. She was obsessed with the past. She didn't live in the here and now.

"Reading between the lines, she was a lonely woman more likely to end her day cuddling up with her cat, a cup of Horlicks and the latest episode of Eastenders, rather than locking lips with some gorgeous Lothario. There's nothing here to suggest she might be typical terrorist material, or even atypical terrorist material," he said with a shrug. "Indeed, right up to her going out in a blaze of glory I would have said Ms. Meadows was, for want of a better word, boring."

"It's amazing what you can find out with Google," Noah joked.

"Actually, to be honest, half of this was out there in the public domain. Given her name and her picture, any one of you could have found it. She had a Facebook page that's littered with pictures of her ginger tom, that links her up with the class of '91 at Newcastle Uni, and had some rather unfortunate photographs dating back to her time as a Cure fan." Lethe raised a wry eyebrow behind his glasses. "You would think an archeologist ought to have known that some things are best left in the past, wouldn't you?" He chuckled at his own joke. "She's written for a number of academic journals. The articles are likewise online for people with insomnia to peruse at their leisure."

"So why burn herself like that? I mean, that's a pretty extreme way to go," Ronan Frost asked, his accent a soft burr now.

"In my country we would be looking for the invisible men," Konstantin said, rather cryptically.

"Precisely," the Irish man agreed with him. "Something about this stinks. A boring woman doesn't just suddenly decide to set fire to herself on a whim. So who is hiding in the shadows? Who are the invisible men?"

"Sir Charles?" Lethe said, indicating the old man should pick up where he'd left off.

The single image on the plasma screens fractured into twelve seemingly identical ones. No, not identical, Noah realized, just remarkably—disturbingly—similar. The center of each screen was dominated by a burning figure. The time-stamp on each read 1500Z. But that was all they had in common.

Working his way around the screens he recognized Dam Square and the white stone pillar of the National Monunmet in Amsterdam, the glass pyramid of the Palais du Louvre in Paris' first *arrondissement*, the red brick façade of Casa de la Panadería in Madrid's Plaza Mayor, the towering majesty of the cathedral in Stephansplatz in Vienna, the obelisk in the heart of St. Peter's Square in Rome, the Vatican hidden behind the flames, and the glass monstrosity of the Sony building in Potsdamer Platz in Berlin. There were more cities and more monuments he didn't recognize. Noah counted them, even though he knew full well there were twelve screens.

"Well *now* it is starting to get interesting," Orla said. An errant strand of hair curled over her brow and across her left eye.

"Thirteen people set themselves alight in very public places all across Europe at exactly the same time? I'd say we've moved way beyond interesting," Noah said. Interesting really wasn't the word he would have chosen though. The whole thing had a fatalistic simplicity to it.

"Oh, it gets better than that, or worse, depending upon your perspective," Jude Lethe told them.

"Don't tell me, more of that Google-Fu?"

"Something like that," Lethe said. He leaned forward and started rapidly manipulating the images on the screen, zooming each one in until the display was filled with their screaming faces. The detail and precision of the digital images was nothing short of horrific. The images were hideously sharp. Noah had seen enough death to last him a lifetime, but something about this, as Frost had said, was different. Wrong.

"Italy, France, Spain, Germany, England, Greece, Switzerland, Austria, Holland, Belgium, Denmark, the Czech Republic and Russia," Lethe reeled off the countries where thirteen martyrs had self-immolated. "You can't really tell the ethnicity from the faces now, too much damage, but the facial recognition software picked up hits for all thirteen here in the UK."

"You're telling me they're all English?"

Lethe nodded. "Passports issued by the UK and Commonwealth Office."

"This is nuts," Noah said, trying to take in the logistical nightmare of forcing thirteen people to commit suicide in public, and in such a violent manner. "What's the news reporting? I presume it's all over every channel in the world." He found himself thinking about the old Smiths song "Panic," though his imagination took it way beyond the streets of London and Birmingham.

"At the moment truth is rather fragmented," the old man said. "As one would expect, the initial reports were very insular. Then within an hour of the event, the scope of the actual event began to come clear. Regional television stations were broadcasting identical CCTV images of the suicides. It's difficult to deny the evidence of your own eyes, of course. No one wants to believe it. The reporters are playing down any connection, for now, but it is obvious for anyone to see.

"The actual content of the telephone calls hasn't been broken yet, but that is only a matter of time. And when it does—and people hear that promise of forty days and forty nights of terror—then as the Americans like to say, everyone will just be waiting for the other shoe to drop. That is the kind of world we live in, I am afraid."

"Thankfully, no one seems to have picked up on the fact that the victims are all British. But that only puts us a few hours in front of the press. Some enterprising soul will put two and two together soon enough."

"We can't worry about that," the old man said. "Right now the only thing we need to concern ourselves with is the facts. What we know from monitoring the newswires is that the major broadcast networks in each respective country received a call precisely one minute before the suicides. In all but two the message was the same."

"And the others?"

"This was the message in Rome." Lethe triggered another audio file. The voice was male. Taut. Barely held together. This wasn't the voice of a man who wanted to die. This wasn't a religious fanatic or some crazed zealot sacrificing himself for a cause. There wasn't a trace of resignation in it. This was an ordinary man, still hoping against hope that somehow he would be saved. *"Roman Pontiff beware of your approaching, of the city where two rivers water, your blood you will come to spit in that place, both you and yours when blooms the Rose."* And then, after almost thirty seconds of silence, *"Tell Isla I love her. Please. Tell her that."*

Jude Lethe didn't wait before playing the final message. Questions could come later. "This call was made to *Das Erste* in Germany." Again it was a man's voice. This one was more composed than the last. He spoke slowly and calmly, as though reciting a script. Each word was enunciated clearly: *"The Holy Father passed through a big city half in ruins and half trembling with halting step, afflicted with pain and sorrow, he prayed for the souls of the corpses he met on his way; having reached the top of the mountain, on his knees at the foot of the big cross he was killed by a group of soldiers."*

"The first message was quatrain 2.97 from the prophecies of Michel de Nostredame. The second is an excerpt from the third secret of Fatima. Both are believed to foretell the assassination of the Pope," the old man put in.

"Okay, so let me get this straight, we are talking crackpot sects and a healthy dose of make believe?" Noah asked. It still didn't make the logistics of this kind of mass sacrifice any less complicated, but fanaticism would go some way to explaining it. He rubbed at the stubble on his chin. No, that didn't jibe with the first man's voice or his plea to tell some woman he loved her. That wasn't in the fanatic's genetic makeup. They were too fired up with the righteousness of their cause to worry about earthly crap like the people they left behind.

"If only that were the case. What we appear to be dealing with here is at the very least systematic and well thought out. You don't burn thirteen people alive like this, with such military precision, without having planned for all of the contingencies. This is a very public opening gambit, Noah. It was designed to be seen, and there's only one reason for that—because whoever is behind it wanted it to be seen," the old man said. Sir Charles changed the display, bringing up the passport photographs of the suicides. As with every passport photo Noah had ever seen, the victims looked somehow less human than they had when the flames had burned away their faces. "With that in mind, Mister Lethe, please continue."

Jude Lethe manipulated the touchscreen computer, bringing up a series of photographs. Some were vacation shots; others were newspaper clippings and the like. "When I saw that all thirteen victims were British nationals my first thought was not only do I dislike this kind of coincidence, I don't buy it. Thirteen people commit suicide in an identical manner in thirteen countries and they all just happen to come from the same place. There has to be a link. So then it was a case of looking for that link."

"Makes sense," Noah agreed. "I take it you found one?"

"Of course," Lethe said, without a hint of hubris. "All of our victims were academics, and, more precisely, all of our victims dabbled in the field of archeology in some way or other. One was a university professor running the history department at Durham. Three were postgrads who have stayed in the field: One worked on that TV show where they dig up old ruins and try to make history sexy; another was a curator at the British Museum; a geophys specialist; a historian with a Middle Eastern specialization. . . . The list goes on, but you can see what I am driving at."

"Looks like you've been busy," Noah said.

"Ah, it wouldn't have looked half as impressive if you'd been here at three o'clock, believe me."

"So there's something to be said for being late, then." Noah smiled ruefully.

"Quite," the old man said, cutting across the banter. There was an awkward silence for a moment as Lethe seemed to forget he'd been in the middle of briefing the others. He triggered the next sequence on the computer and the images on the screen were replaced by a single shot: a lowering sun and a huge orange-red, flat-topped rock formation. In the far right corner was the washed-out blue of the sea.

Noah studied the colored striations that marked the sides of the mesa.

"This place is the one thing they all have in common," Lethe said, gesturing up at the screens. "Masada. It's a World Heritage Site situated along the Dead Sea Road on the eastern edge of the Judaean Desert. According to Jose-phus, who is pretty much the oracle on all this stuff, the original fortress was built by Herod and was a strong-hold for an extremist sect known as the Sicarii. They appear on the face of it to be the world's first terrorists, but Jose-phus was also an inveterate liar and had a habit of grossly exaggerating everything he wrote about, so who knows? One thing for sure though, the Sicarii committed mass suicide rather than surrender to the Romans. The fact that we've got two mass suicides linked to the same place is another coincidence I'm not particularly enamored of."

"All well and good," Orla Nyrén began, "but how exactly does this link our suicides? I'm missing something here." She scratched at her right eyebrow—there was a slight scar beneath the hair—with the thumb of her left hand. It was a curiously awkward gesture.

"I'm glad you asked, Orla," Lethe said in his best wise,

old soul voice. He changed the image on the screen again. This time the displays showed a dozen images of an excavation in progress. "Without a crystal ball I can't tell you how important it is in relation to today's events, but in 2004 an earthquake damaged the crumbling walls of the old fort. The upshot was several previously hidden chambers and an elaborate subterranean network were uncovered. And this, my friends, is where two plus two could either be four or five: all of our victims were part of the team that went to excavate the site."

4

SLOUCHING TOWARD MEGIDDO

"Let me try and wrap my head around this for a minute." Noah looked up at the screens. The faces might have been replaced by the harsh reality of the Israeli landscape, but that didn't matter. His head was filled with Catherine Meadows' digital ghost falling to its knees, arms rising up in a desperate V. He rubbed his fingers against his temples. "You're telling me we're looking at a plot to assassinate the Pope, okay, I'll buy that, but a plot dating back to a sect that committed mass suicide two thousand years ago? Now that's . . . special. And not special in a good way, I might add. And"—he sucked in a disbelieving breath—"as if that wasn't enough, not only has our whistleblower been dead for the best part of five hundred years, he just happened to be a fortuneteller who couldn't spell Hitler and marked Saddam as the Antichrist. Does that about sum it up?" He looked around the table. "I mean, seriously, do you have any idea how bloody ridiculous that sounds?"

Lethe met his gaze full on and held it. He was the youngest of the group by a good decade, and right then he looked it. He touched the black frame of his glasses. "I'd say we're merrily skipping down the yellow brick road into Looney Town," Lethe agreed with a wry smile, "but what we've got here is a link. The modern world is all about links, degrees of separation and joining the dots. The only thing that makes any kind of sense is that something happened at Masada and these people burned themselves alive because of it. I'm not claiming it makes a good kind of sense."

Noah didn't know much about the kid. The old man had introduced him to the team as a researcher. Noah had always assumed that meant hacker. He was the archetypal nerd with his thick-framed glasses and tufts of beard that really didn't seem all that keen to grow through. Lethe took his glasses off. Without them he looked another five years younger, if that was possible. Noah liked the kid, even if he spent too much time jacked into the neural net or whatever it was he did as a substitute for having a healthy sex life.

"I think that's a bit of a leap of logic," Orla Nyrén interrupted his train of thought. Noah looked her way, worried for a moment that he might have said part of what was going on in his head. Thankfully, she wasn't looking at him. Orla brushed that errant strand of hair away from her face again. She moved her cell phone so that it sat exactly perpendicular to her on the table. It was a tiny adjustment that smacked of an obsessive need for order that went beyond needing things around her to make sense. It was all about controlling her world and what happened in it. Noah could respect that so long as it didn't involve turning widdershins three times and rolling up a trouser leg before opening a door.

"That it might be, but anything else would mean a second layer of coincidence, wouldn't it?" Lethe reasoned.

He pinched at his nose. It was obvious he'd been staring at computer screens for hours; his focus had that kind of glazed quality life online brought with it. "If it isn't Masada that links these suicides, then it is either a totally random collusion of circumstance, a coincidence to the power of thirteen, if you like, or somewhere out there, there's another singularity where these thirteen unfortunate souls come together. My money is on Masada though, not a black hole. Occam's Razor and all that," Lethe said.

"Look hard enough and you'll start to see conspiracies everywhere," Orla shrugged. "And forgive me, but I don't exactly see how this falls under our remit. We aren't body-guards. If someone is out to kill the Pope, we should pass on what we know to the authorities and wash our hands of it."

"Very Pontius Pilate of you, my dear," Sir Charles said, settling back in the seat of his wheelchair. "However, our remit is whatever I say it is on any given day. You knew that when you took this particular king's shilling. Now, given the links to Masada and the Sicarii, I believe we are in a unique position to investigate. Perhaps our martyrs did find something on their excavations. It isn't out of the question. And when you consider the fact that Masada is a biblical site, anything they found would very definitely fall under our area of interest, or could be twisted until it did, wouldn't you say?"

Orla Nyrén stewed in silence for a full minute. She did not look remotely convinced. She moved her phone twice, once nudging it slightly out of true, and again to return it back to its perfect perpendicular. Finally she pursed her lips and shook her head. It was a short, decisive denial. "No, not buying it. Sorry, boss. Dress it up any way you like, this isn't our business. This is MI6 and defense of the realm stuff. Suicide . . ."—she paused, catching herself mid-breath. Noah wondered if she had been about to say bombers; it was such a natural extension of her old life the two words would almost certainly have fused together in her mind—". . . and terror threats," she continued, her eyes drifting unconsciously toward the screens, "are way beyond the capabilities of five people. We can't be the last bastions of democracy."

"Nor should you be," the old man agreed. He leaned forward in his chair. It was a subtle shift in his body language that implied complicity. "We will, of course, be feeding any information we discover up the line, and it will be for Control to decide how it is distributed. But there is a convergence of events here that we *will* investigate, and that's my final word on the matter."

Orla shook her head. The gesture was barely perceptible. "Why do I get the feeling you know more than you are letting on here?"

The old man smiled indulgently and spread his arms wide as if to show just how helpless he was. Noah knew it was all an act. Sir Charles had been paralyzed by an IRA bomb in the London Docklands over twenty years ago, and even in the hospital bed in the days immediately after the attack, he hadn't been helpless.

The story was, he'd whispered into the right ear, and in turn the right ear had placed a call to a not-so-upstanding friend of an even less upright gent. And while that chain reaction played out, Sir Charles settled back into the starched pillows, content that his whisper had lit a very short fuse. The chemist suspected of being behind the bomb was involved in a not-so-tragic accident less than forty-eight hours later.

That was the kind of man he was.

He didn't get angry.

He didn't rail against the world.

He got even in his own very quiet, almost understated, way.

And right then the old man's smile was a match for any the Russian had ever conjured. "Because, my dear, I am dreadfully predictable and you know me far too well. It's the curse of spending too much time together. I will admit this much, I have my suspicions. I can only assure you that some very good reasons underpin those suspicions—but I am not ready to voice them just yet. As soon as I am sure, you will be the first to know. Until then, he who speaks first and thinks later has an idiot for a mouth. And contrary to what you may believe, I am not an idiot." This time his smile was both self-deprecating and honest. It was a gentle deflection.

Noah half-expected her to challenge the old man again. She could be like a dog with a bone sometimes. She didn't. Noah understood why. Thirteen burning faces told them all it was an argument for another day.

"Okay," she said instead, "let's think about this rationally. The one question that's begging to be asked is: who else was involved in that dig? For all the conspiracy theory nonsense, the dig is the one thing we know for sure that the suicides have in common. Logically, anyone else who had been there is either in danger themselves, or more likely, is wrapped up in the whole thing somehow. Either way, we need to find them."

Lethe had a partial answer. It wasn't what any of them wanted to hear. "More than fifty locals were used as casual labor. The dig was overseen by one Akim Caspi, who is not, I hasten to add, an archeologist. Caspi is a lieutenant general in Tzahal, the Israeli Defense Force. I sincerely doubt he has a list of names, unfortunately. Archeologists are great for keeping itemized records on fossilized donkey crap, but they don't seem all that concerned about people if they haven't been dead for a millennium or more."

He put up a picture of Caspi in full military regalia on the screens. The man looked like someone a soldier would be willing to die for.

"Okay, so given that we aren't going to be blessed with a convenient list of prime suspects, we need to hit the ground running. What ground though?" the Irishman asked.

"We've got thirteen potentially blind alleys to run down."

"Rome or Berlin," Konstantin said, breaking his silence. "There is a reason those calls deviated from the pattern."

"I am inclined to agree," the old man said, "and because of that, Konstantin, I want you to go to Berlin and walk a mile in the dead man's shoes."

The Russian raised an eyebrow. "Walk in his shoes?" He made his index and forefingers skip across the tabletop to demonstrate his understanding, or lack of it.

"Relive the last seventy-two hours of his life," Sir Charles explained. "Go through it with a fine-toothed comb. Every place he visited, every person he saw. No man is an island, especially in this modern age of emails and phone calls. Lethe will support your investigations from back here, following the electronic paper trail. Somewhere in the middle of everything is his killer—and make no mistake about this, he was killed. They all were. Their murderers might not have pulled the trigger, but that is neither here nor there. Death comes upon his pale horse wielding fire, guns and other instruments of death. Nothing says death needs to be intimate anymore. So take his life apart, climb inside his skin. Become him. Let the dead man tell his last tale."

The Russian nodded.

Sir Charles turned to Noah. "I want you to go to Rome. Whether we consider the threat credible or not, the scant evidence we have points toward the Holy See. To ignore it would be negligent in the extreme," the old man said. "And given the veneration half the world feels for His Holiness, I can't say I am particularly eager to have his blood on my hands. So let's see if we can avoid that, shall we?"

Noah nodded.

"Good. Get out there. Get a feel for the lie of the land. There's a reason these two messages were different. I don't know what it is, but my gut instinct is screaming that it is important. Do what you are best at, Noah, make yourself a pain in the arse. Get in there and ruffle some feathers.

Shake the holy tree. Just do whatever it takes to unearth that reason. And, for God's sake, don't let the Pope die, there's a good man."

"Dig up secrets, don't get His Holiness killed, understood."

"Let's not forget the one thing in our favor right now is the sheer scale of this. Everything about today's events cries spectacle. It's terrorism in the truest sense of the word. It is theater. If ten times the amount of people had died in a plane wreck, the world would barely have blinked an eye. Planes crash. Nine-eleven changed the nature of fear. It made it global. As a society we have become so desensitized to death that anything less is almost mundane. Terrorists bring down planes and bomb embassies. That is what they do. It's tragic, yes, but any way you look at it, it's old news.

The old fears aren't enough in this brave new world. Everything has to be bigger,"—he let that sink in for a moment—"which is a salutary lesson for us. What it means in this case is, they don't martyr themselves in broad daylight without having achieved some obvious goal. So what was that goal? Thirteen people burning themselves alive is not frightening, not on a global scale. It is off the front of the newspapers in a few days, forgotten in a few weeks, which is a crime in and of itself, but not one we can afford to worry about.

"If you want my opinion, it is the threat they deliver right before they burn that is frightening. That's what sends shivers through the strata of society. That's what makes the good people of the world look over their shoulders.

"Forty days of terror is very precise and obviously picked for its religious connotations. It's a common biblical time of transition: *And I will cause it to rain upon the earth forty days and forty nights; and every living substance that I have made will I destroy from off the face of the earth.* Later Moses convenes with God on Mount Sinai for forty days and forty nights, and Mark tells us that Jesus emerged from his forty days in the wilderness reborn, having resisted the temptations of Satan. To my way of thinking this all adds credence to Mr. Lethe's theory about Masada holding the key.

"Ask yourself this: Can our modern society resist forty days of listening to Satan's overtures? Will it emerge from the terror, from the purge, as every living substance is wiped from the face of the earth? And if it does, if society comes out of the flames, triumphant, what will *we* have become?"

Before anyone could answer, the old man turned to Orla. "My dear, I am going to take advantage of you shamelessly,"—there was nothing remotely sexual about the overture, despite the glaring *double entendre*—"I want you to find out everything there is to know about the day-to-day lives of the other victims. Work your contacts. Even though the world has been reduced to ones and zeroes, machines will only tell us so much, no matter how brilliant Mister Lethe is. Paper trails are all well and good, but what paper trail ever had loose lips or guilty body language?

"Frost, I want you in Masada. Track down Caspi, he's the one name we have out there."

"One thing I did find out about Caspi," Lethe said. "In 2004 he received an insurance payout in excess of two million dollars, which he dutifully paid an ungodly amount of tax on."

"Same year as the dig? Well, isn't that just another happy coincidence?" Frost said. "Now, if that's everything,"—the Irishman started to push back his chair—"I think a couple of hours of shuteye before dawn wouldn't go amiss. It's going to be a long day."

"This is bullshit," Orla muttered under her breath. She picked up her phone. For a moment Noah thought she was going to wring the mechanical guts out of it. Instead she pocketed it and pushed herself to her feet. "I spent six years in Israel. I know its heart. I know how it works. I've got a network of hundreds of contacts I can fall back on, people in all walks of life. And you're sending him? This is bullshit."

"Calm down, Orla." The old man reversed his chair away from the table, in the process turning his back on her.

"Don't you walk away from me!" Her voice rose until the last syllable was almost twice as loud as the first.

"I will not be argued with, Orla. Ronan is going to Masada, you are staying here, and that is the end of it."

"No," she said, "it's not." The defiance in her voice surprised everyone in the room. There was an established order to things. No one argued with the old man when he'd had his final word. It was just the way of things. "It's a crock of shit is what it is. But it is not over."

"Orla," the old man said, a hint of warning in his voice. His patience was stretching thin. "I suggest you sit, take a few deep breaths and calm yourself down."

"Don't patronize me. I'm thirty-one years old. I was a field operative for MI6 for almost a third of my natural life, and half of that was spent swimming in the shit of Israeli politics. I've been shot at, and blown up, and I'm still here. The country is in my blood. I know it better than I know myself. And you want me to sit here twiddling my thumbs while Ronan goes trampling all over the place with his size nines?" She shook her head. "You need to understand Israel. It's like nowhere else on earth. And no disrespect to Ronan, but he can't understand it. It's impossible."

She saw Sir Charles was about to naysay her and cut him off before he could get the first word out. "And don't go telling me he lived through Ireland. That was different on so many levels. Now, cut the macho bullshit and send a woman to do the job this woman is best qualified to do."

The old man looked at her, then at Ronan, and for a moment didn't say anything. He seemed to be weighing up the cost of losing face over the value of stubbornness like it was some sort of economic factor-equation where one might somehow balance out the other.

Noah wondered how the hell the old man could say no to her. He knew, roles reversed, he wouldn't have been able to. Orla was all fire and heat, and like a moth, he wanted to get as close to her flame as he could, right up to where her incandescence had his flesh burning.

Sir Charles rubbed at his nose and twisted his lips into an expression that was anything but a smile. "Sometimes arguing with you makes me feel like Sisyphus with his damned stone," the old man said. And sometimes, Noah thought, listening to you two makes me wish I'd paid more attention at school. "What part of 'the end of the discussion' didn't you understand, Orla? No, don't bother answering that one, I know the answer. It was the bit where it meant I was saying no to you. You're like a willful child sometimes. I have my reasons for wanting to keep you out of Israel, but if you are so damned determined to get yourself killed, go to Israel.

"Ronan, that means you're on foot patrol here.

"Now, Maxwell is waiting to drive the rest of you to the airfield."

5

THE ADORATION OF SILVER

The old man grappled with his wheelchair, banging the steel rim off the doorframe as he negotiated the turn into one of the many downstairs rooms. He cursed the damned thing, reversed and twisted hard on the right wheel to make sure he made it through on the second attempt. There was no need for it; the wheelchair was electric. He could just as easily have angled it gracefully between the gap using the little joystick set into the armrest, but right now Sir Charles needed to look frustrated. To finish playing the part, he needed to take that "frustration" out with sheer physical exertion. Anything else would have given his satisfaction away.

He slammed the door behind him.

And then he smiled the smile of a man content that he had achieved exactly what he had set out to.

The room was yet another different world within the confines of Nonesuch. It was part study, part retreat. This was the old man's haven. There was an antique pedestal desk with green leather inlay and matching green glass banker's lamp and blotter. The pedestals were chipped and scuffed where he had caught them with the wheelchair. Above the desk was a mirror. Reflected in the mirror was a Rembrandt, brooding and dark with thick, heavy oils. The painting was priceless—or more accurately, beyond pricing—because the rest of the world believed it to be among the lost treasures of the art world, a variant on his 1629 masterpiece *Judas Repentant*. The painting had fascinated Sir Charles, as had the very notion that there could be no rehabilitation for the penitent sinner. What was it Peter had called Judas' repentance? He remembered: *The sorrow of a world which worketh death.*

It was getting progressively more difficult to recall the little things, the ephemera of life, which frightened Sir Charles. The idea of his mental acuity slipping into darkness was terrifying. He'd promised himself he would shuffle off this mortal coil if he ever forgot his own name. It wasn't a promise he was sure he could keep. That was his sorrow. Age.

He studied the painting for the thousandth time. Everything in it appeared to represent genuine shame—the hand-wringing, which mirrored so many portraits of Peter the sinner, the facial expression, even the damage where Judas had been tearing his hair out. They were all classic representations of shame. The difference between this and the original lay in the coins. In the original Judas had been painted as unable to look away from the silver. In this, he offered the blood money up to Mary Magdalene, looking at her with hope, even love, in his eyes. He wasn't groveling for mercy. Instead, there was a discomforting beauty and truth to the painting that had owned Sir Charles' soul since he first laid eyes upon it.

He was a boy when his father had taken him to see it hanging in Jacques Goudstikker's Gallerie in Paris.

It had hung there until the German occupation when, like so many other works of art, it was spirited away into Hermann Göring's personal collection and thought lost forever in the many vaults beneath the Bahnhofstrasse in Zurich.

After decades of litigation, threat and negotiation, a number of paintings had been recovered, but the process was made all the more difficult. Jacques Goudstikker had left his widow, Marei, a typewritten inventory, but without death certificates the Swiss bankers refused to turn over the treasures gathering dust in their vaults.

Of course, Auschwitz, Belsen and Treblinka hadn't been in the habit of issuing death certificates for the Jews they gassed.

It was all a face-saving exercise for the Swiss, who of course, vociferously denied any wrongdoing.

Sir Charles had managed to secure a copy of Marei Goudstikker's list. The interpretation of *Judas Repentant*, known as *The Adoration of Silver*, or more simply, *Silver*, wasn't on that inventory. Its absence had, in part, been the reason behind his obsession with lost treasures.

It had taken him the best part of a decade to grease the right palms, who, in turn, knew the right vault to crack open. Smuggling the Rembrandt out of the country after that had been a comparatively easy task. And now it hung above his desk, a constant reminder that there were two sides to every story, even the best known of all. He had made arrangements for the painting's return to the heirs of its rightful owner upon his death. That, too, was the kind of man he was.

The rest of the room was dominated by a huge orthopedic bed. Again the mahogany frame was scarred where the chair had caught it again and again. Angels, demons and so many creatures of nightmare were beautifully rendered in the frieze that decorated the headboard. Sir Charles had discovered the carving in Palermo and had it shipped to Nonesuch, where he had employed a seventy-year-old artisan to craft the art from a thing of curious beauty into the bed where he intended to die.

There was a green oxygen tank beside the neatly made bed, a clear, plastic mask hanging from the closed valve. The third wall was dominated by more books. Beneath the window an exquisitely hand-carved globe caught the moonlight. It was the oldest thing in the room, the contours of its map hopelessly wrong in this world of GPS and satellite navigation. It was filled with places that had long since slipped off modern maps and into mythology: Hy-Brazil, Hawaiki, Nibiru, Lemuria, Ys, Thule and more. Places that were filled with mystery and promise, lost, like Rembrandt's *Silver*.

Perhaps, he thought, and not for the first time, they too could be found? There was something curiously soothing about tilting at windmills like Quixote.

Sir Charles angled the chair between the bed and the wall, fastened the mask over his face and breathed deeply as the pure oxygen flooded into his lungs. After several purifying breaths he shut off the valve and hung the mask up again. He closed his eyes. He had always intended that Orla would head up the investigation in Israel. Anything else, as she had so vehemently put it, was a waste of her talents—but he was all too aware of what had happened to her out there. It had to be her choice to return to that forsaken land.

The old man drummed his fingers on the arm of the wheelchair. The rhythm sounded like the funeral march of Geppetto's wooden toys. His nails *clacked* and *clinked* and *thunked* against the leather, steel and wood. He found his thoughts drifting.

He hadn't been there for Orla's debriefing, but he'd read Orla's file a thousand times since.

He knew all of the intimate details of Tel Aviv and exactly what had happened to her. Knowing didn't make it any less potent. It didn't purge or cleanse or offer redemption or retribution.

She had been taken during the second Intifada. After a series of suicide attacks the IDF believed stemmed from the Palestinian camp, she had gone in. They were after Mahmoud Tawalbe, a father of two who owned a record store. He also headed an Islamic Jihad cell and was responsible for a string of deaths through suicide bombings at Haifa and Hadera. Intelligence suggested Thabet Mar-dawi and Ali Suleiman al-Saadi, two other top-level Islamic Jihadists were also sheltering in the camp.

Orla's brief had been simple: infiltrate the refugee camp, establish the presence of the primary and secondary targets, and get out. She made her reports, but she didn't get out. She was dragged away from the makeshift streets of the encampment to the heart of Jenin, the Hawashin district, as the first assault hit on the morning of April 2, 2002. Explosions triggered by the bulldozers as they rolled in buried the sound of her screams.

They had told her she was already dead, that there was no place in heaven for her soul, but promised to keep her alive one more night if she gave herself up to them. They used her. Every night they made the same promise, one more night. They kept her for nine days, and though time lost all meaning for her, she suspected that at least five people raped her every night. Often it was two or three at a time, sometimes one man came alone. She didn't fight them. They would beat her, enjoying her pain. They would taunt her, goading her to tears. They would abuse her, violate her. But they refused to kill her even when she begged. Somehow she had made it through, night after night, until the IDF "liberated" the camp.

She hadn't worked for four months when Sir Charles rescued her. The annotation in her service record said simply: *Torture victim. Unstable. Suggest continued observation. If no change in subsequent months recommend transfer out of active service.*

In less clinical words, Orla Nyrén was the quintessential "damaged goods" that could quite easily keep a psychiatrist fed and watered for years.

That didn't change the fact that during their few years together Sir Charles had grown to think of Orla as the daughter he'd never had. He knew her as well as anyone could, and that natural paternal instinct drove him to at least try and protect her, despite the fact that doing so only served to rile her all the more. His gut instinct had been to send Noah with her. Of all of them Noah was the one he would have entrusted with her life because it was so obvious he shared the same adoration the old man did. Without question, Noah would take a bullet for Orla. But Noah Larkin was every bit as damaged in his own way as she was, and just as likely to get them taken down a dark alley and shot as he was to save the day.

He had deliberately stressed Konstantin's qualifications for the Berlin leg of the operation: his familiarity with the city, with the mindset of the people, his network of contacts from both before the wall fell and after. Everything he had said could equally be applied to Orla and Israel, he'd made quite sure of that. The only difference was their relationships with the places. For Konstantin Berlin mean freedom; for Orla Israel meant torture. And because of that, he had been worried she was going to sit back meekly and let Frost take the Israel assignment. He couldn't begin to imagine the conflict going on inside her mind as she listened to him give her city away. The war of emotions, guilt, relief, anger.

It had been such a relief to see the fire back in her belly. He'd even enjoyed her calling him on his pigheadedness like that, even though on the surface it meant losing face with the others. Frost had been around the block often enough to grasp Sir Charles' game, and Lethe was too in awe of the whole spy culture they had going on to dare jeopardize his place in it. Noah was Noah. Unpredictable.

Difficult to read. Konstantin was different. He came from a culture that respected power, even when that power was incontrovertibly wrong. Still, he had fled for a reason. So even the Russian would find something admirable in the old man being persuaded by her arguments. In truth her flare up only served to cement his position rather than undermine it.

He looked at the grandfather clock, with its tarnished brass pendulum swinging slowly to and fro, *tick, tock, tick, tock*. It made time sound so real, so vital. He heard Maxwell ushering them out, heard Noah saying something deliberately antagonistic to him, the car doors slam and then a moment later the peel of tires spitting gravel as the Daimler accelerated toward the airfield. They would be in the air in twenty minutes and halfway to Berlin, their first stop, before the sun was full in the sky.

How many hours did they have until the first attack? He knew he should have handed everything they had over to MI6. It was stupid not to. But it was 4 a.m. There was nothing the spooks could do that his people couldn't. Indeed, free of the constraints of protocols and hierarchy, there was plenty the Forge Team could do that an MI6 operative legitimately couldn't.

He was tired. There were still a few hours until dawn, and as he had told the others, these few hours might well be their last chance to sleep soundly for the foreseeable future.

Undressing, something that he had taken for granted for so long, was a physical trial. He was gasping and panting as he heaved himself out of the wheelchair and levered himself onto the hard mattress. There was nothing graceful about it. He writhed and wriggled like a beached whale trying to get beneath the covers. Sweat peppered his skin. He lay there staring up at the ceiling. Sleep did not come.

The sun did.

6

FIRST BLOOD

Ronan Frost made the ride to Newcastle in a little over four hours, hitting the rush-hour traffic just as it was getting into full, air-polluting swing. The Ducati didn't adhere to the same rules of motion that stifled the steady flow of people carriers and rusty, old cars. Ronan accelerated along the white line, weaving in between the bottlenecked Fords and Volvos. He skirted the edge of the city, coming in from Gateshead, over the Tyne Bridge and the redeveloped Quayside, swept around the Swallow House roundabout and leaned hard into the corner that took him beyond the university buildings toward the more affluent suburbs of Jesmond and Gosforth.

Lethe had given him the names and addresses of the suicides. Three of them were in the Tyne Valley, making it the obvious place to start. Catherine Meadows, the Trafalgar Square suicide, had lived in Queens Road in West

Jesmond; Sebastian Fisher, the Barcelona victim, around the corner on Acorn Road. He turned off the main drag and drove slowly passed Catherine's apartment. It was a huge white building on the corner that had almost certainly been a nursing home or some such before being converted into luxury apartments.

Luxury didn't extend to the fire escape, which looked like it was held together by rust and a prayer. The street outside was lined with parked cars, but there was a small private parking lot beside the building. Three identical black sedans were lined up side by side. They had government plates, not that Ronan needed to see them to know exactly what the three cars meant. MI5 were already here. Bureaucracy was the only thing in his favor right now.

Five and Six were curious beasts, different sides of the spooks coin, and if Ronan's experiences with the left and right hands of the Secret Services were anything to go by, it would take a little while for the bureaucratic wheels to grind and their forced cooperation to come into effect. So, for the moment at least, they would be at crossed purposes. In an hour or two they would have joined the dots and would be singing from the same hymn sheet. That gave him an hour's head start at best.

Ronan throttled the Monster, gunning the engine before giving the bike its head, and roared down the length of the one-way street. He wove between a series of concrete posts meant to stop cars from entering a quieter pedestrian street, took a left and a second left, doubling back on himself. Acorn Road was on the other side of the main road. It was an oddity of English living, cluttered with shops— everything from the usual slew of estate agents, off-licenses, two faux Italian restaurants and an Indian; the obligatory hairdressing salon and a grocery store side by side with the pretension of an art gallery; a high-cost antique shop with marble statuary in the tinted window; and half a dozen chic, high-fashion boutiques with lines imported from all over the world. There was a pub on the corner, The Three Turtles, and beyond the pub, the entrance to the local subway station.

Sebastian Fisher lived above one of the estate agents with a black horse *passant* on its racing-green billboard. The building was like the countless others the Irishman had driven past in the last hour. They called them Tyneside Flats, a 1920s blueprint for mass-housing projects, and like Ford's Model T, where you could have any color you liked as long as it was black, with the Tyneside Flats you got a standardized design. That standardized design meant that without having to step through the front door, Ronan knew the precise layout of Fisher's home.

Ronan pulled in beside the white door in the white façade of the maisonette and hung his helmet on the handlebars. He didn't chain the Monster up.

He took a moment to reconnoiter the place. He still had an hour before the estate agents would be open for business, which meant probably thirty minutes before anyone was in the office to hear him walking about upstairs. The bakery across the street was open, the aroma of fresh pastries a tug on his hungry stomach. They were playing "Handbags and Gladrags" over the tinny speakers. Ronan bought himself a still-warm croissant slathered in melted butter, traded smiles with the young girl behind the counter and, eating as he walked, went around to the alley behind Fisher's place.

A black Labrador pissed up against a green trash can. The dog was all slack skin and stark bones. It obviously hadn't been fed for ages. Ronan tossed what was left of his croissant at it. The mongrel sniffed it suspiciously, then set about it with laving tongue and sharp teeth.

Ronan counted out the gates, stopping outside the ninth one down. It was painted the same bright green of the door on Acorn Road. He tried the latch. It was locked. The top of the gate was lined with four-inch-long metal spikes meant to stop the city's starlings from nesting, but had the added bonus of perforating would-be burglars. The back patio was walled off, the top of the wall cemented with broken glass. Not that that was a problem. Ronan pulled off his leather jacket and laid it over the shards of glass before he boosted himself up over the wall. He came down on the other side lightly and reclaimed his jacket.

It was like he had climbed the wall back into his Derry childhood. The outdoor toilet was there, and beside it the coal shed, though in this case neither had been used for years. The toilet was filled with the odds and ends of abandoned DIY projects of several tenants. There were two doors, one facing him, that obviously led up a steep back staircase, and one set into the side, which opened into the estate agent's office downstairs.

He tried Fisher's backdoor, not expecting it to be unlocked.

It was.

That immediately set his heart to thumping. Even in the better neighborhoods of the city the door should have been bolted at the very least. He eased it open just wide enough for him to slip through, willing it not to groan as he did so. The place smelled musty, as though it had been a while since anyone had opened a window. That answered at least one question Ronan had been wondering about. He climbed the back stairs slowly, one step at a time, letting his weight settle before he moved up to the next, until he was in the small galley kitchen. The unwashed plates of Sebastian Fisher's last meal were still stacked up on the draining board. There were four dinner plates and they had begun to mildew. How long would it take for mildew to claim the sauce on an unwashed plate? A week? No more than ten days, for sure. It gave him a timeframe at least. Fisher had been here a week ago, and he hadn't been alone.

Ronan stood absolutely still, and listened to the sounds of the apartment.

For a moment there was nothing to hear, then the soft groan of a floorboard in one of the other rooms confirmed he wasn't alone.

He had two choices: go back the way he had come, find somewhere to hide and wait for the burglar to make his getaway, then follow him; or try and sneak up behind the intruder, take him down and find out just what the hell was going on. It wasn't much of a choice.

Ronan moved silently to the door and listened. He had the layout in his head. The galley kitchen opened into the living room. In the standard Tyneside layout the living room would have three doors: one to the second bedroom, one to the hall and the master bedroom, box room and bathroom, and the one he was coming in through.

He opened the door.

The room was spartanly furnished and looked like any of the many that cluttered up the daytime television rosters with their bland interior decorating tips. Sebastian Fisher hadn't stamped his personality on the room—unless his personality was cookie-cutter design and IKEA furniture. The one concession to quality was the Onkyo receiver and Jammo speakers beside the tower of CDs. The sound system was probably worth the same as everything else in the room combined. Curiously, there was no television.

The four unwashed plates suggested Fisher didn't live alone, so the second bedroom was probably just that. He moved cautiously toward the door and listened before easing it open. Bunk beds and cluttered toys explained two of the four plates. There were posters on the wall of soccer players Ronan didn't recognize side by side with costumed superheroes and all of the other obsessions of young boys: dinosaurs, space ships and the death masks of Egyptian pharaohs. The beds were unmade, action figures scattered across the floor. The kids had left in a rush.

Ronan felt his skin prickle, a sixth sense flaring, and turned straight into a clubbing right fist. The hammer blow took him in the temple and shook the world around him. He staggered back a step and felt his legs go out from beneath him. Instinctively, he reached out, trying to catch himself before he fell. He caught at his attacker's coat and earned himself a second straight-arm punch. This one hit low, slamming into the side of his neck and choking him. Frost fell to his knees even as his attacker drove a final merciless knee up into his face to batter the last shreds of fight out of him.

He was only down for a few seconds, but it was enough for the intruder to flee. Ronan heard the back door slam and tried to stand. He needed the doorframe to stay on his feet while the apartment swam around him. He felt the warm trickle of blood down the side of his face and saw where it stained the shoulder of his leathers. He shook his head, slapped his face to sting life back into his senses, and took off after the man who had cold-cocked him.

Ronan took the narrow stairs three at a time and threw the back door open in time to see the intruder going over the wall. He reasoned the next move out in the two seconds it took him to cover the distance from the door to the gate. There were two bolts—one top, one bottom—and a latch on the gate, which would take no more than ten seconds to slip. Going over the glass-topped wall would take no more than three seconds but would almost certainly tear his hands up. In those seven seconds the intruder would have to be an Olympic sprinter to hit the end of the alley and disappear out of sight before Ronan could see which way he had gone.

Ronan slammed back the bolts and threw the gate open.

The alley was empty.

"Bollocks," he cursed, looking left and right frantically. He reached for his cell phone to call it in to Nonesuch, slipping the Bluetooth earpiece into his ear. Lethe could hit the Eye in the Sky and track the bastard over every inch of the city if he had to. That was the joy of technology. He hit the speed dial on the earpiece and slipped the phone itself back into his pocket.

"Go for Lethe," the voice in his ear said. The kid liked to play at soldier.

"Jude, it's Frost. There was someone inside Fisher's place. I'm in pursuit on foot. I could really do with some eyes here, so do whatever it is you do." "Understood, boss. I'll have visuals in a few seconds."

Ronan braced his hands on his knees, using those few seconds to catch his breath.

"Come on, come on," Lethe muttered.

Ronan was breathing hard. He looked up at the sky, as though looking for the satellite looking for him.

"It's like looking for a mouse in a bloody great maze. Maybe a bit of cheese would help. You couldn't have picked a busier time could you?"

Ronan looked anxiously one way down the street, then the other.

Finally Lethe half-shouted, "Yes! I see you. Okay, so what am I looking for?"

There was no way the man could have made it to either end of the alley, which meant he had to have gone over another wall and was hiding in one of the many back enclosures.

"Anyone else out here?"

Before Lethe could answer Ronan heard the sound of breaking glass. The walls were too high for him to see which house it was, but they couldn't hide him from Lethe's godlike perspective. "Five doors down. Your side of the street. He's going in through one of the downstairs windows."

It made sense. It was exactly what Ronan would have done if the roles had been reversed. The shops were empty—less chance of coming head to head with an angry homeowner with a baseball bat—and there was a 50-50 chance the shop was on a silent alarm, meaning he could try and exit with the semblance of normality, making it look like there was nothing more natural than him coming out of the closed shop.

And if he couldn't open the door on the other side, couldn't do it the low-key way, a chair out through the window, onto the Monster and away before anyone could stop him.

A moment later the screech of a burglar alarm kicked in and he knew exactly which house the man was in. He ran toward the sound of the siren. There was blood on the glass where the man had gone over the wall. He didn't have a lot of choice except to follow. He boosted himself up. The shards of glass shredded his hands as his weight came down on them. Ignoring the pain, Ronan Frost heaved himself over the wall and dropped down onto the other side. The place was cluttered with empty cartons stamped with names that meant nothing to him. He tried to visualize the business side of Acorn Road and realized it was the hairdressers sandwiched between the antique store and the last of the estate agents.

"Has he come out the other side?"

"Not yet," Lethe told him. "So watch yourself."

He didn't need telling twice, not with the memory of the man's fist still imprinted on his face. He clambered in through the broken window.

There were no lights on inside, giving the other man plenty of shadows to hide in. The silhouettes of the old-fashioned hairdryers looked like something out of an alien movie as they loomed in the darkness, with their bulbous heads and spindly skeletons all lined up against the wall. He strained, peering left and right into the darkness. He couldn't rely upon his eyes, not in the thick darkness of the salon, so he was forced to listen harder and trust his instincts. "I know you're in here," he called out, not expecting an answer.

"Well aren't you the clever one," a woman's voice whispered, so close to his right ear he nearly jumped out of his skin. She had an accent. It wasn't distinct. In fact it was as though she had deliberately tried to hide it, even in those few words. He turned, reaching up a fist as she drove another sucker punch at the side of his head. He caught her wrist and wrenched it savagely downwards. He felt the small bones snap. She didn't scream as he had expected her to. That heartbeat of expectation cost him.

Instead, she drove the heel of her left hand over the top and slammed it into his mouth, snapping his head back. She wrenched her broken arm free as Ronan stumbled back an involuntary step. He released his hold, reaching around his back instinctively for his Browning Hi-Power 9mm. Even as his hand clasped around the Mil-Tac G10 laminate grip the woman double-fisted his face, screaming when the broken bones in her right wrist grated back across each other. The agony of the blow should have knocked her out by rights. It didn't so much as slow her down. As he doubled up she drove her knee up between his legs. He went down hard.

The pistol spilled from his fingers and skidded across the floor.

She stood over him while he tried to reach it. It was more than two feet beyond his fingertips.

"Have you made your peace with God?" she asked, walking across to the Browning. She picked it up, turned it left and right in her hand, then leveled it, drawing a steady aim on Ronan's face. She was wearing a black balaclava. Curls of black hair crept out from beneath the hood. Cradling her broken wrist, she walked toward him slowly, kneeling until the barrel nestled up against his forehead. All it would take was the slightest shift in pressure and she would open a soul-sucking hole in the middle of his skull. With only the black wool of the balaclava around them her eyes stood out, ice-cold cobalt blue.

He could feel her breath on his face. He could feel the slight tremor of the gun against his skin. She wasn't as cool as she made out. She was going to kill him, no doubt about that, but she wasn't a killer. Pulling the trigger wasn't instinctive. She had to think about it. And thinking about it meant he had a chance, even now with the gun pressed up against his skull.

There was no way he could reach up and wrestle the gun from her before she put a bullet in him, and there was no way he could wriggle out from under her either. Ronan closed his eyes. He pictured her in his mind's eye, focusing on her broken wrist. He had one chance. He had to make it count.

He bowed his head, as though in prayer or hiding. It didn't matter which she thought it was, only that she thought it was surrender.

He let his body go limp, accepting the inevitability of the bullet.

He felt the rhythm of her breathing change. She was mastering whatever last shred of doubt that prevented her from pulling the trigger. It was now or never.

Ronan Frost drove his head straight up.

The gun slipped off the side of his head and she fired into the floor. As the recoil jerked her back Ronan gambled his life on the fact that the surprise would leave her broken wrist unprotected. He grabbed it and yanked down on it mercilessly. She squeezed off a second shot in agony. It went into the wall. He forced her hand back impossibly, the broken bones tearing through the skin. It wouldn't take a lot for one of the jagged edges to tear through a vein, he knew. That was the difference between them—he *had* killed before.

She tried to aim the Browning at him, but Ronan slammed his free arm up against hers, sending the gun spinning out of her hand. It discharged again as it hit the floor, the bullet burying itself in the wall beside his head. Ronan threw all of his weight forward, trying to unbalance the woman. She went scrambling backwards, cradling her broken wrist.

He went for the gun.

She ran for the door.

Ronan scrambled across the floor, grabbed the Browning, and rolled half onto his back. He didn't aim, just pulled the trigger. The shot went high and wide, digging out one of the ceiling's Artex swirls. He hadn't expected it to hit.

The woman caught one of the standing hairdryers and, wielding it like a lance, charged at the plate glass window. It shattered around the ceramic bulb of the dryer's head. The woman didn't hesitate; she threw herself head-first out through the window even as the glass shattered into jagged teeth and came snapping down. She hit the street on her right knee and shoulder, rolling through the broken glass and coming up on her feet, torn and bloodied. She cast a single backward glance his way, then took off across the road, sprinting toward the press of people coming out of the subway station.

Walking through the broken glass, Ronan asked Lethe, "You got a visual on her?"

"Of course I have," Lethe said, as though talking to a technologically retarded child. "Hang on, are you telling me a girl just beat you up?"

"Less of the chat. Just tell me where she is."

Ronan ducked through what was left of the window. People were staring at him as he emerged onto the street. He could feel the blanket of shock that was settling over them. This was sleepy suburbia. Gunmen didn't run out into the street. They melted away from him as he set off after the woman. He could feel their fear.

"Police," he shouted, even though it was a lie. That one word reestablished their natural world order.

Ronan ran hard, keeping his body low, arms and legs pumping furiously as he drove himself on. He could see the woman. She had maybe forty yards on him. She had pulled the balaclava off and was running with it clutched in her right hand. She was running flat out, dodging every few steps between commuters on their way to work.

He did the math: The Browning had an effective range of fifty yards; there were a hundred other people in the street, bystanders; she was a moving target, but it was a straight shot. He could almost certainly take her down with a single, well-placed shot—all he had to do was steady himself before he took it. But that meant shooting an unarmed woman in the back. With so many people in the street there was nothing to say someone wouldn't take a step or two the wrong way, distracted by something in a shop window or one of the newspaper headlines on the newsstand, and cross the bullet's path. It was all too easy for someone to wind up getting hit by accident in a crowded street. The woman knew that; that was why she was running toward the thickest concentration of people. Like the old saying went, there was safety in numbers—it was just a different kind of safety.

Ronan had five seconds to take the shot if he was going to take it. After that she was going to disappear into the subway system, Lethe would lose his visual contact and Ronan would be left chasing shadows.

The crowd opened up to swallow the woman and she was gone. He cursed.

"Tell me you can see her!" he shouted into the earpiece.

"Sorry boss."

"Bollocks!" Frost cursed again. He pushed his way between the people, but it was impossible not to be slowed down by them. On one side of the station's entrance flowers spilled into the street, on the other, newspapers. He ran inside and hurdled the ticket barrier. There was only one way she could have gone—down to the platform. Breathing hard Ronan took three and four steps at a time. He tried to see over the heads of the commuters, but one dark, long-haired woman looked very much like another dark, long-haired woman. She was cool. She wasn't pushing her way through the press of people, she was going with it, which made her all the more difficult to spot.

The PA system announced the impending arrival of the next southbound train in its tinny voice. He felt the ground beneath his feet begin to tremble as the subway rumbled in to the station.

He couldn't let her get onto it, not if he wanted to find out who the hell she was working for. He squeezed between a pin-striped suit and a mohair jacket. The air was thick with perfume, cigarette smoke and diesel fumes. A busker stood in the corner where the tunnel bent around to go beneath the tracks. His riff echoed off the yellow tiles. Ronan thought about shouting "Police!" again, but people were just as likely to close ranks to make sure he didn't catch the woman as they were to let him through.

She had to be hurting. The adrenalin would only take away so much of the pain. A broken wrist was a broken wrist. When her body came down from it she'd be in agony. Every bump and jostle against another commuter had to be sending another lancing pain through every nerve and fiber in her body—unless she's loaded up on metham-phetamines, he thought. It made sense. She hadn't so much as flinched when he shattered her wrist. The thought didn't exactly fill him with confidence. He'd come up against meth-heads in combat before—it was like trying to take down the bloody Terminator.

Ronan pushed passed a couple of school girls in their jailbait uniforms of short, checkered skirts and too-tight blouses.

And then he saw her.

She was halfway down the platform, weaving her way toward the dark mouth of the tunnel at the far end. He pushed past another suit, his eyes firmly fixed on the woman's back. The train's headlights shone brightly, illum-inating the entire platform. He felt the displaced wind hit his face as the train slowed to a stop. The doors came open.

She made no attempt to board the train, she just walked on toward the end of the platform. She looked over her shoulder, and Ronan saw her face for the first time.

She didn't have that crazed look of someone stoned out of her mind. She looked—and he couldn't believe he was thinking it—beautiful. Heart-stoppingly so. She had that half-cast of the Middle Eastern territories and very sharp, very precise features. It bought her a few precious seconds while he tried to reconcile the beating he'd taken with the delicate beauty of the woman before him. She saw him and started to run.

She reached the end of the platform as the train started to pull out. She didn't slow down. She jumped down onto the tracks and ran into the all-enveloping darkness of the tunnel.

He pulled the Browning and dropped to one knee, braced to fire into the mouth of the tunnel. He squeezed off a shot. The report was deafening in the confines of the tunnel, amplified by the weird acoustics. There was no accompanying grunt from the darkness. He walked toward the end of the platform.

He could hear her stumbling footsteps as she ran blindly away from him. Those same acoustics that had turned his Browning into a roaring cannon carried the scuff and scrape of her feet on the chips of stone back to him with surprising clarity. Each sound seemed so close he ought to have been able to reach out his hand and touch her.

Ronan stared after her into the black hole.

The sign said four minutes until the next train was due.

The ground beneath his feet shivered as another train rolled into the neighboring platform, scaring a rat out of its hiding place. The sleek-bodied rodent scurried across his feet and disappeared between the cracks in the wall. Ronan watched it go and lashed out at the wall in frustration. He really didn't want to go haring off into a subway tunnel in the middle of the morning rush hour. He could think of a dozen less painful ways to commit suicide.

Still holding the Browning, he dropped down off the platform. The tunnel was unlit, so twenty feet in it became a solid wall of black. He made sure he was in the middle of the rails and set off after her. Behind him a voice came over the PA system, telling them to get off the tracks. He ignored it.

Ronan followed the woman into the tunnel and prayed to whatever god looked after Irish idiots playing on railway lines that the next train was cancelled.

A dozen paces in the darkness became absolute. He stopped dead still, trying to hear her in front of him. He couldn't. The darkness was filled with the sound of his own heavy breathing. "Don't do this," he called out, still not moving. He heard something then, a soft skittering in response to his voice: more rats. "There's nowhere to run, and in a couple of minutes the next train's going to make this tunnel pretty bloody uncomfortable for both of us. Come on, don't make this any more difficult than it has to be."

He waited. Nothing.

She wasn't coming out. He tried to think. He was really beginning to wish he'd taken the shot when he'd had the chance. She was a professional, which meant, more likely than not, she wouldn't be carrying anything that identified her or tied her in with whoever had hired her to give Fisher's place a going over. But even professionals made mistakes. He'd taken her by surprise. She'd run before she could find whatever it was she'd gone there looking for— which meant it was still back there waiting to be found.

He chewed on his top lip, took a deep breath.

Ronan started to walk forward. He felt out each step carefully, scuffing his toe along the rough stones until he found the safety of the next wooden tie. One step at a time he edged his way deeper into the tunnel. He cast a quick glance over his shoulder to make sure the light wasn't too far away for him to make it back when the skin along his forearms prickled. The air around him stirred ever so slightly.

And then he felt it: the telltale tremor of the train shivering through the tracks. A moment later light swept around the corner. He saw her caught in the train's headlights. She was no more than twenty feet in front of him, looking around frantically until she saw whatever it was she was looking for, and started to run toward the oncoming train.

Ronan knew then he wasn't going to need to take the shot. The train would do his dirty work for him—but there would be nothing left but blood and guts on the tracks for him to pick over, and only then if he managed to get out of the tunnel himself before the train sheered his body in two. He screamed at the woman. There were no words, just this raw explosion of sound from his mouth.

Inside his cabin, the driver leaned on the horn. In the tunnel the collision of sounds was deafening: the screech of the brakes, the shriek of steel sliding on iron as the wheels locked and slid, the blare of the horn as the driver hit it over and over again, the maddening bark of the loudspeaker ordering them off the tracks, and Ronan Frost's screams as he watched the woman running hell for leather straight at the front of the train.

And then she disappeared.

Just like that.

One minute she was there, and the next she wasn't.

But there was no bloody detonation of flesh. No impact. No spray of blood across the headlights. No body strewn in pieces across the tracks.

The sight kept him rooted to the spot a second too long.

He felt the next breath die in his throat.

Ronan realized he didn't have time to run. There was no way he'd make it out of the tunnel and back up onto the platform before the train slammed into his back. He knew what she'd done; she'd run for one of the service stairways.

He looked left and right. The entire tunnel lit up like midday by the onrushing headlights. He couldn't see anywhere to hide. *So much for that god*, the thought flashed across his mind. Of all the "last things" he had expected to flood his final moments—beautiful women loved and lost, friends betrayed, lives taken and saved—cursing a make-believe deity hadn't so much as registered as a possible farewell-to-the-flesh thought.

He thought about throwing himself down and lying flat on his stomach between the tracks and praying there wasn't a trailing hook dangling from the train's under-carriage to gut him like a fish and drag him all the way back to the city center.

The headlights were huge now, filling the tunnel. The tunnel itself wasn't wide enough for him to press himself up against the wall. He looked down at the wheels, then at the tracks and at the curve of the wall, and realized it was his only chance. The horn blared again. Despite the shriek of the breaks the train wasn't slowing anywhere near quickly enough to save his life. He had seconds to think.

Move.

One chance.

It all came down to the width of the tracks and the aero-dynamics of the train itself. All he could do was pray there was an inch to spare.

Ronan Frost hurled himself sideways, hitting the ground hard, and wedged himself into the narrow gap between the iron rail and the concrete wall. He rolled over onto his right shoulder, face pressed right up against the cold concrete. He tried to stop breathing and melt into the wall, making himself as thin as possible. The horn screeched in his ears, so close it could have been inside his head. He closed his eyes, willing himself not to flinch. The wind battered him up against the wall. Suddenly an incredible force tried to peel his head up into the train's path.

Ronan gritted his teeth and pressed his face into the

gravel. The vacuum caused by the displaced air and the train's momentum tore at his hair. His screams were lost beneath the madness of the hellbound train. An agonized sob tore between his teeth. He resisted every impulse to throw his head back to relieve the pain, knowing that it all that was saving his life.

The *duh-duh-de-duh duh-duh-de-duh* of the wheels filled his head.

He couldn't breathe.

The wind displaced by the train pummeled the Irishman up against the concrete wall, and he loved every damned second of that pain because it meant he was alive.

And then it was gone. The train had passed him, and he could breathe again. He lay there for a full thirty seconds, listening to the mad rise and fall of his own breathing, then pushed himself to his feet. He thought about going deeper into the tunnel, chasing the woman up the service stairwell to the surface, but she'd be long gone by the time he reached the top. Still, there was no way she could know he'd survived. In her place he would go back to the apartment to finish what he'd started. He had to assume she'd think like him.

Ronan Frost walked unsteadily toward the light.

He felt a warm, wet stickiness on his cheek and reached up to feel out the damage. He pulled his hand away and looked at it. There was more blood than he would have expected. The gravel had cut up the side of his face.

As he came out of the tunnel, the first of the next wave of commuters had begun to file onto the platform. A few of them looked at him curiously; the others adopted the Ostrich's if-I-don't-see-it-it-doesn't-see-me attitude, deliberately not looking his way. That was what the city had become over the last few years. A decade ago a good Samaritan would have come to the end of the platform to help him up while someone else went for help. Today they watched him suspiciously as he climbed unsteadily back to the platform and walked toward them. He couldn't blame them. He knew what he must have looked like, battered and bloody and, he realized, still holding the Browning in his right hand.

Ronan holstered the gun.

Walking back toward the entrance he hit the speed dial on the earpiece, but he'd lost the network down in the tunnel. He pushed his way through the barriers, ignoring the stares, and hit the speed dial again and again until Lethe answered: "Talk to me."

"Lost her in the tunnels and nearly got myself flattened by the 8:30 to South Shields. All in all not the best result."

"Oh, I'd say the *nearly* part was a home win. So, fill me in?"

"Female. Middle Eastern origin. Lebanese, if I was forced to guess—she had that look. Five eight with a punch like Tyson. Beautiful. And by that I don't mean the kind of girl you want to take home to meet your mother; we're talking life as a willing sex slave."

"I'll run her against Six's active database. If she's running out of the Middle East, odds are Intelligence has got something on her," Lethe said in his ear. "Maybe they've got a 'hot assassin' search string set up."

"She used one of the emergency service stairwells on the southbound rail, maybe fifty yards inside the tunnel. Can you pull up the schematics and see where she'll have come out?" Ronan asked, ignoring him.

"Already on it, Frosty. Looking for live stream CCTV in the vicinity right now. If she came out that way, I'll find her, have no fear."

Ronan walked back toward the apartment on Acorn Road. As he had expected, the police had begun to gather outside the broken window of the hairdressing salon. He had to get back inside Fisher's place, but he could hardly walk up to the front door looking the way he did; and the back alley was already crawling with cops.

A row of magpies sat on the guttering above the

hairdresser's. He counted them, doing the old rhyme in his head: *One for sorrow, two for joy, three for a girl, four for a boy, five for silver.*

He walked on two streets and stripped out of his leathers and stuffed them behind one of the dumpsters. He would collect them later. One of the bystanders was sure to remember the leather-clad biker who had come chasing the woman out of the broken window. They wouldn't remember the gray-haired guy in the designer suit.

He took a handkerchief from his pocket, wadded it up and dabbed at his face, using it to soak up the worst of the blood, then dumped it in a trash can. He couldn't exactly clean himself up properly, but he looked different enough to pass a cursory inspection.

It was all about the instantly recognizable details—that was the way the brain worked. It registered the leathers and more than likely demonized the man holding the gun. Witnesses were unreliable at the best of times. Out of the leathers and tidied up, none of them would identify him as the demon.

"Well," he said to himself, "time to put the theory to the test."

He walked back to the alley behind Fisher's place.

There were two policemen standing guard at the hairdressers gate.

He said hi as he walked past them. That was part of the trick, having the brass balls to look like you belonged there, no matter where there was. He had to keep his back turned away from them. The last thing he needed was one of them noticing the blood stains. The older of the two police lifted his radio and talked into it. He seemed to be taking a little too much interest in Ronan. He didn't want him looking too closely.

Ronan kept his pace regular, resisting the temptation to walk faster. He willed the policeman to look away, but he didn't. *Just look like you belong*, he said to himself. *Keep it natural. You live here. They have no reason to think otherwise. Just walk up to the gate and open it.* He was glad he'd taken the extra few seconds to open the green gate before. Now as he reached it, he thumbed down the latch, pushed it open and walked inside. It was a lot less suspicious than boosting himself up over the glass-topped wall.

Inside it took him less than two minutes to find what he'd been looking for.

Beside the computer in the study there was a photo of Fisher and his two girls, and tucked into the frame was one of those little photo-booth instant snaps. The woman in the smaller picture was unmistakably Catherine Meadows. She was cheek-to-cheek and laughing with Sebastian Fisher, and it was obvious in that one photograph that they were in love.

What could make a man burn himself alive? he asked himself, and this time he knew the answer, the only answer: to protect someone he loved.

Sebastian Fisher had loved three people. One of them had burned alive with him—a different place, but the precise same moment in time. The other two were missing.

He called in to Lethe again. "Found the leverage. Someone took Fisher's kids." Judging by the picture and the toys in the room, he made an educated guess at their respective ages, six and eight.

"Bollocks," Jude Lethe said.

"He was involved with Catherine Meadows, so it isn't out of the question that Fisher's kids were used to keep her in line as well. There are enough signs about the place to suggest the pair all but lived together. We aren't talking an underwear drawer—she's got half the closet space, half the drawers, and a bathroom cabinet full of cosmetics."

"Have I told you how much I hate people?" Lethe said. "What are the chances of us getting the kids back alive?"

It wasn't something Ronan wanted to think about. The

truth of the matter was, the kids were almost certainly dead now that they'd outlived their usefulness. "Not going to happen," Ronan said, rifling the desk drawers as he spoke. "Any joy with the surveillance cameras?"

"Your Jane Bond didn't come out of the tunnels through any service exit within five hundred yards of where you lost her. Sorry, man. Odds are she doubled back after you were gone and hopped on the next train out of there." It made sense. She had been thinking at least three moves ahead of him, and that rattled Ronan Frost.

Ronan opened the bottom drawer. Inside was a photograph album that looked as though it had seen better days. He pulled it out and opened it up. It was full of younger versions of Sebastian Fisher and Catherine Meadows mugging for the camera. He thumbed through the pages, looking at the ghosts of two happy people. On the back of the sixth side he found what he was looking for. The top of the page was marked up *Masada*. The entire gatefold was filled with similar images: the harsh sun, the sand and parched grass and the ruins of the hill fort. He peeled away the film and pocketed each of the photographs. The last one was a group shot of the archeology team. On the back, in neat feminine script, someone had listed the names of the people in the photo. There were thirty in the shot. He recognized almost half of them without having to look up their names.

Four of the Israeli helpers were listed by first name only.

The fifth, shirt sleeves rolled up, eyes like burned-out coals, was labeled as Akim Caspi. Even though he had only seen the one photo of the man in full military regalia, and factoring in the passage of time and unreliable memory, there was no way on God's earth that the Akim Caspi in the picture was the same Akim Caspi that had been a lieutenant general in the Israeli Defense Force.

Things, as Orla Nyrén liked to say, were beginning to get interesting.

Potsdamer Plats, Berlin

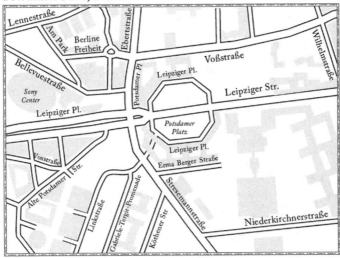

7

GOING UNDERGROUND

They fought as they walked down the street. It was stupid stuff. Sarah wanted to go to Checkpoint Charlie, and he wanted a piping hot Americano and a sickly sweet pastry first. The two didn't need to be mutually exclusive. He'd tried to reason with her. They were on vacation, and by definition that meant there was no need to rush, but Sarah was being Sarah. She had got it into her head she wanted to get to Friedrichstrasse early so they didn't waste the rest of the day.

She wanted to hit the Brandenburg Gate, the cathedrals in the Gendarmenmarkt, and if they could manage it, make Spandau around lunchtime. He wanted to take his time, cross over into what had been East Berlin and try to imagine what it had been like back in '61 when the Russian tanks blocked the road. It was a crying shame they'd torn down the old Watchtower. There was nothing left of the original Checkpoint Charlie buildings, but that didn't stop him from wanting to soak up the history of the place.

It had become something of a pilgrimage for him—and not the usual honeymoon fare. His grandfather had died trying to come across that no-man's land between East and West. He knew it was just going to be a street now, but that didn't matter. It wasn't what it was, it was what it had been. Sarah understood that. That was one of the reasons he loved her. There were plenty of those. They might fight like cats and dogs but she understood him. Hell, she loved him for his flaws, not despite them, and that was worth every stupid fight they'd ever had.

She'd marked the route on the map, they needed to take the U2 east from Potsdamer Platz to Stadtmitte and transfer on to U6 north.

"For God's sake, Sarah," he grumbled, wrestling with the weight of the backpack as he tried to follow her. She was walking too fast for him and he hated talking to the back of her head—even if it was a beautiful back of the head. "It isn't going to kill us if we don't get to the concentration camp by twelve. We can always catch a later train," he said, shaking his head. "I'm hungry, I'm tired and we're meant to be on bloody holiday!" he shouted. He couldn't help himself.

"Go to hell," his wife of seven days turned and yelled at him.

Germans turned to look at them, no doubt wondering at the tourists who lacked the good grace to keep their arguments inside.

"Sarah!" he shouted after her, but it only made her walk faster. "Oh, for crying out loud, woman!"

She didn't so much as break her stride. He hiked the backpack farther up his back and tried to push his way between the unmoving Germans as they gathered around the turnstiles leading down onto the U-Bahn. He didn't have the tickets. She did.

"Sarah!" he shouted above the heads of the Germans.

She ignored him.

He pushed his way over to one of the ticket machines, fumbled with the coins in his pocket and fed them into the slot. It seemed to take forever to print his ticket out. He pushed his way back to the barriers. He couldn't see Sarah, but he knew where she was going. He looked at the signs, trying to work out which platform he needed for Stadt-mitte. He chased her down to the platform, arriving as the train doors shut.

He waved at the driver and ran as best he could with the weight of the backpack slapping against his back and trying to knock him over. Sarah was in the fourth car down. He saw her looking at him through the glass. She was crying. She looked so beautiful and so sad with the tears staining her cheeks. They had only been married for a week. She wasn't meant to be crying. Seeing her like that hurt him. He wished he'd just shut his mouth and kept up with her instead of whining about wanting a cup of coffee and a stupid, bloody muffin. He knew it was important to her that everything was just so. She needed order, and he didn't have to be a prick about it all of the time.

As the train pulled away from the station he tried to pantomime that he was sorry. She stopped looking at him. It wasn't that she was angry—he could live with that, anger came and went—it was that she looked so sad sitting there alone.

He tried his cell phone but there was no reception.

He dropped his shoulder and shrugged out of the pack. The next train wasn't due into the station for seven minutes. He dragged it over the wall and slumped down against it, using the backpack as a backrest. He wanted a cigarette, but the entire U-Bahn was no smoking, so he resigned himself to suffer in silence. He'd light up as soon as he left Friedrichstrasse, and then he'd set about finding Sarah and making it up to her.

The platform didn't take long to fill again.

A woman sat down beside him and asked him if he had made his peace with God. He looked at her. She didn't look like a crazy subway evangelist. She was cute in a Japanese-high-school-girl sort of way with her Heidi-pigtails and knee-length, white cotton socks. She could have been anywhere between 13 and 23 years old, given the bright blue eye shadow and lavender lip gloss. It was impossible to tell. She had a bag slung over her shoulder. There was one of those stylized Japanese cartoons painted on the side of it. He couldn't remember what they were called. It didn't really matter. She was the least likely evangelist he'd ever seen.

She reached into her bag for something. He assumed she was going to read him something from her Bible.

She wasn't.

She pulled a small aluminum thermos flask from the shoulder bag and uncapped it. She up-ended it. A small amount of liquid dribbled out. It wasn't water. It was a tiny amount of liquid sarin. Curls of almost smoky gas evaporated away from the puddle. The thermos hadn't been keeping the liquid cold, it had been keeping the gas just warm enough to maintain its state. The dribble of liquid was all that had cooled enough to condense. Liquid sarin would kill a dozen people, maybe, if they came into contact with it. As a gas anyone who ingested it was dead. On a busy subway system that could mean thousands of people.

"In a moment your nose is going to run. You'll feel a tightness in your chest, and your skin will feel as though it is shrivelling around your body, becoming too tight for the flesh it contains. Then you'll begin to lose your sight. Don't be frightened, it will all happen very quickly," she said, in the most soothing, sympathetic and psychotic voice he had ever heard. She was right, he could feel the snot running out of his nose already. "You'll hardly know it is happening. A few moments of agony and then it will be over. I am going to die with you. I'll hold your hand as we go, if that helps?"

He looked at her. She wasn't mad. She wasn't some raving fanatic. She reached out to hold his hand. He pulled away from her.

"What have you done to me?" he demanded. It hurt to talk. He felt the first flush of pins and needles creeping through his skin and down into his bones. She was right. It was happening quickly. He shivered once, painfully. He felt his gorge rise and leaned over, sure he was going to vomit. "What have you done to me?" he pleaded.

She ignored him. "In a few seconds you're going to find it very difficult to breathe. It will feel like your entire body is shutting down. You'll lose control of your body." Her breath was coming harder now. She was gasping between words. "You will throw up. You will lose control of your muscles. In seconds you will soil yourself. There is nothing you'll be able to do about it. It is death. Every nerve will cry out, and finally your flesh won't be able to cope. You will twitch and jerk, wracked by spasms. The fit will be brief. As you go blind, you will suffocate. There is nothing you can do about it. You are already dead. We all are. Everyone down here is dead."

He looked along the platform. The people were blurs, dark smudges leaning against the walls and each other for support. He could hear them coughing and gasping. Someone cried out, a woman, "Ich kann nicht sehen! Hilf mir, mein Gott, ich bin blind!"

He only understood the last word. He didn't need to know any more to understand what was happening along the platform from him.

It had only taken seconds to spread.

He clutched at the woman beside him, trying to pull her toward him. His lips twitched, but the words wouldn't come.

The world around him lost its shape, the blurred shapes of the damned spreading across his eyes until all he saw was black.

He heard the next train roll into the station, the doors hiss and the screams as people stumbled toward it as though it could bear them away to safety. He couldn't see any of it. He couldn't see the faces of the condemned pressed up against the glass. He couldn't see them clawing at the platform, shivering and twisting as they tried to crawl another precious inch forward. He couldn't see the fear on the passengers' faces as they disembarked. It had been more than half a century since a train last rattled through Berlin carrying so many doomed souls. These passengers were just as dead, and just as unwitting.

He fell sideways, face hitting the floor as another wretched spasm wracked his body, and all he could think as he fought for that last breath was that their stupid argument had saved Sarah's life.

And for that he was grateful.

8

SORROW'S BRIDE

Konstantin Khavin walked through a city in mourning.

The first reports of the horror on the U-Bahn had reached the surface. People stood around in shock, not really knowing if they were supposed to run or go about their everyday routines. Five stations had been hit, and if what he was hearing was to be believed, two of the S-Bahns as well as the city's bus terminus. At least six busses had carried punctured sarin gas bags, dispersing the nerve gas all over the city. It was a brutal way to die.

A radio in an open window played "My Funny Valentine." The vocal strain drifted across the narrow street, transforming it into something out of a Wim Wenders movie. A girl on the street corner sat making Chinese cranes out of scraps of paper. She lined them up along the gutter. There were hundreds of them. She looked up at him, eyes wide with sorrow, and said, "Dies, damit Gott sie nicht vergisst." He knew what she meant: they are so God doesn't forget them. It was a surreal and sad moment, this little girl mourning hundreds, perhaps thousands, of people she had never met. That was the power of a tragedy on such a huge scale. It hurt everyone. The suffering was collective. The mourning public, loud and heartbreaking.

The "other shoe" had dropped in the middle of the early morning rush hour when hundreds of thousands of people were on their way into work across the city, and every level of the public transport system had been hit.

Everything about it made Konstantin angry—he wanted to lash out, hit something, someone—but it was an entirely impotent rage. There was nothing he could do for anyone here, and there was cold comfort in knowing that they were right, that Berlin had been one of the primary targets. It had been a long time since he had left Mother Russia—so long in truth he found it difficult to bring back memories of her streets and her dizzying architecture. Now all he remembered were her crimes.

The world had changed around him in that time. There had been an ethic to terror once, it protected normal people going about their normal lives. They were shielded by some sort of covenant between the oppressor and the oppressed. Strikes were made against legitimate targets: military bases, intelligence operations, weapons stores, and with more localized terror campaigns like Northern Ireland the Provo targets were policemen, political movers and sha-kers, journalists and the like. They weren't kids on the way to school. They weren't mothers pushing baby buggies and balancing groceries. They weren't the city's financial wiz-kids, with their heads full of long-term futures. They weren't the baristas and the store clerks and the bus drivers and the road sweepers that made day-to-day living so much more pleasant than it might have been. The face of terror had changed.

It was more Russian in nature.

Konstantin shivered at the thought.

He felt for these people even though he did not know them.

The old man was right: it was all about the spectacle. This fear was Russian. It dug deep into the psyche of the people. It hurt them where they felt safest—in their everyday life. It was like the KGB arrest squads that battered down the door at four a.m.—it was disorientating, frightening. They came in making noise, shouting, screaming, threatening violence while the suspect, naked and vulnerable, woke to the chaos of their forced entry. If they fought back, they were beaten. If they resisted, they were beaten. If they didn't fall to their knees, beg, confess, they were beaten. If they weren't alone, their wives, girlfriends or lovers were beaten to make them beg and plead. At four a.m. fear broke strong men. That was the Russian way.

He knew that because, once upon a nightmare, he had been one of those four o'clock men.

And now that same fear was being turned upon everyday people as they went about their everyday lives. Konstantin felt curiously at home in this violent society, more so than he ever could have in a world of poets and lovers. But then he had been raised with violence into a world of violence, so it was hardly surprising.

Konstantin was one of the few people on the street walking with a purpose. He was alert, eyes moving quickly from face to face, looking for guilt or complicity in any of the people he passed. Of course it was never going to be that easy. All he saw was shock and disbelief repeated over and over in every face. He knew what they were thinking: How could it happen here? How could it happen to us?

The dossier Lethe had provided him on the man who had burned himself alive in Potsdamer Platz less than twenty-four hours earlier was painfully thin. His name was Grey Metzger, age 34, German father, English mother, born in White Cliff, Whitby. He'd come to Berlin six months before on fellowship to the university, part of an exchange with the University of Nottingham, where he taught Medieval European history. And that, as they say, was all she wrote. No wife, no kids, no debts, no sudden or surprisingly large deposits in his checking account—the balance was a rather uninspiring three thousand and twenty-seven Euros. There was no savings account, no share certificates or other bonds issued in the name of Grey Metzger.

If the paper trail was to be believed, he lived month to month with very little to spare. He paid his bills on time. He had borrowed a grand total of eleven books from the library since coming to Berlin, none of the titles particularly surprising given his specialism. There were no untoward comings or goings registered against his passport number with immigration control. He was the very definition of an ordinary man.

All of that in itself interested Konstantin.

In his world there were no ordinary men.

Metzger maintained a small apartment in Charlottenburg, one of the more affluent boroughs of the old city. It was close to the University of the Arts, so what it cost in increased rent, it saved in convenience. The location might have been an extravagance, but it was an extravagance that was very much in keeping with the kind of man who counted out every penny and measured its worth against its cost. Charlottenburg was an oasis of calm even in the days of the divided city.

He turned onto Schlossstrasse. It was easy to imagine the residents hidden behind those windows, safe in their ivory towers, untouched by the suffering it brought to their city. They would not be so distant today. That too was an element of the new fear—it was intimate.

A newspaper vendor on the street corner was shouting news of the tragedy to anyone who would listen and waving the latest edition, hot off the press, under their noses. Konstantin crossed the street to avoid the man. He counted the other people on the street. There were twenty-seven. One of the busiest streets in the city at what should have been one of the busiest times, and there were only twenty-seven people out about their business. There was a painted red kiosk selling bratwurst and other sausages. A single man sat huddled up against the cold with a half-eaten brat and dried onions slathered in mustard and ketchup. He was the closest thing to normal in the street.

How had it come to this? How had this kind of fear become so commonplace?

Metzger lived on the third floor behind a security intercom, through a marbled foyer and up a curving granite stair. Everything about the building said Old World affluence. He ran his finger down every one of the buttons until someone buzzed him in. People were careless like that, even in the anonymity of the big cities—especially in the anonymity of the big cities. He closed the door quietly behind him and took the time to wipe the street off his shoes on the mat, scuffing each sole backward and forward three times before he opened the second inner door and walked through to the foyer.

It was three degrees colder than it was in the street. The huge iron radiators were at least half a century old, and no doubt the boiler feeding them was just as decrepit. Brass mailboxes lined the right-hand side wall of the small antechamber. Konstantin ran his fingers over the names, stopping at G. Metzger. He didn't have a key for the box. He didn't need one. It wasn't a particularly sophisticated lock. Mailboxes seldom were. The mail, it seemed, was sacrosanct. Again, that was a marked difference from his world, where the mail was monitored, censored and often used to incriminate, no matter that Stalin had been dead for the best part of sixty years. Old habits die hard.

He took his key chain out of his pocket, sorting through them until he found a small enough bump key. Konstantin took his left shoe off and set it down on the small shelf beneath the mailboxes. The theory behind the bump key was simple: all of the grooves filed down to their lowest peak setting. He slipped it all of the way into the lock, then eased it out a single notch. He applied the slightest of pressure to the key, as though beginning to turn it, then bumped the key with the heel of his shoe. The sudden sharp impact caused the pins to jump out of the rotator, giving him the fraction of a second he needed to turn the key. It took him four seconds to open the mailbox.

He sorted through the envelopes as he walked up the stairs. Every groove from every dragged foot was worn deep into the steps, and the wrought-iron filigree beneath the polished-smooth banister had oxidized to the richest red. There were more than twenty envelopes, and the majority of them were computer-generated mass-mailings or this month's bills. Even with three flights of stairs to climb he hadn't managed to read more than half of the dead man's letter. He didn't really need to read any more than that.

Only one envelope was handwritten. People didn't send letters anymore. That made a handwritten envelope something of a curiosity. He teased one of the seams open, careful not to contaminate the glued edge. There was no way of knowing if the contents of the envelope were important, but there was no sense in treating them any other way. If needs be, the old man could get the saliva used to lick the stamp and seal the envelope analyzed, its DNA lifted for comparison or identification purposes. There was so much about this new world that was every bit as frightening as anything that had ever happened in Stalinist Russia.

He reached Metzger's door. The brass number in the center of it had turned green. What he read caused him to check the date stamped on the envelope. It had been posted the day before—the same day Grey Metzger had killed himself. The processing time was stamped at 16:00 CET. The precise moment Metzger had hung up his phone and burned.

It was a love letter, but it talked about him, not to him, as though the writer knew he would never read it but needed to get these words down, to make them exist; as though, like the little girl with her paper cranes, by setting them down God would read them and would remember her man and her love for him—which, Konstantin extrapolated the thought, meant the writer had known Metzger was going to die when she wrote it. He grunted. That meant she had mailed it out with an almost prescient precision. Was she involved? No, he shook his head. This wasn't the confession of his killer. There was no mocking tone, no gloating. Only sadness. Her words were so intense. It wasn't about Metzger at all, it was about his woman. The one Lethe hadn't been able to find on the paper trail.

It was about leverage.

They'd given her the chance to put it all down on paper, and they'd led her to the post office and mailed the letter out at the precise moment the man she loved burned himself alive.

Who were these people?

The strange tense wasn't because she had known he was dead—she wasn't mourning him—it was because she knew she was going to be dead when he read it. It had kept her quiet, given her something to focus on, but she would have known she was a dead woman walking. She hadn't collapsed, she'd written the letter. That took strength. Strength meant she would almost certainly have tried to tell him what had happened to her, somehow, somewhere in the letter.

Did they have pet words? Did she say "remember when we sat on the steps of the Berliner Dom" or "I've never forgotten the rain-filled day we walked hand in hand in the shadow of Checkpoint Charlie"? Something, a reference to a place, a name, anything? There had to be something buried in all of these words of love, a clue that told them who had taken her, or where, something. There had to be. She had been strong enough to write the letter; that meant she had to be smart enough to help them now, from beyond the grave.

He stuffed it into his pocket and kicked his shoe off again. He'd finish it inside.

It only took him nine seconds to open Metzger's front door in exactly the same way he had bumped the lock on the mailbox.

Konstantin closed the door behind him.

The apartment was everything he would have expected from a middle-class existence. The hallway doubled as the library, shelved floor to ceiling with the battered spines of academia and the occasional concession to pop culture. There were very few novels, he noticed, scanning the titles. The books nearest the door were almost exclusively concerned with the Byzantine period. As he moved toward the living room the time line moved with him. The majority of interest seemed to be focused on Medieval Europe, which made sense.

The last bookcase was filled with cheap, trashy airport novels. The spines were creased, the pages dog-eared, as though each one had been read a dozen times. He took one down from the shelf and thumbed through it. On the inside he saw a price written in pencil and the stamp of a second-hand bookstore in the city. He tried three more, selected at random. They all bore the same secondhand stamp.

There was a television, a small portable set that had to be over twenty years old. It didn't dominate the room. Indeed, given the angle it was on, it was almost certainly never watched. There was nothing to say it even worked. Konstantin assumed that these dog-eared paperbacks had replaced the television in Grey Metzger's life. Like Russia, the Germans protected their language obsessively, dubbing the endless reruns of American sitcoms. It would have come as something of a culture shock to an Englishman who probably thought the world revolved around his mother tongue. Konstantin shelved the book.

The hallway opened into a high-ceilinged room. The drapes where thick, heavy green velvet, tied back with a thick gold brocade rope. The hook in the wall had an exquisitely molded lion's head. It was a small detail, but as the KGB had drilled into him, the truth was in the details. There were dozens of tiny details, from the wainscoting on the sash window and the original ropes laid into the side of the frame to the black and white tiles that made a chessboard of the floor, or rather the three broken ones that might have been proof of a struggle. Konstantin walked slowly around the room, then sank into the faux Chesterfield sofa in the middle of the room.

He put his feet up on the granite-topped coffee table. The room barely looked lived in. He had expected it to be strewn with journals and academic literature, with forgotten coffee cups and other signs of the absent-minded professor, but Grey Metzger was meticulously ordered and fastidiously tidy. Like a man who had been a guest here, not the owner.

Or like a man whose life had been purged away before he could come in and look at it, he thought.

There was a single painting on the wall. Konstantin recognized it: *Sorrow*. It was a print, rather than the original, but that was hardly surprising—a school teacher would not have had the wherewithal to own a painting worth upwards of fifty million dollars. It was, Konstantin thought, an ugly image to have on the wall where you did most of your living.

There was a fish tank beneath it, but there were no fish in it.

Konstantin was beginning to get a feel for the man he was following.

He checked the rest of the apartment.

There was a neatly made bed with white silk sheets in

the one bedroom, and a manikin draped with the dead man's clothes stood in the corner, looking like the Ghost of Christmas Past come to haunt the room. The rug appeared to be an elk hide. There was little in the way of personality to the room, not so much as an alarm clock on the side table. He checked the drawers. They were empty. That, more than anything else, convinced him that the apartment had been cleaned by whoever had last set foot in the place. It would be pointless dusting for fingerprints.

In the center of the bathroom was a beautiful antique porcelain bathtub set on pedestal legs. Again, like the details in the curtain hooks in the front room, the legs were molded in the likeness of lions. There were no shampoo bottles, no body washes or facial scrubs. There wasn't a toothbrush in the cup on the sink. He ran his finger along the top of the medicine cabinet—it came away without so much as a speck of dust on it.

The narrow galley kitchen was just as bare. He opened the cupboards one at a time, but after the first he knew it was pointless. There wasn't a single package of junk food in any of them. No boxes of cereal. No tea bags. No dried spaghetti or noodles or any other staple of fast-food living. There should have been moldy bread, curdled milk in the refrigerator, cheese blue with bacteria and many other signs of abandonment. But there wasn't. The purge had been absolute. There was nothing of Grey Metzger left in the place save those few clothes on the manikin and the books.

Konstantin reached into his pocket for the letter. Could they have been so thorough and so careless at the same time? He went back through to the living room, but instead of sitting on the leather sofa he perched on the windowsill so that he could look out over the People's Park as he read it again.

He read the letter through, start to finish, three times. The first thing he noticed this time was that she had called him Graham, his full name, not Grey, not the short, affectionate version a lover might be expected to use. That seemed odd given that Grey used the shortened version of his name on almost every official document Lethe had uncovered. The second thing that stuck out was that she hadn't signed it with her name, rather she'd called herself Sorrow's Bride. That was hardly the goodbye a lover would want to be remembered by.

The rest of the letter was the usual string of sentimental stuff and nonsense that had his eyes glazing over after thirty seconds. He forced himself to concentrate, going over each sentence slowly, looking for an out-of-place word, looking at how the letters themselves rested on the lines in case she'd elevated the occasional letter to spell out some second message within the message—a way of talking to them from beyond the grave. There was nothing that he could see.

He sat there for an hour, the midday sun streaming in through the windows in bright unbroken beams. The heat through the glass prickled his skin. Konstantin looked up from the letter and saw Van Gogh's *Sorrow*, with her sagging breasts, weeping into her hands, and he was again struck by how ugly the painting really was, especially for the only piece of art in the place. He put the letter back in the envelope and the envelope back inside his pocket and went over to the painting. He reached up and ran his fingers over it, feeling for any imperfections on the canvas. He worked his fingers from the top edge of the frame down, slowly. He chewed on his lower lip, not realizing he was doing it. There was nothing. The frame was perfectly smooth. He ran his hand up and down the sides of the frame again, refusing to believe he was wrong. Second time was no more revealing. He hadn't really expected the cryptic epigraph to mean anything, but it had been worth a try.

He grunted.

It had been too easy to think she'd simply point him to the hidden treasure, X marks the spot.

For the sake of thoroughness, he lifted down the picture. There wasn't a safe hidden away conveniently behind the picture, of course. The sun-shadow outline of the picture was stained deeply enough to suggest the picture had hung there for years, not a few days.

Konstantin hoisted it up, tilting the frame to re-hang it when something fell out from the back and clattered on the tiled floor. He put *Sorrow* back down and picked up the white gold wedding band that had fallen out from the back of the picture. There was an engraving on the inside of the ring: a series of digits, probably the date of the wedding, he thought. Only, according to the paper trail, Grey Metzger had never been married. Sorrow's Bride indeed.

He pocketed the ring and flipped the painting over. The USB thumb drive taped to the inside of the frame was so small he had almost missed it. He peeled away the tiny strip of tape and pocketed the stick along with the letter and the ring.

"Who were you?" he asked, rubbing at his chin as he looked down at the painting on the floor. His skin was rough with stubble. It had been forty-eight hours since he had shaved. He knew from experience that that was enough to transform him from human into some atavistic throw-back that could be used to scare the living daylights out of young children—and grown men at four a.m. for that matter.

Who was this woman who called herself the Bride of Sorrow? Everything about her presence of mind in the face of death screamed CIA, MI6, KGB, Mossad, any one of them but absolutely one of them. He might not know who she was, but he was pretty damned sure she wasn't a school teacher.

The answer to that question, and possibly so many others, was almost certainly on the flash drive. He wanted to get a look at it before he turned it over to Lethe. That meant finding a computer.

Konstantin re-hung the picture and left the apartment, knowing he'd found all there was to find in the dead man's home.

9

THE SECRETS OF FATIMA

Dominico Neri was a sour-faced little man with the weight of the world on his slouched shoulders. He was cut from the typical Italian male cloth—interesting features rather than outright handsome, dark-skinned and narrow, his torso an inverted equilateral triangle of jutting ribs beneath a wrinkled cotton shirt. He sat across the table from Noah, sipping at a double-shot espresso in a stupidly small cup.

He looked like he hadn't slept in a week. That disheveled look and the half-awake eyes no doubt made him painfully popular with the fairer sex, Noah thought. Neri looked like the kind of man who didn't so much love them and leave them as he did the kind of man who skipped the whole love thing and went straight for the checkbook to pay the alimony. He stared at Noah. The scrutiny was almost uncomfortable.

That was hardly surprising, Neri was *Carabinieri*.

Rome was burdened by half a dozen levels of police,

from traffic cops to jail cops and forestry police all the way to the normal beat cops. The Carabinieri were set aside from all of them. They were military police.

Only Neri's eyes looked the part, Noah thought, studying the man back openly. If he'd been pushed to guess a career, he would have said journalist. The gun worn casually at his hip killed that career path, though.

"So," Neri said, setting the espresso cup down on the cheap white saucer. The coffee left a near-black stain around the inside of the cup. Noah could only imagine what it was busy doing to the detective's stomach lining. "You think this is all somehow linked to the suicide in Piazza San Pietro two days ago?"

Noah nodded.

News had begun to filter through from Berlin, so Neri was taking him more seriously than he would have even two hours ago. The threat had suddenly become credible, and this was Neri's city. The Carabinieri man pinched the bottom of his nose, both fingers almost disappearing up his nostrils as he thought about what it meant to Rome.

"Forgive my bluntness, Mister Larkin, but an hour ago my office put in a call to your government. They deny that you are working on their behalf, which I admit does not surprise me. When has your government ever owned up to spying?"

"I am not a spy," Noah said.

The Italian wasn't listening to him and carried on as though presenting a case: "And yet despite the fact you have no verifiable credentials to back up your wild claims, you obviously know far too much about what happened in the piazza not to be some sort of intelligence officer. Either that, or you were more directly involved. So I ask myself this: were you involved? You do not look like a terrorist." He grunted a soft chuckle at that. "Not that any of us know what a terrorist looks like, eh?"

"Indeed," Noah said. He decided against saying anything

more. Neri would come to the point, eventually.

Neri reached into his pocket and pulled out a battered tobacco tin. He opened it and took out the fixings for a thin licorice paper smoke, rolling it neatly between his fingers. It was a well practiced motion that needed no thought. Placing the cigarette between his lips he took out his lighter, sparked the wheel against the flint and inhaled with a slow, deep sigh of pleasure as he lit the cigarette. He drew a second lungful of smoke, letting it leak out through his nose before he carried on with his thought. "So then I think perhaps Mister Larkin is a well-known journalist where he comes from and he is here in Rome fishing for a story? It was a reasonable guess. Unfortunately none of the papers in your country appear to know who the hell you are. So not a journalist, not with your government, that leaves me in something of a quandary. What I am saying is, why shouldn't I arrest you right here and now?"

"If you thought I was involved, you wouldn't have come out to meet me in this rather overpriced café, would you?"

"Or perhaps the couple at the table over there are not a young couple in love but are actually my men. And the older gentleman over there, studying the newspaper so intently, perhaps he is actually one of mine waiting for the signal to take you in?"

Noah looked at the young couple. There was a Rough Guide on the table between them. The man was dressed like a fairly typical straight-out-of-university backpacker. His sneakers were a little too clean for someone who'd been slogging around Europe on an Inter-Rail ticket for a month, but otherwise he looked the part. The girl was pretty, blonde, and petite, all the things a younger Noah would have fallen for. They looked good together. They fit. He watched them talk for a moment. He couldn't hear exactly what they were saying above the lunchtime noise of the café, but he could hear enough to know the guy had a fairly broad Mancunian accent and seemed to be spouting the usual bollocks a postgrad on vacation in Rome would. It wasn't the kind of attention to detail he would have expected from an undercover policeman, so he felt relatively confident when he told Neri, "They aren't. I'd know."

"Perhaps," the Carabinieri man said, drawing slowly on the cigarette again. The smell of the licorice paper was sickly sweet. "But that still doesn't tell me why I shouldn't arrest you, Mister Larkin, now does it?"

Noah couldn't argue with him. In his position Noah's bullshit radar would have been firing off warning signals left, right and center. "Call me Noah. Mister Larkin was my father."

"Perhaps later, if we become friends," Neri said. "For now I will call you Mister Larkin, and you can pretend I am talking to your father if it helps."

"Not really," Noah said. "I work for an organization with ah, how shall I put it?"—he spread his hands slightly, as though looking for inspiration from above—"let's say 'concerns' in various countries across the world. We have rather specialized interests and areas of expertise."

"Go on," Neri said, stubbing out the last of his cigarette in the dregs of his coffee and leaving the butt to soak in the tiny cup.

"Because of our interests we have a rather unique network of contacts, and because of our distance from the more political aspects of things, we can sometimes see links between things that others closer to the fact miss, or overlook."

"So you are a spy."

Noah shook his head. "I'm not. Nothing as glamorous. I work for Sir Charles Wyndham. Unofficially my group is known as the Forge Team. We're all ex-military, so we have certain skills. Sir Charles likes to joke that we were forged in the crucible of battle. The old man isn't particularly funny, but we humor him."

"And what might you 'officially' be called?"

Noah thought about deflecting the question, but he needed this guy to trust him if he was going to get through the reams of Italian bureaucracy and get him face time with someone on the other side of the border walls of Vatican City. "Our official government designation, if that isn't a contradiction in terms, is Ogmios."

"So you do work for the British government? Is that what you are telling me, Mister Larkin?"

Noah shook his head. "No. We're, hell, how do I put this? Okay, we're outside the government. We're off the books. If we were still military, we'd be deniable ops. It's the same theory. We are out looking after our country's interests overseas, but if we're compromised, if we're captured or become an embarrassment, we simply don't exist. We're a private concern which just so happens to be comprised of counterterrorist experts and ex-special forces."

"Fascinating, and wholly unbelievable of course. Tell me, what, precisely, does this Forge Team do, then, that Her Majesty's Government reserves the right to deny its existence?" Neri's voice was leery, and it was obvious the real question he was asking here was: *How the hell do you know what's going on while we don't?*

"We're in salvage," Noah said.

"Interesting," Neri mused, "and I would imagine wholly irrelevant."

No flies on you, Noah thought. "You'd be surprised."

"No," Neri said without missing a beat, "I wouldn't. What *would* surprise me would be the unguarded truth slipping out of your mouth when you weren't paying attention."

Noah almost laughed at that. Instead he gestured for the waitress to come over and ordered himself a light beer. She nodded and hurried away. He liked her eyes, the little he saw of them. They promised. There was nothing better than a pretty young thing who promised—and it didn't matter what it was they promised. He looked back at Dominico

Neri. He found himself liking this dour little detective with his doubting mind. He was Noah's kind of guy.

"Now, tell me again why I should listen to you."

Noah leaned forward. He said one word: "Berlin."

That one word was enough. He had known it would be. Neri could bluster all he wanted. He could demand proof that Noah wasn't up to his neck in this whole thing—the killer needing to put himself in the center of the show, needing to see, to feel a part of the fear his murders created. That was the common philosophy of crime fighting, thanks to Hollywood. He could demand Noah turn himself over into his custody while he ran the name Ogmios through their own networks, trying to verify the unverifiable, just to make Noah's life difficult for the sake of making it difficult. All they would find were obscure references to the Celtic deity. What he couldn't do was deny Berlin.

The number of dead was rising by the hour. There was a grossly inappropriate counter on the ticker on the silent screen behind Noah's head that said BERLIN DEATH TOLL RISING and showed the number jumping in small increments as each new fatality was reported. Noah's skin crawled. He didn't want to contemplate where that ticker would finally settle, but wherever that was, it was going to be a number that simply stopped making sense. That much they all knew from Konstantin's very first report from the city. Berlin was in trouble.

"There's nothing particularly secret about what I am going to tell you now, but bear with me." The Italian nodded. "With each of the public suicides there was a message delivered to one of the national news agencies. In London the message was: *There is a plague coming. For forty days and forty nights fear shall savage the streets. Those steeped in sin shall burn. The dying begins now.* It was the same message in eleven of the thirteen cities where someone burned." It was obvious the Italian knew the message off by heart. He wanted to hear something he didn't know.

"And the other two? Where were they, Mister Larkin? Why were the messages different?"

"One was Berlin, the other was Rome." He reached into his pocket for the piece of paper he had written the transcripts of the two calls down on. Noah smoothed it out and read through both short messages aloud. "In Berlin the message was: *The Holy Father passed through a big city half in ruins and half trembling with halting step, afflicted with pain and sorrow, he prayed for the souls of the corpses he met on his way; having reached the top of the mountain, on his knees at the foot of the big cross he was killed by a group of soldiers.* You might be familiar with it. It is a passage from the third secret of Fatima, I believe."

Neri nodded.

"The message in Rome hit closer to home, and I'd take it as a direct threat to the Pope: *Roman Pontiff beware of your approaching, of the city where two rivers water, your blood you will come to spit in that place, both you and yours when blooms the Rose.* It's one of the prophecies of Nostradamus."

Neri nodded again. "That was the message, yes." He let out a short sharp breath, then reached for his tobacco tin again. "I need to smoke," he said. "I am an old Roman, not one of these new children of the city on their damned Piaggios, honking their horns every time they see a pretty girl. It helps me to think."

"Knock yourself out," Noah told him. "As to why the messages were different, we think they were telling us where they were going to hit first. And if we are right, Berlin today means Rome tomorrow."

"Dio ci aiuti," the Carabinieri breathed, part prayer, part absolute denial as he looked over Noah's shoulder at the screen. Noah knew he was reading the numbers and imaging the same tragedy overlaid on his familiar streets. His hand trembled as he raised it to his lips and took a drag on the thin cigarette. It was a painfully human gesture, frail, frightened. This was outside of his philosophy. He was a man made for corruption, *mafioso*, narrow alleyways and the intrigue of an intimate death. Death with honor, as the old saying went. This faceless death was, for want of a better word, un-Italian. For that fraction of a second, when Neri let his guard down, Noah pitied him. He knew all too well the kind of hell that was coming to his city; he'd been shown it all across the television this afternoon. It didn't take any imagination to switch the word Berlin for Rome.

Noah took a swallow on his Nasturo Azzurro. The beer was cold going down, which was just about all he asked of a beer. He wiped his lips and put the bottle back down on the table between them. He didn't turn to look at the screen.

"How do we stop it, Noah?" Dominico Neri asked, using his given name for the first time.

He wished he knew.

"You came to me for a reason, so tell me, how do we stop it?"

He leaned forward, closing the gap between them. It was an intimate gesture, especially for a coffee-shop conversation. Noah didn't want the wrong ears hearing what he was about to say, even if they couldn't possibly know what he was talking about. The old adage of loose talk costing lives had never really been forgotten by the military services. "All of the victims were English," he said instead of answering Neri's impossible question. "We've got people looking into what, specifically, links them. Something has to. And we'll find it. It's what we do. And when we find it, we'll find the people behind it."

"But you won't find them today, will you?" Neri said. It wasn't a question. Not really. "Which means tomorrow . . ." his voice trailed off.

"Look at the messages," he said. "Look at what they say. They're a direct threat against one man, not against the city. It won't be like it was in Berlin." Noah didn't know that was true, but as he said it he realized there was a certain logic to it.

"You really do think they will move against His Holiness?" Neri asked, almost disbelieving. Only the television kept him from dismissing the idea as absurd. "Dear God, you do, don't you?"

Noah nodded slowly.

"Don't take this the wrong way, my friend, but I wish I'd never met you."

"The feeling's mutual," Noah said, without the vaguest hint of amusement.

"I still don't understand why you would come to me rather than NOCS." The Nucleo Operativo Centrale di Sicurezza was the Italian police's counterterrorism unit. They were as good as it got, HALO-trained and worked side by side with the FBI Hostage Rescue, the Israeli YAMAM, the German GSG-9, the Danes, the Dutch, and other special forces groups across Europe. He was right, they were the logical place for Noah to go with this sort of global threat. They were also the least likely to believe him, he thought, but he didn't say that. They might have taken him seriously if he had the weight of Six backing him up, but he didn't. He was as good as alone in this mess.

"I'm just a policeman," Neri said, preparing to start on his third cigarette since he'd joined Noah at the table. "This is outside of my . . . hell, I don't even know what to call it. I'm just a chain-smoking, womanizing Roman, my friend. I don't wear my underwear on top of my trousers." Noah caught the super-hero in tights joke. For all his facetiousness Neri was right, the world could have done with a caped crusader right now. Instead it was going to have to make do with a chain-smoking, womanizing, Anglo-Italian alliance.

"What do you think I am?" he asked, instead.

The Roman laughed. It was a short, sharp grunt of a

laugh, but it was a laugh just the same. "I have no idea what you are. That is part of the problem. And I have no idea what you want from me. You drop this bombshell in my lap and expect me to deal with it, knowing there's nothing me or my people can do about it, not in time. You expect me to single-handedly protect the Pope? Do I look like the kind of man who would take a bullet for God's Messenger? Look at me, Noah,"—Neri seemed happy enough to use his given name again. Noah guessed that meant they were friends now—"I'm not a hero, even without the tights. I do my job. I do it as well as I can without it stripping the humanity from my soul, but the years swimming in the filth of Rome have turned me cynical. I'm tired. I wake up tired, stiff. My bones are trying to tell me it is time to hand the city over to a younger man, and you're presenting me with a secret that is only going to cause me a world of hurt. I don't think I want to thank you for this. And do you know what the irony in all of this is?"

Noah shook his head. He didn't have a clue.

"He's not even in the city right now. He's off on one of his holy pilgrimages somewhere."

Noah looked at Neri. "Are you serious?"

"Does this look like the face of a man given to humor?"

It didn't.

"Well that doesn't change anything," he said, trying to think through the precise implications of an absentee Pope. He hadn't expected it to be a straightforward fix, but it wasn't *Day of the Jackal* either. The original plan had been to make friendly with the locals, get the ear of the captain of the Swiss Guard, convince him of the seriousness of the threat, and get the Pope moved somewhere safe. The odds of their taking him seriously had always been slim at best. And while the religious types might stubbornly cling to the idea of God being their armor, the odds were that the Swiss Guard were a damn sight more practical. They'd be idiots not to take a threat on their man's life seriously—at least until it was proven otherwise.

If the strike was against the Pope directly, his being out of the country would just move the locus of danger. They would be looking to get word to those closest to him, step up security and, more likely than not, arrange an evacuation to a safe house while the threat was neutralized. If it was against the Seat of the Catholic Church it didn't matter if the Pope was in residence or not, the attack would go ahead. The manner of the attack itself would be the only real difference. To be sure one man died, the most effective way was something intimate: a sniper, poison, a car-bomb, something that could be aimed. To take out something as nebulous as the faith itself was moving back into the realm of spectacle. A bomb most likely. A series of bombs. Something big that was going to make a lot of very visible mess.

Noah was back to thinking about terror as a sort of performance art, all the world's a stage and all that. It had to be visible, it had to be shocking and it had to shake the believers to the core. Seeing the rescuers picking through the rubble, desperately looking for survivors while all of their relics and their hopes burned would send a statement to the faithful. He said as much to Neri. The policeman nodded, thinking it through for himself.

Terror as spectacle. That was the one thing that bothered Noah about all of this. These attacks were causing terror, but to what end? What was the cause? What did these people hope to achieve beyond instilling fear in Europe? There should have been videos going viral on the Internet already. Someone out there should be claiming responsibility and telling the world what they wanted in return for ending the fear. That was the way it worked.

"Whichever way it goes, we need time," Neri said. He left the second half of that sentence unsaid. "We can sweep the perimeter of the Vatican, but assuming they've not left us a nice rust bucket with a sign painted on the side that says 'bomb,' it's going to take time. And if they've planted it across the border in the land of Great God Almighty, we're shit out of luck."

"They'll listen to you, surely?" Noah said.

"This is Rome. They'll stick their fingers in their ears and make like they can't hear a damned thing we're saying because they think they're all invincible. They're part of God's Army. There's nothing worse than the grand delusions of True Believers. They either think they're immortal, or they are quite happy they're off to a better place. As far as I can tell it doesn't really matter to them if they're heading there in a million little pieces." Neri's grin was lopsided.

"How long has this trip been planned?"

"No idea. But given the kind of performance a papal visit is, months, six, ten?" Neri shrugged.

Noah tried to think.

How would he approach it in their place?

He covered his entire face with his calloused palm.

"Think, think, think," he grunted, running his hand up through his hair. He shook his head. From the very first calls nothing about this was how he would have done it. For a start he sure as hell wouldn't have broadcast he was going after the Pope. That was stupid. You misdirect with smoke and mirrors, you don't set up that Scooby Doo moment unless you *really* want to mutter "if it wasn't for you meddling kids" as they lead you away in handcuffs. So what the hell was really going on here?

Out of Vatican City the papal bodyguards would naturally be on a state of heightened alertness—that much made sense. Anywhere outside of the Holy See would have to be considered hostile territory in these conflicted days. So, best case scenario, the Pope had people around him willing, as Neri had so eloquently put it, to take that bullet. His daily routine would be less predictable, making it a more difficult hit. You'd need good information flow, someone on the inside feeding schedules to you with enough time to get there ahead of the entourage; otherwise, you wouldn't have been able scout out possible vantage points. Noah closed his eyes. As the assassin you wanted to minimize the random elements, control what could be controlled. The kill was about being patient and methodical. Chance had to be removed from any equation.

In Basrah Noah had lain hidden in a blind for five days, pissing into the water bottles he'd drunk dry, defecating into the wraps that had held his rations. Noah had made the shot on the third day and watched them tear the desert apart looking in all the wrong places for him for another day, but it wasn't until the day after they gave up looking for him that he walked out of the desert. When he tore down the blind he took it all with him. There wasn't a single sign he had ever been there. He heard three of the Mahdi call him the ghost killer. He liked that. He had it tattooed onto his left arm when he got home—it was the only thing he brought out of Iraq with him.

That was the kind of patience an assassination demanded.

The natural-environment kill was easier. The target was at ease. They followed their habits. Habits were patterns.

So if it had been him, Noah would have wanted to walk the land. Study the set up. He would have wanted to be sure he knew where the target was coming from, exactly, and where it was leaving to. Each terrain had its own issues that needed to be contended with. The last thing you wanted was something as stupid as a stray beam of sunlight reflecting off the wrong pane of glass to make the shot any more difficult than it had to be.

Control the variables.

Every way he looked at it, Rome was the perfect location for an attempt on the Pope's life.

"I've changed my mind," Noah said, opening his eyes again. Neri looked at him expectantly. "There are just so many things wrong with this scenario. This can't be about the Pope, not yet. This is about Rome, just like today was about Berlin. It has to be."

"But the quatrain the suicide called in?" Neri said. *"Roman Pontiff beware of your approaching, of the city where two rivers water, your blood you will come to spit in that place, both you and yours when blooms the Rose."* He quoted the piece perfectly. Noah wondered how many times the Roman had read those four lines of prophecy in the last forty-eight hours.

"It's the smoke and mirrors part," Noah said, sure he was right. It was the only thing that made sense. He had let himself become distracted with everything else. "Gets us barking up trees, it has to be. You said it yourself, the Pope isn't here. These guys are meticulous. They have to be to have orchestrated thirteen to-the-minute suicides in thirteen cities, and then duplicate the feat in the U-Bahn today. There's no way they'd make such a blatantly ama-teurish mistake as to not know exactly where His Holiness is right down to the bloody minute. Think about it,"—he shook his head, something approaching admiration in his voice—"the message might have been about the Pope, but we keep forgetting that so was the one in Berlin. Those were the long-term threat; the fact that they were different earmarked Berlin and Rome as targets.

Forty days of terror they promised, and at the end of it all of our gods will die—Christian, Muslim, bloody Norse, it doesn't matter." Noah grunted. "The clock's ticking. Tomorrow they will strike against Rome. I don't know where, I don't know when, but I am prepared to bet my bloody life on the fact it will be spectacular. And in thirty-eight days they'll make their move on the Pope. Right now they're in the blind, waiting," he said, thinking back to Basrah.

"You paint a bleak picture," Neri said. "Assuming you are right, what do you want from my people?"

"This is your city. Where would you hit? What would you do? Think about it. Whoever it is, they're in Rome right now. They will have been here for a while, going over the minutia of their strike, dry runs, timing every twist and turn and exhausting every eventuality, because that's what these people are like. Someone has seen them. Someone knows who they are. Nothing goes unseen in a city this size. You need people out on the streets, asking the right questions. These people will look Italian. They'll sound Italian. They'll have normal lives that they've worked for years to secure. They could be married, have kids in good Roman schools. They're playing a long game."

Neri screwed up his already battered face, as though understanding for the first time that anyone from the young couple with the tourist guide to the old man with the paper to the waitress with her promising eyes, or the guy in the street wrestling with a hot, overly tired toddler could be their terrorist. You couldn't tell just by looking at them, you couldn't read their thoughts. They were just like everyone else, perfectly so, cultivated to be so.

"And with that, I think it's time for me to go haunt my countryman's ghost." Noah pushed back his chair and made to stand. Neri stubbed out the dog-end of his latest cigarette.

"The victim rented a garret in one of the poorer parts of the city proper under the name Nick Simmonds. No doubt you already have the address. You seem very well connected for someone who doesn't work for your government," Neri said wryly, "but there's nothing there. The place was empty when we got there. And not just empty. It had been thoroughly disinfected and every last trace of Nick Simmonds removed. There was absolutely nothing left of a personal nature. Nothing to say he had ever lived there. Not so much as a strand of hair to run against his DNA."

That gelled with what Konstantin had found in Berlin. That similarity in itself made this garret in the poor quarter worth following up.

"His work?" Noah asked. He knew that Simmonds had

been interning with the Vatican archivist, but beyond that it was anyone's guess.

"I've got one of my team trying to make inroads over there,"—he nodded across St. Peter's Square toward the dome of the basilica—"but between you and me, I suspect Dante was writing about that place when he designed his Purgatory."

"That good?"

"Trust me," Neri said, reaching for his tobacco tin yet again. "It's enough to make a guy like me believe in the Devil." He nodded to the older man reading his newspaper. The man returned the gesture and folded the broadsheet neatly before paying his bill and leaving the table. Smiling wryly, Neri nodded toward the young couple who, likewise, put away their Rough Guide and settled their bill, leaving a generous tip as they vacated the table.

"They were your people?"

"They were."

"Trusting soul, aren't you?" Noah said.

"This is Rome, Noah," Dominico Neri said with an almost friendly smile. "You can't trust anybody. Faces of angels, morals of devils."

10

SOME DEVIL

Konstantin had been on both sides of enough black-bag jobs to know when something was wrong.

He liked that euphemism, black bag. It was just a polite way of saying burglary. The British were peculiar like that, they liked to use words like cut-outs, false flags and honey traps instead of calling a robbery a robbery. It was all terribly 1950s, stiff upper lip and all that.

From the surveillance side the set-up with most of these jobs was simple: you baited the trap, sat back and waited. Something would shake loose. It invariably did. Surveillance was all about patience. You sit, you wait, you see who shows up.

Metzger's apartment was the baited trap in this case, and he'd just walked right into it.

There was nothing sixth sense-ish about it. No prickling hairs on the nape of his neck. No instinctive mental alarm tripped to warn him. It wasn't his reptilian brain or anything like that. Konstantin was a practical man on all levels. He had no time for the stuff and nonsense of superstition. That didn't mean he dismissed well-honed instincts, though. A trained man would recognize things on a subconscious level that a normal man would more than likely miss. That was simply the way of it. It was all about tradecraft. Konstantin Khavin knew he was being followed because he was observant. There was no great mystery to having your eyes open. Konstantin had learned to interpret the signs left by careless people. More than once, being observant had kept him alive.

He had picked up the tail as he left Metzger's building on Schlossstrasse.

There had been three tells that gave the watchers away, and each of them was surprisingly obvious (and therefore amateurish) given the level of sophistication the U-Bahn attack had demanded. That was something to worry over later. Right now his first concern was learning as much as he could about the people following him—which meant turning the whole thing on its head and following the followers.

The first tell was as thoughtless as an unshielded lens cap in an upper window across the street from Metzger's place. Whoever was up there in the otherwise darkened room had been taking photographs of everyone coming and going from Metzger's building. It was a grunt job. Observe and log for further investigation. Someone else would do the foot work, and they'd probably relieve each other on eight- to ten-hour shifts up in the dark room to alleviate the boredom of staring out into the street if nothing else. As the noonday sun hit the camera's beveled lens it sent a momentary splash of glare across the window. It was just careless. He imagined they had been up in their rented room for days without a break. That was when sloppiness set in.

He would have dismissed it if it hadn't been for the second tell, the engine of one of the cars across the street gunning as he walked toward the kiosk at the end of the street. The two together were more than mere coincidence.

Konstantin was tempted to go pay the watchers an unexpected visit and bust a few heads. That was his Russian blood. He turned away from the apartment without so much as an upward glance. There would be time enough to return to Schlossstrasse later. A four a.m. visit would satisfy his heritage.

The final giveaway was the guy on the corner who still sat on one of the red benches in front of the sausage kiosk, still eating a bratwurst sprinkled with dried onions. Konstantin had noticed him sitting there, hunched up against the cold, when he had turned onto Schlossstrasse looking for Metzger's home. In the time it had taken Konstantin to go through Metzger's apartment the sausage eater hadn't managed a single bite—probably because he had bought it in the early hours, and now it was cold and greasy and more likely to make him throw up than to sate any real hunger he might have.

The devil was in the details.

Konstantin decided he was hungry.

He walked up to the window and ordered himself a brat with all of the fixings, then made a show of licking his fingers as he enjoyed it. The sausage was hot and tasted twice as good for it. He washed it down with an apple spritzer. Konstantin nodded to the cold man with the half-eaten sausage and said, "God, I needed that," before he walked away. He smiled. It was unnecessary—a game—but he liked the idea of letting the man know he'd seen him, twice. Konstantin was interested to see how they would deal with the knowledge that they had been compromised. How they reacted would tell him how good the team he was up against really was.

He stopped on the corner, ostensibly to retie a shoelace. He checked out the street. The sausage eater hadn't made a move to follow him, which was unsurprising. There was no point in the one face he would recognize tailing him if they had someone else on the street.

The car rolled slowly up to the end of Schlossstrasse and indicated a right turn. He watched it make the turn and drive away. There were two ways the car could play it—it could drop off another watcher once it was around the corner, allowing them to follow him from the front, or it could hope to pick him up again later and assume one nondescript sedan was much like another in this city of nondescript BMWs and Mercedes, Volvos and Saabs.

There was an element of risk in trying to drop back onto his tail that Konstantin himself would never have allowed if he had been running the operation, so he had to assume whoever his opposite number was, the man was every bit as methodical as he was. And that meant they had at least one more man on the street that he had missed.

Konstantin took his time. There was a green *pissoir* fifty feet further down the road. Berlin's elaborate city crest was embossed on the swing door. He walked toward it, counting out his footsteps on the paving stones. Each step sounded crisp in the chilly air. Twenty feet away the reek of urine came his way as the wind picked up. It was one of a thousand unpleasant smells in the city. Some cities had a thousand stories, he thought, remembering the old TV show—Berlin had a thousand reeks. Konstantin grunted. He decided to relieve himself.

The *pissoir* was built in such a way that he could see over the top into the street as he urinated. It was a rather peculiar idea, very German. It did, however, give him a full minute to watch people, see who was moving, who was slowing down, and who the sausage eater was watching— because it wasn't him. Konstantin tried to follow the direction of the man's gaze without dribbling on his shoes.

The man seemed to be looking intently at Grey Metzger's doorway.

That was when Konstantin saw the woman in the red

dress—it looked like some sort of evening wear, beautifully cut around her full curves—walk out into the street. She was coming his way. He zipped up and timed his exit to meet her on the street as he stepped out of the green urinal.

She regarded him openly, her gaze drifting slowly from his head down to his feet and back again. Konstantin inclined his head slightly and gestured for her to pass. She did. She walked slowly. He followed her for six blocks, enjoying the luscious, ripe curve of her ass as the material clung to it. He allowed her to lead him another block before ending the game. She broke away, ostensibly drawn like a magpie to the bright, shiny glitter of jewels in a shop window, while he crossed the street. He didn't wait for the lights. He had heard a second set of footsteps just out of rhythm with his own as he followed the woman in the red dress.

Just as he would have done in their place, they were leading him front and back. Shepherding him.

So, knowing what was happening, he decided there was nothing else to do than appreciate the view—there was something hypnotic about watching the gentle sway of her hips as she walked. That, Konstantin was sure, was the purpose of the red dress. It was the honey on the trap. As pleasing as the view was, it didn't take his mind off the fact that he was being led like a lamb to the slaughter. Tailing front and back was professional. It took numbers and discipline and, given that the Berlin cell had already sacrificed at least seven from their ranks with the U-Bahn strike, the fact they had the manpower to spare on Metzger's apartment was more than a little interesting to the Russian.

It wasn't some random coincidence. There were no random coincidences in his world.

They had been watching for someone. Why? Well he could make an educated guess: it was down to Sorrow's Bride. They had had the woman for at least a week, perhaps two, and no matter what she was, what her training had prepared her for, there was one basic truth to espionage Konstantin had brought with him over the wall: everybody talks in the end.

The films and books made it glamorous and painted portraits of the hero with the iron resolve and trembling lip who withstood any amount of pain to hold onto his secrets before eventually breaking free. That was all silver screen bullshit. Given time, everyone broke. Everyone talked.

So they knew who she was, who she worked for. They knew what she knew about them, and they had come to see who came looking for her. Again, it was exactly what he would have done. Konstantin had to admit a grudging amount of admiration for these people. They were thorough, organized, thoughtful and disciplined. All traits he would have associated with professionals, not some homegrown terror cell based around a core of fanaticism. If he had been a gambling man, he would have put a substantial bet on them being ex-military.

What it came down to was this: Konstantin needed to know more about the woman in the painting. She was the key, but he had no idea to which lock.

He had his suspicions, but they were essentially groundless. This case of mistaken identity was only serving to reinforce them. They were looking for whoever came to claim the information on the thumb drive. Who would have known it was there? Her handler? If she was an agent, it made sense—but then why would an agent from one of the Secret Services have latched on to Grey Metzger? Until yesterday there had been nothing remotely interesting about the man.

While the woman disappeared into the antique jewelers, the second ghost set of steps followed him across the road.

Konstantin didn't look over his shoulder, not even once.

He wanted to see how serious this person was; that meant changing the nature of the game.

He turned the corner and stopped dead in his tracks. He had fifteen steps on the man behind him. He pressed himself up against the wall, taking a second to calm himself, center his breathing and focus before exploding into action. He counted the steps out in his head, tensing.

As the man came around the corner Konstantin stepped into his path. Recognition flashed across the man's eyes, followed a split second later by blinding pain. Konstantin moved instinctively. Violence was his trade. He knew how to hurt people. He stepped in close, getting right up in the man's face, feinted as though to slap the man, drawing his eyes to the flurry of motion, and drove the heel of his shoe through the man's knee hard enough to shatter the cap and tear the cartilage as he forced it to bend the wrong way. The man went down in the fetal position, clutching his ruined leg up to his chest and screaming.

Konstantin stood over him.

"You'll be lucky to be walking in six months. Be grateful I didn't kill you. Next time I will."

He left the man lying in the middle of the street. He crossed the road again, weaving between the slow moving cars. A yellow bus indicated that it was coming to a stop. Konstantin hopped on board and took up one of the window seats that allowed him to see down the length of Schlossstrasse for a few seconds as they drove past the mouth of the street. The man was still lying on the cobbles. The woman in the red dress stood over him, talking quickly into her cell phone. Konstantin couldn't read lips but he could guess what she was saying: the job was botched, the target got away and they had a man down. It wasn't the kind of call any operative wanted to make. There would be repercussions. Konstantin didn't feel the slightest bit of sympathy for them. The woman looked up, and for a moment their eyes met. Then the bus carried him out of sight.

He rang the bell and hopped off less than three hundred

yards up the road.

The last thing they would have expected was for him to double-back and switch from hunted to hunter. He walked briskly past the usual line of personality-less shops with their blind windows, then saw the bright yellow sign of a charity shop and ducked inside. It took him less than a minute to pick an oversized sheepskin coat and flat working man's cap from the rack of dead men's clothes at the back of the store. He paid in cash and left his own coat as a donation. He pulled the cap down so it covered most of his face and buttoned the sheepskin all the way up to the throat as he stepped back out onto the street. The entire transaction had taken less than two minutes.

He looked, to the casual observer at least, like a different person from the one who had walked out of Grey Metzger's apartment building less than ten minutes earlier. That would be enough for what he had in mind.

Konstantin had always been happier as the hunter.

He walked back toward Schlossstrasse, head down, hands stuffed in the old man's coat. He could smell the stale flavor of cigarettes that permeated the sheepskin. It had that comfortable worn in and worn out feel. He felt the first few fat drops of rain fall. Each one seemed to release another forgotten odor from inside the coat.

He saw the red dress before he saw anything else. It stood out like a beacon in the gray street. Konstantin leaned up against the nearest wall, positioning himself beside one of the many bus stops along the street and watched.

Less than five minutes later the sedan pulled up along-side them, and the woman helped the fallen man up and into the car. Konstantin smiled wryly, enjoying the panto-mime of pain that went with the whole maneuver. But it was the sedan's license plate that caught his attention, or rather the zero where the location code should have been. Berlin plates, for instance, had a B prefix followed by a six-digit string of numbers.

The zero marked the sedan as a diplomatic car.

He memorized the number. It would be something to keep Lethe busy, if nothing else. Diplomatic plates could have amounted to just about anything, but on the most basic level it meant friends in high places.

Konstantin pulled the brim of his new cap down over his eyes as the car swept past him.

The rain started to fall in earnest.

He needed to find out what was on the thumb drive.

11

GHOST WALKER

"All right Koni, talk to me," Jude Lethe said into the headset. He wiped his lips with the back of his left hand and put the empty drink can down beside the rickety pyramid of other empty cans.

Half a world away, Konstantin Khavin sat in a dingy Internet café nursing a straight black coffee. He looked over his shoulder three times in as many minutes. Jude could see the stern-faced Russian through the blurry pixilation of the webcam. He enjoyed watching other people while they sat in front of computers, especially when it was so obvious that they were lost in space.

"What do you need me to do?" Konstantin asked, eying the screen as he would a viper.

"I'll need the IP address of the terminal you're using," Lethe explained, knowing it was going to sound like double-dutch to the big man.

"And in a language I understand?"

"I'm going to take over your computer from here. It'll be just like magic," he said, grinning.

"You can be a complete ass, Lethe. Did anyone ever tell you that?"

"If you're going to do anything, do it all the way, eh? What say we hack this computer, then, shall we?" He talked Konstantin through the process, directing him through the control panel into the network settings until he found the computer's unique Internet address. In less than a minute Konstantin read him a string of numbers.

"Perfect," he said. He tapped in the digits and triggered a string of commands that allowed him to take remote control of Konstantin's machine. He didn't use the operating system's built-in helper. His code was much more invasive. "I'm sending you a piece of code, Koni. All I want you to do is execute it, and we'll be cooking with gas."

"Just tell me what to do."

"Click on the smiley face when it pops up. It's as easy as that."

Konstantin did as he was told. A second terminal window opened up on the bank of monitors in front of Lethe. In it he saw exactly what Konstantin saw. "Fantastic. Okay, plug the USB stick in. I'll take it from here." A few seconds later he was moving the cursor and launching a browser to explore the contents of the thumb drive Konstantin had recovered.

Of course it was never going to be that easy.

In the digital heart of Nonesuch Jude Lethe stared at the encryption key that froze his screen. His grin turned feral as the image on the screen shivered and broke up. The terminal window closed, the connection severed. This was his world. He'd built an entire ghost network that allowed him to come and go through the mainframe corridors of power at will. The ghost network data-mined Ministry computers. If he so chose, he could fire up webcams from hundreds of the laptops used by politicians and high ranking civil servants just to see what they were doing then and there. An eleven-digit encryption key wouldn't take long to break through, no matter who built it. People were predictable; they used family pets, nicknames, favorite books, things that were memorable. Some tried to be clever and used random number strings. Either way, it didn't matter to Lethe.

He reestablished the connection.

This time he didn't try to crack the encryption over the remote connection. He ran a cloning program, making a perfect copy of the small memory stick, encryption and all.

"Got it."

"So what does it say?" Konstantin asked.

Lethe had been so focused on the screen he had forgotten the Russian was on the line. "No idea, but I'll find out."

"Do you need anything else from me?"

Just give me two seconds," Lethe said, punching in the command that would erase the memory stick. Most people didn't realize that erasing something on a computer was pretty much the same as using an eraser on a block of legal paper: you could pull off the top sheet and use the edge of the pencil to highlight the impression left on the page beneath. Or, in other words, deleting a document didn't take it away. Not if you knew how to go snooping through digital files. Of course if Lethe wanted something gone, he could make it happen. He had designed his own data shredder. It wasn't perfect, but without the restructuring code he didn't believe there was a programmer in the world who could put Humpty together again.

To finish the job he uploaded a virulent piece of code that would inflict a whole world of hurt on the first machine that tried to unravel it. It was his parting gift.

"Okay," he muttered, "it's all yours, Koni." He didn't tell the Russian the drive in his pocket was now worse than useless. He figured it was better for the big man to think he was protecting untold secrets in case someone over there picked him up. The less he knew the better. Lethe's grin was fierce as he kicked the chair back. It twisted slightly as it glided on its small wheels. He killed the connection and pulled the Bluetooth set out of his ear.

The room was floor to ceiling with server racks and drives, ribbon connectors, USBs, and trailing wires that seemed to have fused together into some sort of grotesque Transformer.

Lethe reached over for the remote and cranked up the volume on his iPod. It was hooked into an expensive speaker rig. Even at quarter volume the speakers had enough power to deafen every living thing within one hundred yards of Nonesuch. Musically, Jude Lethe was born out of his time. The jazz refrain of Hue and Cry's "I Refuse" faded into Stuart Adamson's powerful Dunfermline burr as it came up screaming "In a Big Country." The entire playlist was all mid-80s but avoided nerve-jarring pop jingles and focused on iconic tunes like "Love is a Wonderful Color" and "Sixty Eight Guns." These were the songs that defined a generation.

He cracked his knuckles and stretched back in the chair, enjoying the dead singer's voice as he sounded his battle cry. He leaned across for the alarm clock on the shelf above the computer, checked it against his watch, and set it for forty-five minutes time to make things interesting. He put the clock back on the shelf and turned his full attention back to the screen.

Lethe triggered a string of commands, his fingers moving with staccato-grace across the keyboard. Without knowing anything about the woman who had built the encryption he was running in an algorithmic darkness like a blind mouse.

That was just how he liked it.

It didn't take him anywhere near the full forty-five minutes to unlock the cloned disc. The encryption wasn't meant to deter a stubborn investigator, only to put off prying eyes.

The woman's codename was Ghost Walker. Her real name was Grace Weller. All of the documents were signed GW. There was enough information hardcoded into the file system for Lethe to know as much about the woman as her own mother by the time he'd finished digging. Even his cursory scan revealed enough for him to know Grace was anything but an unfortunate girlfriend in the wrong place at the wrong time. As far as Lethe could tell she'd engineered herself into exactly where she wanted to be. Her machine was registered as property of Her Majesty's Government, which meant she was almost certainly with MI6. The fact that the tech boys still insisted on properly registering their bulk licenses for various software was mildly amusing. There had been a time back in the '90s where the core government offices developed their own database, accounting and word processing software rather than buy in services. Now, like the rest of the known world, they paid the Great God Microsoft a small fortune for the privilege of keeping the nation's secrets electronically.

Given the extent of the dossier Grace had assembled on Grey Metzger, Lethe figured he was what Six liked to call a "person of interest." That was a euphemism for prime suspect for something or other. In this case Lethe had no idea what for, but the answer was almost certainly buried within the hundreds of pages of words and numbers he'd just unlocked. He'd find it. It was what he did. The others might flex their muscles and work up a sweat playing soldiers, but what happened in this little room beneath Nonesuch was every bit as vital as all of the running about and fighting that went on up there in the "real world."

Judging by the creation dates of the various files, Grace had been working Metzger for the best part of three years.

Lethe sat back in his chair, processing what, exactly, that little nugget of information meant in terms of the big picture. He thought of life as a huge, multi-million-piece mosaic, each tile offering an action, a reaction, an inter-action, a person, a place, an event, and it wasn't until all of the tiles were laid down that this thing called life began to make sense. He figured that the whole life flashing before your eyes at the end really just meant for once you could see the entire mosaic instead of just those few tiles closest to you.

That Grace Weller had been following Metzger for three years meant one thing in terms of the big picture—for three years Metzger had been doing something worth watching.

Lethe browsed quickly through the files, scanning for key words that caught his eye. They were surveillance reports on Grey Metzger, logging his movements for almost two and a half years. There were hundreds of low-res and high-res photos taken in smoky bars, lecture halls, beside national monuments, at digs, in cafés and restaurants, shaking hands, kissing, hugging. What he wasn't doing was trading any suspiciously wrapped packages or meeting men with briefcases on park benches while the fog set in. It was a life in pictures. Metzger's life, to be precise. It looked decidedly normal.

There was a comprehensive journal that covered every-thing from contact lists, emails, phone numbers, and logs of phone calls in and out. Grace had shadowed his life with a thoroughness that bordered on the obsessive.

And then, seven months ago they made contact.

It was all there in her report.

She had seduced Metzger, ingratiating herself into his world.

They had become lovers.

There was something incredibly cold about the way she reported it all, like there was no emotion in any of it. Get-ting close to Metzger was a job, and she was determined to do it to the best of her ability. Lethe wondered what it would be like to live your life that way, disassociated from even the most intimate of things, reducing everything to assignments and lies.

Looking at the paperwork, she had moved in with Metzger three months ago—four months after first contact—but her surveillance hadn't stopped. If anything it had become even more detailed. Midway through the autumn she had noted her fears that Metzger was involved with someone she called Mabus.

There was something familiar about the name. Lethe stared at the screen. "Mabus," he said, tasting the sound of it on his tongue. He'd heard it before. He didn't know where, but he'd definitely heard it before. He said it again and a third time as if it might be a charm. It was. He hadn't heard the name before, he'd seen it. And he knew exactly where.

Mabus was the name Nostradamus had given the third Antichrist. Napoleon, Hitler and finally Mabus. He switched screens and ran a search for Mabus, cross-referencing it against Nostradamus. The results were pretty much what he had expected, page after page of theories, conspiracy and crackpot, about the rise of the Antichrist, the Mabus Code, the Mabus comet and so much other stuff and nonsense.

Lethe read the original quatrain, Century 2, Quatrain 62:

Mabus will soon die, then will come
A horrible undoing of people and animals
At once one will see vengeance, one hundred powers, thirst,
Famine, when the comet will pass.

It wasn't exactly damning stuff—comets, the undoing of animals, powers thirsting. It was all pretty vague.

Most of the articles he found turned Mabus around and called the damned man Sudam, and much as the Hister of

Nostradamus' earlier quatrains was reinterpreted to mean Hitler and Napaulon Roy became Napoleon Bonaparte, they turned Sudam into Saddam. It was a small step, then, to declaring the execution of Hussein the beginning of the end that Nostradamus had foreseen.

He came across another quatrain, Century 8, Quatrain 77:

The anti-christ very soon annihilates the three,
twenty seven years his war will last,
The unbelievers are dead, captive, exiled;
with blood, human bodies, water and red hail covering the earth.

Reading through the stuff it was fairly obvious that all of the so-called prophecies were vague enough that absolutely any and every meaning could be shoe-horned into them neatly enough if you were determined to impress a certain interpretation. A twenty-seven-year war of vengeance for the death of Saddam Hussein? Hussein transformed into the martyr for the Arabic world? Instead of ensuring peace, could cutting the head off that particular snake usher in the End of Days? There were enough people out there that seemed to think so. They pointed at the escalating nature of the terror attacks that had plagued the West following his execution in the last days of 2006, but that didn't mean they were right. Hell, it didn't mean they were anything other than kids in their back bedrooms with a few books and a crush on Armageddon. That was the joy of the Internet— it gave everyone a voice even if they had nothing to say.

Still, the very notion sent a chill running down the ladder of Jude Lethe's spine.

For the next hour he immersed himself in Grace Weller's world. From what he could gather from her reports, this particular Mabus was—at the time of writing at least—very much alive and well, a fact which jarred with the Hussein theory.

He couldn't shake the feeling that all of this went back to Masada and whatever Grey Metzger and the others had found there. But what tied the archeological dig at the home of the Sicarii assassins, the herald of the Antichrist and thirteen suicides together? One thing was for sure, whatever it was, Grace Weller believed Metzger was up to his neck in it. She'd been putting the case against him together for three years. That meant this thing had been going on even longer. All the way back to '04 and the dig at Masada, perhaps? He needed to know more about the woman and what she was working on, and that meant using the ghost network to dig through Six's files. But first he needed a smoke to clear his head. It was going to be a long night.

Lethe printed out everything onto a hardcopy for the old man. He'd want to see it. Lethe couldn't shake the feeling that he was staring at three of four pieces of the mosaic instead of seeing the picture in all of its glory. Maybe the old man would be better placed.

He put the Bluetooth earpiece back in place and called up to Sir Charles. Max answered the phone on the second ring. "This is not a good time, Mister Lethe," the butler said without missing a beat. "Sir Charles is taking his early evening constitutional."

"Tell the old man I need to see him. We're talking a shit-and-fan moment."

"You do have such a colorful way with words, young sir."

"Just tell the old man that MI6 has had one of our suicides under surveillance for three years."

"And where there is one, there are likely to be others. I assume that is the gist of this message?" Max said, filling in the blanks.

"Add the fact that Koni had some trouble in Berlin, that that trouble was collected in a diplomatic car, and I'd say things are just starting to get interesting."

"I shall inform Sir Charles immediately."

"I thought you might."

12

ALLIGATOR MAN

Orla Nyrén deplaned at terminal three of Israel's Ben Gurion airport.

She emerged from the air-conditioned hull into the mid-70s heat of the Tel Aviv afternoon and lifted her face to the sky. The sun felt good. Honest. It had been a long time since she'd set foot on Israeli soil, but for a while it had been her second home.

The ground crew swarmed over the asphalt, dragging the hose from the refueling vehicle toward the underside of the G5. They were all dressed identically in white coveralls and looked disturbingly like a hazmat team going to work. They moved with the efficiency of drones, each doing their part. The nearest gates were occupied by commercial airliners, tail fins showing their allegiance to each and every flag imaginable. Farther along the hardstand a huge Airbus 380 was taxiing toward the gate. The Airbus dwarfed every other plane on the ground.

Orla adjusted the lie of her skirt. Her heels *tunked* hollowly down the steel stairs onto the hardstand.

Her escort waited for her at the bottom of the stairs. He was a good-looking man, typically dark, with an olive cast to his skin, and carefully cultivated two-day stubble that was neatly trimmed. He wore a light linen suit and a white shirt that was rumpled around the collar. He held out a hand to her as she reached the bottom step. It might have been misplaced chivalry, or an offer to shake hands, she couldn't tell. Orla took his hand and turned the gesture into a brisk handshake. His grip was uncomfortably firm. "Orla Nyrén," she said, stepping down on to the blacktop.

"Uzzi Sokol," her host said, smiling tightly. "Walk with me." He turned on his heel without another word and led her toward the terminal building. Sokol moved with the arrogance of a military man. Orla had to walk half a step faster than was comfortable to keep up with him as he steered her toward the special customs gate. She had met his type before a dozen times a day when she'd been operating in the Middle East. It was that arrogance that marked her as a second-class citizen. It was rooted deep in the male psyche. It was the usual kind of pseudo-sexual, dynamic bullshit that really infuriated her. Orla had known the guy less than sixty seconds and he was already trying to imprint his dominance over her.

Well, screw that, she thought to herself, and stopped trying to match his pace. She turned to look back at Sir Charles' Gulfstream. It might have looked like the runt of the litter alongside the Airbus, but it really was a majestic piece of aeronautical design. She saw Ryan, Sir Charles' man, on the stairs. His white shirt immaculately starched despite the long-haul flight, looking every inch the dashing pilot. He flashed Orla a smile and tipped her a two-fingered salute. She smiled back, knowing the few seconds she had taken out of chasing Uzzi Sokol should have been just enough to exasperate the Israeli. That was her intention, after all.

Sokol waited for her beside the security door. He could barely mask his impatience. Orla smiled, which just seemed to annoy him all the more. She followed him through the door into the terminal. They walked through a narrow glass corridor. She could see the hubbub of passengers through the glass walls as they milled around, waiting for their flights to be called. Before she was halfway through the corridor announcements had been made in five languages.

Sokol didn't say another word until she was on the other side of the customs gate. The diplomatic tags on her briefcase prevented them from interfering with her luggage and meant she could bring her service piece into the country. He whisked her away into a waiting black Mercedes sedan bearing the insignia of the IDF intelligence Corps, *Heil HaModi'in*. He closed the door and came around to the other side of the car.

"We'll be with Lieutenant General Caspi in a short while. I trust your flight was comfortable?" If this was his attempt at small talk, Orla thought, it was rather woeful.

"It was fine," she said, looking out the window. Airports across the world were all a much of a muchness, she decided, as the car swept around a line of waiting taxis. A snake of cars crawled up the on-ramp into a multistory parking garage. The barrier was down and the sign read full, so for every car that went in, one had to leave. Out of the airport the streets were depressingly familiar with their low buildings and spray-painted facades. Five minutes out of the airport compound they passed a man selling stacks of eggs from a rickety roadside table. Two minutes beyond that a grandmother—every damned day of her hard life engraved deep into the creases of her face—sat selling fruit from a handbasket. A little girl on a bright red bicycle pedaled hard, the frame swinging from side to side as she raced toward the row of buildings. She had her head down and wasn't watching the traffic. Twice other drivers sounded off their horns as she came dangerously close to cutting across them. There was no uniform design to the buildings. They seemed to have grown haphazardly from out of the desert, all different sizes and different shapes. She saw black spray-painted graffiti on most of them and recognized the word Yahweh, one of the seven names of God, repeated over and over amid other Hebrew words she couldn't decipher.

Another two minutes down the road the houses gave way to empty desert-like fields of scrub. In one field, solar panels sprouted up like corn, their glass panels reflecting the sun back brightly. In another were the tents of a gypsy camp. This was Israel encapsulated in a few short minutes, the privation of the common people right beside the wealth of the high-tech industries.

As they neared the city proper she felt the car begin to slow.

She watched the yellow and red painted curb flash by with hypnotic regularity.

The driver indicated a right and slowed. He made two more tight turns. Telephone wires were strung up overhead. As the street narrowed, the houses towered over either side of the car, the wires loaded with washing. It wasn't something he expected. Washing lines, yes, but on the telephone wires? It was peculiar enough for him to notice.

The next turn took them off the main road. Palms lined the road leading up to a hill. A vast area had been cleared out, and construction workers were busy working with girders, rebar and concrete, setting the foundations for what would almost certainly become another skyscraper dominating the Tel Aviv skyline. It took Orla a little while to get her bearings. A lot had changed even in the few years since she had last been in the city.

They were driving up Shaul Hill—Saul's Hill. There were no IDF buildings up the hill, or there hadn't been when she'd lived in Tel Aviv. If she remembered right, the only military establishment anywhere on the hill was Kiryat Shaul, and that wasn't anything to do with the Intelligence Corps. It was the military cemetery where, among others, lay the victims of the Yom Kippur War.

She looked quizzically at Uzzi Sokol. The Israeli ignored her scrutiny, staring straight ahead. He reached forward and tapped the driver on the shoulder. The man nodded and slowed the car, indicating a left turn into the cemetery gates.

"Where are we going?" Orla asked.

"To see Lieutenant General Caspi, as per my orders. You do want to see Akim Caspi, do you not?"

"He's meeting us in the cemetery?"

"It is as good a place as any in the city," Sokol said, without the slightest trace of humor. "Unless you are frightened restless spirits might eavesdrop on your conversation?"

Nothing felt right about this.

Orla shook her head.

A moment later the driver brought the car to a stop beside the visitor's center. "If you would be so kind?" Sokol asked, indicating the door. Orla opened the door and climbed out. High on the hill the sun was the same, but the wind brought the temperature down markedly. It was that, or the fact they were in a cemetery, Orla thought. Sokol indicated for her to follow, and he led her through the graves.

Finally he stopped in front of a small stone. The grass around it was neatly trimmed, and a fresh bunch of sunflowers were in the small glass jar beside the headstone. Someone obviously still tended the grave regularly. She read the name and dates carved into the headstone. *Akim Caspi, beloved father, cherished husband, loyal servant.* There was an engraving of what appeared to be an alligator at rest at the base of the headstone. According to the dates,

Caspi had died in June 2004, age 56. And if Lethe was right, that meant he was pushing up daises a month before two massive insurance payouts had been made in his name.

"There are several people who are very keen to know why the hell you're so eager to talk to a dead man. Perhaps you would care to explain," Uzzi Sokol asked.

She looked up from the grave to see the Israeli's Jericho 941 pistol drawn and pointed at her. The slide was cocked and locked, Sokol's finger a hair's breadth from squeezing down on the trigger. The move didn't surprise her. She'd been expecting Sokol to pull something the moment he had met her off the plane. Lethe had uploaded both sides of the photograph Ronan Frost had found in Sebastian Fisher's Jesmond flat to the G5's onboard computer. He had drawn a red ring around one of the faces. On the back he had underlined Akim Caspi's name. The second photograph he had uploaded was taken directly from Caspi's IDF file. Akim Caspi had either undergone radical reconstructive surgery and simultaneously turned the clock back about a decade, or she was looking at two very different people. In this case she was pretty sure it was the "or." She had made a hardcopy before the plane landed. Given this turn of events, she was glad she had. Orla turned slowly so that the pistol's black eye pointed squarely at the center of her chest.

"I think a gun is rather like a cock," Orla said, inclining her head slightly toward the black eye. "Just because you have one doesn't mean you have to stick it in a girl's face."

"Cute. You'll excuse me if I don't laugh. Now, answer the question."

"It's better if I show you," she said. "Assuming you aren't itching to pull the trigger on that penile extension of yours as soon as I make a move?"

"It's a risk you will just have to take."

She interpreted his curious inflection as an invitation to test him. Moving slowly, Orla knelt beside her case and broke the diplomatic seals. Sokol had to know that the whole purpose of the seals was to allow her to bring her Sig Sauer P228 compact into the country. "I've got a gun in here," she said, releasing the clasps and opening the briefcase's lid. "I am not going for it, but the papers I need are beneath it."

"Open the case," Sokol said.

Orla nodded and stood again. She lifted the lid so the case opened facing toward the Israeli. "The photographs are in the manila envelope beneath the gun. There's more information in the files, but for now you need to see the photograph."

Uzzi Sokol reached into the case with his free hand. His Jericho's aim never left her heart. He teased the envelope out from beneath the Sig Sauer and stepped back, reestablishing the slight safety of distance between them. Orla could have taken the man—she was relatively certain—if she had had the inclination. And the moment to do it was now, as he was distracted taking the photograph from the envelope. It would have been easy, throw the briefcase in his face, and as he instinctively recoiled sweep his legs out from under him. She would have had less than two seconds to disarm him, but she wouldn't have needed more than one. Orla had no intention of turning this into a fight. Akim Caspi's death only served to ask more questions, and the whole point of her coming to Tel Aviv had been to find answers, not get bogged down in a wild goose chase for the truth.

She waited for Sokol to slide the photograph out of the envelope.

Sokol studied the image, then grunted. "What is this supposed to prove?"

"It is a photograph of an archeological dig at the Sicarii fortress of Masada. It was taken in 2004. You might recognize some of the names on the reverse, if not their faces. They have been in the news over the last few days."

Sokol looked at the back side of the photograph. He shook his head. Then paused, turning the photograph back over so that he could study the faces of the young archeologists again. It was obvious he was having trouble reconciling the name Akim Caspi with the face of the lieutenant general he had served under.

"This is not Caspi," he said, finally, looking up from the photograph. "But you know that, don't you?"

Orla nodded. "I do, although it is a fact my people have only just learned."

Sokol made a curious clucking sound in the back of his throat, his tongue clicking against the roof of his mouth as he weighed up what he was about to say. "This is the man you wished to speak to?"

Orla nodded again.

"Why?"

"The other people in the photograph are dead," she began. "It is the circumstances surrounding their deaths that we're interested in."

"And you believe this false Caspi can help you somehow?"

"Something like that. Though, of course, we thought he was the real Akim Caspi less than five hours ago."

"How do I know this is not some sort of elaborate ruse concocted by your government?"

Orla breathed deeply and let that breath out slowly. "At precisely 1500 hours Zulu Time yesterday, thirteen people committed suicide in thirteen different European cities."

"I watch CNN," Sokol said. "The whole world knows what happened yesterday, and what happened in Berlin this morning. This is not news. Why should any of this be of concern to Israel?"

She pointed at the photograph.

"You're telling me this is a photograph of those people who burned themselves alive?" He waved the photograph imperceptibly.

Orla nodded again, slowly this time. "The Masada dig is, as far as we can tell, the one thing they all have in common. I'd hoped talking to Lieutenant General Caspi might shed some light on what happened yesterday, but . . ." She looked down at the well-tended grave and trailed off.

"But you said this photograph was taken over five years ago. Why would you think the lieutenant general would know anything about what happened yesterday?" Uzzi Sokol stopped talking then and looked at Orla Nyrén— really looked at her. His scrutiny made her uncomfortable. She felt dirty beneath his gaze. "Unless, and now I am reading between your rather unsubtle lines, you believe Israel is somehow behind this latest wave of terror attacks in your country? Is that what you are telling me?"

"I'm not telling you anything, Uzzi," she said, using his name for the first time. "I don't *know* anything. I'm looking for links. Leave no stone unturned. It's the only way to do this. You'd be doing exactly the same in my place. Don't pretend you wouldn't be. Masada is the one constant in these people's lives, the one place and time that links them all together. What it means, if anything, I don't know; but if something happened there, anything that might help make sense of what's happening now, this man, whoever he is, could be the key. All of the official records list Akim Caspi as leading the dig. That's why I wanted to talk to him."

"I don't think you will find your answers in Israel," he said without conviction.

She hadn't expected him to say anything else. Israel was a country of secrets, and its dirtiest it kept to itself. "But you understand why I have to ask?" He nodded. "So you're not going to shoot me, then?"

"Not today. Maybe tomorrow, if you go stirring up trouble in my country."

"I can't promise anything," Orla confessed. "There's a second set of papers in the case. Do you trust me to take them out?"

Sokol nodded again. Orla fished a second manila envelope out of the case and took a thin sheaf of papers out of it. She handed the first two to Sokol. "In July of 2004 two substantial payouts were made to Lieutenant General Akim Caspi, one by The Silverthorn Trust and the other by something called Humanity Capital."

"Payouts to Caspi's widow, no doubt."

"It's feasible. Humanity Capital are global underwriters. They specialize in insuring troops in war-torn areas, including Iraq and Afghanistan among others, and have close ties to the UN. That's what they mean by human capital. But Silverthorn? As of this morning our man hasn't been able to find anything on this so-called trust—and believe me, what Lethe can't find isn't there to be found in the first place. So, Silverthorn deposited something in excess of seventeen million dollars into a numbered account in Hottinger & Cie, one of Zurich's oldest private banks. The holder of that account, opened, coincidently, three days after his death, was one Akim Caspi." She handed Sokol another print out.

"How did you get this stuff?"

"As I said, anything Lethe can't get isn't there to be found. He has a knack for finding out other people's secrets."

"So I see," Uzzi Sokol said. "I would imagine someone like this Lethe of yours could be dangerous if he put his mind to it." He chuckled at that. Orla didn't contradict him. She knew enough about how numbered accounts worked to know that with some of the older Zurich banks the number was all you needed to make a withdrawal. It was all part of the arcane secrecy of the Old World banking system. Some were password protected, but she was in no doubt Jude Lethe could find that just as easily if he set his mind to it. What he did was rather frightening when she considered it. It went beyond invasive and into Orwellian Big Brother. These numbered accounts were meant to be among the

133 SILVER

most closely guarded secrets of a secret-obsessed nation, and Lethe had followed the money all the way back to the vaults of the Bahnhofstrasse in less than an hour. There were millions of reasons why anyone in their right mind might be tempted to try their luck.

"As you will see, withdrawals have been made as recently as three months ago. Deposits appeared to have ceased six months prior. That nine months of inactivity ended six days ago when a substantial deposit was made." By substantial she meant another eight-figure sum.

Sokol flipped over the page and scanned the rows of numbers. She could guess what he was thinking as the balance turned into a numerical string longer than the account number that protected it. "None of this looks like a widow's pension," he admitted. "At least not an Israeli widow. I don't mind telling you if my wife was in line for this kind of payout, I'd be looking over my shoulder while we spooned."

Orla knew exactly what he meant. There was enough money in Akim Caspi's account to finance a small war. That was what frightened her. These last few days didn't feel like random acts of violence anymore; they felt like the opening salvos in a war. And given that, it made even less sense that Sir Charles had chosen to make it their war.

Someone had access to the account and was using it regularly, and if the real Akim Caspi was as dead as the headstone made him look, it was a safe bet this other Akim Caspi from Fisher's photograph was the man spending all of that money.

A hooded crow settled on the stone cross beside Caspi's grave. Orla chose not to take it as a sign.

"Can I ask you something, Uzzi?"

"You can ask."

"Do you really expect me to believe the IDF would send out an Intelligence officer on a grunt mission like this if it didn't already have an inkling as to what was going on with the dead general's money?"

"Lieutenant general," Sokol corrected, instinctively.

"That doesn't change the question."

"Contrary to what the song says, it isn't all about the money," Sokol said.

"That sounds like an answer I'd love to have explained. You know who this man is, don't you?"

Instead of answering her, Uzzi Sokol said, "I know a lot of things. First, tell me, have you heard of the Shrieks?" He watched her intently, looking for any sign of recognition.

Orla shook her head. "No."

"Then you need to know about the Shrieks." Sokol scratched at the back of his neck as though he'd just been bitten. It seemed to derail his train of thought.

She looked at him, expecting him to go on, but Sokol was clearly no longer in a confessional mood.

"Then tell me about the Shrieks," Orla said, steering him toward the tidbit he'd dangled so tantalizingly. He looked at her.

Above them the sky filled with a flock of migratory birds on their way from swathes of European fields for the warmth of a North African winter.

"Not here," he looked over his shoulder as though he expected the dead to be eavesdropping on them. Orla followed the direction of his gaze. An old Jewish mother was laying flowers on her soldier son's grave. "And take the gun out of your briefcase. It is no good to anyone in there."

13

DON'T DRINK THE WATER

He watched the woman drink.

Botticelli would no doubt have considered her exquisite. As she bent over, raven black hair cascaded down around her face. Her breasts spilled white over the red-laced top of her bra. He enjoyed looking. He had always had a thing for fuller-figured women. It was something about the extra flesh that promised excess, like there was so much body for him to lose himself in. The woman wore a thin cotton blouse made translucent by the sweat that clung to the curves of her body. He delighted in the flesh. Unfortunately for her there were fewer and fewer men like him in the world; the ideals of beauty had moved on. Beauty was leaner, a work of art now, anorexic over ample. It was all about carving away the curves, turning beauty asexual, boyish. What was beautiful to the old Italian masters was nothing short of obese in this new world. He despaired at the kind of world that couldn't enjoy the sensation of sinking into that warm softness only a big body could offer.

Rome loved its water, even more so than Venice. There were the fountains, the horses of Trevi, Bernini's Four Rivers in Piazza Navona, the tridents of Neptune in Piazza del Popolo, the Fountain of Books, the Fountain of the Porter in Piazza Venezia, Triton, and then there were the springs and drinking fountains. Every street tapped into the water, every tap filled tourists' water bottles and slaked thirsts as the sun burned hotter. Spring in Rome was given over to the sound of water pouring from the fountains, people laughing as they turned their backs on the Trevi and tossed coins over their shoulders, hoping for the new romance promised Maggie McNamara in *Three Coins in a Fountain*. He wondered how many of those wishers knew the actress wound up dead after a deliberate overdose. It rather took the Tinseltown shine off the story.

He watched the woman walk away from the drinking fountain. She brushed her hair back out of her face, and seeing him looking at her, smiled. Her cheeks were flushed slightly red from the spring sun. Rome was like that now. A few years ago there had been four defined seasons; now there were two. And a few weeks either side that fluctuated between freezing and sweltering. She had a wonderful smile. The kind of smile that stirred his mind as well as his body. He inclined his head slightly, his own smile knowing.

It was a pity she was already dead, though actually there was no pity in it. He thought about going over there and seducing her. He knew he could. He could be with her when she died, then. He could watch that last beautiful sigh as the life left her glorious body. He could share that most intimate of moments, that final breath. He could see the fear in her eyes as she looked up at him, see the horror and the inevitability as she surrendered. He could smile down at her, touch her cheek perhaps. Kiss away the tears of fear, knowing he had given her both *la petite mort* and *la grande mort* in one sweet day. He was good with words and knew what most women wanted to hear, how to gently brush his fingers against places most men were too lazy to touch and how to use that gentle pressure to turn a woman's lips toward him. He knew how to seduce, how to play to both vanities and insecurities, and more importantly, he looked the part. Like her, he had been blessed with classical features, but for men the ideal of beauty had remained unchanged for centuries so he was every bit as beautiful today as he would have been in the Renaissance. That was just another small cruelty of this male-driven world.

She was with two other women, both thinner, both prettier on the new scale of beauty. He imagined she enjoyed his attention simply because she was used to being overlooked in favor of her friends. He blew her a kiss across the cobbles of the piazza.

When he looked back toward the drinking fountain a father was helping his small daughter stick her tongue out to catch the splashes.

Over the course of an hour, over two hundred people had drunk from that one fountain—students, tourists, locals, men and women of all shapes and differing beauties, and children. He enjoyed watching, counting them all as they stooped over the dripping fountainhead.

He gave up his seat and went for a walk, and everywhere he went instead of admiring the Baroque grandeur of Bernini or Lombardi, Peruzzi or Michelangelo, he watched the people as they stopped to drink and said a silent prayer of thanks to whatever god of the old pantheons brought the sun out on this day of all days.

Dominico Neri stared at the clock. He had run the permutations in his head all day—the number of seconds in an hour, the number of seconds Rome would be bathed in sunlight, the number of seconds she would gleam alabaster-pure under the moon. He had counted his heartbeat as it drummed against his ribcage, knowing it was its own clock. It didn't matter which one he obsessed over, both left him feeling like Nero with his damned fiddle. But for all that, it was less than forty-five minutes until today officially became tomorrow, and Rome was still standing.

He felt an inordinate sense of relief as each new second ticked by without all hell breaking loose in the incident room. His desk was piled high with case reports, witness statements and anything else he had been able to pull from the files that matched the Englishman's concerns.

Neri had a sixth sense for trouble, and the Englishman was trouble. He knew the sort, he might not be the insti-gator, but Noah Larkin had the air of a man used to walking hand in hand with death. The fact that Neri hadn't been able to find anything beyond Larkin's sealed military records and that every query he made ran up against proverbial brick walls only added to that sense of unease.

Likewise none of his searches for Ogmios brought any joy, but then he hadn't expected them to. Somewhere, no doubt, his queries had raised red flags and the surveillance was turning back on him, wondering who the hell he was to be asking about Ogmios and Noah Larkin. That was the joy of this clandestine world. And Neri was under no illusion that he had stumbled into some sort of secret world here. He didn't believe Noah Larkin was in salvage any more than he believed Santa Claus was a big, chubby white guy who looked disturbingly like God. Neri was a good Italian boy, he believed in crime and corruption and his mother's cooking; beyond that everything was open to doubt.

All he could do, for now, was take Larkin at face value.

That meant in the next forty-five minutes people were going to start dying in Rome.

He didn't know what to expect. None of them did. He'd

had his men working the streets, looking for suspicious activity, but how the hell were they supposed to see a potential terrorist when he looked just like the next man? These people weren't walking around with *Jihadist* tattooed on their foreheads. They were normal people— well, normal on the outside. There was nothing normal about their psychology. They were blonde, blue-eyed; they were olive-skinned Italians with five o'clock shadows and dangerous smiles; they were university students and businessmen. What they weren't was a bin-Laden caricature swathed head-to-toe in desert robes, with the gleam of madness in their eyes.

He looked at the clock again. Forty-three minutes. He wanted to believe nothing was going to happen, that Noah had been wrong in his assessment of the threat to Rome. Neri was still learning things about himself. Today he had learned that he was by nature a pessimist.

Forty-one minutes.

He took a sip from the coffee that he'd allowed to go cold on the desk. It didn't taste any better for his neglect.

Two hours earlier Neri had taken a risk. He'd called in a favor, setting up a meeting with Monsignor Gianni Abandonato for Larkin. The Monsignor oversaw work on several of the sacred texts and was one of the three archivists who worked closely with Nick Simmonds in the days leading up to his suicide. If anyone had an inkling as to the dead man's state of mind it was Abandonato. Neri put the Styrofoam cup down. He needed another drink to wash the taste of the coffee from his mouth. He circled Abandonato's name on the notepad beside the phone. It meant The Forsaken in Latin—a curious name for a man of the faith—but maybe it just went to prove the Holy Father had as rotten a sense of humor as the next man.

Rina Grillo poked her head around the door. "You need to see this," she said. He didn't like the way she said it, especially as there were only thirty-nine minutes left until midnight, and safety.

"What is it?" he asked, pushing himself up out of his chair.

She came across the squad room and offered him the file in her hand.

"San Gallicano Hospital in Trastevere just reported its third death in an hour from what they believe could well be thallium poisoning."

"Thallium?"

"The Poisoner's Poison; it's arcane stuff. It was popular during the Renaissance. The Medici family's weapon of choice. It isn't a 'nice' poison." She shrugged, almost as though embarrassed by the notion that there could be anything considered a nice poison. "Symptoms include vomiting, hair loss, blindness, stomach pains. Then the brain misfires, and the victim is subjected to hallucinations before they die."

Neri looked at the clock. Three people dead wasn't bad, considering how Berlin had suffered yesterday. Three people he could live with, even if the symptoms of their death were as horrible as Grillo had outlined. As soon as the thought had crossed his mind he felt guilty for it. Grillo's next sentence drove that guilt home, and the good Catholic in Dominico Neri couldn't help but think God was punishing him for it.

"I've checked against other hospital admissions, we've got reports of over five hundred admissions in the outer districts in the last hour alone. There seems to be a concentration around Torrenova, Acilia, Rebibbia, Primavella and San Lorenzo, but I am not sure that tells us anything, really."

"It gives us somewhere to start looking," Neri said, knowing that wasn't true, knowing that all that would achieve would be to make them feel as though they were doing something. "How do you poison five hundred people in a city like Rome without being seen?" he said, more to himself than to Rina Grillo.

"The water," she said. "It's the only way that makes sense. You contaminate the water supply with some sort of heavy metal halide solution, lethal in even small quantities, and with the sun out people are drinking. And the more they are drinking, the worse their deaths are going to be. It's evil, Neri."

He thought about the implications of what she suggested. He wasn't going to argue with her; it was evil, as pure an evil as any he had ever encountered. How long had the water been poisoned? How long did it take for the symptoms to manifest? Could these people have been poisoned even before the suicide in St. Peter's Piazza? And the implications that went with that line of thought: How many more people had drunk the poisoned water? How many more were already dead and didn't know it?

He stopped himself as he was about to take another mouthful of cold coffee. The taste wasn't worth dying for. He thought about all the coffee he had drunk in the last week. Like most Italians he took his caffeine intravenously. He tossed the Styrofoam cup into the trash can beneath his desk. His hand was shaking. Neri had no idea if that was one of the symptoms of thallium poisoning, or if it was just one of the more banal side effects of fear. He was frightened, and not just for his city now. Now his fear had a name; it had symptoms, and a pathology. Worst of all, it had a death toll.

Thirty-six minutes.

They had been so close.

14

SAFE IN SORROW

Ronan Frost looked up at the huge painting of the girl in the red coat that dominated the side of the building. She dwarfed Frost, easily ten times his size. He didn't understand how the urban artist had worked his art, but he appreciated the finished product. There was a certain sadness about her and the toys scattered around her feet, or so it looked at first glance, weren't toys at all. They were all political statements, the broken constructs of state and society scattered around the spoilt child's feet. Frost didn't like the picture. It reminded him too much of the kind of disaffected street art that lined the Falls Road in Belfast, and that just brought back other memories he didn't want to be reminded of.

Further down the street came the usual gang tags and swastikas spray-painted on the weeping walls. Beside the little girl in red there was something infinitely more infantile about the swastikas, like children playing at politics, shouting for the sake of shouting but with nothing to say.

Ronan Frost had found eight of the thirteen victims' houses. The story had been the same at each of them. The places had been ransacked. There were signs of family but no actual family to be found, and in each place it looked as though they had left in a hurry. There was food untouched and moldy on the plates in front of the TV. The DVD menu in one house played the same mindlessly chirpy thirty seconds of music over and over and over again. Frost knew it had been playing like that for at least a week. It was a wonder the relentless happiness hadn't driven the neighbors insane. Despite the fact that the houses had all been scoured, there were still things that linked them back to Israel. This puzzled Frost. If they weren't trying to hide the links to Masada what *were* they trying to hide? What was the purpose of ransacking the houses if it wasn't to purge it of any links to the dig? It was a good question.

Frost checked in with Lethe for the latest situation report from the others. It was difficult running an operation across four countries. The sooner they were back together, the better. Still, they had limited resources, the scarcest of which was manpower. They weren't the Army. They couldn't dispatch a dozen agents into the field. What they had was Lethe. Lethe gave him a brief rundown. Rome had fallen, meaning they'd been right in their interpretation of those first two targets, but from here on in they were running blind. Tomorrow it could be any of eleven cities.

Of everything Lethe said, it was the fate of Grace Weller, the MI6 agent who had ingratiated herself into the life of the Berlin suicide, that interested him the most. She was almost certainly dead, but she'd had the wherewithal to leave them a trail like Gretel following the witch off into the woods. The documents on that USB stick were her breadcrumbs. In other words Grace Weller was something tangible. She existed. She had a personal file. She had a desk, a home, all of the clutter of life. She might have spent years watching Grey Metzger, but that didn't mean she had spent years without going home. He needed to know where she lived; he needed to know who, exactly, she worked for. He needed to talk to her contact here in the UK. He needed to know what she was doing out there in Berlin. He needed to know why Six had marked Grey Metzger as a person of interest. Was Metzger somehow at the center of this? Less a victim than an instigator?

He didn't need to tell Lethe to keep on digging.

Come dawn they'd know everything there was to know about this Ghost Walker woman.

But it was still a long time until dawn, and he had a ninth house to visit.

He had talked to neighbors, trying to build up a picture of the victims' last few days, but they were city people. City people kept to themselves. It wasn't like even fifteen years ago when everyone knew everyone else's business. Now the doors closed, and what went on behind them was anyone's guess. Door-to-door inquiries were a waste of time. Even if they had seen something, people pretended temporary blindness. There was no sense of civic duty anymore. There wasn't even a milkman doing a daily delivery anymore. Everything had become so anonymous.

Ronan Frost walked down the street. He pulled his jacket closer. The night was cold on his skin. It didn't feel like spring had finally arrived. It felt like winter had killed any trace of warmth. Cars lined the side of the road, parked bumper to bumper. There were no expensive sports cars in the long snake of Fords, Fiats, Mazdas and Citroens. These were all functional vehicles. None of them were new. This was a part of the city where a new car came in a poor second to feeding the family.

Most of the houses had alarm boxes up above the doors. It was a good bet that more than half of them were dummies. It was that kind of place.

He looked for a twitching curtain, a Neighborhood Watch sticker in a window, anything that would suggest a nosy neighbor who might just have seen something out of the ordinary. But the curtains were drawn and the lights dimmed. People didn't look out into the street because they knew what was good for them. Frost walked down the middle of the road, breathing in the city smell. He could almost taste the danger pheromones in the back of his throat. This place had more in common with the Belfast of his early 20s than just the graffiti.

He counted the numbers down until he reached the white door of the ninth house. The windows were dark. Weeds had grown up between the cracks in the pavement, and the bare bulb of the outside light was broken. It was the right street, the right house, but it was quite unlike any of the other eight he had visited. The others had all been in better parts of their various cities, more expensive houses in the up-and-coming suburbs if not the heart of the cities themselves, but not this one. This place smacked of poverty. He could feel the desperation crawling up and down his skin like mites.

Of course, the benefit of a street like this was, if the curtains didn't twitch, he doubted very much if anyone would call the police either.

He walked up to the door, and taking the Browning from his belt holster, broke the small window with the butt of the gun. He knocked out the jagged glass teeth left behind and reached through for the lock. He had assumed the deadbolt wouldn't have been set if the occupants had been bundled off in a hurry. He was right. The door swung open.

Frost stepped inside, closing the door behind him.

The first thing that hit him was the smell.

He gagged and had to fight back the urge to vomit, the stench was that intense.

He knew the smell. There was only one thing in the world that owned this odor: new death.

At least a week's worth of unopened mail spilled across the mat, along with the newspapers. He knelt down and counted eight days' worth of unread news. So, nine days ago the inhabitants of this small two-up two-down terrace in the middle of the wrong part of town had been taken. The feel of this place, even in the dark, was different. He didn't turn on the light as he walked, trailing his fingers along the wall to make sure he didn't stumble. He found the end of the balustrade and worked his way carefully up the stairs. The house was quiet. The higher he climbed the worse the smell became. Moonlight streamed in silver through an upstairs window, casting a long light slash through the shadows of the dark house. In the light he saw the swirls of wallpaper that had been hung back in the mid-70s. It felt coarse and heavy beneath his fingers.

He heard his own breathing and realized it had become shallower and sharper with each new step. He knew what was waiting up there. But that didn't mean he could just turn his back and head off looking for house number ten. Indeed, the fact that he knew what was waiting for him meant it was all the more important that he face it. It was exactly what he had come looking for: proof.

His first thought as he reached the landing was that something had gone wrong. The open area didn't feel right. It wasn't Feng Shui. It was far more instinctive and pre-dictive than that. People had a way of arranging the things in their life so that they were simple, functional. Furniture placement was repetitive. He could go into rooms blind and know even before he stepped through the door how a good number of those rooms were laid out. But the first floor landing was wrong. It was out of balance.

It took him a second to realize why. The chair that should have been in the right angle, where the balustrade met the immersion cupboard at the far side of the landing, had been dragged out so that it half-blocked the way into the bathroom. Its back was toward him. He tried to picture the struggle that would have turned it. On the opposite wall the blanket box had a thicker band of shadow on the side nearest him, meaning it hadn't been pushed back up against the wall properly. In his mind's eye Frost pictured someone on their back, thrashing about as they were dragged toward the stairs. They caught the chair and tried to hold onto it as it twisted away from the wall. They kicked out with their right foot, trying to get some sort of leverage as they lost their grip on the chair. It might not have played out exactly like that, but he knew it was close enough to make no difference.

The floorboards groaned beneath his weight.

He walked toward the first of three doors, to the smallest bedroom. He couldn't tell what color it had been painted in the moonlight, but a mobile with elephants and toucans and other exotic animals hung over a cot, and most of the floor was cluttered with cuddly toys and stuffed bears. There was no sign of the baby. That, he knew, was the only moment of blessed relief he was going to have until he left the house. He was well aware of the numbers: ninety percent of all kidnap victims were dead within thirty-six hours of being taken. There weren't going to be any happy endings in this house.

There was a body on the bed in the next room. She lay sprawled out across the bed sheets. Her blood had turned them dark. Dark specks crawled across her face, stomach and legs: flies. They would have started laying their eggs in her already. In another day or two her flesh would be crawling with maggots.

Frost covered his nose and mouth and moved into the room. Up close, the stench made his eyes water.

She hadn't just been killed, she'd been opened up. Twenty, thirty, forty cuts—it was impossible to tell where one entry wound ended and another began. They had sliced into each other and across each other. Frost didn't want to think about the frenzy that must have driven the attack. No one deserved to die in so much pain. He looked at her lying on the bed, stripped of dignity as well as life. There was no way she hadn't suffered. She'd been fighting and screaming through each and every knife thrust until her system shut down in shock.

All he could think was that she might have been beautiful once, but not anymore.

He looked at the ruin of flesh that had been a wife and mother nine days ago, and he wanted to break something.

He continued to walk around the room. For the sheer amount of violence there was very little out of place in the room. There was no sign of the baby. Was that the leverage they'd used against the guy to make him burn himself? Murdered his wife and kidnapped his baby? Or did he think they were both still alive? Did he think that by burning himself he was saving them?

Of course he did. How else did you keep a guy compliant? Kill his wife and he's going to be thinking all the time about how to hurt you, how to turn on you, even if his child's life depends on it, because he isn't stupid. He knows that if you've killed one, you'll kill the other as soon as he's given you what you want. So no, the guy had to think his wife and child were safe. The poor bastard went to his death thinking he was buying their lives.

The woman's mobile phone was on the bedside table. He tried to turn it on but the battery had discharged. He cracked it open and took the battery out so he could get at the SIM card.

Frost pressed his finger against the headset in his ear and triggered the call-home auto-dial. Lethe answered on the first ring.

"What do you need, boss?"

"Run the number on this SIM card for me, last call made, last one received." He recited the three strings of numbers printed on the back of the card and waited while Lethe did his thing. It took a couple of minutes. In that time Frost looked around the room. Even discounting the body on the bed it was an utterly sad room, white built-in wardrobes around the bed, from corner to corner and up to the ceiling. He opened a few of the cupboards and the night stand drawer. There was nothing particularly out of place in any of them, clothes and the junk of life shoved away in drawers to be forgotten about. She had been reading Agatha Christie. She'd never know who did it, Frost thought. He walked across to the window and looked out over the backyard. The word yard (in terms of grass and flowers and greenery) was a bit of a misnomer. It was a patch of cracked paving and unruly weeds fenced in by rotten wood that had been painted with brilliant white emulsion. The slats of wood looked like Papa Death's rictus grinning up at him.

"Okay, here we go," Lethe said in his ear, breaking his macabre chain of thought. "Last call in was from a cell phone registered to one Miles Devere. You recognize the name?"

"Doesn't ring any bells," Frost said, running the name through his memory. "Check him out though, just to be on the safe side."

"Will do. Right, so, last call out, now this is interesting . . ." Lethe broke off. Frost could hear the sound of his fingers rattling off the keys beneath them. "Last call out was to the Nicholls Tobacco Warehouse, a bonded warehouse down by the Canning Docks. And what's interesting about that, I hear you ask? Well, that was abandoned in 1983 and condemned in 2006. It's a ruin. They had a campaign in the '90s to try and stop the decay of all these old buildings that were built during the Industrial Revolution. Stop the Rot it was called. They made a lot of noise about preserving our heritage, but I don't think they had a lot of luck—certainly not in this case. Nicholls is due to be torn down and replaced by luxury apartments. The phone was reconnected twelve days ago. So riddle me this, boss: why would a derelict building suddenly need a working telephone?"

"Running a line into the site office as they get ready for the demolition," Frost said.

"Oh, go on then, take all the fun out of it with a practical answer, why don't you?"

Outside, Frost heard the doppler of a siren rising and falling as it raced through the night. It could have been more than four or five streets away, and it was getting closer all the time. He resisted the urge to run. They weren't coming for him. Sirens were as common as takeouts in this part of the city. He could think of a dozen reasons off the top of his head why they were heading anywhere but here, to this two-up two-down terraced house with the dead woman lying in a whorish sprawl on her bloody sheets. But with each heartbeat the sirens grew louder, and he knew each of those dozen reasons was wrong.

"Okay, Jude. I think I'm in a bit of trouble here," he said, walking over to the door. The sirens couldn't have been more than a street away. "Tell me the plod aren't on the way here. Lie to me if you have to."

"You really want me to lie?" Frost could hear the humor in his voice. He was enjoying this far too much. "Well, then, three squad cars most definitely haven't been scrambled to number 11 Halsey Road, the last known residence of one Tristan James, ex of this parish, and his wife Wilma and their eight-month-old son, Marcus. No police on their way whatsoever. You might as well put your feet up and watch TV. Nothing exciting is going to happen whatsoever."

"You're not a very convincing liar," Frost said.

The door downstairs opened.

Frost backed into the room. Whichever way he looked at it, being found in the house with the dead girl wasn't good. He moved slowly toward the window. "Can you see out there?"

"In two seconds I'll be able to."

Frost didn't know how Lethe did what he did, probably hooking into a Defense satellite and or something equally illegal and frightening. The boy had a way with machines. All that really mattered to Frost right then was that Lethe was his eyes and ears. He wouldn't be able to get out of the house without him.

"Give me their positions," he whispered into the headset, barely daring to vocalize the words. He tried the window, but it had been painted shut. He pushed against the frame but there was no way it was going to give without making a god-awful racket. The last thing he wanted to do was let everyone in the house know exactly where he was.

He crept back to the bedroom door, doing his best to keep his weight distribution even so that the floorboards didn't betray him. He could hear them moving about downstairs, working their way through the rooms. They sounded nervous, pumped up, ready for a fight. They were talking loudly, barking instructions at each other. He stood absolutely still. No way this was going to end well. They'd be listening for the slightest out of place sound. The way he figured, he had at best a minute before they came upstairs. The place wasn't that big, and there weren't that many places to hide. It would take no time to sweep through the downstairs, and given the all-pervasive reek, they all knew they were in a death house. They were expecting to find a corpse. They weren't expecting him to be there. If he startled them, it could all go south very quickly. "Lethe," he breathed, "please tell me they didn't send a Tactical Response Unit."

"No guns," the voice in his ear assured him.

That was one less thing to worry about. He heard them clumping about beneath him—which meant he had less than half a minute to get out of the house. He couldn't just run down the stairs and out the front door, no matter how much the simplicity of the idea appealed. They would be on to him before he was halfway down the stairs. He didn't really want to have to explain what he was doing in the house. But, for that matter, he didn't really want to shoot anyone either. So it was all about not being caught.

"Three cars in the street out front," Lethe whispered in his ear. Frost almost laughed at the younger man's theatrics. It wasn't as though it was Lethe who was standing over a corpse, separated from half a dozen policemen by a few inches of wood and plasterboard. "Two men are still outside. One is heading around the side of the house, going for the backdoor. That means three are inside."

Three wasn't a good number.

"I'm getting too old for this shit," Frost whispered, rubbing at his forehead. "Can you do something? Cause a distraction?"

Without waiting for an answer, Frost crept across the landing. He ignored the baby's room; the window there looked out onto the front of the house. That left the bathroom which, as he had expected, had a tiny fly-window that was neither for use nor ornament. Frost started to reach around for his gun, ready to shoot his way out if he had to, when he saw the chair half across the bathroom doorway. Again he was struck by how out of place it was. He looked up. There was a small loft access hatch in the ceiling directly above it. The hatch was barely wide enough for him to squeeze through. He didn't have a lot of choice. It was that or charge down the stairs guns blazing straight onto the evening news.

Frost heard the downstairs backdoor opening.

The cops had done the first sweep.

They were talking now. He could hear every muffled word they said.

"You check upstairs," one of them said. Frost heard the crackle of a radio. They were sending in a situation report: downstairs all-clear.

Frost didn't wait for the sound of the first footsteps on the stairs. He stood on the chair and reached up. Placing the flats of his palms on the wood he pushed slightly, lifting it less than an inch clear and eased it aside. Moving quickly, he gripped the sides of the loft hatch and pulled himself up, swinging his legs inside the hole as he heard the heavy sound of the policeman climbing the stairs. He didn't have time to slide the hatch all the way back in place. All he could do was ease it across so that it covered most of the hole and hope no one looked up. Frost lay on his back in the dark, listening to the sound of the search beneath him. The chair was still directly under the hatch, but there was nothing he could do about it so it wasn't worth worrying about. He lay on his back, his Browning cradled against his chest.

"Oh, sweet Lord," he heard, followed by the hacking sound of a man heaving his guts up. More footsteps on the stairs, running this time. Frost risked rolling onto his side, and put his eye to the crack. He couldn't see much through the narrow gap, the shoulder of one uniformed officer and part of the back of another. "Trust me, you really don't want to go in there."

"Damn," another muttered, backing out of the room.

Frost didn't dare breathe. All it would take was for one of them to realize the chair was out of place and to look up. And because he didn't dare breathe, the smell clawed its way into his lungs, trying to force him to. He closed his eyes, willing them to go back downstairs. He couldn't exactly hide in the loft space forever, and soon the place would be swarming with forensics and crime scene investigators. One of them *would* look up. They would see that the hatch was out of place, and there wasn't a damned thing he could do about it. He tried to think. His prints were all over the house, but he hadn't touched the woman or the bed. But he had touched the window, her phone, the door handle. Had he touched the balustrade? Had he touched anything downstairs? He cursed himself for being an idiot.

"What kind of animal would do something like that to a woman?"

That was a damned good question.

Frost had spent enough time around killers to know that this kind of murder needed hatred to fuel it. It wasn't just about killing. Using a knife made it intimate. Slashing once or twice was hard, being forced to look into the eyes of your victim while they fought you, but slashing forty or fifty times? Opening up the woman like she was some kind of medical exhibit? That was more like an autopsy than a killing. That took rage.

"Vince," one of the voices beneath him said. "I think you better take a look at this."

They moved out of his line of sight. They were in the nursery.

Frost licked his lips.

The darkness above him was filled with the sound of his breathing. It was so loud in his ears he couldn't believe they couldn't hear it down there.

"Now would be a really good time to give me that bloody distraction," Frost rasped. The words came out like a prayer.

Lethe was listening.

15

THIS GARDEN
Then - The Testimony of
Menahem ben Jair

The boy looked up at his father, adoration in his eyes.

Jair had never been able to look up at his own father that way. What did it feel like to look up into the face that you would grow into? It was a simple right every boy deserved. But then, Jair had never known his father. He had been murdered before Jair was born. This garden was the only place he felt close to him. Jair came here at night sometimes and imagined the sigh of the wind through the olive branches was his father's voice. His mother had begged him time and again not to come, not to dwell in the past. It was a place for ghosts, she said. He didn't know whether she meant the past or this garden, or both. It didn't matter. She was a ghost herself now. When he picked up one of the scattered stones he couldn't help but wonder if it had been the one that had killed his father. He felt out the sharp edges with his thumb. More than once he had clutched a stone and driven it against his temple, trying to feel the same pain Judas must have felt, but he couldn't. All the stones in the world couldn't capture his father's pain because it wasn't physical. He knew that better than anyone.

Father and son walked hand in hand through the olive arch into Gethsemane.

The garden was in bloom. All around them color rioted, the clashes ranging from the subtle to the raw. He took a deep breath and led Menahem across the garden toward a small, white stone shrine. The grass was mottled with golden spots of light where the sun filtered down through the canopy of leaves. Every fragrance imaginable surrounded them. Despite the heat, the man shivered. The shrine had seen better days. The face of the saint had mildewed. A few trinkets had been laid out around the shrine in offering: a figurine made out of olive twigs and bound with reed, a nail, a fragment of slate marked with the cross, and a coin. That was his offering, a remembrance of the second man in the garden's tragedy. Everyone remembered the betrayal but forgot the sacrifice. His son clutched his hand tighter, as though sensing his discomfort. There was a simple affection to the gesture, but it wasn't strong enough to save a man's soul.

He ruffled the boy's hair. It was a rare moment of affecttion from the man. He didn't know how to be a father. It wasn't that his mother, Mary, had not loved him. She had. She had loved him more than enough for any child. But he wore his father's face. Every day he grew more and more like the man she had loved, and it reminded her more and more acutely of what she had lost. He was a living ghost. Just by being close, by sitting in her lap and looking up at her, by smiling the same smile his father had smiled, he brought it all back. He was her grief as well as her joy. How could that not damage the bond between them?

"Do as I do, boy," he said, and knelt, bowing his head in quiet reflection. He stayed that way for the longest time.

Onlookers might have thought they were offering a prayer to the betrayed Messiah like so many others who made the pilgrimage to the garden. They weren't. Jair was remembering the father he had never known while the boy was enjoying the closeness of his. It was the simplest of all pleasures. "The others may forget, but I will remember," Jair promised the ghosts of the garden. "Others may hate, but I will love." The words were more than just a promise; they were the gospel of a dead man. "Others may be blind, but I shall see." He looked up. His eyes were red-rimmed, but there were no tears. It was so strange to think that this was where love ended.

He looked at his son then, and all he felt was sadness. The boy was growing up so quickly. He was old enough now to know truth from lie. That was why he had brought him here. "Come here," he said, opening his arms wide. The boy scurried forward and threw himself into his father's embrace. The hug seemed to last and last, until finally the man broke away. "It's time I told you what happened here."

Jair reached into the folds of his road-stained robes and withdrew the battered leather pouch his mother had given him. He had been the same age as Menahem when she brought him here to tell him about his father. Until that day she had never talked about him. He felt the weight of silver in his hand. The coins had fascinated him when he was younger. Now he found them curiously comforting. He set the pouch on the ground between them. As best as he could remember they were sitting in the same corner, perhaps even under the same tree. She would have approved. She was one for symmetry, signs and circles.

"This is where my father died," he said. "Twice."

"I don't understand," the boy said.

And why should he? Jair thought, looking for the words to explain. "He died once in spirit, and then again in flesh, blood and bone. They talk about the resurrection of Jesus, they glory in the man who lived twice, but they forget my father, the man who died twice. First they broke his soul, forcing him to honor a promise, and then, when he was reduced to a shell of a man they broke that shell, battering it with stones. But we few, we remember. My father was an agent of Sophia. Do you understand what it means to say that?"

The boy shook his head.

"Sophia is Divine Wisdom, the Knowledge of God. So when I say Judas Iscariot was an agent of Sophia, I mean that he worked for the Divine Purpose."

"He was carrying out God's will?" the boy asked.

"Exactly. Think about the story you know, the Messiah on the cross, the resurrection—without your grandfather's betrayal there could be no resurrection. Without the death and the resurrection the sins of man could never have been cleansed. There could be no new faith without Judas, Menahem. Don't ever forget that truth. He gave everything, and is reviled for it." He emptied the silver coins onto the grass and spread them out with his fingers. "All because of this."

"Money?"

"Money given to him by the High Priest, Caiaphas, in return for the kiss that identified his friend, Jesus. They paint him as a villain now, because of these coins, but it was never so. Here, on the night before the kiss, Jesus drew my father aside and begged him to be strong, for already he was beginning to falter. You see, this betrayal, this agony thrust upon him, was not of his doing." Jair had so much he wanted the boy to understand but it was so hard to find the words. "They were like brothers, their love thicker than blood. Your grandmother stood between them. She adored them both, these two great men. All these new lies have risen, but this is her truth, and from today it is yours to remember. Do not let the world forget, boy, and don't let them convince you otherwise; they were friends into death. That is the only truth. Do not let the world forget it."

"I will not, father, I promise," the boy said solemnly.

Jair smiled gently. "I know, my son. I know."

"Then what happened?" Menahem asked, as though it was any other story he had heard and wanted to know the end of.

"After the fighting in the temple Jesus was a marked man. The Pharisees could not abide this man who walked among the poor people, spreading a message of love without fear. Without fear, boy, that is the important thing here. Love without fear. Love without avarice. Love without stricture. He took them out of the temples, bringing them back to the earth. He was their teacher. He hated what they had done to his god, how they had taken him away from the people and hid him in their huge temples and their false idols. He wanted people to worship the natural wonder, not its manmade face." Jair picked up one of the stones and turned it over in his hand so the boy might see. "Look at this stone, see it properly, see the miracle of time and attrition and earthly forces that had to come together to press it into this final form. That, boy, is a miracle worthy of God. Putting them two by two atop one another to make a wall, that is just sense. Do you see the difference?"

The boy thought about it for a moment. "Yes, father," he said, eventually. "The stone was always there, whatever shape we choose for it. Like the tree. By itself it can offer comfort and shade, bear fruit and provide, or the carpenter can reshape it to match his needs."

Jair smiled. The boy had a sharp mind. "And which is the miracle?"

"The first, the tree."

"But they are both creations, are they not?"

"No father. One is creation, the other is recreation."

"Very good, Menahem. Very good." Jair's smile widened. He wondered if he had grasped the concept so readily when he was the boy's age. He doubted it. "The Nazarene was recreating the god of their book, taking him out of the temples and into the fields, back to his original wonders, and reminding them that they did not need stone temples to glorify him. That frightened the Pharisees. Inside the temples they had control of the people. Strip them of their temples and you strip them of their power. Worse, change the way people think of their god, make him this caring father instead of some distant wrathful deity who purged the world with flood and plague, and you take away the fear. Without power, without fear, these men were nothing. And that more than anything frightened them."

"So they wanted Jesus dead?"

"Exactly. They wanted to strip away everything that made him special, assuming that whatever remained would prove to be as craven as they themselves were. They couldn't grasp the notion of sacrifice. It was outside of their philosophy. So to make him suffer, they made the people who followed him suffer. After his attack on the money-lenders the Pharisees turned their anger onto the people who listened to the message of this new caring god, and they hurt them.

"So here, in this garden, Jesus turned to your grand-father and begged him to help put an end to their suffering. Even though it meant ending his own life. Judas did not want to betray his friend. What man would? But what choice did he have? The people he loved were suffering. The Pharisees were persecuting them in his name, promising that the suffering would only end when Jesus was silenced. They spread lies and hate. They used both to undermine the truth enough to have people turning back to the temple for protection. It was all about fear with them. Always fear.

"So, together these two friends conceived of a plan that would end the tyranny of the temple once and for all. And they did it here, in this garden, the same place my father would surrender his friend to the soldiers, the same place the stones of the disciples would end his life. Here, in this garden."

Eyes wide, the boy looked around as though seeing the place for the first time. Where there had been trees and shrubs he saw ghosts. Jair remembered that sensation. He remembered thinking he had seen his father incline his head just slightly and smile as his mother gave him the coins. The mind had a way of giving you what you needed most. He wondered who the boy saw.

"That promise destroyed my father. It killed the man he had been. Killed the kindness and the humor and everything mother loved him for. For the rest of his life he was a shell, a husk, a broken man. Not that there was much life left to him. Mother met him on the road here. He knew they were waiting for him. He knew they were going to kill him. She begged him to leave, to run, but he wouldn't because he wanted to die."

Something bothered the boy.

"What is it, son?"

"Why didn't Jesus surrender himself? Why did he need grandfather to deliver him?" Menahem asked earnestly.

That was a question that had bothered Jair for most of his adult life. He had seen people spit at his mother, so called holy men, and curse her and call her a whore. It had cut deep. The Pharisees looking to smear her. He had asked his mother why Judas had to die for this other man with his new religion. Because she knew both men better than anyone, he thought she might have the answer. She gave him the only answer that made any sense: "Because he doubted himself. He doubted his own strength. Jesus needed someone at his side to be sure he went through with it. He wasn't merely surrendering, he was sacrificing himself. He needed to know he wasn't alone. So that was the sacrifice your grandfather made. He gave himself so that his friend could end the tyranny of the Pharisees." And for that she allowed them to spit at her and call her whore.

"Grandfather must have been brave," the boy said.

Jair nodded, lost again in memories that weren't his. "Even his own friends turned on him because he couldn't tell them the truth. Like everyone else they thought he had betrayed Jesus. They didn't understand. There was so much they didn't understand. They thought he had acted out of jealousy and greed. They thought it was all about these damned coins. It wasn't. It never had been. You know that now. He lost everything because he was the best of them, the strongest, most faithful. And now they call him faithless." Jair closed his eyes. The real betrayal was still fresh inside him.

"He was about to become a father, yet for the sake of his friend he gave up the chance of ever knowing me." He looked at his son, trying to imagine himself in his father's place. All of the choices he had made in his life paled beside that single choice Judas had made in this garden. It would have been so easy to flee, to take Mary and start their new family. Again that familiar swell of bitterness rose inside him. "I can't imagine never knowing you," Jair said, glad he had been spared that agony at least.

He gathered up the silver and handed the pouch to his son.

"These are yours now. Think of them as the last reminders of your grandfather's sacrifice. We cannot forget the truth. We owe that much to him, don't we?"

"I'll never forget," Menahem promised.

16

BURNING DOWN THE HOUSE
Now

The first siren blared almost immediately.

The second and third came only a second later. In less than five seconds every alarm box in the street was wailing. Half of them might have only been for show, but the other half were doing the best to raise the dead. In thirty seconds they had joined into a single wall of noise.

"What the hell's that racket?" one of the uniforms said.

"Not sure, Sarge. Sounds like burglar alarms."

"You trying to tell me every bastard in this street just got robbed? I don't like this. Go and check it out, Hollis."

Ronan Frost listened to one set of booted footsteps clump down the stairs. That still left two uniforms upstairs. They were better numbers. He could take two, quickly, if he had to. Still, with a little bit of luck there would be no need.

"What the hell's going on out there?" the uniform was talking into his radio, Frost realized. He couldn't hear what the crackling voice said in reply. He didn't doubt for a minute that Lethe had the ability to mess with their frequencies if he wanted to. If the boy could trigger every damned burglar alarm in a square mile, he could sure as hell dampen a radio signal. "Say again?" the officer repeated, shouting to be heard over the caterwauling alarms.

Just go down there and check it out, Frost willed the man to do his job.

They had a corpse here, but the one indisputable thing everyone knew about the dead was that they didn't get up and walk unless it was a Romero film. She wasn't going anywhere. Outside, it could have been the first salvo of the Third World War if the racket was anything to go by. They were policemen. It was their duty to go out there and investigate.

Frost waited, counting the rhythmic *dub-dub dub-dub* of his heartbeats.

Street by street more alarms sounded until they formed their own grotesque dawn chorus across the city. It was pandemonium. Still he didn't move. His skin prickled with anticipation. He felt the tension coiling up inside him, desperate to be released in a fury of action. Still he waited, lying on his back, listening to the cacophony. It was music to his ears. He'd asked for a distraction and Lethe had delivered. He could picture people beginning to stumble out of their houses in the pajamas, rubbing their sleepy eyes and wondering what the hell was going on.

With a bit of luck a few more minutes of this and he'd be able to slip downstairs and out of the backdoor unnoticed. He wouldn't need to be Harry Houdini to disappear into the crowd of woken sleepers grumbling about the bloody noise.

He heard more footsteps on the stairs.

It was hard to tell if it was one man, or if both of them were going down.

Frost waited until he couldn't hear them, then whispered, "Talk to me Lethe."

"You can say thank you any time you like. No, no, seriously. Any time you like. I live to serve."

"Yeah, yeah, just tell me what you see."

"Five plod standing around, looking worse than useless. I think I confused them. That or all the noise is interfering with the neural relays and their brains are shutting down to protect themselves."

"Meaning one's still inside the house," Frost mused, ignoring everything after the word five.

"No fooling you, boss."

"Remind me again why we keep you around?"

"Because I'm brilliant, obviously, and because without my little bit of techno-magic you'd be spending a good chunk of the foreseeable at Her Majesty's Pleasure. Now, it's good to talk and all that, but how about you get the hell out of there, Frosty."

Frost holstered his pistol.

He reached up for one of the rafters, caught a hold of the beam with both hands, and lifted himself silently to his feet. He stood, one foot either side of the loft hatch. He couldn't stand fully upright because of the confined space. He bent down all the way, working his fingers beneath the wooden board, then very carefully lifted it out of the way. The alarm chorus hid the occasional scrape and scuff of wood on wood as he put the loft door down. He could see the landing lit up beneath him. Frost lowered himself back down to his stomach, then leaned ever so slightly down through the opening to see exactly what he'd be lowering himself into.

The last uniform still stood in the bedroom doorway, unable to pull his gaze away from the mutilation on the bed. The odds were the poor guy had never seen a corpse before. That his first looked like one of Andrei Chikatilo's victims spread out there on her bed didn't help his brain process the horror of the room. But it did help Frost. He breathed deeply, once, twice, steadying himself, before he lowered himself slowly, and soundlessly, down. Frost took all of his weight on his forearms like a gymnast on the parallel bars. As his shoulders came level with his elbows every muscle in his arms began to tremble violently. He expected the police officer to cry out, but he didn't. Frost twisted slightly, allowing his body weight to lower him further, until it felt as though the muscles in his shoulders and upper back were going to tear, then he dropped down the last few inches to the floor silently behind the uniform.

He reached around to the holster at the base of his spine and drew his gun.

He took two steps across the deep pile carpet, quickly bringing himself up to no more than a few inches behind the policeman. He saw himself over the uniform's shoulder, in the mirror on the wall behind the bed. The uniform's eyes widened and he started to turn. Frost didn't hesitate. He pistol whipped the uniform across the side of the head, dropping him like a stone. It was that or putting a bullet in his temple. He caught the man as his legs buckled and lowered him gently to the floor.

Frost took the stairs two and three at a time, then froze at the bottom, caught by a moment's indecision. "This is such a bollocks job. That guy saw my face, and my prints are all over this place," he said, looking at where his left hand still rested on the ornamental acorn-carved knob at the bottom of the balustrade.

"Three choices," Lethe said in his ear, without missing a beat. "Get the feather duster out, play chemist and burn the place down—it's easy enough, trust me. There's a gas main, and there's enough explosive stuff in the average kitchen to take out a tank. That kills two birds with one stone: no eye witness, no prints to worry about. It's surprisingly easy. All you need is some lard, the crystallized oven cleaner and the gas hose. Couple of minutes and the blaze will be out of control. Or I can make it look like you never existed. No fingerprints, no military records, nothing. You'll become a non-person in about twenty seconds flat. Your call."

Frost saw faces moving in the broken square where the small window had been inset in the front door. They couldn't see him, but they would in about five seconds. "You're a scary bastard," he said. He had no doubt the kid could wipe every trace of him from the face of the world as easily as he claimed.

"Obi Wan taught me well, but you are my Lord and Master, Frosty. And as your faithful servant I feel obliged to remind you it's time to make like a shepherd and get the flock out of there."

Ronan Frost knew the kid was right. He turned and started to run. He heard the front door opening behind him. He didn't risk a backward glance, knowing it could be the difference between making it out of the house and not. He hit the backdoor running. Outside was chaos. Alarms blared, people were shouting, confused, worried. Frost didn't break his stride as he ran straight across the tiny backyard and launched himself at the painted fence. He hit the Grim Reaper's grinning wooden teeth right foot first, caught the top with his hands, and boosted himself up over the fence in one fluid motion. He dropped down onto the other side and stood there for a second, back pressed up against the fence, looking left and right.

The Monster was parked streets away.

"All available cars have just been sent your way, boss. In a few minutes the entire area is going to be teaming with the law."

It didn't have to be a problem. They had no idea they were even meant to be looking for him. As far as they knew there was a dead body and a lot of alarms ringing. He didn't have any blood on him, and other than being in the wrong place at the absolutely wrong time, he'd done nothing wrong. Still, there was nothing to be gained from sticking around.

He started to walk toward the far end of the alleyway that ran between the narrow terraces. People had begun to congregate around the alley's mouth and on the street corners. No one had a clue what was going on. There was a chill to the night that had them permanently moving as they tried to keep themselves warm. Some of them had dressed hastily, pulling coats on over their pajamas. Others were in jeans and jackets and whatever else made up their normal daywear. In less than twenty feet he passed all body types, from the anorexic to the bloated belly hanging out over the waistband of straining pajama bottoms. Lurch tall to Cousin It short. There were more than their fair share of Uncle Festers out there as well. And of course, there was the one staggeringly beautiful Morticia with her died-black hair, piercings and Gothed-up eyeliner, who had no right to be living among this freak show of inner-city life. Frost smiled at her, risking the wrath of her very own Gomez. Charles Addams would have been proud of how his old cartoons captured this slice of dystopian, happy families so well even all these years later. They were all out there on the streets, and none of them looked very happy with their life right then.

"One last trick," Lethe said in his ear.

Frost had no idea what he meant until the first street-light exploded in a shower of glass. Each bulb detonated in quick succession, sounding like a series of shotgun blasts. Shards of glass fell like jagged rain. Frost walked down the center of the street, feeling like some dark avenger who had stepped out of a B-movie. Lethe laughed in his ear. Darkness chased down the street, passed him and raced on. In thirty seconds the stars in the sky were suddenly so much brighter because there wasn't a single streetlight burning in the entire city.

"I don't want to know how you just did that," Frost said.

"Liar," Lethe said. "But don't worry, I'll let you in on the secret. All I did was redirect some electricity. It's amazing what you can do with a computer. I overloaded the transformers and something had to give. The bulbs are built to blow. It's cheaper than replacing the entire wiring. Looked good though, didn't it? Give me that much, at least."

"It looked good," Ronan Frost agreed.

He saw two policemen getting out of a squad car. He walked across to them, pretending to be a curious resident. "Hey fellas," Frost called out, "what's going on?"

"Nothing to concern yourself about, sir," the shortest of the two uniforms said, slamming the car door. He locked it. Trust in their fellow man, it seemed, had yet to reach the local police force.

"It's a bit hard, sounds like all hell is breaking loose," Frost spread his arms wide, taking in the whole cacophony.

"Yeah, some sort of outage in the power grid shorted all the alarm circuits. I don't pretend to understand, mate. I just do what the gaffer tells me," the taller uniform said, smiling almost conspiratorially.

"Ahh," Frost said, as though that made perfect sense. "Well you have a good night, guys."

"You too."

"You know the deal, no rest for the wicked."

He went in search of the Monster.

Finding the warehouse wasn't difficult. Neither was getting close to it. Getting in was a different matter.

The Canning Docks were one of several along the river. Once upon a time, the river had been the heart of the city. While the river thrived, the city thrived. It was a symbiotic relationship. Every import and every export came in somewhere along the waterfront. Huge cranes still towered over the riverbanks, relics of a bygone age when the men in this country had worked with their hands and industry had been dominated by shipbuilding, coal mining and the old trades. But there wasn't enough trade coming up the river to keep all eleven of the river's docks working. The flour mill didn't grind flour anymore; the side of the building advertised itself as The Oxo Gallery. When Frost was growing up Oxo had made gravy granules. It seemed odd to him that now that it was being rebranded as an arbiter of beauty.

It had been decades since the last ship had been built on the river. Likewise it had been decades since the men of the city walked with their heads up, filled with pride and accomplishment. Now their football teams gave them their identity and sense of self-worth. With the collapse of the traditional industries, too many men, in their forties at the time, had never worked again and had finally died, stripped of dignity, beaten by life. Other industries had risen up, of course, ones where these men needed to be able to answer phones and use computers and do the kinds of things the girls in the office used to do. They weren't making things. They weren't creating. And because of that, they weren't happy.

To the left of the access road the iron gates of the steel mill had closed for the last time fifteen years ago. Now the huge shell of the building was in the process of being converted into luxury apartments for kids with too much money and not enough sense. The bonded warehouses that had been the heart of the import trade were boarded up, windows blinded. Inside, no doubt, the floorboards had been torn up and the lead and copper piping stripped and sold on the black market.

Frost slowed the Ducati to a gentle 15 mph, crawling through the labyrinth of alleys around the docklands. It was as though he had driven into a post-apocalyptic wasteland. None of the buildings had survived intact. Walls had crumbled. Bricks wept dust. The cranes might have been the towering exoskeletons of Martian war machines. The tarmac petered out into hard-packed dirt in places. Weeds had started to grow up through the cracks, nature reclaiming this part of the city for itself. He could hear the crash and retreat of the tidal river. He could see the silhouette of the Nicholls Tobacco Warehouse ahead of him. It must have been an impressive building back in the day. Now there was something tragic about the figure it cut in the night. For all its size, for all of its glorious red brick symmetry and its history, it was every bit as redundant as the men who had worked so hard building the ships, hauling the containers, beating out the sheet metal, and grinding the flour. It was a remnant of another time. So perhaps it was good that it was going to find another life, Frost thought, pulling up alongside the gates.

An ostentatious padlock secured the chains that secured the gate. He found it wryly amusing. The chain links of the fence could be bent apart with bare hands and a bit of determination, but the padlock would surrender to no man.

For a building that was supposedly abandoned, there were an awful lot of tire tracks leading to and from the gates. Frost drove on. He had a bad feeling about the place and wasn't about to go walking in through the front door.

He found a dark, secluded spot out of sight of the warehouse's windows and dropped the kickstand. He took off his helmet and hung it on the handlebars. He called Lethe.

"So what can you tell me about this place?"

"Not much, to be honest. Like I said, it's scheduled for redevelopment. The officer of record for the development is one Miles Devere. Yep, the same Miles Devere who was the last number to call James' wife's cell phone. So we've got a nice little coincidence there."

"No such thing as coincidence, my little ray of sunshine. What we've got is a link. We may not have both sides of the puzzle, but we've got the bit in the middle. Tell me more."

"Devere Holdings has its fingers in a dozen pies all across the city. The man's something of a property magnet. He's bought up a handful of the old warehouses and mill buildings along the docks, and not just Canning Dock. He's got plans in with the planning department for the development of an entire Docklands Village. We're talking multi-million investment in urban regeneration and land renewal here. He's claiming huge subsidies from the authorities too. He bought the Nicholls building for a one pound consideration and the promise that he would invest in local labor to rebuild it. That one pound has already brought him in over thirty-three million in government aid, and he's not had to lift a finger."

"Got to love big business," Frost said. "So what, if anything, does Miles Devere have to do with this?"

"Maybe nothing. Like I said, it could just be a coincidence. I'm still looking for the link between Tristan James and Devere. There has to be one. But as of now, I've got nothing."

"Maybe Devere hired him to excavate something?" Frost mused, thinking aloud. What other use would a property developer have for an archeologist?

"Looking for a pirate ship run aground on the muddy riverbank?" Lethe said, chuckling.

"Maybe not." In the distance, Frost heard a dog bark. A moment later he saw the dark shape of one man and his dog walking through the debris-strewn yard of the Nicholls building. The man's flashlight roved across the darkness erratically. He hadn't seen the Monster approaching, but the dog had picked up Frost's scent. It knew he wasn't supposed to be there.

Frost crept away from the bike, crouching low to make his silhouette as small as possible. The dog's bark grew more aggressive the closer it came toward the chain-link fence. He had two choices, get on the bike and get out of there, or shut the dog up. Frost braced himself against a concrete pillar. He watched the beam of light skip across the rough ground. The dog, a sharp-snouted Doberman, strained on its leash, pawing at the ground. Frost eased his way around the pillar, making sure there was as much concrete as possible between him and the devil dog.

The guard said something into his radio. Frost couldn't hear what. He didn't need to. The man knew someone was out there. He'd be assuming it was kids playing in the grounds of the disused buildings. Frost closed his eyes and listened. He kept his breathing regular: deep and slow. Gravel and broken stones scuffed, too close for comfort. He didn't dare move.

What did a disused warehouse need with this kind of security? He hadn't seen any sign of building materials having been moved onto the site, so there was nothing worth stealing. The dog barked again, deep in its throat. It was the aggressive sound of a hunter that knew its quarry was near. The flashlight beam played across the ground less than five feet from his hiding place.

Frost pressed back harder against the concrete pillar as if it might somehow make him smaller.

The pitch of the growl shifted.

And then the night exploded in a flurry of noise. The guard slipped the dog's leash and the Doberman sprang forward, claws scuffing up the hard scrabble in a desperate attempt to gain purchase as it launched itself toward his hiding place. Frost didn't move so much as a muscle. With the chain-link fence between them the dog couldn't get at him. There were several ways this could play out: eventually either the handler would re-attach the leash and move on with his rounds, in which case he would see Frost's Monster and realize he wasn't dealing with kids—which would mean Frost would be forced to take care of both man and beast before things got out of hand; Frost could make a dash for the Ducati and get the hell out of there, but then, if they were up to something in the old warehouse, any element of surprise he might have had would be gone for good; he could try to slip away and come at the place from the other side; or he could just slip out from behind the pillar and pull the trigger twice. Frost was a lot of things, but he wasn't a cold-blooded killer. There was nothing to suggest the night watchman was anything more than that, a retired policeman paid minimum wage to walk around the deserted warehouse and stop vandals from getting inside. In that case two bullets was not just overkill, it was murder.

He took a deep breath and began to move away from the pillar when Lethe's voice crackled in his ear. "Well now, isn't that just fascinating?" Frost couldn't risk making a sound, he just had to hope Jude Lethe would elaborate. He settled back against the concrete, waiting for Lethe to speak again. "In the last three years Miles Devere's various concerns have opened offices in Berlin, Rome, Prague, Amsterdam, Lisbon, Madrid, Paris, Vienna . . . need me to go on and list all thirteen? Devere's started operations in every city where our archeologists burned themselves alive. They're all shell companies, and the paper chase is a mile long and whisper thin. Someone doesn't want these links found.

"And the best part? My very favorite discovery so far today: in 2001 Miles Devere volunteered as a relief worker in Israel. He was part of a United Nations program to improve the camps. He was in Gaza for almost a year before moving across to Jenin. That means he was in Jenin when Orla was there, but we'll come back to that later. Here's the interesting stuff: he left Israel in July 2004, having worked on a reconstruction project that ran in tandem with an archeological dig in Megiddo overseen by— you know who I am going to say, but I'm going to say it anyway, I'm just pausing for dramatic effect—Akim Caspi. And there, my oh so quiet friend, is our smoking gun. Aren't you going to say something?"

Frost didn't say a word. He could hear the dog prowling along the line of the fence.

"Suit yourself. I'll just have to do the talking for both of us. Now, Megiddo is an interesting spot all of its own. According to the Book of Revelation, Megiddo is where it all goes down at the end. We're talking big ass battle, the amassing of forces, the children of light fighting the minions of the Antichrist. Armageddon. The word literally means the hill or mountain of Megiddo. You can't tell me this isn't just a little bit cool."

Frost made a decision then. He was going to count to ten in his head, slowly, and then he was going to step out from behind the pillar and shoot the damned dog. He'd take his chances with the guard.

One. He breathed deeply, tasting the river in his throat.

Two.

Three. The dog clawed at the chain-link fence, pushing back against it and barking.

Four. He drew the slide back then eased it forward, chambering the bullet. He let out the breath he had been holding.

Frost didn't make it as far as five.

The night watchman's voice carried to him easily. "You're getting old, stupid bloody dog. There's nothing out here but the ghosts of dead ship-wrights. Come here." Frost risked the briefest of glances around the edge of the pillar. The man was on his knees and had the Doberman by the scruff of the neck. He appeared to be playing with the animal. It always surprised him the way men bonded with the animals they used, ascribing all of these human qualities like understanding and aging minds to dumb animals. He watched the pair for a few more seconds, then the man clipped the leash back in place and dragged the huge dog toward the front gates.

Frost released the Browning's slide and holstered the gun at the small of his back.

He waited for them to disappear from sight then spoke in a hushed whisper, "Good job, Jude."

"Thought it'd make your day, boss," Lethe said in his ear.

"I'm always happier chasing the money than I am worrying about some holy bloody relic. Fanatics give me the creeps, but money I understand. Greed I understand. These things make sense to me. So we can link Devere to every city that's been threatened, and back to Caspi. I think we've found our man in the middle, so someone needs to pay our Mister Devere a visit."

"One step ahead of you, boss. Devere chartered a private jet to Winningen airport, Koblenz, yesterday. He cleared customs eighteen hours ago."

"Germany," Frost mused, thinking about it for a minute. "Konstantin's still in Berlin, right? Get him to take a detour. See if he can't lean on Devere. Find out what he knows."

"I'm on it. What are you going to do?"

"I'm going to find out what the hell's going on on the other side of this fence. If I don't check in within the hour, send in reinforcements."

"Erm, boss, you do know we don't have any reinforcements, right?" Lethe said.

"I know that, kiddo. It's an expression, that's all. It basically means if you don't hear from me, start to worry."

"Well that I can do," Jude Lethe said with a nervous little laugh.

Frost killed the connection. He needed to concentrate, and Lethe babbling in his ear wasn't exactly conducive to focus. He walked over to the chain-link fence. A coil of barbed wire topped it. These guys were pretty serious about keeping people out, which made Frost all the more eager to find a way inside.

He took off his leather bike jacket and threw it up, still holding onto the cuff of one sleeve, so that it fell over the wire. He took off his silver-gray suit jacket and lay it on the ground. Frost was no fool; there was nothing to identify him in either set of pockets. If he needed to run, the most they'd learn about their intruder was that he had impeccable taste and wasn't afraid to spend money to look good.

Stepping back, he rocked on his heels, then took a short run up of four steps and launched himself at the fence. He grasped the top, the leather jacket saving his hands from being shredded by the teeth of the barbed wire, and boosted himself up over the fence. It wobbled violently beneath him as his weight shifted. He dropped down on the other side and crouched, listening. Mercifully, the dog didn't bark.

Frost pushed himself up from the ground and started to run, hard, and kept low. He kept his eyes straight ahead, focusing on the warehouse. His stride ate up the ground. His feet scuffed across the hardstand. There was nothing he could do about the noise. Inside fifty feet he was breathing hard. The windows all along the ground floor were either boarded up or barred. He couldn't see any doors. He forced himself to run faster, barely slowing before he hit the wall. He turned so that his back was pressed up against it and began to edge around the building, looking for a way in.

The moon was a silver slice above the rooftops of the city on the far side of the river. There wasn't a cloud in sight. Somewhere in the distance a train horn sounded its lonesome mating call. Frost jogged around the side of the warehouse. The skeletal limbs of scrub bushes swayed gently in the breeze. The first entrance he found was large enough for two trucks to drive in side-by-side. It was covered by roll-down doors. Like the main gate, it was secured by a thick padlock. He rattled the doors but the padlock didn't budge, so he carried on around the side, looking for a more conventional door.

As he neared the far corner a flicker of movement caught his eye.

Frost dropped into a tight crouch, instinctively reaching around for the Browning.

It wasn't that kind of movement, he realized a moment later. Something had flickered in his peripheral vision. He studied the boarded-up window just above him and found an inch-wide crack in the wooden planks. The faintest of lights danced erratically through the small crack. It took him another moment to realize that the reason the light was so erratic was because of the draft. There was no glass in the window. The candle burning on the other side of the boards was down to little more than a stub. In a couple of minutes it would be dead and the room dark. Frost pressed his eye up against the crack.

There were a dozen mattresses in the small room. Frightened people lay huddled up on each one. Most of them were sleeping. He had found the leverage. Whoever was behind the suicide burnings had taken these women and children as insurance to make sure the "suicides" went off according to plan. Frost felt sick to his stomach. This kind of trade in human life was vile, but he was beginning to understand the kind of people they were up against, or more importantly, the limits of the people they were up against.

On the far side of the room he saw a woman holding two young children close to her chest. He couldn't tell if she was asleep, but he guessed not. Her body was tense; he could see it in the muscles of her arms as they draped protectively over the kids. Another young girl, this one no more than 9 or 10, was looking up at him. He had no idea if she could see him in the dim light. He whispered, "It's all right, I'm here to help you." His voice rippled through the sleepers, causing them to stir. A third girl, this one closer to 16, sat up on her mattress. She rubbed at her eyes and seemed to have trouble focusing.

"Who's there?" she called out. Her voice spiraled on the last syllable, becoming dangerously loud. The young girl pointed toward the window. She had seen him.

"Shhh," Frost cautioned with his finger to his lips, worried someone would hear her. It was a stupid gesture given that she could only see part of his cheek and his right eye. Others started to look toward the boarded-up window. "I'm going to get you out of here."

It was as though he'd said the magic word. The older woman stood, coming toward the window with her two children clinging to her legs. "Oh, thank God. Are you with the police?"

"No," he said, softly. "And not the Army, either," he cut her off before she could ask too many questions. "But I am here to help you. I need you to do something for me. I need you to tell me how many people are in there with you. How many hostages and how many people are holding you. Can you do that?"

The woman nodded hesitantly. "I don't know if there are any others—they don't let us out of this room—but there are sixteen of us in here, four adults, three teenagers. The rest are under ten."

"All girls?"

The woman swallowed and nodded. "There were boys, but they took them. We heard the gunshots. I think . . . I think . . . they executed my son." She broke down then and started to cry. He gave her a few seconds to gather herself, but he couldn't wait for her to cry herself out.

"I need you to hold it together, just a little while longer. What's your name?"

"Annie."

"All right, Annie, my name's Ronan. Right now I am your new best friend, and as your new best friend I'm going to make you a promise. I am going to get all of you out of there. And I am going to make you a second promise now, just between the two of us, I am going to make them suffer for what they did to your boy. Okay?"

She nodded.

He looked at her through the narrow crack in the wooden boards. "Do you trust me, Annie?"

There was another short hesitation, then she nodded again.

"Good. I trust you as well. Now, try to remember if you

can, how many guards have you seen?"

She thought about it for a moment, biting on her lower lip. "Six. Eight. I am not sure." She wrapped her arms around herself. She was shivering. Frost wished he could reach through the window and hold her. There was nothing more reassuring than human contact, especially in a situation like this. Noah was good at the human stuff, he wasn't. He had to make do with his voice.

"That's great, Annie. Good girl. Now I want you to get everyone ready so when I come through that door you'll all be ready to move. Can you do that for me?"

She nodded again.

"Are you going to kill them?" she asked.

This time it was Frost's turn to nod.

"Good," Annie said, emphatically. She looked down. When she looked up again he saw the shock in her eyes. Her need to be strong for her two girls was swimming up against a need to just collapse and mourn her son. She had already decided they were all dead and had been curled up in the corner with her girls, waiting for their killers to open the cell door again and take another one of her children out into the darkness. And then he had arrived, and suddenly she dared to hope. But now she was starting to come apart because of it. When there was nothing, it was easier for her to be strong. Those last hours, however many or few they might have been, were all about staying strong for her girls. Now there was hope and hope meant a life beyond their cell. If she started to believe they might escape, that they might have a life left together, losing it would hurt all the more. She had to trust her life to this stranger on the other side of the wall, and it was all she could do not to crumble. Frost had seen it before. He just prayed she could hold it together long enough for him to get them out.

As far as what happened next, six or eight didn't matter. Even with the element of surprise the odds were stacked against him. As Orla was wont to say, that only made it more interesting. He double-checked the Browning for a chambered round.

"You're going to be all right," he promised her. He needed her to believe that. He needed hope to galvanize her, not paralyze her. "In a few minutes it will all be over." He pushed away from the window before she could answer him, glanced over his shoulder to be sure the night watchman hadn't doubled back, and then set off around the corner.

There was another wide, green steel overhead door and beyond that a small door. He crept up to it. He saw a small weather-worn fire exit sign and beneath it, the warning that the door was alarmed. He doubted the alarm was still functional, but given the fact they had a night watchman and a Doberman prowling the grounds, he wasn't about to take any chances.

He looked around for another way in.

Then he looked up.

An old rusty fire escape stair dangled just out of reach.

He smiled. People were a lot laxer about security on the third, fourth and fifth stories than they were on the ground and first floor. He backed up a couple of steps, then took a running jump. Reaching up, Frost snagged the last rung of the ladder and hauled himself up hand over hand until he got his first foot up on the fire escape. The rusty metal made a god-awful racket as it groaned under his weight. He didn't have time to worry about it.

He ran up the first set of stairs then along the wire-mesh platform to the second set of steps. He didn't try the first, second or even third fire door. He went straight for the fifth-floor, not looking down as he ran across the wire platform. The door was locked, but the wood around the lock was so rotten it didn't take a lot of persuading to open. He bumped his shoulder up against the door, once, twice, straining the woodworm-riddled frame, and on the third bump the frame splintered and the door swung open. It wasn't quiet. All he could do was pray that it was quiet enough.

Frost stepped inside. The vaulted ceiling of the old warehouse was cathedral-like, panes of frosted glass with iron girders holding the whole thing together. The moonlight streamed in through the glass, casting shadows that stretched to every corner of the wide-open warehouse floor. The crane gib and winches were all still in place, though the mechanisms had almost certainly seized up with two decades of disuse. He wasn't about to risk swinging down on the dangling chain like some sort of comic book hero.

He took a moment to scout out his immediate surroundings. He was on a gantry that ran all around the top floor of the warehouse. There were maybe half a dozen doors on each side of the building which, he surmised, led to the old offices. All of the windows along the gantry were dark. Down in the center of the concrete floor five stories beneath him, he could see two men sitting on packing crates. They appeared to be sharing a smoke.

The Browning was accurate enough over this kind of distance that they were a comfortable shot, but he had no intention of taking it. The next few minutes were all about silence. He ghosted along the gantry, looking for the stairs down to the next level. He found the stairwell in the far corner, meaning he had to cover the entire length of the warehouse floor. He kept looking down over the side. Neither man looked up.

Frost took the stairs, keeping his shoulder pressed against the wall as he half-ran down the ninety-degree turns of the stairwell. He didn't go all the way to the bottom. He wanted to know as much about what he was up against as possible, so he crept out onto the second-floor gantry. Like the one much higher up, the gantry ran around the entire circumference of the warehouse. He could see down through the floor all the way to the ground. Conversely, that meant anyone who happened to look up would be able to see him.

As trades went, it was one he was happy to make. The pair he'd watched from the fifth floor told him all he needed to know about these guys and their operation. They'd been watching their hostages for over a week now without incident. They were complacent.

He moved out along the metal gantry. Two more men came out to join the others at the packing crates. They were big guys. One had a Heckler & Koch MP5 slung casually over his shoulder. Frost watched the way the man moved. There was an easy confidence about his posture as he sank down beside the others. He took a packet of cigarettes from his shirt pocket and lit up. Frost waited and watched. He tried to think through the numbers. If Annie had seen eight guards, the odds were they were running two shifts, four and four. He didn't recognize any of them as the night watchman, which meant there was at least one more out there whose whereabouts was unaccounted for.

There was no way he could take them all at once. He was going to have to pick them off one at a time like the ten green bottles accidently falling. *Not so accidentally*, he amended silently. These would have bullet holes in the back of their heads. That made falling the only natural thing to do.

The MP5 guy stubbed out his half-smoked cigarette under his boot.

It would be easy to move along the gantry and squeeze off two quick shots, taking out a couple of the guards, then make his way down to the ground. They wouldn't know what had hit them, and in the panic that followed he'd have time to clear up the loose ends. What he didn't know was when they changed watches, when the relief would arrive, how many of them there actually were in the old warehouse, and if the sound of the gunshots would carry to the watchman outside. These were variables he couldn't control. Adding more guns to the mix meant more room for things to go wrong. The situation became harder to control.

All he needed was for one of the kidnappers to go through to the room they were using as a cell and start shooting.

His instinct was to dictate the scenario.

That meant striking hard, fast and, if possible, remaining unseen.

He crept along the gantry, conscious that the slightest movement could catch a kidnapper's eye at any time. He kept as close to the wall as possible. It took him a full minute to get into position. Frost crouched down. He had a perfect view of the killing ground beneath him. The Browning felt heavy in his hand, hungry. He'd carried the gun for what felt like all of his adult life. He had a parasitical relationship with the thing. It had kept him alive more than once, but sometimes it felt as though it thirsted for blood. This was one of those times. He breathed deeply, forcing the rise and fall of his lungs to stay steady.

Frost raised the Browning, drawing a bead on the man with the MP5. The kidnapper turned away from him, as though challenging him to put the bullet in the back of his head. Frost didn't care about cowardice or seeing the whites of his victim's eyes. That was Hollywood bullshit. A dead goon was a dead goon. It didn't matter how he got there. He wouldn't score points in goon heaven for taking the bullet face first. Honor was for the Samurai. It had no place in saving the lives of these women and children.

He kept the gun steady, breathing in, breathing out. He wanted to time the shots with the exhale for accuracy.

Beneath him, the kidnapper threw up his arms and spun on his heel. The MP5 banged off his hip. He looked up, and seemed for a heartbeat to be looking straight at Frost. Frost squeezed down on the trigger, slowly increasing the pressure until it was a hair from firing.

And stopped himself.

At the last moment the gunman looked away, barking something at his compatriots. Frost expected an explosion of gunfire. It never came. Their voices carried, loud in the huge space of the empty warehouse. It took Frost a few seconds to realize what had them so agitated—they were waiting for instructions. They were arguing about whether they should go in there and kill the hostages. Their contact hadn't called in and they were getting fractious. The joker with the MP5 seemed to be the one with the itchiest trigger finger.

Frost put him out of his misery.

The back of the man's head exploded in a spray of blood and brains.

Frost squeezed off a second shot, taking one of the men sitting on the crates high in the forehead. His body jerked back, a crack opening above his right eyebrow as his eyes widened in shock. It was a comical expression caught between surprise and fear, not the kind of look you'd want to carry into the afterlife. The dead man slumped sideways, falling from his perch on the crate. His leg kicked out as he fell and twitched uncontrollably for a full thirty seconds before the last vestiges of life convulsed out of his body.

Frost didn't wait for that to happen.

While the other two reacted, diving for cover from this unseen threat, he made a run for the stairwell. His boots clattered loudly off the metal gantry, his footsteps echoing through the confines of the warehouse. The report of a gunshot cracked. He neither knew nor cared how close the shot came. The bullet didn't hit him. That was all that mattered. Another shot sounded. Frost threw himself forward, hitting the gantry hard and rolling on his right shoulder. This time he saw the puff of concrete dust as the bullet buried itself into the wall six inches from his head. He came up running.

The staccato cackle of machine-gun fire tore through the warehouse. Bullet wounds strafed the wall, ripping through the brickwork. Frost half-stumbled half-ran across the last few yards of the gantry to the stairwell. He felt the wind from the rush of bullets against his face and the sharp sting as one nicked his cheek.

He ignored the sudden flare of pain and dropped to his knees.

A second burst of gunfire ricocheted off the metal gantry, spitting sparks. Frost pulled away from them, slamming into the wall. He pushed away from it, throwing himself through the mouth of the stairwell. He was breathing hard. He was shaking as the adrenalin pounded through his system. Shouts chased where the bullets couldn't follow. He realized the stupidity of what he'd just done as he charged around the first ninety-degree turn of the descent only to hear shouts from down below chasing up the stairs to meet him. He couldn't exactly run back up the stairs, and there was only one place the stairs were going to emerge. He needed to mix things up.

They would be expecting him to come down shooting. In their place he would have placed shooters either side of the stairwell, covering left and right, with a good view all the way up to the first turn. There was no way he'd get down the last ten steps without being cut down in a hail of machine-gun fire, so there was no way he was going to go down those last ten steps.

As he reached the first-floor landing he stopped running. He leaned out, looking down through the mesh grill of the lowest gantry, then up at the glass ceiling. Each of the huge plate glass panels was more than twenty feet across by twice that long and slotted together with iron girders. He squeezed off three shots inside a second, each aimed at the weak point in the center of each sheet of glass. For a split second he didn't think it was going to work, then the strain pulled the glass apart. The glass around each bullet hole spiderwebbed and splintered, each crack running deep. Then the first shard fell, and suddenly the hole it left undermined the fragile balance of the entire twenty-by-thirty sheet. And following a crack like brittle thunder a lethal shower of glass rained down. Amplified by the confines of the warehouse walls, the noise was incredible.

Frost didn't wait to see what happened. Blowing out the glass would buy him a few seconds at best while the kidnappers took cover and shielded their faces. He charged down the final flight of stairs. One of the kidnappers lay sprawled out at the mouth of the stairwell, jagged splinters of glass buried in his chest and neck. A viscous black pool of blood spread on the concrete like some kind of mocking halo around his head. He appeared to be very dead. Frost didn't take any chances. He put a slug in the middle of the man's face and walked out onto the central floor of the warehouse, glass crunching under his feet.

He couldn't see the final gunman.

He felt out the cut in his cheek. It wasn't deep, but it was bleeding freely. He'd been lucky.

He scanned the warehouse quickly, looking for any sign of movement, any out of place shadow. Something that would give the last man away. A section of the warehouse floor was given over to forty- and smaller twenty-foot metal shipping containers. They offered plenty of places to hide. It wasn't an exact science, but nothing in the spread of glass across the concrete floor suggested anyone had run across it so he turned his back on the containers. If he could take the last guy alive, great. If he couldn't, he wouldn't shed any tears. Frost licked his lips. He could taste his own blood on his tongue.

He heard a woman's scream and realized the last gunman had gone for the hostages. He didn't stop, he didn't think, he ran. He wasn't about to lose anyone—not now, not when he was this close.

The gunman stood in the doorway. "You!" he yelled, waving the muzzle of his machine gun around threateningly. "Here!"

Over his shoulder Frost could see the terrified face of the woman he had spoken to through the window. She stumbled toward the man, eyes wide with fear.

The man grabbed her and pulled her close, then started to turn. He was trying to use Annie as a human shield.

"Let her go," Frost said, keeping his voice calm and reasonable.

The kidnapper shook his head wildly. His eyes bulged, filled to bursting with the blood pumping too fast through his body, driven by his racing heart. His fear was palpable. He started to bring the snub-nose of the MP5 up toward the side of the woman's head. Frost took a step toward him, and another, even as the man shook his head. He didn't look like evil incarnate. He looked like an everyday Joe. Unremarkable. Unmemorable.

"It doesn't have to end like this," Frost said.

Less than ten feet separated them. He could smell the man's sweat. It was rancid, like he hadn't washed in days. Maybe he hadn't. Maybe there were no replacement guards. Maybe he and his dead friends had been the only ones involved after all. He stank every bit as badly as the hostages he had kept penned up in that tiny room for a week.

"Back! Stay back!" His voice broke on the last syllable.

Frost ignored him, taking another step toward him. Nine feet.

"I'm serious! Get back!"

Frost took another step. He made no pretense of offering peace.

"I'll kill her! I'll kill them all!"

"Then I'll kill you," Frost said, quite matter-of-factly.

Seven steps.

"Truth is, it doesn't matter what you do, I'm going to kill you. You know that, don't you?"

Six steps.

"I'm going to kill you for what you did to her son," he nodded toward Annie. "I'm going to kill you for what you did to their fathers and their husbands. I'm going to kill you because you deserve to die. Make it easy for me, go on,"

Frost urged. "Make a move. Pull the trigger."

Frost raised the Browning. The muzzle rested less than five feet from the center of the man's face. The madness of fanaticism blazed in his eyes.

"I'm not going to miss from here. And no matter how quick you are with that thing"—Frost's eyes drifted toward the MP5—"I promise you, I am faster with this."

He expected the man to beg for his life.

He was disappointed when he didn't. The man stared at him belligerently.

"Tell me who's giving the orders here," Frost said.

"Go to hell!" the man snapped. He shook his head. He was wired. Every muscle trembled beneath his grimy skin.

"You're not the man here," Frost said. There were three steps between them now. He could taste the man's halitosis and see every pore opening as the sweat came. "You're the muscle. You're a goon. You didn't plan this. Who do you answer to? Who's your boss?"

"Do you think I will tell you?" the man sneered. "Are you really so stupid?" He shook his head.

Without breaking eye contact Ronan Frost lashed out with his left hand, grabbing a fistful of the man's greasy hair and pulling down hard. The move dragged him off balance. Frost pressed the gun into the center of his forehead. "Last chance. Talk."

"I will *never* betray my people."

"That's all I wanted to know," Frost said, pulling the trigger.

The man's head jerked back and his body went limp. Frost's grip on his hair stopped him from falling. A ring of powder burn circled the entry wound. There was surprisingly little blood and almost no damage. The back of his head was a different matter. The exit wound was a mess of bone fragment, brain tissue and blood. Frost pushed the dead man aside and holstered the Browning.

Behind Annie, the women and children were looking at

him as though he were some kind of avenging angel—they needed him, they knew that, but he scared them. He smiled at one of the older girls. She sobbed, a great heaving breath that stuck in her throat, and then as the tide of relief swarmed over her, started to cry. Her entire body shuddered. One of the women walked over to her and just held her. The sense of relief in the room was palpable.

"Okay, folks, time to go home," he said, holding out his hand. Annie took it. She looked at him with the most intense mix of grief, thankfulness and horror. Her two girls clung to her legs. Frost reached down and scooped one up and cradled her in his left arm. She clung with both arms around his neck. "What's your name, sweetie?" he asked the girl.

She leaned in, pressing her lips up close to his ear and whispered, "Vicky."

"Lovely to meet you, Vicky. In a few minutes I am going to tell you to close your eyes. You'll do that for me won't you?" The girl nodded. Frost smiled down at her. "You just screw your eyes up real tight and everything'll be fine. I promise you."

He drew the Browning and held it in his free hand. He wasn't taking any chances.

He ushered the women and children out of their makeshift cell one by one. More than half of them had lost their shoes. "There's a lot of broken glass out here; you might want to carry your kids," he told them. They did what he said without a word. He led them through the ruined warehouse toward the huge green overhead door at the far side of the floor. He heard the devil dog barking before he saw it. "Close your eyes, sweetie," Frost whispered in Vicky's ear. He felt her scrunch up against his shoulder, burying her head in his collar. A moment later the Doberman came barreling around the shipping crates, claws scrabbling on the concrete as it ran. Its incredible gait devoured the distance between them in three seconds flat. Frost waited until the last moment, as it reared up to launch itself at his chest, jaws snapping, teeth ready to tear out his throat, and pulled the trigger three times. The bullets tore into the dog's hide in a tight cluster, ripping through the muscle and bone to rupture the animal's racing heart. The moment of its charge wasn't stopped by death. Frost twisted sideways, trying to get out of the animal's way. All he managed to achieve was presenting it with a smaller target.

The dead dog slammed into Frost hard enough to stagger him back three steps, and off balance, before he fell. The girl in his arms screamed. He realized she'd opened her eyes to see the wild glass-eyed stare of the dead Doberman inches away from her face. Frost covered her eyes with his hand and soothed, "It's all right, it's all right. It can't hurt you now."

He struggled to rise.

The fact that the dog had hit them here, inside the old warehouse, meant the night watchman couldn't be far behind.

He had dropped his gun in the fall. Annie stood beside him holding it.

He saw movement in the periphery of his vision: the night watchman. The last man between them and their freedom.

"Give me the gun," he said holding out his hand.

Annie didn't seem to hear him. She only had eyes for the night watchman.

"You don't want to do it," Frost said, sensing what she was thinking. It wasn't difficult. Here was a chance to strike back at one of the men who had ruined her life. Who wouldn't want to kill him given the chance? The gun empowered her. Her arm trembled. Frost knew what was happening. It had happened to him the first time he had contemplated killing. Suddenly the gun weighed so much more than the sum of its parts, so much more than the metal and the polymer. It weighed a life. She wasn't just pulling the trigger, she was pulling against the weight of all those unlived days, all of those unexperienced joys and sadnesses. "Let me," Frost said, calmly. "This is what I do. You don't want to live with his death inside your head."

"I do," Annie said. "I need to."

She pulled the trigger and kept on pulling it until the man went down. The first two went wide, hitting the metal door and raising a shriek of echoes with their impact. The third hit him in the shoulder. The forth in the leg. Neither would kill him. The night watchman lay on the floor, screaming and begging.

Frost held out his hand for the gun.

This time Annie gave it to him.

He checked the chamber. There was a single round left.

It was all that he needed. He walked across the floor, his footsteps echoing, hollow in the funereal expanse of the huge old building. Frost stood over the bleeding man. "One chance," he said. "Who do you work for?"

The man lay on his back, squirming in his own blood. Frost was wrong. He clutched at his thigh where Annie's bullet had opened a major artery. That one would kill him.

"You're already dead," Frost said. "If I don't kill you one of the Goon Squad will. And the only way I am *not* going to kill is if you give me a name. Now, who do you work for?"

The man gritted his teeth.

Frost raised his gun, aiming it squarely between the man's rapidly glazing eyes.

Frost felt sure he was going to hold out on him and die stubborn and determinedly silent. He had to know he was dying. His eyes were glassy as he looked up at Frost. "Mabus," he said.

Frost put the bullet between his eyes.

He had a name. Mabus.

Frost holstered the Browning and walked across to the shutter. On the wall beside it was a large red button. He hit it. Gears groaned to life and the door began to rise slowly, the metal grinding as it was forced to turn.

Beams of light streamed into the warehouse beneath the metal shutter, throwing shadows across the concrete. The chill of the coming dawn raced in. Frost carried the girl out into the open air. The sun rose red over the city on the other side of the river. The lights were headlights. Six cars were pulled up outside the chain-link fence. He could hear voices shouting, but he couldn't make out what they were shouting. He could barely make out the silhouettes of the men behind the headlights. One of them walked forward so that that he was back-lit by the cars as he reached the heavily padlocked gate.

Frost ushered the women forward.

They were hesitant at first, lost now that they were outside. The women seemed particularly wary, moving cautiously toward the light, like someone might suddenly snatch it away from them and force them back into that hellhole. When they realized the headlights were police cars they started to run toward the fence. Frost was less happy to see the boys in blue.

He thought about setting the girl down and trying to fade back into the shadows. There was a chance he'd find his coat and jacket and, in turn, the Ducati, but all he needed to do was look at the ground beneath his feet and the pool of light there to know that trying to make a break for it now was a dumb idea. Instead he walked slowly toward the gate, resigned to his fate.

By the time he reached it they'd cut through the padlock and were beginning to take care of the first women and children to reach them.

"I can take her, sir," a WPC said, holding out her hands for the girl. She had a pretty smile but a harsh face. Frost handed Vicky over, ruffling her hair as she squirmed out of his grasp. Another officer walked over, and Frost thought he heard the gods laughing at him from on high. It was the short surly one of the pair he had talked to after getting out of the James house on Halsey Road.

The man made straight for him, and as Frost started to turn away said, "Well, well, well, fancy seeing you here," and shook his head slowly, as though to say pigs really had started to fly as far as he was concerned. "It's quite some coincidence, don't you think? I feel like I am seeing more of you than I do my own mother. First you're outside a murder house while all hell's breaking loose, which, let's face it, is worthy of a raised eyebrow all by itself. And now here you are rescuing all these women and children like some sort of superhero. You know, all that's missing is the burning building to make the whole thing complete. So why don't you start by telling me who the hell you are, Mister Superhero?"

Frost looked at the detective. It took him all of two seconds to have the measure of the man. He had Little Man syndrome. He was bitter, angry, and looking for a scalp. "Frost," he said. He didn't bother lying. "Ronan Frost."

"Should I have heard of you?"

"I don't see why you would have."

"Well then, Mister Frost, let's go for two for two. Who are you? I mean, you're not one of us—you're not police—that much is bloody obvious. So who are you? Government? Intelligence? Five? Special Forces? Counterterrorism? Justice League? Who *are* you?"

"I'm just a Good Samaritan," Frost said.

"Bullshit."

Frost said nothing.

"I'm not an idiot, Mister Frost."

Again Frost said nothing.

"Okay, let's try again. How did you find out about this place? How did you know what was happening here when no one else had the slightest clue?" He shook his head. "We're still not sure, and here you are saving the day."

"I suggest you stop wasting time asking questions I am not going to answer," Frost said, "and start thinking about what happens in the next hour or so." He looked toward the rising sun. "There are five bodies in there. Six if you count the dog. I know because I killed them. And no, you aren't going to arrest me for it, before you starting getting any ideas. You said it yourself, I'm a bloody hero. Now, what is it, almost five? Anytime soon their relief are going to turn up, expecting to take over babysitting duties. I suggest you get someone in there to clean up, fix the damned gate you just broke, and think about bringing in the rest of this mob. So we can either stand here measuring our dicks, or we can shut these people down. Me, I know how well I'm hung. How about you?"

That shut the little man up.

Frost turned his back on him and hit the dial-home on his earpiece.

"Don't you walk away from me!" the policeman shouted at his back as he walked away.

Frost ignored him.

"I said don't you dare walk away from me!"

Frost continued to walk away. He'd told the man all he was going to tell him.

When Lethe picked up all Frost said was, "The idea is to call in the cavalry *if* I am in trouble. I'll be here all bloody night trying to explain this away."

"And here I am, thinking you were going to say thank you," Lethe said. "So? What happened? Tell me, tell me. Come on. The only excitement I get is living vicariously through you lot. I want all the gory details."

"We got a name: Mabus. There's not much else to say. A normal day at the office."

"Ah, man, you take all the fun out of life, Frosty, you do know that, don't you?"

17

THIRTEEN SHRIEKS

Orla Nyrén followed Uzzi through the warren of offices that made up the IDF Intelligence Building. Inside the world of spy versus spy, the Intelligence Directorate was better known as *Aman*. More than seven thousand people plied their trade in this world of Israeli secrets. Uzzi was *Modash*, IDF Field Intelligence. Field was something of a euphemism for special measures, which in turn meant collection and elimination. Uzzi Sokol dealt with national security issues inside the Israeli borders. Security, planning, dissemination of intelligence and overseeing foreign emissaries. He was much more than a babysitter.

Despite his warning, the drive over had been uneventful.

She had holstered her gun as they entered the building. Her heels clicked sharply on the linoleum-tiled floor.

He gestured with a finger over his shoulder for her to keep up. The man really grated on her nerves, but he knew things she didn't, and she was prepared to put up with his macho bullshit until he told her what she needed to know. He knocked sharply on the glass pane in the center of a door, once, and opened it without waiting for whoever was inside to answer.

"She's here, sir," Sokol said. He stepped back to allow Orla to enter the office first. It was the first trace of chivalry the man had shown since she had gotten off the plane.

The man squeezed in behind the desk barely even looked like a man anymore. The top button of his shirt wouldn't button up because there just wasn't enough material in the shirt for it to reach all the way around his enormous neck. He did his best to hide it with a navy blue necktie that looked like a noose. The huge black circles beneath his eyes only added to the illusion. His complexion was sallow, his hair salt-and-peppered at the temples.

The toad looked deathless. He could have been anything from fifty to one hundred and fifty years old. The only real clue to his age was the memorial plaque to his son, killed in the Yom Kippur War. Shimon would have been fifty five now, which meant he had to be in his early seventies at least. He licked his lips. The way his tongue slipped out put Orla in mind of a toad. He reached out a hand for her to shake.

His grip was clammy but surprisingly firm for a man of his age. He was the parody of the fat incompetent general right up until the moment he opened his mouth. His voice was like honey. She could imagine thousands of women spending a lot of money to listen to any sex line the man voiced.

"So pleased you could join us, my dear," he said, his accent perfect Old School Tie English. "Please, sit down. Make yourself comfortable." He turned to Sokol. "Uzzi, close the door on your way out. There's a good man."

Sokol didn't look pleased, being dismissed so matter-of-factly, but he didn't argue, which meant the toad outranked him comfortably. The IDF was like any sort of military organism; it lived and died by its respect of rank and structure. Sokol was never going to argue with the toad. He closed the door and left them alone.

"So, tell me, Miss Nyrén, how do you like being back in our fair country? It must be very difficult coming back here after what happened in that camp, no?"

They had done their research. She expected nothing less from Aman. They were methodical. Circumspect. And every bit as dangerous as they were careful. There was nothing hot-headed about Aman's modus operandi. Stealth, cunning, reason and malice of forethought—those words best described her experience with the organization.

Orla looked around the room as though admiring the beauty of the landscape beyond these four walls. The toad had decorated in the familiar military austerity chic. He had a row of black-and-white pictures and a single color one of himself. There was a line of books with battered cloth spines and faded gold lettering, and a faded globe with the old territorial boundaries of the fifties. The only concession to decorative softness was a scale model of a soft top 2CV. It was a curious thing to be the only decoration, and then Orla remembered who the toad was, and why the car was significant to him.

Gavrel Schnur. It was the car she remembered. The tiny 2CV and the woman. His wife, Dassah, had been killed in a car-bomb attack outside their home in the Ramat district to the north of the city. Gavrel had been a rising star in the Likud party back then. She looked at the figures in one of the black and white photographs and realized it was Menachem Begin, the former Likud prime minister. There was another of him with Shamir and Netanyahu. She remembered Gavrel Schnur as being particularly vocal in his opposition to Palestinian statehood and in support of Jewish settlers in the West Bank and Gaza.

The PLO had placed the bomb in his car, not expecting his wife to be the one to drive it that day. Not that it really mattered to them one way or the other. Her death had achieved one thing—it had turned Gavrel Schnur into a poster boy for his party. He had stood on the platform in the days immediately after her murder and decried the Palestinians as cowards. He had sworn a vendetta against his wife's murderers. His rallying cry had been that the Palestinians were a nation of godless terrorists, that death was in their blood, and that he would not rest until they were driven out of Judaea, Samaria and Gaza. And now here he was, guardian of the state's security. There was something almost ironic about it.

"It feels like home, Gavrel," she said, enjoying the slight smile he gave her. They were like players on opposite sides of a card table, each keeping their cards close to their chests.

"Very good, my dear. You do not disappoint. Tell me, what was it that gave me away?" He licked his lips again.

"I remembered the car," she said.

"Of course you did, of course you did. Everyone remembers my great tragedy. Few remember the great triumphs of my life, but I do not blame them. Sometimes I can barely remember them myself, but Dassah, Dassah I never forget. Even after all these years I still expect her to come home from shopping. That is my great tragedy. But you didn't come here to talk about my dead wife, did you?"

She shook her head.

He shifted his weight in his seat. The leather and wood groaned.

The story, if she remembered it right, was that Gavrel had gone after his wife's killers personally. She found it hard to believe, looking at him spread their in the chair, but he had apparently hunted down the bomber and the chemist that had built it, as well as taking out the man who had given the order. Gavrel Schnur did it the Aman way. He watched, gathering intelligence, making plans, until over the course of one long night in Tel Aviv everyone in any way remotely connected with his wife's death fell victim to what on the surface appeared to be unconnected accidents and random acts of violence. The coincidences racked up and, come dawn, everyone knew Gavrel Schnur had had his retribution. That, more than anything, cemented his place within the political spectrum of the city.

"I am sure Uzzi explained our interest in your inquiries. Most odd, someone asking after my old friend Akim after all this time. I had thought the world had forgotten him like it has forgotten so much else. But suddenly there his name was. You understand, I am sure, why it raised a red flag with our office. We, of course, did our homework. You're a very well connected young woman, Miss Nyrén. Friends in those much vaunted 'high places.'"

Orla nodded. She didn't say much. She waited to hear what the toad had to say. In this world, she knew, knowledge was hard currency. The adage that knowledge was power had been invented for the hallowed halls of spydom. Sharing knowledge was a matter of quid pro quo: giving on both sides. She had to decide how much she was willing to give up, and how much she thought she might get in return. She began with the bare minimum, repeating what she had already told Sokol back at the graveside. She outlined the insurance payouts from Humanity Capital, the numbered accounts at Hottinger & Cie, with their irregular deposits and withdrawals made by the dead man, and as a *coup de grâce* showed the toad the two different Akim Caspis in the photographs she carried. When she was done she said, "Sokol said I needed to know about the Shrieks? I think now would be a fine time to find out what it is, exactly, that I need to know."

The toad nodded, the folds of flesh around his neck rippling. He didn't seem the least bit surprised to see this second Caspi, or likewise, the least bit curious as to why the impostor had drawn the attention of foreign intelligence. There was something unnerving about the fat man. He seemed far too sure of himself. Orla didn't like it.

"They call themselves the Disciples of Judas," the toad said. "They've become known to Aman as the Thirteen Shrieks."

"As in screams?"

"Yes. It is some sort of unholy chorus, I believe. When all of their voices come together, the world will listen. You get the idea. It is all very portentous and not a little insane. What the world is meant to listen to, well, that is not even particularly interesting. They claim that Judas Iscariot was the true Messiah, not Jesus Christ. Shock, horror, I know. It seems the new millennium, even a decade old, is still obsessed with pseudo-historical-religious nonsense. You have to remember, in those days every man and his dog was walking around claiming to be the son of God. Tinker, Tailor, Candlestick Maker, Messiah, Beggar Man, Thief. What's the difference? That was just the way it was." The toad shrugged. "I always imagine it was like something out of that Monty Python movie, *The Life of Brian*, every street corner boasting its own Savior." He smiled wryly.

"But, I must admit I have a certain amount of sympathy for their argument. If you think about it rationally, there would be no Christianity today without Judas, would there? No resurrection. No redemption for the sins of the world. No clean slate for humanity. Of course being the Great Facilitator doesn't automatically make you divine, does it? But, think about it for a moment, if Judas was the true Messiah, I would ask them, what did his death do for mankind? How did his sacrifice redeem us? It didn't, did it? Or am I missing something?" Schmul said, reasonably. "I look around me today at all of the wars, all of the sense-less killing and all that random violence, and wonder if we weren't actually damned."

Orla looked at the fat man as he spread his arms wide.

"I know, not a terribly fashionable sentiment. I am sorry. Some days I miss Dassah more than others. I find myself given over to melancholic rambling. I have thought about this a lot, though. It is the curse of living in this place and time. What do you think messiah means, Orla?"

"The son of God," she said. She knew she was wrong, but she wanted to hear what he said to that.

"In Hebrew it means Anointed One. There have been any number of messiahs. Did you know that? In the Jewish tradition it was said that a son of the line of King David, a *ben yishai*, would return to lead the Jews from Exile, rebuild the Temple in Jerusalem and bring about a period of prosperity and peace. In that sense, belief in a messiah was nothing more than a belief in the restoration of Israel and an end to the troubles. Now would be a good time for a new messiah, I think. The messianic ideal changed through time, especially when Judaea was conquered by the Babylonians and under the rule of Emperor Hadrian. New gifts were associated with the word and suddenly they were talking about raising the dead, which is supposed to mark the end of days.

"In Christian terms the Messiah was the divine one who would initiate the Kingdom of God on earth. Then you have the Ephraitic Messiah, a concept which existed in ancient Judaism and the book of Zerubavel, which tells of a woman named Hephzibah who accompanies the messiah ben Joseph into war with the enemies, where he is killed, and after his death she will save Jerusalem. In our own time the Rabbi of the Lubavitch Hassidim was worshipped as messiah. He never claimed to be the son of God. It's such a strange thing that it has become so corrupt in meaning because of the rise of Christianity. The concept of messiah is not part of biblical Judaism, did you know that? No, why should you? It was developed from folk tradition with countless variants, countless understandings of what it truly meant.

"It's the subject of Hassidic songs and even occurs in the Babylonian Talmud, but there it is about the time when

Jews will regain their independence and all return to the land of Israel. It even says that all prophecies regarding the Messiah are allegorical, and the only thing important is that all religions return to the true religion, that Jews are free and we know the wisdom of the Torah. It's all a bit different, isn't it? So even the word messiah is just another thing Christianity has corrupted."

Orla didn't know what to say. She hadn't come here for a religious studies lesson, but she couldn't help but think she'd just learned something, even if she wasn't sure what. "Fascinating," she said, more out of politeness than true interest.

"Of course, on a personal level, I always found it fascinating that Judas isn't mentioned once in the Gospel of Peter. Think about it. What does that tell you? The so-called great betrayer doesn't even warrant a mention in the first saint's gospel? That 'betrayal' bought this whole mythology we've swallowed whole, and it doesn't even appear in one of the main gospels? But,"—the toad chuckled at the thought before he shared it—"if one is to believe that Judas was in fact the divine object, the—for want of a better word—Messiah, then surely that would turn the thirty pieces of silver that bought our religion into the most holy artifacts known to man, wouldn't it? Instead of the cross people would be worshipping money." He placed a single coin on the table between them. It was a new Israeli shekel with the word *Yehud* written in ancient Hebrew. Silver. "It almost seems like it is that way already, doesn't it? Money, money, money. Still, they're all just stories, aren't they? But it is an interesting turnabout, don't you think?"

"Who are they?" Orla asked.

The toad shrugged, his entire upper body undulating in place with the roll of his shoulders. The flesh of his forearms dug into the edge of the desktop as he leaned toward her. "Who are they indeed? We have as many guesses as there are days in the week. More. There have been a number of suicide bombings and other attacks in Jerusalem and Tel Aviv over the last few years that the Shrieks have laid claim to, but in terms of concrete knowledge we know very little. I would say they are ghosts, but they're not—they're more like wraiths. They feed on despair.

"What we have managed to work out is sketchy at best, but we believe each disciple has his own followers. So rather than one cohesive organization we're talking about splinter cells that have grown like offshoots from the core group. Essentially you're looking at thirteen separate organisms, each with one purpose—to spread terror. And when you have that image firmly rooted in your mind, then, my dear, you are beginning to understand the nature of the Shrieks. Think about the scope of it for a minute."

She did. She thought about the thirteen innocent people who, by burning themselves alive in thirteen European cities, started this entire chain of events she found herself caught up in.

"Last year we did a sweep of the city based on an anonymous tip we'd received. We brought in two men we believed to be fairly well placed within one of the chains. They might have been dog's bodies for all the use they were to us. If we think of each Shriek as a self-sufficient organism, each one seems to be structured in such a way that no one knows who the next step above them in the chain is, or who is two steps below them. They are each responsible for recruiting one man, and one man only, who works directly below them and reports only to them. The identity of their recruit is reported to no one—not even the disciple himself—so no one has a complete picture of how wide-spread the network is, what positions of authority have been infiltrated. They're all working blind.

"That kind of organizational set-up makes it damn near impossible for us to crack open. If we take out one man, we break the chain, but it doesn't take long for it to grow a new tail. And those left behind simply become a new head for their own serpent. You try infiltrating that kind of set-up. It's paranoia at its finest. It also means it is damned near impossible to stop them. We're chasing our tails half the time, their shadows the other half. We hit them, they cut their man free and we're left with nothing. It's as simple and frustrating as that."

Orla nodded. She'd come across similar protection mechanisms in sleeper cells in Western Europe. It was part of the modern philosophy of fear. It was based upon distrust. No one could afford to trust anyone around them. They expected to be betrayed at any moment, so there were no secret hideouts, no conspiratorial meetings of gun-powder, treason and plot. It was difficult to be betrayed when people didn't have the slightest clue who you were or, when it came right down to it, whether you even existed. Everyone focused on their own place in the chain.

In a structure protected by distrust it was amusing that all any of the individual conspirators had to go on was the word of the man above them in the chain that they weren't alone in what they were doing. She wanted to ask how the disciples disseminated their orders, how the word to fight was passed from link to link without it taking forever. How did the disciples make their will known to others in the chain? It was a basic thing, but in such a fractured chain of command it was hard to imagine them picking up a cell phone and calling the first man on the list beneath their name. She almost laughed at that. She didn't. Instead she asked, "So the men you caught didn't talk?"

The toad shook his head. "On the contrary. They talked plenty. They begged. They pleaded. They swore blind they didn't know anything. It was all we could do to stop them talking. Unfortunately they were telling the truth. They had nothing of use to say. We had hoped that by taking one of them we might work our way up the chain, get the name of his contact, track down the next man in the line, bring him in, break him, get the name of his contact and so on. It didn't work out quite like that." The toad licked his lips nervously. She was naturally uneasy about people who licked their lips. It was a furtive thing, a reflex that smacked of nervousness. "The first name on our list was found floating in the Yarkon estuary the morning after we brought his man in. It was a quite literally a dead end."

Orla nodded again. It made sense that someone would be making sure they kept their house clean. Given the nature of the Shrieks, either the disciple himself, or more likely, his right hand, would have seen to it that Schnur's men couldn't simply kill their way up the chain to the top.

"This is all very interesting, but, and forgive me for being blunt, Gavrel, how exactly does this all link up with our two Akim Caspis?"

"A few days ago I would have said it didn't," the toad admitted, shifting in his seat again. She pitied the chair. "I wasn't even sure it did until you showed me that photograph of your man. Then, as they say, it all became clear."

"You recognize him?"

The toad nodded slowly, as though deciding how much it was reasonable to share. "I do," he said. "He was one of us."

Now that had her attention. "You mean Intelligence?"

Gavrel nodded again. And again the gesture was painfully slow and drawn out, as though it physically hurt him to share even that much. "Now he calls himself Mabus. When I knew him his name was simply Solomon. He was Akim Caspi's protégé." He looked at the photograph of the Masada dig again. "The fool took him under his wing, taught him everything he knew. I think he saw him as the son he never had. It is a common flaw among childless men of a certain age. Curious that Solomon chose to pass himself off as Akim. This was taken when?"

"Around two months after the real Akim Caspi died," she said. "It was taken at an archeological excavation at Masada after the '04 earthquake."

"Meaning, if I understand you right, two months before these mysterious payouts from Humanity Capital began?"

She nodded.

"Curious."

"You could say that," she agreed, "but I'm still not seeing how this all ties together. I feel like I am missing something obvious, something staring me right in the face."

"From here on, what I am about to tell you is pure conjecture. It has no basis in fact. I have no real reason for believing it, but I do. I believe Mabus is not merely a self-styled Disciple of Judas, but rather he is the First Disciple, the man who stands above them all. That he should be reborn at Masada, well, perhaps that is not so surprising. How much do you know of the place?"

"Some," Orla said, leaving it to the Israeli to work out for himself what she did and didn't know.

"For a while Masada was a Roman fortress, then it was occupied by a group who called themselves Sicarii. They wanted to expel the Romans and their partisans from Judaea. One could argue it is the same fight we are having today, but isn't that always the way? People fight about territory. Anyway, the Sicarii were dagger men, assassins. That's where the name comes from in point of fact. *Sicae* is Latin for dagger. Sicarii, men of the dagger. They were forerunners of the Arab *Hash-shashin*. Patient killers. They worked their way close to their target, ingratiating themselves into their service, becoming trusted friends. Confidants. Allies. They would become indispensable to the Roman generals they sought to kill. They worked away in the background. Then, when the guard was down, they struck and faded away into the chaos of the murder scene, often calling for help for the dying man and holding him like the friend they were supposed to be.

"Does any of this sound familiar? It ought to. It is the story of Judas, or at least a version of it, after all. Even his name Iscariot is interpreted by some scholars as a

Hellenized transformation of *sicarius*. The suffix -*ot* could be interpreted as denoting his belonging to the Sicarii. Of course, it's only a theory, but it is a theory that is supported by the knowledge that Menahem ben Jair and his brother Eleazar, the last known leaders of the Sicarii, were the grandsons of Judas. And, interestingly enough, the brothers died together at Masada in AD 73 when the entire sect committed mass suicide rather than be captured by the Romans. So why wouldn't Masada be the perfect place for the first Disciple of Judas to be reborn? There's a certain sick symmetry to it." He shook his head.

Orla didn't really understand half of what he had said. She had stopped listening halfway through when something the toad had said had derailed her train of thought. Something wasn't right about this.

"Mabus has been their mouthpiece for the last five years. He is the one obsessed with taking terror to a new level in this country. He makes hate films and distributes them via the Internet. They call it Viral Fear. In them he claims responsibility for attacks in Jerusalem, Tel Aviv, Gaza and along the West Bank. He taunts us openly. He goads our investigators as we hunt his people. Last year they instigated a one-of-them—one-of-us policy.

"After we captured their two men, they snatched two of my men, good men, and showed their beheadings on the Internet. It makes me sick what this man does. I watch the filth he spreads, and it makes me want to crush his windpipe with my bare hands, Miss Nyrén. As I am sure you appreciate, I am not a violent man. For Mabus I would make an exception. For Mabus, I would get blood on my hands. What frightens me most, though, is not the films or the beheadings—we all know the risks when we enter this line of work. No, what frightens me most is he knows us; he knows how we think, because he was one of us."

Orla understood that all too well. No one wanted an enemy who shared their mindset and knew the ins and outs of their protocols. It meant he could anticipate every response, every action, and compensate for it. It wasn't just that it gave him an advantage; it was as though he could reach into their minds and pluck out each and every measure and countermeasure even before the first strike had been made. It made their enemy omnipotent. Godlike. But what she didn't understand was how the toad knew it was him.

Gavrel Schnur reached down and opened one of the drawers in the pedestal legs of his desk. He pulled out a dossier marked "Mabus." He flipped it open and laid it down on the desk between them. "We never found the man responsible for my old friend's death," the toad said. "But now,"—he tapped the photograph on the table with a thick stubby finger—"I think we have. I think I am finally beginning to understand a lot of things that have bothered me for a long time, Miss Nyrén, and for that I thank you.

"Now, I believe I have upheld my end of the bargain and told you all we know of the Shrieks." He pushed the folder across the table toward her. "It should prove interesting reading, if nothing else. This is every last scrap of information we have gathered on Mabus and his people. It's yours. I wasn't sure what arrangements had been made for your stay, so I took the liberty of booking a junior suite for you at the Dan Tel Aviv. It's one of the nicest hotels in the city, with a stunning view of the water. And I really do mean stunning. I'm not just quoting a line from the sales brochure." He chuckled at that. "I don't know about you, but I appreciate a little space when I travel." The toad cupped both sides of his pendulous belly with his hands and wobbled it. It was an oddly self-deprecating gesture. "But, don't get me wrong, there's nothing quite so enjoyable as a little bit of indulgence, either.

"Take the dossier, digest it. There is much in there. I will arrange for Sokol to collect you in the morning. If there's anything you don't understand, or want to go over, we'll pick it up tomorrow. How does that sound?"

Orla took the folder from the table and slipped it straight into her bag, as though she was afraid he might change his mind and take it away from her. She couldn't imagine someone in a similar position in MI5 making the same offer. Perhaps she had misjudged the toad? "That is most considerate of you," she said. "All of it. Obviously I hadn't had the chance to think about where I was going to sleep tonight, so thank you. A bit of pampering is exactly what the doctor ordered."

"Think nothing of it. You have flown a long way to solve the riddle of my friend's murder. It is the least I can do to thank you. I am told the shiatsu massage is to die for. I wouldn't know, personally. It has been a long time since I allowed anyone to touch my body." His eyes momentarily drifted toward the model car on the bookshelf.

She understood.

She started to stand, realizing that her meeting with the toad was over.

"One last thing, if you would," Gavrel Schnur said, looking up at her. "Before you go, perhaps you might tell me why this thorn in my side was prickly enough to draw you to my city?"

He's good, she thought. He'd saved his fishing expedition until the very last moment and she was on her way out of the door. It was all about catching her off balance. She continued to rise, pushing the chair out behind her. The chair legs grated on the floor. She smiled at the sound; it was a petty rebellion that said he wasn't going to get it all his own way. Gavrel Schnur wanted to know what they knew. It was as simple as that. He'd revealed their hand, and now, to continue the poker analogy, he was calling her. She wasn't about to lay all of her cards on the table though, not yet. Nothing had changed since she walked in to the toad's lair. In this world information was still hard currency. It was that simple. He might have just given her a

SILVER

small fortune, or he might have tried to pass off a few counterfeit notes. Without checking out the file Orla had no way of knowing. Of course, to sell her the deal, he was pressing for something in return *now*. He didn't want to wait. Quid pro quo.

"Let me read this tonight," Orla tapped her bag. She kept her voice neutral, light, and made sure she didn't allow her doubts to creep into her tone. She didn't want to offend the toad, but neither did she want to tell him everything that she knew.

She reached the door and turned back toward the fat man, deciding, as her hand closed around the door handle, to offer him a little something to whet his enormous appetite. "We believe that this man you call Mabus could be behind the deaths of those people in the photograph with him." She didn't say how they had died, or what it was about their deaths that had brought it to Sir Charles' attention. If Gavrel was as good as she suspected, he already knew and was just looking for confirmation. That, too, was the nature of information in this clandestine world of deceit, half-truths, shadows and eavesdropping. "It's a link we are very interested in following up. When we get together tomorrow perhaps we can compare notes?"

"I'd like that very much, Miss Nyrén," the toad said.

18

THE WATER WASHES AWAY HER SOUL

Orla didn't check into the junior suite at the Dan Tel Aviv.

There was something about the offer that just didn't sit right with her. She couldn't put her finger on why it felt off, but try as she might she couldn't imagine a British spymaster being so considerate or so extravagant. That was enough for her.

Instead she crossed the port and used her "flexible friend" to check into the Dan Panorama.

She had no luggage, but the porter insisted on accompanying her all the way to the room, then held his hand out expectantly. She tipped the guy, apologizing that she didn't have any local currency. He assured her it wasn't a problem. The air conditioning was on, and the TV screen welcomed her to the Dan Panorama and hoped she enjoyed her stay. The wide windows looked out over the crystal blue water. The balcony door was half open and inviting. She went out onto it and stood there for a full five minutes, hands braced on the balcony rail, just drinking in the incredible view.

The suite itself was three rooms, a lounge area with two small couches arranged around the flat screen TV and a coffee table. A varied selection of magazines from *Business Today* to *Architectural Monthly, What Photo?* and *Harper's* were fanned out across the coffee table, light reading for every possible palette. A luxurious robe hung on the back of the door. She ran a hand over its thick plush. Behind the couches was a nicely proportioned dining area. On the table there was a full bowl of fruit stacked high with everything from apples, oranges and grapes to kiwi fruits, guava and papaya. The cooler was stocked with miniature bottles of champagne, San Pellegrino, orange juice, Absolut Vodka, a decent half-bottle of both red and white wine, the usual bags of nuts and enough chocolate for even the sweetest tooth.

She pulled her blouse off, glad to feel the air on her skin, and threw it onto the nearest of the two couches.

She rooted around inside her bag for her cell phone and called in. It was a short conversation; she updated Lethe on what she had unearthed, which, when it came to spelling it out, was very little. The Disciples of Judas, that name again, Mabus, a history lesson and a lot of dead ends. Gavrel Schnur hadn't said anything about Masada or why the real Akim Caspi had been murdered. She hoped the truth was inside the Mabus dossier, but somehow she didn't think it was. Truth was an alien concept in this city.

She hung up on Lethe and went through to the bedroom.

It was like something out of *A Thousand and One Nights.* The bed was covered in sumptuous silks and piled with a dozen pillows. The furniture was rich, black wood, handcrafted with incredible detail. It looked more like a rich man's brothel than a hotel room.

She put the dossier down on the nightstand, kicked off

her shoes, pushed away more than half of the pillows, and lay back on the huge bed.

The mattress fashioned itself to her shape, cocooning her in its soft embrace. A ceiling fan rotated lazily in the heat. Unlike a cheap motel where the fan would have driven her insane with its irritating background groans, this one was oiled precision. She couldn't rest. She felt itchy in her own skin. After two minutes lying on her back she pushed herself up off the bed. She felt exhaustion sweeping up to meet her thoughts, but she didn't want to sleep yet. She needed to think. She went through to the bathroom and started to run a bath instead.

Orla set the lights down low and emptied an expensive bottle of bath salts and luxury foam into the water, swirling it around with her hand until it started to bubble up. On the way back out of the bathroom she set the air conditioning to bring the temperature down to a comfortable 68.

In the bedroom she stripped out of her clothes. They smelled like she had been wearing them for two thousand miles. Naked, she stretched, bending her back supine and cracking the vertebrae by leaning first left and then right. She walked across the room to the phone and made arrangements for the maid service to collect her clothes and have them laundered and ready for the morning.

On the wall in the bedroom, there was a motion-sensitive Bang and Olufsen surround sound system. Orla waved her arm across the onyx face, amazed at the luxury money could buy, and the case opened up. The hotel room was better equipped than her entire flat. It ought to have been for the best part of a thousand bucks for the night. Schnur had been right about one thing, sometimes a girl did want a bit of pampering. Inside the surround system, instead of a CD player there was a four-inch touchscreen that listed the various genres preloaded onto the rig. She set it on '80s shuffle, adjusted the volume and set the speakers to the bathroom, and went back through to the bath. The bubbles in the water were close to overflowing and the mirrors were blind with steam. She turned off the taps, moved the largest of the towels to within reaching distance of the tub, and sank into the suds.

Orla closed her eyes and savored the stinging heat on her bare skin.

Haircut 100 sang "Fantastic Day" to her through the small speakers set into the tiled wall on either side of the fogged mirror. It didn't feel fantastic, unless the meaning of the word had been changed to never-ending. She let the water wash over her, cleansing her skin. The tiredness threatened to take her under. She scooped up a handful of suds and massaged them into her arms. She slid down so the water rose up over her face, holding her breath while she counted to twenty in her head, then came up, shaking the suds out of her hair like a dog. She popped her ears, working the water out of them with her little finger. Then she soaped herself thoroughly, just enjoying the feel of the lather forming on her skin. Again she submerged, letting the water rinse her clean. When she came up again the song had changed. Duran Duran were "Hungry Like The Wolf."

Then she heard someone moving about in the other room. Her first instinct was panic. She knew she had locked the door. But then she remembered the laundry. The maid service had master keys. She shouted above the music, "The clothes are on the bed!"

She lathered shampoo in her hands, then worked it into her hair, massaging it in all the way down to the roots, then slipped beneath the surface again. She worked her fingers through her hair over and over while she held her breath. The lather formed a film on across the surface. She came back up for breath, then submerged again.

Something had been bothering her ever since she left the toad's office. It wasn't just that he'd taken the liberty of booking her a room in the Dan Tel Aviv. That *could* have been old-fashioned human kindness. It was something else. She couldn't say what it was, just that something, some nagging doubt, chipped away at the back of her mind. Something he had said or something he hadn't. She rose to the surface again, letting the breath leak out of her mouth and nose. She inhaled and exhaled five times, slowly, then went under again. It was like one of those elaborate finger puzzles that had been popular when she was younger, where you put your fingers in at either end, and the harder you tried to pull them out, the more stubbornly the trap clung to them. She worried away at it, but her mind refused to make the connection.

Then it hit her: how could Gavrel Schnur know so much about this Mabus character? He was good, but was he *that* good? Was it possible? Schnur had said that even those recruited to the Shrieks were limited in their knowledge. They only knew two others within the entire terror cell—the man who recruited him and the man he recruited. Schnur had looked at the photograph of Solomon—only Solomon, he hadn't even given the man a second name—and recognized him. Had he simply fed her the lines about Mabus and his terrors, she might have believed it; after all *they* knew about Mabus. His name had come up again and again, but they didn't have a face to put to the name. He was a ghost. Like the toad had said, that was how he worked. No one knew who he was, not the real man behind the codename.

She shook her head at her own stupidity. She thought she had been so clever, holding out on the toad. She had been so preoccupied with not letting on what she knew she hadn't listened to what he was saying. That the toad recognized Solomon as Mabus meant he had to be the man above or the man below in the food chain. There was no other way he could know him. He'd told her as much when he said he sympathized with their cause. He'd outlined their beliefs in detail. He'd even put a silver shekel on the table between them. Judas had supposedly been bought with Tyrian shekels.

"I am an idiot!"

He hadn't just taken the liberty of booking her a room, he'd tried to put her somewhere where he would be able to find her when he needed to. A hotel room was more comfortable than the average cell, but that's exactly what it would have been.

Orla decided to get out of the bath.

As her head broached the surface she saw a masked face leaning down over her. Leather gloves fastened around her throat and pushed her under the water. She lashed out, kicking and flailing and swallowing water as she tried to scream. As she felt the fight draining out of her body the masked man hauled her up out of the water and slapped her across the face, forcing her to breathe. She coughed up a lungful of water. Without a word he pushed her back under the water. She tried to grab his wrists and pull them away from her throat, but he was too strong. She splashed up water, kicking frantically. She slapped at the surface, spraying bubbles, then slipped down the length of the tub. Her head hit the bottom.

Orla opened her mouth to scream for help instinctively and choked again as her mouth filled with soapy water.

She slapped helplessly at the side of the tub, trying to reach something, anything.

The masked man hauled her up again. She coughed water, spluttering and trying to see through stinging eyes. She couldn't focus on anything in the room. There was steam, and in the steam there were shadows, blurs. She could have been seeing three masked men or one.

"Were you really stupid enough to think you could hide from us anywhere in this city?" She didn't recognize the voice. The accent was thick, heavy, but that could have been the water and the fear distorting what she heard.

She was helpless. She was naked. She reached up for the

man's face. She wanted to see him. Her fingers barely touched the wool of his balaclava before he grabbed her wrist and twisted, using his grip on her wrist to push her under the water again. As she went down she heard someone behind him say, "Don't break her."

She tried to push her head back above the water. She couldn't. The masked man reached down, his hand closing around her throat, and kept her under.

"The boss wants the bitch alive."

She knew that voice.

She knew it because she'd been listening to it all day.

She knew it because she had been stupid enough to trust it.

Uzzi Sokol.

The toad's man.

19

CONTROL

Sir Charles Wyndham made the call at close to midnight. The ring signal was broken on the third cycle. A sleepy voice demanded, "This better be good."

"If the bald man has a chain through his tongue, how can he sing?" Sir Charles said, careful to enunciate every syllable clearly. It was a stupid opening gambit. Anyone monitoring the line would be immediately curious.

"Say that again," the man on the other end of the line said. The old man could almost hear the sleep slipping from his effeminate voice.

"If the bald man has a chain through his tongue, how can he sing?"

"Oh, for pity's sake, do you have any idea what time it is?"

Sir Charles had no sympathy for the man. He had become safe, comfortable in his life. Like so many others in the upper echelons of the trade he'd come to think that the nine-to-five daily grind was his right. Late night calls, safe words and clandestine meets were for the grunts doing the leg work.

"We need to talk," he said.

"We *are* talking."

"The line isn't secure. Meet me at Fagus sylvatica. First light. There are things we need to discuss that can only be said face to face."

He hung up before the other man could object.

Max, the old man's butler, pushed his chair through the soft wood chippings of the bridal path known locally as Rotten Row. The name was more colorful than the reality of the path. The birds were up, the dawn chorus breaking out all over the city of London. The neatly trimmed grass of Hyde Park still glistened with diamonds of dew. The air was crisp and clean. It was one of the few hours of the day when London didn't feel like it was suffocating under the smog of pollution.

A little way ahead riders from the Household Cavalry were giving their mounts a run out. The drum of horse's hooves shivered through the ground beneath them. Sir Charles felt it through the steel frame of his wheelchair. He had a blanket folded over his lap and a newspaper folded over the blanket. A few early morning joggers crisscrossed the path—Brownian Random Motion made flesh. A woman with a short-clipped, black bob walked beside them for a hundred yards, a miniature black poodle skipping along beside her. It always struck the old man as amusing how a certain type of dog owner seemed to subconsciously model themselves on their pets. It was almost as though they were breeding little versions of themselves. *Two legs good, four legs bad*, he thought to himself wryly as he watched the seductive sway of her hips as she moved away.

Sir Charles liked the park in the morning. It teamed with all sorts of life, not just joggers or birds, flying squirrels and red foxes. It was a microcosm of the city itself. In the distance he saw a tall man in a pin-striped suit and bowler hat walk through what had once been the Tyburn Gate down by Speakers Corner. Even from this distance he was instantly recognizable. He walked with what could only be described as an old school, jaunty bounce to his stride. He looked preposterous as he twirled the silver-tipped cane he held in his right hand. Even from where he sat, Sir Charles could hear the faintest strains of his whistling. All the old man could think as he watched this caricature of British gentry stroll through the park was how on earth had Quentin Carruthers ever survived out in the field. Of course when he was a younger man he had been quite the dapper bon vivant, a dandy, happy to work, rest and play hard with the boys. The boys back then had included Kim Philby, Burgess and McClean. The Cambridge crew. It still fascinated the old man that Quentin had managed to come out of that fiasco clean while all those around him were busy losing their heads or defecting. For all his affected effeminacy, the old queen had always had a well-honed sense of self-preservation. Somehow though, as the '60s became the '70s and the '70s the '80s, he had become a parody of himself. In the new millennium he was nothing short of a relic.

The man cut toward the bench beside the old upside-down tree, Fagus sylvatica 'Pendula,' and sat himself down. He opened his case and took grease-proof-paper-wrapped triangles of tuna sandwiches out. He didn't eat them. He used them to feed the birds while he waited for the old man to join him. It was their familiar meeting point. It had been six months since Sir Charles had last visited the old tree. Fagus was really quite something, a weeping beech. It looked like children had gathered a huge stack of fallen branches and built a cave out of them. He liked to think that only a few yards away the wretched villainy of old London had hung by their necks while the crows fed on them, and it amused him that the new city was so eager to hide from the old that it renamed Tyburn Marble Arch. It was probably one of the earliest examples of spin doctoring he had ever come across. It seemed a fitting place for two old spies to sit and share the early morning.

Maxwell pushed the old man's wheelchair alongside the bench and made his excuses to leave him alone for a few minutes. Sir Charles took the folded broadsheet from his lap and made an elaborate show of opening it up and turning to the financial pages. Time had not been kind to the man sitting beside him.

"Oh, for heaven's sake, Charles, dear boy. Do we need to go through this charade every time? It's all well and good to play at being spies when you are seventeen, but when you are pushing the wrong side of seventy, well it is getting to be something of a chore, I must confess. The fun has quite gone out of the game."

"You always were a spoilsport, weren't you, old boy?" Sir Charles smiled.

"If by that you mean I was one for propriety, I think you must have me mistaken for someone much more interesting. Well, I assume you have a terribly good reason for dragging me out here?"

"Grace Weller. One of yours?" the old man said without any preamble. He folded the top of the newspaper over so the masthead disappeared.

"I couldn't possibly—" Quentin began to offer the standard deflection of secrecy, protection and the good of the State when Sir Charles cut him off.

"Of course you could. You can pretend to be retired all you like. The truth is you can take the boy out of Vauxhall, but you can't take Vauxhall out of the boy. You can't be Control for twenty-five years and just give it up, *old boy*," Sir Charles said, mimicking his companion's affected tones. "Now I am willing to bet a pound to a penny you know what's going on with your people better than anyone, even the poor sap who's trying to fill your glorious patent leather shoes. Now, I might be getting on, but you can't fool me, old friend; you're still connected." His tone changed. "This is serious, Quentin. I need your help." What he wasn't saying was it was serious enough to drag the man who had given him the mandate to go off the books with Ogmios in the first place out of retirement.

"I assumed as much when you woke me so rudely at midnight, with that nonsense about Ogmios. There has to be a certain amount of decorum in life, dear heart. When you start making midnight calls and you aren't either Bela Lugosi or a particularly striking cabana boy bearing fruit there, is something terribly wrong with the world. Now, how on earth is this old queen supposed to help you, bearing in mind I've already got one foot in the grave? I'm not really sure I am up for the excitement of illicit ren-dezvous anymore, more's the pity."

"Grace Weller," the old man said again.

"You're getting tiresome. I can neither confirm nor deny whether the lovely Grace is fighting for the side of righteousness."

"Which means she is," Sir Charles said. It was always wordplay and games with Quentin Carruthers. But then, Control had never been the sort of man you'd expect a straight answer from.

"Well if she is, you can understand I can hardly go blathering willy-nilly about what she is doing for Her Majesty, now can I?"

"Was," Sir Charles said. He took a facsimile copy of Grace Weller's last letter from his inside pocket and handed it to Quentin Carruthers.

"Well that's just a damned tragedy," the ex-spymaster said, seemingly genuinely shocked by the news.

"What was she involved in, Quentin?"

"By which you mean, what was she doing in Germany that would get her killed?"

"A rose by any other name," Sir Charles said softly,

dipping his head in acknowledgement.

"I really don't know the ins and outs of—"

"Don't be coy, Quentin. Her mission notes date back to 2004," the old man lied, playing a hunch. "That puts you back in the chair as Control when she was sent out into the world. Don't try to tell me you don't know exactly what you wanted her to do. I won't believe you for a minute."

"Your suspicion cuts deep, old friend. If you prick me, do I not grin and say more?" Quentin Carruthers laughed at his own inglorious jest. "Yes, yes, very well, Grace was my pride and joy. Is that what you wanted to hear?"

"What she was doing in Berlin?"

Quentin Carruthers half-snorted, his entire body trembling. It took a moment for the old man to realize he was stifling a sob. He twisted his face. "Is that where she was? It's been a long time since I last heard from her."

"So what was she doing out there?" Sir Charles pressed. He wasn't about to let this go.

"It was a bad business, Charles. Dreadful. Are you aware of a corporation, Humanity Capital?"

"I've come across the name," he said, giving nothing away.

"They insure soldiers in combat zones. It's all above board. They profit by our boys managing not to get themselves killed; they pay out when things go wrong. They're parasites essentially, but then what insurers aren't? Anyway, we believed Humanity Capital a front for other less savory businesses. The usual exploitation stuff. You go into a new area, ingratiate yourself with the general populace, take a little bakshish for doing a few favors. That sort of thing. Then it escalates, and soon you are moving medical supplies and food to places they shouldn't be. Then it's guns and ammunition. Then it's a sidewinder missile. Then, like the name says on the tin, it's human capital. It's all about escalation—grease the right palm and you get things done. You know how it goes. Supply and Demand."

"They were providing mercenaries to fight our own boys?" Sir Charles said, following the old spymaster's wandering chain of cause and effect to its natural conclusion. "But surely that makes no sense? If their mercenaries were successful, they'd have to pay out on the combat insurance policies."

"You would think, wouldn't you? But you would be surprised at just how wriggly these chaps can be when it comes to holding on to their pennies."

"Right, so you sent her to work for Humanity Capital?"

Quentin Carruthers nodded. "I did indeed. She was a star, dear boy, a star. Within a month she was Fraiser Devere's girl in more ways than one. Humanity Capital was Fraiser Devere's baby. You know Devere right? The Devere dynasty. Old money. Inbreds. It's all uncle marries third cousin twice removed with the blue bloods. You know me, Charles, I never explicitly tell my people how far they have to go when they're under, but the good ones get it, they make it real. Grace made it real. It was a hot steamy affair. And then, for no reason, he broke it off."

"He got suspicious?"

"I doubt it, but something spooked him. Maybe he was afraid of love. Plenty of people are, when it comes right down to it. Maybe he just got tired and wanted a new plaything. You know how the rich are. Whatever the reason, he cut her off completely. We've got the transcripts of her debriefing, but there was nothing in there as far as I could tell. Then she met the son, Miles. He was off on some building project in Israel, trying to prove to daddy just how independent he was. Grace found a way to get herself on the project. Like father like son, I suppose. They became lovers, but unlike Devere senior, junior was completely infatuated. He kept trying to impress our girl with how much he knew about the old man's dirty secrets. Needless to say, as far as these things go, it was really rather useful."

"Quite," Sir Charles said.

"She went with him when he started Devere Holdings, and for a number of years she was party to the ins and outs of every deal they struck. She began to notice anomalies in the corporate accounts, not just hiding pennies from the tax man, you understand, but some rather large offshore deposits. There were meetings. At first she assumed it was the usual corporate espionage kind of thing, but Grace was nothing if not thorough. Turns out Miles Devere wasn't just mixed up with some bad people, he was the bad person others were mixed up with, if you catch my meaning. His money brought a lot of pain to the world. Everywhere daddy's corporations spread war, junior came in their wake, snapping up contracts to rebuild the infrastructure, the buildings and the schools. He liked to open the school himself, great photo opportunities for the benevolent capitalist and all that. No mention of all that blood on his hands, of course. That didn't make for good copy."

Sir Charles nodded. He was getting a picture of Devere now, and an understanding of how it all hinged together. Some aspects still didn't make sense, not completely, but as ever it seemed that money, money, money—and the things in life that money could buy—were at the root of it all. Wasn't that always the way?

"The last time Grace checked in, and it was quite some time ago, more than a year in fact, she left a rather enigmatic message for her handler. She had found patient zero. You're aware of patient zero—that first disease carrier who walks around, blissfully infecting others, without ever exhibiting symptoms of the sickness himself? Grace had found him, in Berlin it seems, if that is where this sad story of hers finally played itself out. Poor girl. I don't mind saying I was really rather fond of her. She played the game as well as any of us old boys ever used to. She was prettier too, if that was your sort of thing."

The old man had a very good idea who patient zero was in this case. Grey Metzger. How he linked Devere, war profiteering and clean-up with the Akim Caspi impostor, who may or may not be Mabus the terror-master, he wasn't sure, but he would find out. There was something, one last piece of the puzzle to drop into place. He would find it.

It's what he did.

He found things out.

"Are we finished here, then? Because as much as I am enjoying our little reunion I can think of a lot prettier faces I'd like to be looking at, no offense."

"She didn't die well," the old man said. "I thought you ought to know. It wasn't clean, but even at the last she was professional enough to get a message out. We found all of her journals. Everything she had dug up, the entire paper trail. My boy is going through it right now."

"Do you know who did it?"

"I have my suspicions."

"Now who's being coy. You've had my tit, you owe me your tat. Who killed her, Charles? Who killed my brilliant little girl?"

"One of two men: an Israeli who calls himself Mabus or Miles Devere."

Quentin nodded. "Will you promise this old man something, Charles?"

The old man raised an eyebrow. "I would say it rather depends on what it is you want me to promise, my friend."

"When you know which one it is, don't wait for justice to take its course. Kill them for me. No one kills one of my people and lives to tell the tale. I'm old fashioned like that."

20

VIDEO KILLED . . .

Jude Lethe stared at the screen. The video clip had gone viral. In a matter of hours from its first being posted on the net to when he'd found it just now, some three million people had seen it.

The picture wasn't good. It was the usual kind of fuzzy, grainy image with poor-quality lighting and terrible audio distortion. It didn't matter. The content was hypnotic. Hypnotic in the same way as a car wreck where the paramedics are loading up the body-board as you drive slowly past. You can't help but look, even though you know what you are seeing is someone else's tragedy.

He watched again, trying to be sure, but it was so difficult because of the poor resolution and bad light. He knew in his gut though. Just knew. On the small screen a man in black walked backward and forward, ranting every so often at the camera. Behind him slumped a woman in chains, her head down, hands trussed up over her head. Her body was sliced with red welts where she had been whipped and beaten. She didn't look up once. The masked man pulled a blade and held it up to the camera. Lethe couldn't understand what he was saying, but it had that fanatic's rising pitch that sent a shiver, bone by bone, down his back. Normally Orla would have interpreted the madman's rant for them. Nothing about this was normal.

The dagger man paced back and forth.

Lethe studied the blade in his hand. It was old, that much was obvious. It wasn't Damascene, but it was quite similar.

The dagger man walked up to the chained woman and drove a fist into her stomach. She barely reacted. Off screen someone laughed. It was the single most chilling sound Jude Lethe had ever heard. The man took a sheet of paper from his pocket and walked toward the camera. He read what Lethe assumed was a list of demands, then walked back across to where the woman hung. Someone off camera moved the light source, casting an eerily bright glare across the woman's tortured body. She looked wretched. Her body was covered in bruises, and her bones stood out like an anorexic's against her wax skin.

He ran the blade from her temple, down her cheek and neck all the way down to her hip, drawing the thinnest line of blood that welled in the cut. He tangled his hand in her hair and yanked her head back, forcing her to stare at the camera. He spat another outburst of bile at the screen. Lethe didn't understand a word of it. He didn't need to. He knew exactly what was going to happen next.

The man took the blade, leaned in close and cut her throat.

He couldn't watch.

Equally, he couldn't look away.

The man didn't stop cutting until he was through the windpipe and the blood was streaming down his hands. Then, holding her head up, he finished the job with a thicker machete-like blade, cleaving through the bone. Her body still hung there, suspended by the chains. The masked man picked the woman's head up from the floor and showed her face to the camera.

He paraded his trophy back and forth, with more ranting in whatever language it was. This wasn't the part that had stunned Lethe. It was the last ten seconds before the camera died, as the picture roved wildly around the makeshift dungeon.

He froze the stream.

In the shadows, barely recognizable for the beating she had taken, he saw another woman chained to the wall. He pushed the image on, frame by frame, until she looked up. For a single frame she stared straight at the camera.

Orla.

He called up to the old man and told him. For a moment there was only silence. Then the old man said, "Are you sure it was her?"

"As sure as I can be, sir."

"Bring Frost in. We need to deal with this as cleanly and simply as possible. She is not ending up on some bastard's propaganda movie, Mister Lethe. Believe me, hell will freeze over before I allow that to happen."

"Yes, sir. Do I recall Koni and Noah?"

"The world doesn't stop because Orla's in trouble, Mister Lethe." The old man sounded cold. Detached. Fire and ice. Just a second before passion had been driving his tongue. All it took was a second for the tactician to take control. Jude was immediately reminded of the half-played-out game of chess on the board beside the great fireplace. The Saavedra position. It was the old man's favorite endgame for a reason. "And Mister Lethe, whatever happens, under no circumstances are you to inform Larkin about any of this. Do I make myself clear?"

"Crystal, sir."

"The fact of the matter is that Larkin is too unpredictable

as far as she is concerned. I can't be worrying about him going off message," which was the old man's way of saying Noah was in fact far too predictable in this case. He'd wage a one-man war to bring Orla home. He wouldn't care about casualties or collateral damage—he would bring Orla home, and God help anyone who tried to stop him. It was precisely the kind of thing that made Noah so vital to the team; but sometimes one's greatest strength can become their greatest weakness. The old man wouldn't be able to control him.

In one breath Lethe had heard the best of the old man, and the worst.

"Understood."

"Good man. After you've contacted Frost I want you to run a few queries for me. Specifically, I'm after information concerning Humanity Capital. I want a list of territories where they have insured fighters, and if there is a paper trail, I want to know all of the places where they have supplied mercenary fighters."

"There's always a paper trail," Lethe said. "If they sent a private army out there, you'll know before lunchtime."

"Good. When you've done that, I want you to cross-reference these against any contracts won by companies Miles Devere has a stake in. I want to know exactly how much Little Man Devere has made out of the suffering of others."

The old man hung up on him.

21

THE WORDS OF THE PROPHETS WRITTEN ON SUBWAY WALLS

Noah Larkin had spent the night alive and well and living in hell.

Each one of his personal demons were within arm's reach. There was a bottle of thirty-year-old McCallan scotch whiskey on the nightstand, a plastic cup beside it. The bottle's top lay on the nightstand beside the bottle. The cheap hotel room beside the Rome Stazione Termini reeked of alcohol. He had drunk a third of the bottle but felt like he had downed the lot. He sat on the windowsill, watching the girls out in the street. It would have been easy to call down, and one of them would come up to help him take his mind off things. Sometimes that was all he wanted.

He had music playing simply because he couldn't stand to be alone with his own thoughts. It got like that some nights. The dead started talking to him with the voices of his imagination. The music helped to drown them out, but it didn't silence them completely. That was what the drink was for.

The girls on this side of the world were the same as the girls back home. They congregated on the street corners and in doorways and walked up and down the street, advertising their wares. Every creed and color was out there to be bought. A car trawled the gutter, driving slowly from woman to woman as they walked up toward the rolled-down window. Watching was uncomfortably voyeuristic and made Noah feel distinctly dirty. He poured himself another slug of whiskey before he went back to the window. He thought about Margot, the middle-aged whore he'd found in Kings Cross.

He'd paid her to stay off the street for a night. She wouldn't, of course. She was one of these creatures. This was her life. It was all she knew. Like the song said, it was a hard habit to break. But that was what the money was all about. It wasn't about the sex. He hadn't enjoyed sex for a long time. Now he used it to punish himself. He'd given up on the dream of beautiful flesh and candles and soft music and all of that nonsense. It was hard to lose yourself in beauty when inside your own head it was so ugly. He knew his own psychology as well as anyone could.

He looked at the clock blinking red beneath the small portable television set, with its little round aerial poking out from the back: 2:47. The night was slipping remorselessly into morning. He had a little under seven hours until he was supposed to meet Dominico Neri's man from the Vatican. He could sleep. He could drink. He could screw. The truth was he didn't feel like doing any of that.

He decided to go for a walk and picked his coat up off the bed.

Rome at night was a dangerous creature, but what city wasn't. The mood Noah was in, if any local boy had decided to push his luck, he would have ended up hospitalized.

He took the stairs down to the lobby. It was another

personal quirk. He had no love of elevators. It wasn't the confined space, he wasn't claustrophobic; and it wasn't the height, he didn't suffer from vertigo. But somehow, with the two put together, all he could think about were the metal cables above sheering away and the elevator car plunging, so he took the stairs.

Noah walked all the way down the hill of Via Cavour to the ruins of the Forum. Even in the dark, Rome was a spectacular place. But like the prostitutes at the top of the hill, there was something worn down and seedy about the place. It had seen better days. Almost two thousand years ago to be precise.

An occasional car cut through the streets, heading down toward the Coliseum and Constantine's Arch. He walked in a circuit, following the beaten tourist tracks along Via Teatro Marcello and over to the Pantheon and then back around toward the hotel. He heard the revving engines of boy racers, proving that Rome was just like any other city in the Western Hemisphere— full of idiots with fast cars. The entire circuit through the old Rome took him the best part of three hours. The area around the railway station was the one part of the city that didn't sleep. News vendors were up already, pasting up the day's headlines.

One of the girls walked toward him, her smile and the sway of her hips inviting.

He didn't see her.

He only had eyes for the thick black ink of the headline.

One word: *Veleno!*

Poison.

Rome had fallen silently while he drank his whiskey and watched the whores. He had been looking for fireworks. An explosion on the horizon. Something big. Bright. Bold.

He felt sick to the core.

He turned his back on the woman as she started to ask if he wanted company for the long, hot night.

Despite the drink, Noah was suddenly clear headed.

Noah could see Monsignor Gianni Abandonato was anxious. He shuffled about from foot to foot. He stood at the top of the steps of St. Peter's Basilica. Behind him the white travertine stone of Maderno's facade gleamed in the morning. The statues of John the Baptist, Christ himself and the eleven Apostles looked down on the Monsignor. Noah couldn't help but look around himself at the Baroque stonework marvels Bernini had fashioned. There was something truly awe-inspiring about the approach to the cathedral. Bernini had somehow managed to balance heaven and earth in his grand design of a split plaza, with its elliptical circus and trapezoid courtyard. It had soul.

In contrast, Maderno's facade seemed flawed. Instead of inspiring awe and reverence it smacked of mankind's vanity. While Bernini had reached for the heavens, Maderno's work lacked line and symmetry—and its cardinal sin . . . it lacked any form of vertical feature to draw the eye as the pilgrim approached the holiest of holies. That was left to the dome in the distance.

Noah squinted against the rising sun. The attic where the statues stood watch over the great square was too cluttered with detail for its relative lack of height, he realized. It was trying too hard to force grandeur into the white stone. But then Maderno had been frightened by the notion of original thought, almost as though by definition it became original sin, and had clung to the proportions of the rear of the basilica drafted by Michelangelo.

Noah walked slowly toward the Monsignor, who stood across the piazza. He was suddenly at a loss as to how he was supposed to greet the man. Did he call him Father? Eminence? Excellency? Just Monsignor? Gianni? Piazza di San Pietro itself was empty save for a few early morning tourists up with the crows. He counted five crows in the dry basin of the fountain as he walked past it. That made one crow for every early bird. There was no water in either of the fountains. They had been drained at first light, as had every other fountain in the city.

Noah hadn't been able to reach Neri, which was hardly surprising. The Carabinieri man had been working all night, dealing with the effects of the poisoned water. Rome was a city under siege.

The Witness, the ancient Egyptian obelisk that had supposedly seen the crucifixion of Saint Peter, cast its shadow all the way to the dry fountain. Noah crossed the shadow. It felt as though he had passed some sort of boundary. On the other side, this world of God and Saints and Souls seemed so much more real.

He took the opportunity to study the man on the steps. He was wearing the robes of his office but lacked the serenity of a man at peace with his place in the world. Noah recognized the telltale signs of a man on the verge of breaking. How much was he risking by meeting with Noah? Surely not so much as to be looking over his shoulder every few seconds? Noah wondered who was back there, hiding in the shadows? There was someone back there, he knew. One of the Swiss Guard perhaps? Another holy man? Who would he be more frightened of? The archivist was obviously eager to sweep him away from prying eyes and into the labyrinth of the cathedral itself. Curious then that he would choose such a public place to meet, especially as the doors wouldn't open for pilgrims for a few hours yet. He held up a hand and waved in greeting. He reached the stairs a few moments later.

"Monsignor Abandonato?"

"Gianni. This way please, Mister Larkin," he gestured not toward any of the three doors that led through to the nave, but rather toward another smaller passage that led toward the barracks of the Swiss Guard.

"Noah."

"A propitious name if ever I heard one. Some of us are not so blessed," he shrugged slightly. They turned one corner and then another, walking along the side of a narrow, yellow painted wall. There were a number of small doors set into the stone. He opened the fourth they came to and led Noah through into a small vestibule. It lacked the grandeur of the main basilica, but this was part of the administrative buildings not the holy face. "As you can well imagine, being called 'The Forsaken' in this place can prove rather, how shall I put it, convenient for jokes." He looked up at the ceiling. It was a very theatrical gesture, practiced no doubt over many, many years. It was a long-suffering "why me, Lord?" look. Noah found himself rather liking this nervous priest.

Noah followed the Monsignor through a number of narrow passageways, and then the nature of the building seemed to change. For want of a better phrase, Noah thought it went from functional to holy. The ceilings raised. Plain walls became exquisitely painted with frescos, and every raised detail seemed to have been gilded with pure gold. Instead of being beautiful, it was staggering; instead of being calming, it was intense. Like Maderno's façade, there was just too much going on, too much for the eye to see. Did the priests believe that by owning every single work of art they could prove themselves most holy? Most worthy? Was that what it was? Noah could suddenly understand the attraction of minimalism.

He felt very, very small as he followed the priest across the marble floor. Every few feet they crossed a new geometric shape laid into the stone. The sun streamed in through the windows set high above his head. Because of the angle of the sun, they didn't reach the floor, but lit somewhere halfway down the wall on the right side of the passageway. Dust motes danced lazily in the beams. Noah half-expected to hear monks chanting in the distance somewhere or choirboys practicing their harmonies, or something. He knew he was getting his denominations all muddled up, but it felt like there really ought to be singing of some sort, even if it was only a single voice raised in hallelujah.

"Terrible business, this thing with the water," Abandonato said, leading him onto a long, straight passageway that seemed, almost like some optical illusion, to go on and on and on into the vanishing point of the distance. "All these people poisoned. Have many died?" Before Noah could tell him that he didn't honestly know, the Monsignor continued, "How could anyone do that? I don't understand. How could anyone knowingly poison all of these helpless people?" He had a handsome face, black hair swept back in a widow's peak, and dark circles under the eyes. His skin had a vaguely waxen tint to it that suggested more than just a passing familiarity with the library stacks and darker corners of the Holy See.

"I think we're having this conversation backwards, Gianni. I'm meant to be the one asking how can something so horrible happen, and you're meant to be the one assuring me it is all part of God's ineffable plan." Noah smiled slightly to show he was joking. The archivist looked uncomfortable despite the gesture.

"Sometimes it is hard, even for us," he admitted. "Our faith can be tested in the most surprising, and sometimes most human, of ways. What man could think of all those children queuing at the water fountains, thirsty for a drink yesterday, and not feel angry that today they are fighting for their lives and losing? But yes, the innocents will find their way to His side, where they will be safe and welcome. There is comfort in that, but the man in me still smarts, Noah."

Noah wasn't certain what he had expected, but he wasn't comfortable taking Abandonato's confession. He thought about making a joke about everyone inside the Holy See being fine because obviously they could just have a word with the Big Guy and get him to do his water-into-wine trick. Thankfully, he played it out in his head before he said it, realized exactly how flippant it would sound and thought better of it. It was one thing to share a wry observation—it was quite another to mock the man's faith—especially when he wanted something from him. Instead, Noah tried to steer the conversation in another direction, asking about Nick Simmonds and what he had been doing during his tenure at the library.

"Nicholas is a good man," the Monsignor said, defending the dead man even though he hadn't been asked to. It was obvious he suspected Simmonds was accused of something. What other reason could Noah have for digging into his background? "He has a good heart. He has been with us for almost two years now, I think. He is quiet, keeps to himself, but then that is rather a bookish trait, is it not?" Noah nodded where he was expected to. "Obviously young Nicholas shares our passion for the preservation of literature. I find it hard to imagine he could have done anything wrong."

"Well, with all due respect, Gianni, didn't you also just say you found it hard to believe people could poison the same water children drank? Sometimes ours is not to reason why."

"Indeed," Abandonato said through tight lips. He gestured to one of the side passageways. "We have been going through something of an upheaval here. The Biblioteca Apostolica has been closed to the public for the best part of three years now. It is undergoing some significant restorative work. Nicholas has been helping us with that. Not the restorative work, obviously, the preparation of texts for storage. Did you know we house over seventy-five thousand codices and over one million printed books within these walls? Think about how many shelves you would need for those." He chuckled. "On top of that we preserve no less than eight and a half thousand incunabula." The Monsignor read the look of incomprehension cross Noah's face. He smiled softly. "Forgive me, sometimes I forget that not everyone is obsessed with books in the same way that my colleagues and I are.

"*Incunabula* means 'cradle,' as in a baby's cot, or beginning. Think of it as the first traces of anything, that spark of life where it all began. In this case we are talking about the first printed books, even single-sheet manuscripts, anything that wasn't handwritten. You would be surprised how many—or perhaps how few—of these first printings have survived. In the library we preserve extant copies of the very first books manufactured by your countryman, Caxton, for instance. Some of our texts are utterly unique, but in many cases several copies have survived. Take the Gutenberg Bible, perhaps the most famous of all 'first books.' There are almost fifty copies of this known to exist still—forty-eight or forty-nine depending upon who you believe—making it a fairly common book, but of course quite valuable. We have the original hand-written cantos of Dante's *Purgatorio* and *Paradisio* as well as *La Vita Nuova*. Then we have *Codex Vaticana*, the oldest extant Bible, and *Libri Carolini*, King Charles' response to the Second Council of Nicaea. It is more commonly known as "King Charles against the Synod," which probably tells you all you need to know about its contents. The library contains the single most important collection of books in the world. Believe me when I say it really is quite some collection."

"If books are your thing," Noah said with a shrug. He managed to keep a straight face. "I'm more of a movie guy myself."

"And even if they are not," Abandonato said, "it is difficult not to be overwhelmed by the sheer scale of everything within these halls, as you will soon see. We need to employ over eighty staff here just to oversee the protection and preservation of these works of art. Eighty people!"

The narrow passage led into what must have been a part of the library itself. There were no bookcases, but at various intervals across the floor there were simple straight-legged wooden tables with glass cases displaying various irreplaceable books. These were perhaps the least ostentatious of the long room's furnishings. Every other table was overwrought with gold and bore expensive vases, themselves almost certainly every bit as irreplaceable as the books. The room was a headache of colors, reds and oranges and rich blues with a black-and-white checker-board floor.

Noah didn't know what he had expected, but considering Abandonato's boast, it seemed odd that he couldn't actually see any bookshelves, just lots of paintings of robed people holding books open.

"And it isn't just books," Abandonato continued. "We are responsible for over one hundred thousand prints, drawings, engravings and maps, as well as three hundred thousand papal coins, medals and so forth."

Gianni Abandonato led him through two more corridors, these opening into a final room that finally looked like it ought to be part of the world's most extensive library. Banks of card index files went back into the distance. Each one probably catalogued twenty-five thousand items. The banks went back as far as the eye could see. Two tiers of shelving and a gantry filled one wall, each tier packed floor to ceiling with abstracts and indices and other leather-bound texts bearing surprisingly uniform binding. No doubt they were books about the books the library housed. There were reading lecterns arranged conveniently along the gantry and booths set aside for scholarly study. There was an unerring uniformity to everything in the room.

"I had heard," Noah began, looking around to see if anyone was in listening distance, "that the Vatican library had the largest collection of, ah—okay, this is going to sound stupid no matter how I say it—I had heard that you had the largest collection of erotica in the world?"

Abandonato burst out laughing. He had a deep, rich, laugh. It reached all the way down into his belly and came out of his mouth, filled with proper mirth. The sound swelled to fill the entire chamber, echoing off each of the walls. He looked immediately contrite and seemed to shrink about three inches in height. When he continued, his voice was barely above a whisper. "Someone has been pulling your leg, I am afraid, Noah. Unless you are willing to consider the odd Renaissance nude as pornography? Our tastes are far more prosaic.

"Now, Nicholas, Nicholas. What can I tell you about his work here? Nothing particularly glamorous, I am afraid. Nicholas is one of nine volunteers we have working in the archives at the moment. With the renovations we have been forced to transfer many of the Lateran and Pre-Lateran texts down to the subterranean archives. Moving this many books, many of which are so fragile they can be damaged by the merest touch, is a monumental under-taking."

"I'm sorry?"

"Ah, we divide our texts up into five historical periods for ease: Pre-Lateran, marking the earliest days of the Church; Lateran, which lasted up to the reign of Boniface the Eighth in the 13th century; then there are the Avignon texts—there was a time from 1370 onwards when the Popes were in residence in France; Pre-Vatican, and Vatican, when, in 1488, the library moved here. From then until now the collection remains unbroken. But of course you didn't come here to listen to me wax lyrical about old books. It is difficult. I could talk for hours about this place and what happens here. Nicholas has been helping with the preservation and storage of some of the oldest Hebrew codices."

"Like the Dead Sea Scrolls?"

"Like the Nag Hammadi codices, yes, though obviously not those particular texts. The scrolls are housed at the Coptic Museum in Cairo, after all."

"Ah, show's what I know," Noah admitted. "I thought they were locked away down in the deepest vaults because they proved the bloodline of Jesus?" Noah offered Gianni Abandonato another lopsided grin.

"I'm not quite sure what you believe we're hiding down here, but it isn't all the *Da Vinci Code*, I'm afraid. We aren't keeping earth-shattering secrets from the world."

That the archivist had a passing familiarity with the popular novel only made Noah like him all the more. "Not that you would tell me if you were," Noah said, tapping the side of his nose with his finger. "They're secrets, after all."

"Quite. The library houses several—more than several—of what we would call heretical texts. These are what I am assuming you are talking about. They aren't all grimoires bound in human skin, though. You won't find incantations for summoning the Devil or whatever else you might have heard, despite the persistence of such rumors. In the early days of the Church vast amounts of materials were gathered to be destroyed because they preached what were considered heresies. Of course, it should come as no surprise to hear that a great many of these texts were never destroyed, but were in fact brought to the library. The library existed even then to preserve knowledge, not destroy it. The surviving documents are almost entirely stored in the Pre-Lateran and Lateran archives."

"Which is where Nick Simmonds was working?" Noah said, following the conversation right back to where it began.

"Yes."

"So what you're saying is Simmonds was working with these heretical texts?" Noah licked his lips, thinking. "Could he have been looking for something directly? There's a lot of stuff here. Could he have come in looking for something in particular?"

"I am sorry, I don't follow."

"I'm trying to put several pieces together at once," he said, and then an idea came to him. He had no reason to think it might be true, but he asked it anyway. "Would any of these works be from Israel, around the time of the Sicarii?"

"No doubt there are copies of Josephus, who, as I am sure you know, was the preeminent historian of the time. As to anything else, I am afraid I couldn't even begin to guess. No doubt there are testimonies and such, but you have to remember that very little from that time was written down. I haven't read close to a hundredth of all the ancient texts. I doubt anyone has. Many of these texts have not even been looked upon in decades. It is not like picking up a book to read down on the beach. In translation each word, and how it sits beside the next, can lead to varying interpretations of the precise meaning of every sentence. Miracles can happen rather unintentionally if someone decides the preposition is *on* instead of *beside,* for instance, which would make the miracle of Bethsaida slightly less miraculous."

Noah didn't really follow, but nodded because it seemed like Abandonato expected him to. "How about Simmonds? Was he comfortable enough to read something like that and understand the significance of the linguistics?"

"I couldn't possibly say. Sorry." The Monsignor shrugged. "We did not work that closely. As I said, we are all very solitary people down here. We work our own specialisms and keep to ourselves."

Which translated in Noah's head to: *of course he could, and he could have walked out with any text he wanted, because this whole place functioned around trust.* "Do you know what books, precisely, he was working with?"

"As I said, Pre-Lateran and Lateran Hebrew codices."

"Right, and you have a list of these books?"

"Yes, of course, but as I said, the library is undergoing a massive refurbishment. It would be almost impossible to ascertain one way or another if an individual text were missing; and it would take weeks to be sure. As I am sure you can understand; nothing is where it is supposed to be right now."

"Great," Noah said, barely keeping his frustration from bubbling over. Simmonds' working with Hebrew texts couldn't be a coincidence. Nothing else he had learned in the last four days had been, so why should this be? He needed to think of everything as though it was all connected, not strings of random events. It was pointless asking if any books had gone missing recently; the Monsignor had already said it would be nigh impossible to tell. And there was nothing to say the book was a recent find. Simmonds had been working in the library for the best part of two years. He could have found it at any time.

Noah pursed his lips, wondering how best to proceed. There was only one thing left to say and he knew it. He blew out a sharp breath. "Nick Simmonds committed suicide four days ago. You might have heard about it. He set fire to himself in the main square outside."

"Goodness."

"Unfortunately there's very little of that out there anymore, Monsignor."

"And you think his work here had something to do with his killing himself?"

"It's a distinct possibility," Noah said. "Would he have recorded somewhere what books he had already prepared for the move?"

The archivist nodded. "Another of the volunteers has developed a computerized ledger system for the move. Every book, as it is prepared, is entered into the system."

"So everything he laid his hands on ought to be registered in the system?"

Abandonato nodded.

"Halle-bloody-lujah."

Noah sat with Abandonato in a small walled garden in the heart of the Vatican. The Monsignor had offered to show him the Sistine Chapel and other treasures to help pass the wait, but Noah didn't feel like feigning interest in the clouds that had been painted in to preserve the modesty of the angels by men far more prudish in nature than those who had commissioned the work of art in the first place. But wasn't that the truth of all occasions? It seemed indicative of the modern world that any amount of violence was fine so long as it was cartoonish in nature, like the Road Runner dropping that anvil on Wile E. Coyote's unsuspecting head from a great height, but a flash of genitalia needed to be covered to protect the fragile innocence of the young, lest they become sexual delinquents. He could *almost* understand the reasoning of the Muslim men who wanted to hide women behind burqas to avoid temptations of the flesh. *Almost.* Next to painting over angelic dangly bits to preserve the piety of the chapel, it seemed positively reasonable.

Instead, Noah decided to talk to the priest about the suicides, and more specifically, the messages that pointed toward Rome.

"You are aware, of course, that every generation has its own apocalypse it believes is going to wipe out mankind? Some cite Mother Shipton who claimed the world would end in 1881, some the Mayan Prophecies who give us until 2012, others Nostradamus. This isn't something new to us. According to Josephus, Theudas declared himself the Messiah in AD44. He was beheaded. In AD53 the Thessalonians believed they'd missed the Rapture. Hyppolytus calculated the world had only six thousand full years, and should have ended in AD600. Rabbi Judah ha-Nasi and Rabbi Hanina both predicted the Second Coming would be around four hundred years after the fall of the Temple in AD70. Adso of Montier's Treatise on the Antichrist in AD950 prophesied an end-of-the-millennium apocalypse. In AD964 Cartulaire de Saint-Jouin-des-Marnes wrote: *Dum saeculum transit finis mundi appropinquat* . . . . As the century passes, the end of the world approaches. Millennial end-of-the-world panic has always been rife.

"Abbo was another AD1000 End of Days advocate. And of course everyone was seeing signs: monstrous children, famine, and mortality. The pale rider was sighted in the sky—a comet no doubt. Of course when nothing happened, when Christ did not return, it led to an outbreak of heresies in France, Italy and the southwest Mediterranean regions, which in turn were believed to be the unleashing of Satan as written in the Book of Revelation. These predictions go on and on, all ultimately useless. There's no evidence of the new star supposedly sighted in heaven, or the rain of blood as the sun turns red and fails to shine for three days, or the natural disasters of the world returning to its natural chaos. Believe me, Noah, none of this is new to us.

"In AD1186 the Letter of Toledo warned everyone to hide in the caves and mountains because the world would be destroyed and few saved, and yet we're all still here. The Taborites of Czechoslovakia predicted every city would be annihilated by fire and only five mountain strongholds would survive. Again, this great burning failed to take place. And of course your own people believed AD1666 was the end of all times, hardly surprising given the bubonic plague and the Great Fire struck in the same year; and the presence of the 'number of the beast' in the date did little to help allay their fears, but that's all they were, fears.

"In 1914 the only reason the world did not end was that Michael had defeated Satan in heaven, if you believe Jehovah's Witnesses, that is. The Tribulations began again in earnest in 1981, and continued rather hysterically all the way until the new millennium. We're no less superstitious as a people now than we were in AD1000, and no less gullible, it would seem. Now, it appears, the next 'great event' is actually prophesied in the Pentateuch, and predicts a comet will crash into the earth in 2012 and annihilate all life. The Church preaches calm in the face of all this insanity, Noah." He spread his arms wide.

"Is that why it withheld the third secret of Fatima?"

"Ah, yes. Sometimes a date is just a date, and no man can tell the will of God. But to answer your question, yes, the Church did officially withhold the third secret of Fatima long beyond 1960, when they believed it would be better understood by the world. But no, it doesn't foretell a single event. The first secret was merely a vision of Hell; the second has been interpreted to mean the Virgin appeared to warn of World War II. The third talks of prayer as the path to salvation for our souls. But of course, by its withholding, it made the so-called revelation so much more controversial. That is the way of things, is it not? If people believe you are hiding something, they want to discover its secrets all the more."

Noah nodded.

"True, certain quarters believe that the Church has not in fact released the third secret at all, because the text released in 2000 does not contain any words from the Virgin; neither does it talk about a crisis of faith in the Church. People can and will see conspiracy in every corner. It is the way of man. After so much anticipation it is only natural they believe the Church is still withholding things from them."

Noah was very careful about how he phrased his next question. "Could the third secret foretell the assassination of the Pope?"

"Ah, the Bishop in White? As I said, these things are always open to interpretation. The most recent I heard was that the Bishop in White was Ximenes Belo, and the city trembling in ruins was in fact Dili in East Timor. Of course the secret falls down because Belo was saved from certain death, but almost anything can be squeezed into these prophecies and predictions if the interpreter is looking to make a point. While the Church will not openly acknowledge these interpretations, let's put it this way, she won't take any unnecessary chances with the safety of the Pontiff. *Roman Pontiff beware your approaching, of the city where two rivers water, your blood you will come to spit in that place both you and yours when blooms the rose.* That one is the work of Nostradamus," Abandonato said. He couldn't have known he had just repeated Nicholas Simmonds' last words. It was the one quatrain of Nostradamus that Noah was familiar with.

"It's suitably vague that it could mean just about any Holy Father in any city of two rivers. There's nothing to date it, nothing to make it even remotely insightful." Abandonato breathed in slowly, then looked around the small garden as though he was about to whisper some heresy of his own. "However, in 1999 John Paul II intended a pilgrimage to Ur, birthplace of Abraham, to meet Saddam Hussein in Baghdad. Iraq is a land between two great rivers, the Tigris and Euphrates. That pilgrimage was cancelled. Subsequent pilgrimages in 2000, 2001, and 2003 were also cancelled despite His Holiness' desire to visit Ur. I am not saying they were cancelled in response to Nostradamus' quatrain, but they were cancelled just the same. The city of the two rivers could just as easily be Paris, fed by the Seine and Marne. Should we cancel the Pontiff's visit to Paris? Or is that a step too far? Are we jumping at shadows?

"There are similarities, of course. Both so-called prophecies refer to the rose. But is that rose a way of saying springtime and grounding the prophecy with the time of blooming? Or could it be a person? Some have tried to say the rose was Princess Diana, England's rose. It is a possible interpretation, just as Hitler was a possible interpretation of Hister and *'from the roof evil ruin will fall upon the great man'* could relate to the Kennedy assassination. His only outright and correct use of a name was in the quatrain relating to Franco.

"And for all the similarities there are glaring and irreconcilable differences. The third secret of Fatima talks of a city almost destroyed while Nostradamus sounds like a pleasant papal visit in spring. You tell me, because your interpretation is every bit as valid as mine, Noah. Are you seeing the problem with accepting prophecies here?"

"I think I'm getting the picture," Noah said. In truth he was. He might not have understood even half of what Abandonato had told him, but he didn't need to. The priest was doing a damned good job of convincing him that fate was fickle, unpredictable, and basically everyone and his aunt had predicted the end of the world a dozen times. But that didn't change the fact that four times the Vatican had cancelled the Pope's pilgrimage to Iraq due to fears for his safety. Fears almost certainly put there by scare-mongers pointing at the Nostradamus prophecies and asking why tempt fate? Of course this was different; the secret and the quatrain had been used not to predict an attack on the Pope but to threaten one.

Noah was about to explain when a third man bustled into the small garden. He shuffled with his head down and hands clasped. His feet brushed over the stones. As he came closer Noah realized the young priest was holding a printout. "The results of the search you requested, *Monsignore*," he held the paper out for Abandonato.

"That will be all, thank you," the priest said, taking the sheet and reading through the list of codices Nicholas Simmonds had signed off on during his time in the library. The young librarian shuffled back out of the garden. There were eighty-seven texts listed by name. Abandonato pursed his lips as he read through them quickly. Reaching the bottom of the page, he shook his head. "As I said, he was working on the Pre-Lateran and Lateran Hebrew codices. There's nothing here I wouldn't expect him to have handled." He turned the sheet over and continued to skim the list of titles. Midway down something caught his eye.

"Well now, perhaps this is something. You mentioned the Sicarii zealots, yes? According to this, Nicholas worked with one specific text that would be of interest for several reasons, *The Testimony of Menahem ben Jair*. If it is the text I am thinking of, it was in a dreadful condition when it was brought in a few years ago. I would need to check the precise date, but I believe the bequest came to us after it was discovered in an earthquake in the Masada region of the Dead Sea. I would need to check with my colleagues to be sure. I do know that our restoration team have been working on reassembling the original papyrus for quite some time."

"2004," Noah said, as another piece of the puzzle slotted softly into place. Simmonds had been sent in to look for this book. Noah was certain of it. It made stone cold sense. Not only that, it was the only thing that made sense. The testimony had been recovered from the site during the Masada dig. Now Mabus wanted it back. What could it possibly say to make it worth all of these lives? "You said there were several reasons people might be interested in this testimony?"

"Indeed. Ordinarily I would say with something like this the main interest has to be the historical nature of the find. Any document from the time helps provide us with a picture of the world as it was. Let's not forget that even the most highly educated of men were not in the habit of recording their thoughts in writing. Thoughts were for thinking, for speaking, but not for writing down. Wisdom was passed on from father to son, in parables and stories. Anything that adds to our understanding of the time is precious. But, discoveries like this? Something like this doesn't just cast a little light on the final days of the assassins' cult, though that in itself is a priceless gift to our generation. No, this is far more because it was written by Menahem himself. And why was Menahem important?" Abandonato asked rhetorically. "I'll tell you, Menahem ben Jair was important because not only was he the leader of the Sicarii zealots, he was also the grandson of Judas

Iscariot. Tell me, who wouldn't want to know the final mortal thoughts of this man? His secrets? Everything he held dear and wanted to set down for time immemorial? I know I would."

Noah thought about it as he followed the Monsignor back through the labyrinth of illuminated corridors toward a door that led out to Rome proper.

"So, what do you think the testimony says?" Noah asked.

Abandonato shook his head. "Truthfully, I do not know. I would not expect much wisdom—the man was a killer, his band of zealots little better than terrorists, though they would have called themselves freedom fighters, like the IRA, no?"

Noah could see the comparison. The Sicarii wanting Judaea for Jews wasn't dissimilar to the IRA wanting to reclaim Northern Ireland for the Irish, but sectarian attacks and bombs at Bishopsgate and Warrington and Canary Wharf, where children and two shopkeepers, ordinary decent people, died, made it difficult for Noah to think of them as freedom fighters.

He made a noncommittal gesture.

"Perhaps Menahem's testimony was nothing more than a list of his beliefs? A manifesto of sorts so that anyone who found it could pick up his cause and fight for an unoccupied Judaea?"

As a guess, it made sense, but Noah wasn't entirely sure he believed the priest when he said he hadn't read it. Skepticism was natural, but at some point it shifted into paranoia, surely?

"So it wouldn't be like finding a new gospel, then?"

"In one sense, possibly. The word gospel is derived from the Greek *euaggelion*. It means quite literally 'good news.' In the sense you mean, though, the gospels include the four canonical books of Matthew, Mark, Luke and John as well as some extra-biblical gospels written in the second century. These gospels are the 'good news' written about Jesus the Anointed and organized as connected narratives that focus upon the *kerygma*, that which is proclaimed, and the *Sitz im Leben*, the situation in life. What motivated the gospel writer to put down his words? The intentions of the author are fundamentally important in the gospels," Abandonato explained.

Noah vaguely remembered the uproar surrounding the Gospel of Judas when it was recovered. The Judas Iscariot of his own gospel was both the betrayer of the Bible the world knew and simultaneously the hero of his own life. It was that aspect of the story that captured the imagination of the world—from being the most infamous traitor of all time Judas was suddenly presented as the most loyal and faithful companion, the only one who could be trusted to make the great sacrifice.

It was the same with all of the so-called Gnostic gospels. They seemed to paint everything we knew in a different light. In Thomas, God didn't need great houses of worship, since Thomas promised that God was beneath every stone and in every split piece of wood. God was in the details. God was in the stuff of life. That was the nature of His creation, and it was there in the middle of it, beneath the heavens, that He should be worshipped, not in houses of brick and stone.

It was as Abandonato had said, subtle changes in translation of an existing text, or a subtle shift in the message of a "new" one could send tremors out through the world.

Did the Church really *want* a sympathetic Judas?

Wasn't it easier for him to be vilified as the betrayer, motivated by greed and jealousy and all of these most human of sins?

Did the martyring of Iscariot change the importance of the resurrection and the other miracles central to what had become the day to day faith of Christianity? Noah wasn't a theologian, but it seemed to him that it did. It was a subtle shift, but it was a shift just the same. And then the natural extension of that line of questioning became: was that enough of a change for the Vatican to bury the secret?

Noah wanted to think it was, but surely, then, Abandonato wouldn't have mentioned the *Testimony of Menahem ben Jair* at all? He didn't have to say Nick Simmonds had had anything to do with the document. After all, it was easier to hide something when no one knew it existed. Abandonato had broached the subject himself, suggesting that some people believed the third secret of Fatima had been doctored before its publication. Why wouldn't the Church do something like that? And if it would do that, why wouldn't it hide any documentary evidence that might prove dangerous to its fundamental belief systems?

Noah's head was spinning with it all.

The only thing he knew for sure was that Nick Simmonds had been on the dig at Masada, where the Testimony had been unearthed, and he had followed it here to the Vatican two years later. That went beyond circumstance into still-hot smoking-gun territory. The rest was irrelevant.

"Here we are," Abandonato said. "If there is anything else I can do, you only have to ask."

"I'd really like to know what is in that testimony," he said, knowing he was asking the impossible of the priest.

One of the Swiss Guard stood watch over the exit. He was dressed in his regular-duty uniform of simple blue with a flat white collar, knee-length black socks and a brown leather belt. He wore a black beret tilted slightly to the right. The simple uniform marked him as a newer recruit to the Guard. The blue was a lot less gaudy than the red, yellow, orange and blue motley of the Guard's official dress. Of course, had he been stationed on the other side of the door, that is exactly what he would have been wearing, along with a ceremonial sword and halberd like something stepped out of Renaissance Rome. The guard's face was impassive to the point of being sorrowful.

Abandonato didn't answer him. Instead he opened the door.

The guard nodded slightly to the priest and stepped aside to allow Noah to leave.

Noah wasn't quite sure what he was seeing at first, but instinct quickly took over.

The door opened onto the piazza, a little way beyond the two dry fountains. Noah had expected to slip out of the same small side door he had entered the Vatican through. This door led out into the grand piazza of San Pietro. He was aware of the long snake of tourists lining up to go into the basilica, but that wasn't what he was looking at.

Noah stared, fixated at a man as he lurched through the line of shadow The Witness cast across the center of the piazza. The man wore a long flapping raincoat completely out of keeping with the season. The coat was open and his body seemed to bulge disproportionately beneath it. The man clutched something in his right hand. Noah couldn't see what it was. Something about the way the man was moving set all sorts of alarm bells ringing inside Noah's head. He held his hand out in front of him like whatever he was holding was contagious. Noah saw the C4 strapped to his body before he saw the fear in his face. The packages of explosives were strapped around his belly with thick bands of gaffer tape. Noah couldn't see the wires from where he was, but he knew that the device in his hand *had* to be a detonator. He didn't hesitate. He couldn't afford to wait for the Swiss Guard to react, and he had no idea whether they had a means to take the suicide bomber out anyway.

He stepped out into the piazza. The sun streamed down, suddenly, horribly bright after the darkness of the Vatican's endless corridors.

"On your knees! Get down *now!*" Noah yelled, drawing

his Heckler and Koch USP 9mm and pointing it straight at the bomber's chest. He tensed, ready to pull the trigger. He couldn't allow himself to think, not with hundreds of people in the piazza queuing up to file into St. Peter's. Judging by his misshapen body, there was enough C4 strapped to the bomber to make a hell of a mess. One life for many; it wasn't even a question.

The man stumbled forward another step.

And then another.

People in the square were starting to look, drawn by the sound of Noah's voice. Even if they didn't understand his words, their delivery cut across the chatter and stopped them dead in their tracks.

"You don't have to do this!" Noah shouted at him, moving a step closer to meeting the bomber halfway. "Just put down the detonator, get down on your knees and put your hands behead your head!"

He locked eyes with the man, willing him to open his hand and drop the detonator. But the man didn't. He took another step closer to Noah. Noah could see the red of the button poking out from his clenched fist.

"This doesn't have to end this way!"

The man shook his head violently. Noah could see the strain in every inch of his body. He was wired. Sweat peppered every inch of his skin, streaming down his face. He looked down at his hand and started to raise it.

Noah dropped him. Three shots punched a neat triangle into the area around the bomber's heart. The man jerked and spasmed, his body thrown into a violent pirouette. He twisted and hit the ground hard, face first. Blood spread around his head where his nose had opened up from the sickening impact. Noah walked toward the bomber, his H&K still aimed directly at him. He wasn't taking any chances, not with the detonator still clasped in the man's hand. All it needed was the slightest twitch and the whole place would go up.

He didn't hear the screaming. He didn't hear the shouts of the Swiss Guard yelling for him to put the weapon down.

He knelt beside the would-be bomber and pulled open his coat. There were wires sticking up from the blocks of C4, but they didn't go anywhere. They were cut. The C4 wasn't connected to the detonator in his hand. There was no way the bomb could have gone off. Noah tried to pry the detonator out of the man's fist but couldn't. It had been glued around the detonator. He couldn't have dropped it if he had wanted to.

Everything about this stank.

He had killed an innocent man.

Noah couldn't afford to think about it.

Even as he knelt down to rifle the dead man's pockets, looking for a wallet or some form of identification, he knew he was missing something. Something important. Why did he keep walking? All he had to do was kneel down. He couldn't detonate the C4 strapped to his body, so why did he carry on walking? There was only one reason for that: someone made him. Noah scanned the piazza. There were literally thousands of people, and they were all looking his way. One of them had scared this man so much he had carried on walking even though he knew the next step would be the death of him. Which meant it had to be more than fear for himself that kept him moving. Noah scanned the faces closest to him as though he might be able to pick the monster out of the crowd. Real life wasn't like that. As long as the real terrorist in the square did nothing to reveal himself he could have been any Tom, Dick or Harriet looking at him.

"Close the square off!" he barked over his shoulder. He twisted to see the guard. The man stood rooted to the spot in shock. "Snap out of it! I need you to close off the damned square. The man who poisoned the city's here!"

"Where—" the guard started to ask when Noah cut him off.

"Move!"

The Guard snapped to attention and stepped back through the door. He picked the radio up from the table and called in what had just happened.

No one seemed able to believe what they had just witnessed. The bloodshed had shattered the sanctity of the place. Two more of the Swiss Guard had left their station and were running across the square toward them. He saw others moving, gesticulating that the piazza should be closed off. Behind him, Abandonato was rooted to the spot. A look of abject horror twisted his face. This was not in his philosophy. This kind of madness made no sense to the holy man. It was, however, the world in which Noah lived.

Noah used the frozen moment of shock to get things done.

He found a wallet and went through it quickly. There was no driver's license, no credit cards, no store cards or Blockbuster cards, nothing that might identify the man. The only thing in the wallet was a single piece of folded paper. He teased it out and opened it up. It had two short lines written on it: *We have tested your faith. Today we break it.*

He stood up and looked around the square again, slowly, his eyes moving from face to face. He didn't know what he was looking for, but he hoped to hell that he'd recognize it when he saw it. Horror? Fear? Shock? He chewed on his bottom lip. He had three thousand, four thousand possible suspects, and they were all just milling around like little lost sheep.

Then, halfway across the square, he saw a solitary figure leaning against The Witness. Their eyes met for half a second and, smiling, the man saluted him. The gesture was laced with irony so thick it smacked of loathing. The man, dressed simply in jeans, plain white sneakers and a gray tee-shirt and blue hoodie was utterly unremarkable with his close-cropped, dark hair and five o'clock shadow. He had wanted Noah to see him. He pushed away from the obelisk. He was well built, muscular. The gray material of the tee-shirt strained across his pecs and biceps. Possibly ex-military, Noah thought, watching the way he moved. The notion was only reinforced by that mocking salute. He turned and started to walk toward the thickest part of the crowd.

"Call Neri," Noah shouted, taking off after the man. He knew it was a trap, but he really didn't have a choice in the matter. He wasn't about to leave it to the jesters of the Swiss Guard in the motley to chase the man through Rome, and he wasn't about to let him disappear into the crowd. So even if it meant chasing him all the way into whatever trap he had waiting, that was exactly what Noah was going to do. "Tell him I'm about to get myself killed!"

22

THE BIRTH OF THE TRUTH

The ICE train from Berlin to Koblenz took six hours.

Konstantin Khavin chose the first airline-style window seat in the silent carriage. The seat backed onto the restroom, meaning no one could sit behind him and he could see anyone walking toward him. It was an ingrained habit. He didn't want noise. He didn't want people pretending they were important and talking into their mobile phones for the entire journey. He didn't want kids with their annoying little computer games chirping and bleeping at him. And most of all he didn't want someone sitting next to him and talking at him for six hours. He wanted to be alone with his thoughts, either looking out of the window at the world rolling by or with his eyes closed, pretending sleep.

The carriage was five degrees cooler than it was outside, and maintained at a constant sixty-eight by precision German engineering. The air was lifeless, pumped into the car as though it were an airplane.

Konstantin breathed deeply, letting the manufactured air leak slowly out of his nose.

Lethe had briefed him an hour ago. He had filled him in on everything the rest of the team had discovered. It was a lot to digest.

When Lethe finally stopped talking Konstantin said simply, "And I am to kill them, yes? That is what the old man wants?"

That was the Russian way. Already his mind was running through possible scenarios. He could walk into Devere's office and take him out of the picture. One bullet was all it would take. Not even that, men like Devere were seldom fighters. Konstantin could simply walk up behind him and snap his neck as brutally and efficiently as that. Or he could wait for him in the street, drag him down a dirty alley and leave him in a stack of garbage sacks for the rats to gnaw on. He could rent a car, run Devere off the road, then stand over his flashy sports car while it burned. There were as many different ways to die as there were hours in a year. The end result was the same. That was all that mattered.

There was a certain elegance to the Russian solution sometimes.

It would be different with Orla. Extraction not execution. It would need more thoughtful planning. He didn't have time to thoroughly case the area, so he would have to rely upon shock. Hit them before they had a chance to react. Come at night. Make lots of noise. Full of fury. In the dark of night fear was as good a companion as a second shooter. But he would need more than just his Glock 19.

Lethe killed the fantasy before he could lock the slide on the imaginary gun. "No. You're not to kill anyone, Koni. At least I hope you're not. The old man's got other plans for you. Devere's in Koblenz. He's the money—he isn't likely to do the thing himself, but he's going to want to watch what he's paid so much for. He won't be able to resist. It'll be like the Kennedy Assassination. Everyone will say 'where were you when the Pope got shot?' and Miles Devere wants to be able to say 'I was there. I saw the whole thing with my own two eyes.' Koblenz fits the prophecy—it's a city split by two major rivers, the Rhine and the Moselle—and the Pope is scheduled to be in the city for the next forty-eight hours before moving on to an engagement in Krakow. Your job is simple," Lethe said without a hint of irony. "You stop it from happening at all costs. Whatever it takes, Koni. Keep him alive. It's as simple as that.

"I'll be raising flags on the Bundeskriminalamt INPOL database. I'll give them every face from that photograph in Masada, every name from the dig. I'll build them as com-plete a profile to work off as I possibly can in the time, and meanwhile the old man will be calling in the cavalry. You won't be alone, Koni, but here's the kicker: you won't be able to trust anyone. As far as we can tell Orla spoke to no one outside of the IDF in Israel, and Mabus took her. If they can infiltrate the Israeli Defense Force, they can sure as hell infiltrate the BKA, or at least know how to pose as some down-at-the-heel German detective. Trust no one, my fine Russian friend."

"It will be just like old times," Konstantin said.

"I thought you'd like that," Lethe said.

Konstantin thought about it.

It made sense.

Orla was in trouble. But Orla was a big girl, big enough to look after herself. She had done it before, and she would do it again. She was a soldier. She was trained for this. She was resourceful. Capable. The old man had chosen her for a reason. He trusted the old man's judgment. For that reason he shunted her out of his thoughts. He needed to focus on the things he could influence.

"I appreciate the irony of the situation," Konstantin said, "but I do not like it. I would be much happier going to Tel Aviv and killing the men who have taken our girl."

"Me too, my friend. You doing the killing, obviously, not me. I could barely crush a wasp. Look after yourself, Koni. I'm going to send a data packet to your cell phone in a minute; it's got the Pope's itinerary on it for the next forty-eight hours—who he's meeting, where, and how he's getting there. I'll also send you the parade route. His Holiness is scheduled to lead prayers tonight in the Florinsmarkt. The dais is being constructed on the exact same spot where the gallows used to stand. Part of the prayer service will also be to sanctify the unholy ground. I'm thinking, if anything is going to happen, this is the most likely place. It's a crowded square overlooked on all sides. Plenty of angles of opportunity."

"Precisely why it is least likely, then," Konstantin said. "It is where security will be tightest. What about the parade route?"

"The cavalcade will run along the riverside and through the Old Town. The route's a little over three miles with plenty of meet-and-greet spots. It's going to be pretty exposed from what I can see on the computer screen. Hardly any of the streets have the same sort of blanket surveillance camera coverage we're used to, so I'm not going to be a lot of use when the shit starts hitting the fan."

"You do what you do, I will do what I do," Konstantin said, and hung up.

The rhythm of the wheels on the tracks was soothing. He found himself dropping into a thought pattern that coincided with the *duh-duh-da-duh duh-duh-da-duh* vibration that shivered through the floor beneath his feet.

Provided the train ran according to the schedule, he would arrive around two and a half hours before the Pope was scheduled to deliver evening prayers. That gave him a little time to walk the parade route, looking for possible vantage points a sniper might use and that kind of thing, but crowds would be gathering at the same time, making his job more difficult.

There was corruption here. The entire thing reeked of it.

Humanity Capital was big business. Devere Holdings was bigger business. That Miles Devere had been in Israel at the time of the quake and worked with the real Akim Caspi put him right at the middle of this particularly tangled knot Konstantin was trying to unravel.

He didn't doubt for a minute that Lethe was right; Devere would want to see the endgame played out, but he wasn't an ideologue like Mabus. Devere was a money man. Devere had money. Money bought people. It was a fairly simplistic worldview, but he'd yet to have it disproved. He had corporate muscle. He developed corporate strategies that exploited the system, and he loved the system quite simply because it allowed him to exploit it.

Mabus was a different beast entirely. He didn't hire mercenaries to prolong a conflict or bribe men to hit a civilian ward so that he could be hired to rebuild it. He wasn't a profiteer. He didn't need to be. He was a zealot, just like the Sicarii had been two millennia ago. And like any zealot he relied upon fanaticism as his stock in trade. Mabus had a single core belief: the Church was founded upon a lie. The man history loathed as the great betrayer was in truth the real Messiah, a religio-martial liberator who made his sacrifice out of love, sealing it with a kiss.

That belief had caused Mabus to bring together thirteen others and forge them as self-styled Disciples of Judas. Those thirteen had cast their nets out, recruiting others to their faith. Together they formed the Shrieks. Their purpose? The only one that made any sort of sense to the Russian was an attack on the very foundations the Catholic Church was built upon. After all Judas was their Messiah, not Jesus. Why should the world pray to the cross and drink the blood of Christ if his entire life was a lie? What salvation was there in that? It was a seductive way of reasoning.

He felt his phone vibrate in his pocket. He checked it.

Lethe's data packet had arrived. He opened it, checking the locations, dates and times, and realized there were far too many for comfort. Protecting the man was going to be a nightmare. Even without walking the parade route he knew there would be far too many places an assassin could hide. Modern sniper rifles made it possible for a skilled shooter to be so far removed from the scene that chasing them was next to impossible if so many of the variables of the murder weren't already fixed. So, of course, the last thing Konstantin was going to do was waste his time trying to protect the Pope. Besides, he had his personal guard, willing to take a bullet for him and earn their place in heaven. And of course, the entire BKA would be on high alert from the moment he stepped out into public. No, Konstantin would put his particular skills set to a slightly different use. As the old football adage went, attack was the best form of defense.

He would find the man and kill him before he could pull the trigger.

That gave him anything from three hours to two full days to find the assassin, depending upon when he had decided to take the shot.

The train rolled on. Konstantin found himself drowsing. He let himself slide into a shallow sleep. He had no idea when he might sleep again.

While he slept he dreamed in Russian. In his dream Mabus was the snake in the darkness, whispering with its forked tongue. He held his Glock but couldn't see what he was aiming at. And then he saw it, the snake coming out of the darkness. He pulled the trigger again and again and again, making the snake writhe. He shot ten, twenty, fifty, a hundred bullets into its cold skin. He was a snake charmer, making it rise. Then the creature arced forward and bit him. He fired and fired and fired again.

He woke with a start, lurching forward in his seat.

The ICE train was pulling into a town that looked like it

had been lifted straight from the fairy tale world of Grimms' fables.

The driver announced the next station. It wasn't Koblenz. He closed his eyes again. This time he did not allow himself to sleep. He was hungry, he realized. He couldn't remember the last time he had eaten. He walked along to the restaurant car and ordered a too-hot cup of black coffee and a microwaved pizza slice in a silver-lined box along with a cinnamon bun dripping white icing, and a candy bar. It was all sugar food. Fast energy junk. But he didn't feel like a sit-down silver-service dinner, which was the only alternative, so it would have to do.

He worked his way back through the train, rolling with the motion of the car as it leaned into the long curves in the track, until he was back in his seat. He sipped at the coffee. He ate the pizza in six bites, barely taking the time to chew before he swallowed, he was so hungry. He licked the stringy cheese from his fingers.

If he thought like a Russian, it made sense that the Disciples of Judas would want the Church's "papa" dead. It was a bold move. It was a strike right at the heart of their false messiah. It obeyed the Moscow Rule: come hard, come fast and leave them frightened. It was just like breaking down the door at four a.m. and dragging a man out of bed, naked, kicking, screaming and, most important of all, helpless. But more than that, with the eyes of the world watching, it turned the murder of one man into a spectacle.

The driver announced Koblenz Hauptbahnhof.

Konstantin wrapped the bun in the napkin it came with and crammed it and the candy bar into his pocket and moved toward the door.

He stepped off the train straight onto the set of a macabre morality tale straight from the Grimms' repertoire. It was fitting, given the gingerbread quality of the houses and the quaint narrowness of the cobbled streets. There were police waiting at the end of the platform. Instinctively Konstantin reached for his pocket for his papers. The fear was ingrained in him. It took him a moment to remember this wasn't Moscow and these men weren't looking for traitors to the Soviet cause. They didn't care if he was a defector, but it was hard for him to forget that he was exactly that. He walked toward the station house. Not too quickly, not too slowly. The policeman nodded slightly as he past. Konstantin inclined his head a fraction.

The station house had that unique railway station smell, a combination of flowers, fast-food grease, diesel engines and the desperation of a place where people were forever saying goodbye.

There were ten uniformed officers that he could see spread out across the platforms and the main entrance. In the few minutes it took him to walk across to the coffee stand beside the ticket office, buy a piping hot Americano that came served in a paper cup thin enough to burn the fingers, sit down on a bench and drink it, they didn't challenge a single traveler. He didn't know what they were looking for, but they obviously didn't see it in the faces of the bald businessmen, the skinhead in the torn Clash tee-shirt that said London was calling, or the woman in the high heels and A-line skirt whose powerful calf muscles turned all the heads as she walked by. They didn't see it in the bearded man in his college professor jacket with worn-out elbows, or the lanky student with his sunglasses and dyed-black hair that hung down past his shoulders.

He took the crushed bun from his pocket and unwrapped the napkin. The icing stuck to the tissue, the tissue stuck to the bun and then both stuck to his fingers as he tried to tease them apart. Konstantin took his time, savoring the bun. A tramp came and sat down on the bench beside him. He smelled as though he hadn't bathed in a month; it was that sour stench that reached down his throat and made him want to gag. Konstantin took the candy bar from him pocket and offered it to the man, who took it, peeled it out of its wrapper and ate it hungrily. Pigeons gathered around their feet. One hopped up onto the bench beside the tramp. A woman came and sat on the other end of the bench and started to read a newspaper. The tramp spread his arms out, trying to shoo the birds away, but that only brought more. Together they looked like a curious reworking of the Last Supper: Jesus, Mary, Judas and the birds.

Konstantin finished his coffee and threw the sticky napkin in the bin.

The police guarding the station watched him walk toward them. The timetables and maps were on the wall beside them.

They didn't stop him.

He took his phone from his pocket. At less than two inches squared the route map was almost useless, but it was enough for him to check up against the street map beside the timetables and ICE, Inter City and regional rail schematic maps. He studied the two for a few minutes, committing them to memory. "Do you need any help?" the nearest of the uniformed officers asked, seeing him staring at the street map.

"I'm fine, thank you," Konstantin told him without looking away from the map. The parade route followed the line of the Rhine for two of its three miles before turning in toward the Old Town. There were several landmarks, including, of course, the massive Ehrenbrietstein citadel on the opposite bank of the river. Then there was the aluminum factory and the automotive brakes manufacturing plant. Both had a lot to offer in terms of isolation, but without seeing them he had no way of knowing whether they presented a genuine shot. Office buildings, hotels, boarding houses—those were the kind of places he was most interested in. Places offering a view, which meant they had to be a few stories above ground level. That almost certainly discounted a lot of the older buildings of the Old Town, meaning the shooter would probably favor the new town with its wider streets and higher buildings. But again, he wouldn't know for sure without walking the parade route.

Beyond the main portico of the station a curious glass roof rippled out into the center of the main square. The road curved around a paved area. To the right of the entrance a bright yellow DHL van was collecting the day's deliveries. To the left was the short-term parking lot. It was filled with almost identical "people carriers" and family cars. Bicycles were chained up against every post that supported the glass roof. Even through the glass, the sky above was like some crystal blue mountain stream. Across the street was one of those chain-store cafés that had turned the simple pleasure of drinking a coffee into visiting an emporium. On the far side of the square he saw a building almost entirely constructed of glass. It might have been a design school or a fancy office block, he couldn't tell. It was at odds with almost every other building around it.

There were signs pointing every which way. He followed the pedestrian route down to the Rhine. The path divided into two, half for cyclists, half for walkers. There was no one for three hundred yards ahead of him. Konstantin took his time walking, looking left and right like a tourist drinking in the medieval architecture. A small café spilled out into the street. The eight wooden tables were empty, but two of them had dirty espresso cups on them and the corner of a napkin that fluttered in the wind. Next door, buckets of tulips, sunflowers, velvet-headed roses and other colorful bunches of flowers had been arranged around the doorway. There was a white handwritten sign in the door saying "Closed," but a striking middle-aged woman stood in the window, fixing the display. Seeing him, she smiled.

Konstantin smiled back. The windows of the first floor were dark, as there were no skylights. He turned to follow the angle of trajectory from the first floor as best he could, but it was far from ideal. In the shooter's place he wouldn't have used it. That was enough for him to dismiss it.

Down at a waterfront kiosk he bought a packet of unfiltered cigarettes. The man took his money. They exchanged pleasantries. Konstantin mentioned the barriers and the shopkeeper burst out laughing. "Where have you been for the last month, my friend? The Pope's coming to cleanse us of all of our sins," he said, still grinning. "In a few hours you won't be able to walk here for people. It'll be crazy." He didn't smoke, so he didn't have a lighter to light the cigarette he put in his mouth. The barriers ran all the way along the riverside. A few people had already taken their places at the front as though they were queuing for pop royalty at a sellout concert. They had their picnic bas-kets and neat little tripod stools. He liked the way a father took a chocolate bar and broke it into squares, giving one each to his wife and the two children.

"Any trouble?"

The shopkeeper kept on smiling. "Here? Trust me, the only reason kids hang around on street corners is because they're waiting for the lights to change."

Konstantin smiled at that. Most people believed the towns they lived in were safe, at least averagely so, but looking around him he knew he could probably take the shopkeeper at his word. There was some industry, so that meant there was probably some friction, and given the tight economic climate all across Europe, that friction probably escalated into the odd fist fight on a Friday night. Fairy tale twin town didn't look like it had a high instance of breaking and entering, car thefts or other antisocial crimes. There was very little in the way of graffiti that he had seen, even on the tunnel walls or along the wall that kept pedestrians back from the water's edge. Of course that could have been due to clean-up crews for the papal visit.

And as idyllic as it looked on the surface, plenty of nastiness could be happening behind those cookie-cutter windows and he would have been none the wiser.

Konstantin hopped over the metal barrier and walked down the center of the road. He intended to walk the parade three times before the Popemobile drove the Pope to the steps of St. Florin's.

Contrary to what he had told Lethe there was almost nowhere along the entire riverside part of the parade that would make for a good, clean shot. He walked over to the wall and looked across the water up at the citadel. If the shooter was up there, he didn't have a prayer. It made sense from a tactical standpoint. The Popemobile was a specially adapted Mercedes Benz M class SUV. There was a special glass-enclosed "room" built onto the rear of the vehicle. The glass would be bulletproof, of course, and the roof reinforced with armor plating. To pierce the glass, the shooter would need to be good enough to fire a fatal triangle—three shots in a triangle so tight they literally joined the dots. An experienced sniper would be capable of making the shot in the right conditions, but then it came down to trajectory, distance, wind, whether it was a moving target, reaction times of the security detail and all of these other intangibles the shooter couldn't know before he lined up the shot.

Taking the shot either as the principal entered or exited the protection of the bulletproof cage made more sense but lacked the spectacle. In an intense moment of paranoia he wondered if someone couldn't have tampered with one of the windows, prepping it for the shot? The agents riding along would be expecting the glass to protect the Pope. They wouldn't expect it to betray them.

He reached for his cell and called Lethe. "Two things," he said before Lethe finished saying hello. "One, get the security detail to triple check the integrity of the glass on the parade car. Two, run the utility bills on every address in a mile radius of the route. I'm thinking the shooter will have found himself a spot two weeks, ten days ago. He could be the kind of cold pro used to privation, but the guys in Berlin were a joke. Which means it is unlikely—but it's possible—that this guy might have turned the water on. No phone, the cell coverage is fine. Three, look for buildings that are supposed to be empty, leases out, that kind of thing."

Lethe didn't point out that he was only supposed to say two things, not three. "Will do."

The more he thought about it, the less likely it felt that he was looking for a shooter.

The window of opportunity was so small, and certainly this waterside route didn't offer more than one or two possible vantage points, which in itself discounted them because any shooter good enough to hit a fatal triangle on a moving target from the kind of distance they were talking about would be good enough to know that statistically only one or two possible vantage points meant, barring miracles, a zero chance of getting away from the scene. It was uncommon that really good shooters went on suicide missions.

Fanatics went on suicide missions.

This brought him back to thinking about Mabus and Miles Devere.

"Four things," he said, calling Lethe back up.

"Fire away."

"You've got Devere's cell, can you trace it?"

"As long as the battery is connected I can run GPS tracking, sure. Wonders of modern technology. There's no such thing as off the grid."

"Don't tell me you can do it, tell me where he is," Konstantin said. He turned the cigarette over and over again in his fingers. He could understand why nervous people smoked: it gave them something to do with their hands.

Lethe gave him an address in Jesuit Square, part of the Old Town.

Thirty minutes later Konstantin was staring up at one of the curtained windows, sure that the shadow looking back down at him through it was Miles Devere. There was a beautiful symmetry to it. Hunter and hunted locking eyes without either man quite knowing his role in the play of violence. Who was the hunter? Who was the hunted? It appealed to Konstantin's overdeveloped sense of the theatrical. He was the first to break eye contact, walking toward the building. He wondered if Devere even knew who he was. But of course he did, the Russian reasoned. A man like Devere had to be a control freak. This was his game. He wouldn't have been able to bear not knowing all of the pieces that were in play.

But how much did he know?

The answer, of course, depended upon how good Devere's people were. Konstantin Khavin's service record was sealed, as was everything Her Majesty knew about him, right up until the moment his feet landed on the western side of the Wall. But someone like Lethe would have been able to tell Devere what he'd had for breakfast the day before, the color of his boxers that morning, the last time he'd taken a dump and everything in between. And knowing Lethe, it would have taken him less than five minutes to gather those little gems of personal hygiene. So Konstantin had to assume Miles Devere knew everything two governments held on him and a fair bit beside. He had no idea how that would affect the way things played out, but a good strategist knew what he was going up against and planned accordingly. So again, Konstantin must assume Devere would be building his plays around a detailed knowledge of who he was up against.

Was it hubris on Konstantin's part to think that Devere would give a rat's ass about who he was and what he'd done during his forty-something years on the planet? If this was

Moscow, the answer would have been obvious—even in the microcosm of Nonesuch it was obvious—but out here where people played by money's rules? Devere had proven he could do whatever he wanted, and not even within reason. He wasn't averse to buying the guns that killed the men who built the house that Jack built, then he'd sold the mortars that razed the house, meaning someone else had to come along and rebuild it. It was all good business so long as you didn't care about poor old Jack. Devere had proven he could buy people as easily as he could buy places and things, and that he cared just as little about them. The oligarchs in his country were no different. Perhaps it was the gift of money that did this to people?

Konstantin walked up to the door. The small silver plaque beside it read Devere Holdings was on the third floor. Two of the other businesses in the house belonged to Devere as well. Only the restaurant downstairs wasn't part of his property portfolio. He pressed the buzzer and, when the voice crackled back unintelligibly through the small speaker, he leaned in and spoke into a concealed microphone: "Konstantin Khavin to see Miles Devere."

He counted to five, listening to the silence, when the door buzzed open.

Konstantin went in.

He hadn't intended to confront Devere and had no idea what he would say now he was inside the building. He walked up the narrow marble staircase rather than take the caged elevator, using the two minutes it took to ascend to formulate a plan. The next few minutes were going to be interesting, if nothing else, especially with the opening gambit he had in mind.

A pretty young thing stood in the open doorway waiting for him. She looked him up and down, then held out her hand as he stepped onto the landing. "Konstantin, Mister Devere is expecting you. Is there anything I can get you? Tea? Coffee? Something a little stronger?"

She had a disarming smile. He could easily imagine that smile making otherwise sensible, rational men moon about like love-struck fools.

"Water is fine, thank you," he said.

"Not a problem. Sparkling or plain?"

"Straight out of the tap is fine."

"Of course. Please, take a seat." She showed him through to a small reception area that was in complete contrast to the Old World charm of the rest of the building. It was all glass, steel and sharp angles. There were two black leather couches, one beneath the window, the other against the side wall. On the circular steel-framed coffee table lay the usual clutter of well-thumbed magazines. Other than the magazines there was nothing in the small room to suggest that business was ever actually conducted there. The pretty young thing came back through with his water, a bottle of Perrier along with a tall glass and a slice of lime. He'd had worse service in hotels.

Devere made him wait for nine more minutes. It was nothing more than cheap psychology, Devere attempting to establish dominance before they even met. Konstantin uncapped the screw cap on the water and poured himself a small glass. He sipped at it, then walked across to the window. He looked down into Jesuit Square, reconstructing the view in his head and reversing it. This was the window he'd seen Devere looking out of a few minutes earlier. Taking another swallow, Konstantin shifted his attention from the square to the waterside. Even given the relative elevation he couldn't see more than a few feet of the parade route at a time between the rooftops. For a sniper to take a shot from up here he'd need someone down on the ground giving him a countdown so he knew when to expect the converted white Mercedes to come into view and didn't end up snatching his shot. Even then, creating a fatal triangle to blow out the bulletproof glass was going to be virtually impossible in the fraction of a second the car would be in view.

At least he could discount the building as a possible base of operations for the shooter. No serious pro would deliberately take a shot three or four times as difficult just for the sake of convenience.

Behind him, Miles Devere entered the reception.

He knew it was Devere without turning. The weight of his footsteps was different. He could smell the cologne—too much of the stuff. And compared to the pretty young thing's, a considerably richer signature.

"Mister Khavin? It is Mister Khavin isn't it? How can I help you?"

Konstantin didn't turn. Facing the glass he said, "I believe you're planning on killing the Pope in little over an hour. I am sorry to be the bearer of bad news, but I thought it only fair to warn you, it's not going to happen."

"Oh? And why is that?" Devere said, seemingly amused by this turn of events.

"Because I am going to stop you," Konstantin said, reasonably.

Now he turned.

Miles Devere was a chiseled sculpture of a man; a David with too-soft features, too perfect a tan and one of those orthodontically enhanced smiles made for the glossy ad pages of *Vogue* and *Harper's Bazaar*. He was pretty, not handsome. Too pretty to be taken seriously, Konstantin thought, looking at the man. And too pretty not to be hated by half the people who ever saw it. It was the kind of face that no doubt got Devere whatever he wanted, whenever he wanted it, be it the smile from the pretty girl behind the shop counter or the head of John the Baptist on a plate. The world liked the pretty ones.

Devere didn't seem the least bit perturbed by the Russian's unexpected appearance in his office, nor his allegations. He licked his lips, his smile spreading. "How dreadfully exciting," Devere said. "Do go on, I love a good story. Come through, make yourself comfortable. I can't wait to hear how this one ends."

"There's only one way it can end," Konstantin said.

"Oh, do tell?"

"In tears," Konstantin said. He hadn't really thought of what he was going to say beyond this point. His sole intention in coming here had been to rattle Devere. It didn't appear that it had worked quite as well as he had hoped it might.

"Well, well, it seems we agree on something, after all. There was me thinking this was going to be a thoroughly boring afternoon. I do so hate waiting, don't you?"

They walked through to Devere's office, though office was something of a misnomer. It was like a geek boy's nerdvana, floor to ceiling gadgets. There was a miniature robot on his glass-topped desk that swiveled its head at the sound of their voices. The shelves were book-ended with silver Daily Planet globes. He noticed smaller memorabilia from other science fiction movies, and it took him a moment to realize they were all mechanical, like the golden androids of *Metropolis* and *Star Wars*, Maria and C3-P0, Dewey from *Silent Running*, Box from *Logan's Run*, Robbie the Robot from *Forbidden Planet*, K9 from *Doctor Who* and others he didn't recognize. It was strange that a grown man would surround himself with toys. The decor no doubt said a lot about Miles Devere the man.

"Sit, please, make yourself comfortable."

Konstantin sat in one of the two armchairs in the room while Devere sat behind his desk. It was another subtle power play, the desk between them, the slight height difference between the armchairs and the desk chair all combined to give Devere dominance over the situation. Konstantin didn't care. He sat back in the armchair, crossed his right leg over his left and breathed deeply, stretching the muscles of his back.

"Perhaps you could answer a question for me?" Devere

asked, quite reasonably. "Why, if you are so sure I intend to kill the Pope, would you come here and start annoying me? I am not quite sure I follow the logic of it."

"Because that is the way it is done in my country, face to face. Death is man's business, not a coward's."

"So you're saying you are going to kill me now? You really are quite unbelievable. What was your name again? I think I should learn the name of the man who is going to kill me, don't you?" Devere shook his head slowly, as though he couldn't quite believe what he had just heard.

"Konstantin Khavin."

"Konstantin Khavin," Devere repeated, saying it slowly.

"Yes. First I will stop your man, then I will come back for you. That is a promise. When you hear that first gunshot you should start running, Mister Devere, because the second one won't be all that far behind; and as the villain says in all the bad movies, it will have your name on it. I doubt that someone who still likes to play with toy robots will be all that hard to kill, no matter how much money he has. What do you think?"

"I think you should leave now," Miles Devere said. The smile had left his lips.

The meeting had been rash, and unwise, and so many other words that meant "really bad idea" but Konstantin couldn't help smiling as he walked out onto the street of Jesuit Square. He had enjoyed rattling Devere, but there was more to it than that. He called Lethe.

"Fifth thing," he said.

"Like the Hatter, five impossible things before breakfast. That's me, Jude Lethe, Mad as a Hatter."

"Trace every line in and out of Devere Holdings' office here from about two minutes ago."

"May I ask why?"

"I just told Devere I was going to kill him," Konstantin

said. Beside him, a woman turned and gave him the weird-est of looks, halfway between horror and embarrassment. She obviously didn't know if she was supposed to take him literally at his word—after all people threatened to kill each other every day and didn't actually mean it—and was clearly ashamed she'd been caught eavesdropping. Konstantin shrugged and she hurried off.

"Smooth," Lethe said. "Nothing like putting the cat amongst the pigeons."

"He's going to make a call, or he already has, depending upon how much I upset him," Konstantin said. "Find out who he calls."

"You know I will."

Konstantin hung up.

How the next hour or so would play out depended very much on who Miles Devere called. If he called the shooter, it would act to trigger one chain of events. If he called Mabus, it would trigger a very different one. And if he called someone else, then it would mean Konstantin really hadn't got the measure of who he was up against and would necessitate some thinking on his feet as he improvised a third one.

More people had begun to congregate for the papal visit. The parade route was beginning to look quite crowded. If Konstantin had judged the route right, and the crawl of the Popemobile, he had about half an hour before they reached here. Looking at the majority of them he found it hard to imagine any of this flock had a religious bone in their bodies.

The difference in the quarter of an hour or so that he had been off the streets was noticeable. He checked his watch. The parade ought to have started a few minutes ago. In a little over half an hour the benediction would begin.

Konstantin closed his eyes, recalling as best he could the layout of the city, and headed in what he thought was the direction of the Florinsmarkt. Five minutes later the phone in his pocket began to vibrate. He answered it. "Who did he call?"

"I love you, Koni, in a very manly way, of course. I don't think I've said it before, but I just wanted to make sure you knew."

"Yes, yes, who did he call?"

"Not one, not two, but, wait for it, three calls in as many minutes. The first was to the mothership in Canary Wharf, the Devere Holdings building. That one took me by surprise. It certainly wasn't the call I was expecting. The second was more interesting, to an unlisted pay-as-you-go cell phone which was part of a bulk order placed in London a month ago. I think it is safe to assume this one was to your shooter. The third call was the shortest of all of them, to a landline in Switzerland. Again the number's registered to another branch of the Devere corporate network; this time, though, it was one of daddy's."

"Spit it out."

"There you go spoiling my fun again. The third call was to the Humanity Capital offices in Geneva. Happy now?"

Not really, but he didn't say anything to Lethe. He needed to think. He hadn't expected Devere to call daddy—that threw his thinking for a loop. London made sense because it was the base of operations for the multinational concern; information would traffic through the hub and filter out to wherever it needed to be. Calling the shooter to warn him made sense as well. It was the call he had hoped to illicit with his impromptu visit. That was the call that told him he had read Miles Devere correctly. The man was used to being in control. He hadn't been able to resist checking in with his man.

No, what surprised him was that he had expected one of the calls up the chain to Mabus, meaning a number out in Israel. Tel Aviv, most likely. It was possible that Mabus was in either London or Geneva, but it was unlikely. Given the level of mystery around the terrorist's identity he couldn't imagine Devere entrusting that call to one of his grunts, especially considering Devere's psychology.

"Could you trace the second call?" Konstantin asked, still thinking.

Lethe sucked in a wounded breath. "I'll let you off this once, Koni, but only because I just professed my love for you. That's how good I am to you, remember that. *Could* I trace the call, indeed? Sheesh. Does a naked Pope shit in the woods?"

Konstantin said nothing.

"The answer you're looking for is 'of course' because he's Papa Bear, get it? Goldilocks? Sometimes I think my genius is wasted on you, Koni. Yes, I triangulated the signal from the cell phone to a building on one of the approach streets to St Florin's. Mehlgasse, number 13."

"Unlucky for some," Konstantin said, killing the connection. He pocketed the phone.

It took him seven minutes to cover the ground from Jesuit Square to Mehlgasse. It wasn't one of the streets cordoned off for the papal visit, making it ideal for the getaway. Konstantin walked along the sidewalk. The buildings rose higher here, up to five and six stories. He scanned row after row of blind windows as he walked down the street.

He checked his watch again. Less than thirty minutes before the benediction was due to begin. He didn't like the way time seemed to be accelerating on him.

There was nothing remarkable about number 13, nothing that said this was the house hiding an assassin. It was an utterly average facade, with row after row of plain windows. There were no balconies. He studied the top row of windows. A flicker of movement below caught his eye. A curtain moving in the window furthest from the Square. The window was open six inches. Enough clearance for a shot.

Konstantin turned, following the trajectory from the

window as best he could from below. The angle of the shot was tight. The shooter would only be able to see a fraction of the square itself, but he had a partial view of the stage that had been constructed. Assuming the steps up onto the stage were on the left, what the shooter had was an unobstructed view of the Pope as he climbed them up onto the stage and his first four or five steps across the red cloth toward his papal chair.

He pictured the scene, the white Mercedes Benz pulling up beside the dais, the Pope and his guard climbing out, and being escorted to the stage. For the short time it took to get from the car to the chair the old man was a sitting duck. The bottom of the street closest to the church square was blocked off. He saw two BKA agents standing by the barricade. Worshippers had come to stand beside them. By the time the Holy Father arrived the crowd would be twenty or thirty deep.

Konstantin looked back up at the window.

There it was again, the slight movement of the curtain as though whoever was behind it was checking the stage area obsessively. It was oddly amateurish, but not out of keeping with the debacle of their surveillance efforts in Berlin.

He counted the windows: fifth floor, forth window across.

He shielded his eyes, trying to see more of what was going on behind the glass, but he didn't have the angle to see much more than a patch of the ceiling.

He checked his watch again. Twenty-five minutes until the parade was due to reach the square. He thought about calling in to Lethe, alerting the BKA officers, playing it by the book, but not only would that have made a liar out of him, it would have risked compromising him. It wasn't only that he had told Devere he was going to stop the assassination, and then he was going to go back and kill him—which pandered to his overdeveloped sense of justice—his movements put him in Berlin before the sarin gas attack, and now he was here. It was too much of a coincidence, and he couldn't call on the Service to help him out. It also meant he was a prime suspect. They'd close off the road and rail, hit every lodging house and hotel, turning the place over. He was alone. Which meant making the best out of a bad job. It was as black and white as that, as far as he was concerned. That didn't mean he was happy with the situation.

He tried the street door. There was an intercom on the wall beside it. Assuming the buttons mirrored the layout of the building, he pressed his way down the line, skipping the buttons for the fifth floor. Thirty seconds later someone buzzed him in. It never failed. He tried to tell himself this was one of the good things about living in the West, but really all it meant to him was if he wanted to go on a killing rampage, statistically speaking, some idiot would let him into whatever building he chose. It didn't matter how secure or safe it was supposed to be.

Again he took the stairs, but as a precaution he opened the door on the cage elevator, breaking the circuit so it couldn't be called.

He climbed slowly and steadily.

He didn't draw his gun until the third-floor landing.

He carried on up to the fourth, the muzzle of the Glock 19 leading the way.

He stopped before he reached the fifth floor and leaned against the elevator cage. The steady rise and fall of his own breathing was the only sound he could hear in the entire stairwell. He moved up to the landing, keeping his center of gravity low, his stride powerful as he climbed the stairs three at a time. The stairwell came out in the middle of the landing. There were two doors to the right, two to the left. The two farthest doors opened into apartments that looked out over the back of the street, the two middle doors onto the front. The doors themselves were old-fashioned heavy wood, but the locks were nothing special. He could have bumped it in thirty seconds flat. Instead he put a shot right into the middle of metal ring and kicked it down. The wood around the latch splintered under the force of the blow and the door flung inwards, slamming off the wall.

He felt the timing ticking away from him.

Konstantin stepped into the apartment, gun aimed straight ahead.

The place had that musty unlived-in smell that only comes with months if not years of emptiness. The carpets had been ripped up, leaving bare wooden floorboards and, in places, patches of old newspaper that had obviously been used to line the floor before the carpets had been laid. They were yellow with age and brittle beneath his feet as he walked over them.

He checked left and right, clearing each room as he went.

The kitchen and bathroom were empty. He tore back the shower curtain. There was no one there. The shooter hadn't passed him on the stairs and he hadn't been able to call the elevator, so he had to be in the room. He stepped into the lounge, the room overlooking the corner of the Florins-markt.

It took him a split second to process what he saw.

There was a sniper rifle on a tripod by the window, a cell phone on the windowsill, a little, plastic toy robot dog that yapped while he stared at it, the sudden burst of noise star-tling him. He stepped back instinctively toward the nearest wall, cutting off the number of angles he could be attacked from. On the windowsill the sudden motion of the dog caused the curtain to twitch. It barked twice while he was watching, then fell quiet. There was nothing else in the room.

Heart hammering, he checked the two bedrooms.

Both of them were empty. There was no furniture and no cupboards for the shooter to hide in.

The apartment was empty, but it didn't look like it had

been abandoned in a hurry, unless the shooter had incredible discipline. There was no trash, no drink cans, no sleeping bag, nothing to suggest anyone had been in the place since the sniper rifle was set up on the tripod.

He leaned down, checking out the shot through the scope. It wasn't lined up on the stage or any of the area around it. In fact it seemed to be aimed at one of the five trees in the main square, a fair distance from the stage itself. It seemed odd to go to the effort of setting the shot up early and not have it lined up precisely, but it was possible the shooter had knocked it as he'd cleared the room. Or perhaps it was a superstition thing and he didn't want to aim at the target until there was something there to kill. He squinted at the tree itself and realized a dozen or more bird feeders had been strung up from the branches. The tree was hiding an entire flock of hungry birds.

That was interesting.

There was quite a crowd gathered in the square already. He checked his watch yet again, feeling like an obsessive compulsive. There was less time on it than before and no shooter. Individually, both facts were bad enough; together they were the worst of all possible worlds.

He checked out the gun itself.

That was when he knew for sure the entire thing was a set-up. There was a small timer set on the side of the stock and attached to the trigger guard. The timer was ticking down. It had 27 minutes left on it. Twenty-seven minutes would not only have placed the Pope in the square, it would have put him up on the stage. Konstantin checked his watch to be sure. The benediction was due to begin in 21 minutes. This gun was never intended to kill the Pope. Devere's call to the cell phone here had triggered the timer, setting everything into motion. It was like that kids' game, Mouse Trap. The shot would go off, itself triggered by the timer, the bullet would fly straight into the tree where it would startle the birds nesting there. The sudden explosion of movement and the ricochet of the gunshot would trigger panic in the crowd. In the seconds immediately after the shock of the gunshot someone close would then step in and kill the Pope while everyone else was looking frantically left and right for a shooter that didn't exist.

He took the cell phone from his pocket and called Lethe to fill him in.

"I hate to say it, Koni, but it makes sense," Lethe said in his ear. "Think about who we're dealing with here. If they've modeled themselves on the Sicarii, surely they'll mirror the Sicarii MO: get close, be trusted, and slip the knife in even as you're calling out for help."

"Great," Konstantin grumbled. "Trust no one."

He looked at his watch again: 19 minutes.

"What doesn't make sense is why Devere would trigger the remote timer immediately after your visit. . . . He must have known we'd trace it and find the gun. He's not an idiot, you said so yourself. You don't plan something as elaborate as this and then blow it on a single phone call."

"But it wasn't a single call was it? There were three. He played us. *Mudak*," he cursed in his mother tongue. "He hid the important call in plain sight, giving us something closer to home to worry about." He slammed the side of his fist off the window frame and cursed again. "Geneva!" he spat, the pain focusing his brain. "Swiss Guard! Every member of the Guard have to serve in the Swiss Army, right? That was the call. It's one of the Guard. The inner circle's been breached." Konstantin realized the implycations of what he had just said. He had 18 minutes before the papal cavalcade arrived at the stage, and the people he needed to trust the most to do their job, to protect the Pope, were the ones he could trust the least to do their job.

He looked out of the window. There were perhaps a thousand people congregated in and around the square now.

"What do we do?" Lethe asked.

The truth was Konstantin had no idea. He knelt and started to strip the timer away from the gun, but stopped. Devere had warned the assassin—that's what the call to Geneva had been about—but it didn't mean he had called the man off. But if the gun didn't go off, the assassin wouldn't strike. That was a stone cold certainty. If the assassin didn't strike in the next half an hour, when they knew where he was, he could strike tomorrow or the day after or the day after, anywhere along the pilgrimage's long road. And if he was right and the assassin was part of the Swiss Guard, he could wait until they were "safe" in the Holy See and no one would be any the wiser. No, this was the one place they knew something was planned to go down.

Knowing gave them a hand, if not the upper hand. There was a chance the assassin could take the gunshot to mean Konstantin wasn't as good as he was, wasn't as close. It was a risk. All he could do was get close to the stage. That way when the gun went off and the birds exploded from the trees in a flurry of wings and screams, he would be the one person watching the stage. It was a dangerous game to be playing, but he wasn't about to throw his hand in now.

"We use the Pope as bait," he said, realizing, even as he said it, the stakes of the gamble he was about to make. It wasn't just one man's life he was playing with here.

23

THE BEAST WITH 13 HORNS

He wore the dagger in a ceremonial sheath nestled beneath his left armpit.

The crowds cheered and waved their flags as they pressed up against the barriers, hoping to get a glimpse of the Pope. The noise of the people sent a thrill through his skin. It had been so long in the planning, so long since there had been honesty in the world. But it was coming. It was close. And when it returned they would have something to see.

His fingers strayed toward the dagger. He felt its weight so close to his heart. It wasn't an ominous weight. It wasn't portentous. Like his task today, it was an honest weight.

They had found the silver dagger in one of the suicide tombs unearthed by the earthquake at Masada. It had been returned to them while the world adjusted to the new millennium. No truth can lay hidden forever. That is the way of great truths.

The tomb had contained the desiccated skeletal remains of a man, along with a document. They had no way of knowing exactly what the roll of papyrus actually was, what it said and whose words they were, because by the time they had unearthed it, it had been in such a wretched condition the individual folios had fused together, forming a thick pulp.

But they had suspicions.

How could they not?

The world knew what had happened as the Roman legions had built their ramp up the side of the mountainside of Masada. It was the last fortress of the Sicarii, the freedom fighters bound to the service of the bloodline of the true Messiah, Judas Iscariot.

And on the day when they took their own lives and ended the bloodline, it had been home to Menahem ben Jair and his brother Eleazar, the grandsons of Iscariot. If either of them had penned the testimony, the wisdom it contained would be priceless. What truths might it contain?

But the papyrus was ruined beyond anything they had the resources to salvage. Mabus had wanted to try anyway. They had skills, they could find people they could trust. But the other man—the one who had taken the name Akim Caspi after they had found the dagger—had said no, that they could not risk the truth, so long lost, being destroyed.

Caspi had brought the truth to him, and entrusted the silver dagger to his care. He welcomed the truth, pledging himself to the Disciples of Judas. They didn't know the secret of the blade until they deciphered the Testimony.

They had turned it over to the Vatican's experts, knowing even as they did that there was no way the Church of Lies would release the truth it contained. That meant they would have to steal it back, but not until it had been restored and translated. It had involved careful thought and planning, like everything else, but because it was driven by truth, God had seen them through. Of course, he had never doubted. Why would He not want the truth known? After all it was His truth. They had put their own man on the inside, a priest who worked in the library. He monitored the restoration, then, when the text was ready to be deciphered, sent word to Caspi so he could send in his own expert to oversee the translation and spirit the Testimony out of the Vatican before the truth could be buried again.

The first revelation was its writer. What they had discovered in the hidden tomb was no less than the *Testimony of Menahem ben Jair*, grandson of Judas Iscariot, founder of the Sicarii zealots. Menahem ben Jair was the grandson of the true Messiah.

The second revelation came in the body of the text itself. Learning the truth had not been easy. There were levels of truth in the words: first the bloodline itself, Menahem son of Jair, Jair son of Judas and Mary, the same Mary Magdalene the Church of Lies had painted as a harlot. The truth played out in the garden at Gethsemane, where he begged Judas to stay strong, to deliver him to the Romans, knowing to do so would break his friend. How could any man ask someone who loved him to deliver him to death? Still faithful to his friend, Judas shared that last kiss knowing he was damning himself because of the guilt he felt; because he knew he would not be able to live with it.

He never met the son he fathered. But instead of being father of one he proved himself father of many. In that act of love not merely was Judas a saved man, he became the Messiah, the true Messiah in the Judaic tradition, the man whose sacrifice bought salvation for his people, the man who reunited them and offered them peace. There was nothing about Jesus, the Christian Messiah, being God the Father come to earth in the skin of a mortal man. The truths differed starkly.

This was the truth that Menahem had cherished and

held close, the promise he had made to Jair that he would never forget his grandfather's story, and in turn would not let the world forget. From that promise he had forged the Sicarii, men of the dagger, named for his grandfather's sacrifice.

The third secret had been the forging of the dagger, what it was made from and the truth it represented. The blade had been fashioned by Eleazar and Menahem in the armory of Masada from the silver shekels paid to Judas Iscariot, the coins that bought the sacrifice—for it was not a betrayal, not remotely, it was a sacrifice—that an entire religion was founded upon.

Even for its age, the dagger forged by Eleazar ben Jair was an exquisite piece of craftsmanship. To think this silver had been held by the true Messiah.

Again his hand strayed to the dagger at his side, lingering over the blade.

He wished he could read its story with his touch.

He wished he could understand it all.

Akim Caspi had found him in Geneva. He was young, impressionable, ripe to be imprinted with idealism. He had been drawn to Caspi. The man was enigmatic, but more than that he was inspirational. He talked about the lies of Matthew, whose Gospel sought to force the truth of Judas into fitting some Old Testament prophecy and how the Bible itself contradicted the death of Judas Iscariot. In the Acts of the Apostles he is said to have fallen down head first in a field and burst asunder in Akeldama, the field of blood. Matthew had Judas hang himself from a tree—and in doing so doom himself as a suicide to exile from heaven. He listened while Akim Caspi talked with such passion about how Matthew's words sought to bury the truth, how so much of these lies of the Church was founded upon were the reworkings of reality. Why paint Mary Magdalene as a whore if not to take away her importance to the true Messiah? Why not even mention Judas, most loyal, most beloved at all, in the Gospel of Peter?

That Peter did not mention Judas of course led others to believe the silver itself could not exist if the man himself didn't; after all, how could you buy betrayal from a man who had never walked the earth?

But why would anyone be surprised by this? Victors wrote the words remembered by posterity, which is why the *Testimony of Menahem ben Jair* was so fundamental to what Caspi believed. It was more than just words; it was the truth delivered first hand, truth that supported the Gospel of Judas itself. Jesus told Judas: *You shall be cursed for generations. You will come to rule over them. You will exceed all of them, for you will sacrifice the man that clothes me.* Matthew and Mark excoriate Judas: *Alas for that man by whom the Son of Man is betrayed. It would be better for that man if he had never been born. But who gains from these lies?* the would-be assassin asked himself. *Who gains from these twisted truths?*

Caspi had been passionate in his sharing, and he clearly believed his truth. And even now, with the white Mercedes Benz nearing the stage, the young Swiss Guard knew it was a truth worth believing.

It was a truth that made his heart race, his skin creep with anticipation. It was a truth that the world needed to know, needed to understand, simply because it was honest.

It had taken almost a year before Caspi had shared his plan with him.

It was a simple plan, filled with tragic symmetry.

Two millennia after the silver brought about the death of Jesus those same coins, melded now into the form of a dagger, would be used to kill the Bishop in white, the Pope of the Church of Lies. If Matthew wanted to twist lies about the Messiah to fit prophecies from Zechariah, then they would take prophecies of their own, from every man who had predicted the rise of the Antichrist, and use this death of the False Father to prove these prophecies true.

There were patterns within the patterns. The Prophecy of the Popes given by Malachy, the 12th-century Bishop of Armagh, offered 112 future Popes, according each an enigmatic phrase to identify them. The list, like all so-called prophecies, was enigmatic and open to interpretation, but there were truths in it that Caspi had identified. Truths that helped him believe their path was preordained, that now was the time. Those short phrases were important: Paul VI, Flower of Flowers; John Paul I, the Middleness of the Moon; John Paul II, the Labor of the Sun; Benedict XVI, the Glory of the Olive; and finally, the 112th name on the list, the final Pope, Petrus Romanus.

The signs all pointed to the truth. The Flower of Flowers bore the Fleur-de-lis on his coat of arms, the flower of purity and chastity. The Middleness of the Moon, Albino Luciani as he was born in Belluno, so close to *bela luna*, Beautiful Moon, reigned for only 33 days, dying before the new moon. The Labor of the Sun, born and died within a solar eclipse. The Glory of the Olive that would bring peace to a troubled world by demanding a sovereign state for Palestine, one might have reasonably thought, yet Caspi taught him otherwise. The Glory of the Olive, he argued, was the glory of the Olivet Discourse in the Gospel of Matthew, that the time of Tribulation was at hand. The prophecy of the Popes led them by the hand to the truth, that the true Messiah's return was at hand, the one who was everything this Christ of the Christians was not.

The car turned into the square and the faithful began to cheer.

His heart burned with the birth of the truth.

Soon the world would know.

Soon.

KNIFE
THEN - THE TESTIMONY OF MENAHEM BEN JAIR

He crept up behind the holy man. The air was thick with musk meant to hide the filth of humanity. Sunlight streamed in through the narrow windows and scattered across the floor like gold coins given up in offering to the greediest of gods. Yitzhak, the priest, was on his knees, hunched over before the altar, mumbling his devotions in the temple's inner sanctum. The holy man didn't break away from his prayer. He crept closer, listening to the shallow rise and fall of Yitzhak's breathing and the gentle rise and fall of his prayer. There was hope in it, love, and strength. In a matter of heartbeats there would be nothing but empty silence where all of that had been.

The Sicarii paused one step behind the priest.

Yitzhak turned and looked up, startled, hands clasped in his lap. "The god you believe in is a lie," he told the holy man. *They were the last words the priest would ever hear. Yitzhak's eyes blazed feverishly with fear as the Sicarii grabbed his hair and pulled his head back. In one smooth motion the dagger sliced across his throat. A death rattle escaped Yitzhak's lips. He clawed at the gash, trying to force the air and blood back inside the flaps of skin. But there was no salvation. The Sicarii released his grip and Yitzhak fell. He was dead before his corpse sprawled across the blood-slick floor.*

Menahem never did forget that promise. It burned inside him as the world turned and he grew into a man. It shaped everything he believed. It echoed in every act he performed and every decision he reasoned. In many ways his grandfather's truth was the core of the man he had become: bitter, brooding, a loner. Menahem ben Jair was an outsider. He took comfort in solitude. He drew strength from isolation. He called no man friend. He had no time for the sects and their new religions. There were thirty or more already in Jerusalem, everyone worshipping their own brand of messiah. Menahem didn't worship any false gods. He had a mind of his own. He believed one thing, one truth—that his land should be for his people. He had seen his father suffer. He had sat at his knee and listened to tales of the Pharisees spitting at his grandmother and calling her a whore for loving the wrong man.

And then they had killed Jair. That day had changed the boy into the man he was always destined to be.

Menahem ben Jair was Sicarii.

A dagger man.

The world might have turned him into a killer, but in his heart he still yearned to be the boy who had walked into the garden to listen to his father's lesson.

His mind raced. He looked down at his hands. Shaped like the wings of an angel they were coarse, hardened by life, but they were still beautiful. The blood was gone, but no amount of scrubbing with lye could remove its bitter iron tang from his mind. Still, it did not matter. He scrubbed them for a fifth time. It was strange . . . usually it was so easy to forget the faces of those he killed, but not this time. The face of Yitzhak Ari burned inside him. He saw it every time he closed his eyes. He couldn't get it out of his mind.

Menahem was no stranger to death, but this was the first time he had taken the life of a priest.

Yitzhak Ari's murder wasn't about faith or fury. It had another purpose entirely. The motivation was as coldly rationalized as the deed itself. His murder was a political killing. It was the opening gambit in a long game of murder and sacrifice where the glittering prize was freedom. The holy man's blood would be used to rally the faithful against the faithless. The Herodians and the other Roman sympathizers were already venting their outrage at the killing. They were already out in the streets shouting blue murder. Come sunrise that outrage would have brewed over into fervor and fury, and by dawn Jerusalem would run thick with blood.

It was that simple.

But there was still so much Menahem needed to think about, so much that could go wrong before then.

He paced back and forth. Behind him the door opened. The sun behind him transformed his visitor into a solid black silhouette. Menahem recognized his younger brother.

"What do you want?"

"Well, for one thing, I want you to stop pacing up and down like an old woman," Eleazar grumbled. "Anyone would think you were losing your nerve, brother."

"Just thinking," Menahem assured him, though thinking was different from remembering. Thinking was active, remembering was passive. Menahem was not one for passivity. He lived his life. He was committed to it. He made things happen around him. He did not sit back and simply allow things to happen to him.

"No you're not. I know you. You're stewing over what the mad whore said, aren't you? I know you. Look at me. Now listen. She wasn't a soothsayer, she was raving. Sickness had got into her mind and undone it. That's the difference. Not all madness is a glimpse of the future. Sometimes it's just plain old insanity."

"And sometimes it's not," Menahem said. In truth he wasn't sure what he believed anymore. And that, more than anything, disturbed him. He was used to a life of absolutes.

The mad whore, as Eleazar so colorfully put it, had come stumbling up the siege ramp to the gates of the Masada fortress that morning, and stood there, hammering on the huge wooden doors until her fists were bruised and bloody. At first they had ignored her, assuming she would go away. She didn't. Instead she had hit the doors all the harder. One of the others had emptied a slop bucket over her head, thinking it would shut her up. It didn't. She had kept on hammering away on the massive iron-banded doors.

Finally Menahem had opened the door.

Swathed head to toe in rags that barely hid the sores of leprosy, she staggered forward and clutched him by the scruff of the neck. "You'll be dead before sunrise if you kill the priest," she rasped. Her breath was rancid. "Listen to me, Menahem son of Jair, listen to me!" He pushed her away. She went sprawling in the dirt. She lay there, her dress hitched up around her waist, dirt getting into the open sores that wept down her thighs. "I have seen your death!"

"And I have seen yours," he said, turning his back on her. He slammed the heavy door. He stood with his back pressed against wood, breathing hard. He could hear her through the thick wood.

Menahem drew the beam down to lock her out. It didn't help. She was already inside his head.

Menahem and Eleazar walked out of the small room together and climbed the narrow stair to the ramparts of Masada. The wind howled around them. Despite the plain lying over a thousand feet below the mesa the stronghold was built upon, Menahem could still feel the sand in the wind as it hit his face. The wind had a name: Simoom. The poison wind. It was an apt name. The air was thick with dust. He watched, fascinated by the giant dust devils that were constantly being whipped up and scattered again. They could just as easily have been the ghosts of the desert, the souls he had sent on their way to oblivion. It was easy to see where stories of the great Djinn originated. All it took were a few superstitious minds, the baking desert sun, Simoom, and a supernatural force was born.

He rubbed at the coarse hair of his close-cropped beard. Eleazar was right; the woman's curse had gotten to him. Now that her words were inside his head they continued to worm away at his confidence. Doubt festered inside him.

There were no birds, he realized, staring into the lowering sun. He wasn't sure what that meant, but it was a rare enough occurrence for him to notice. Yesterday Menahem would have said he didn't have a superstitious bone in his body. Today all he could think was that yesterday he had been a fool.

"Walk with me, brother," he said, turning his back on the Dead Sea and the empty sky that rolled away into the middle distance. "It feels like tonight is a time for truth."

"You're not going to die," Eleazar said again, shaking his head.

"I am, you are, it's the one given in this life," Menahem said, managing a wry smile that didn't reach his eyes.

"Ah, so now you are a philosopher? Next you'll be asking if I ever consider the morality of what we are doing." Eleazar shook his head. He was more than a decade younger than Menahem. He could see his father in every line of his brother's face. Sometimes he suspected he could see the old man looking out through Eleazar's eyes, the similarity was that disconcerting.

"We don't have the luxury of worrying about morality while our people are still prisoners in their own land. If we don't kill them, they will kill us. That is just the way it is. Until we are free I am nothing more than the dagger in my hand."

"So, dagger, why don't you share this truth of yours, then?"

He did.

They walked a while in silence, Menahem gathering his thoughts. There was a lot he needed to tell, a lot that would have the ring of lies about it, and he needed his brother to believe. For the first time Menahem shared with his younger brother the truth of their grandfather Judas Iscariot. He showed him the thirty Tyrian shekels that were his legacy, and told the true story of the agony of the garden. After all these years protecting the secret, it sur-prised Menahem how good it felt to unburden himself and to have someone else understand.

"I want you to have the coins," he finished. "Take them, they are yours."

Eleazar braced himself against the wall, staring out over the plain. "No," he said, finally. "If what you say is true, we should use them to honor grandfather, not hide them."

"And how do you propose we do that?"

Eleazar thought about that for a moment. "We are Sicarii, brother. We are men of the dagger. What better way to preserve his truth than use them to commission the greatest blade ever?"

"Were you listening to anything I said? These coins are cursed. They cannot be spent. Grandfather couldn't even give them away."

Eleazar rubbed his thumb and forefinger across the stubble of his chin. He did not have an answer for that. What good were coins that could not be spent? They stood in silence for a few moments longer, until Eleazar grinned. "Humor me a moment," he said. "So the coins can't be used to pay a master weapons smith, but that doesn't mean the coins themselves can't be forged into a dagger, does it?"

"A silver dagger?" He thought about it for a moment. There was a certain righteousness to the idea, given that the coins—or rather what they signified—had been one of the major influences behind the founding of the Sicarii. To turn the shekels into a dagger seemed somehow fitting. But silver was such a soft metal, any blade made out of it would be almost useless. But then perhaps a dagger never intended to kill was even more apt a tribute to Judas Iscariot? "Let me think on it."

He lost the remains of the day in thought. The notion of the dagger appealed to him, so he had Eleazar light the forge fire and promised he would join him soon.

His mind refused to rest. All he could think about was tomorrow and tomorrow and tomorrow. It promised to be the defining dawn in the dagger men's struggle. The harridan's curse gnawed away at the back of his mind. In killing the priest had he damned them all? No. He refused to believe that. The plan was good. He had gone over it a thousand times. It was simple—misdirection, subterfuge and bloodshed.

Come first light the Sicarii would hit Jerusalem's supply lines. They would burn the fields and slaughter the cattle. Without food the city would collapse in a matter of days, forcing the people to turn on the besieging Romans. There would be no more weak men out there trying to negotiate peace for the hungry. They would be out there on the streets with one thought: food. That was the shadow play. It turned the eyes away from what they were really doing, and allowed the dagger men to disappear into the ghettos. Once they found the shadows they would be able to orchestrate the true rebellion from the streets, striking only to fade away before the dying was done. Again and again, like vipers, they would attack, sinking their steel teeth into the pilgrims as they shuffled toward the Temple Mount looking for salvation, hitting the priests and the soldiers and leaving them clawing at the dust as they bled out into the road. And they wouldn't stop until every last Herodian and Roman sycophant was either dead or driven from the city, leaving Jerusalem for the Jews.

It would be glorious. Righteous. More, it would be a fitting memorial for both his father and his grandfather, and would mean even more souls to join them wherever they were now. He refused to think of heaven or some beneficent Maker tending to the spirits of the dead. In Menahem's mind the afterlife was a place of torment and suffering, Gehenna, with the gates of *teshuvah* firmly closed. How could it be anything else, built as it was on lies? There was no caring Christian God, no everlasting life in *Olam Habah*. The only deity he believed in was vengeful, the one who brought the flood to purify his creation, who demanded Abraham murder his own son to prove his fidelity. That was the god who owned the afterlife, the god capable of imagining such hells as the great fiery lake that existed solely to burn the sinners.

And that was a god he could kill for.

Menahem stopped his pacing. The red sun was a fiery glow behind the mountains in the middle distance. This land was his land. He felt a fierce attachment to it. When he died he wanted his blood drained and poured into the dirt so that he could become one with it. Was the woman right? Would he join them in Gehenna tomorrow? Was that his fate? Curiously the thought didn't frighten him. It wasn't that he hadn't resigned himself to dying, more that he was at peace with it. He would leave the world a better place for his people than it was when he had entered it. That was all any man could ask of his life.

Menahem disappeared into one of the dark tower doors that led out of the sun. His footsteps echoed as he rushed down the spiral stair. The air was different, older. It was so much colder than outside, his scalp prickled and his skin crawled. It was only a few years since they had taken Masada by force. The blood of the Romans still stained the sandstone where it had been spilled. It leant the stairs a second set of shadows. How many ghosts still walked the walls? How many death rattles did the old stones remember?

At the bottom of the stairway the passage opened up into an antechamber. Like much of the fortress, the room was devoid of any decoration. There was an archway, lit by flickering torchlight. A draft blew through from outside. Beyond the arch three doors led off into other rooms. Another stair led down deeper to what had been the Romans' dungeon, and a passage led toward the courtyard. Menahem followed the passage. The torches in two of the sconces had burned out, leaving dark shadows in their place. The passageway curved slightly, following the contours of the mesa. Around the corner, the passage branched into a second one, which in turn led out to the courtyard.

The heat hit him immediately. The temple stood in the shade of Herod's three-tiered, round palace. When they had taken the fortress they had stripped it of much of its luxury. The bath house had fallen into disuse. The huge palace itself served as barracks for the assassins. Menahem hurried across the courtyard. Like Herod's great temple in Jerusalem, this one had a variety of entrances. Even here the servants could not worship their Lord side by side with their masters. There was a door for the women, a door for the first-born sons, a door for the priests with their offerings and a door for the commoners. The Sicarii had stripped the temple of all religious trappings and turned it into a sheep croft for no other reason than it amused them.

He pushed open the temple door and went inside.

The air was hot. Uncomfortably so. And it stank of animals. Eleazar had brushed the straw away from around the altar. Behind it sandstone bricks had been built up around a wooden fire to trap the heat. The wood had already burned down to charcoal. His brother was hunched over the fire, feeding it.

Eleazar was the Sicarii smith—the dagger men's dagger maker. He moved with quiet economy, every movement precisely measured. He didn't look up as his brother entered. Menahem saw he had made a crude sand cast to pour the molten silver into. It would give the dagger its basic shape. The smith's hammer lay on the altar. On the floor beside the altar was a bucket of luke-warm water.

Eleazar took the silver coins from Menahem and emptied them into the crucible and fed them to the fire. It didn't take long for the metal to begin to fuse together. Eleazar removed it from the fire, allowing it to cool slightly, turning his wrist so that he could better see the lump of metal the coins had become before replacing it. This time he left it there until molten, then took the crucible from the flame and emptied the swirling silver liquid into the form. The metal began to solidify immediately, swelling to fill the bar-shaped cavity hollowed out in the sand. As it cooled it lost its luster.

Menahem lost all concept of time as he watched his brother take the silver bar with tongs and beat the metal flat, turning it over and over, each hammer blow shaping it a little more. Sweat dripped from every inch of his brother's skin. The veins stood out angrily against his muscles. He didn't stop for a moment, not even to wipe the stinging sweat from his eyes. He returned the silver to the fire, heating the metal until it began to soften and lose its shape, then moving quickly laid it flat on the altar. He took up the hammer and beat it towards its final form. Again and again he turned the silver, beating first on one side and then on the other, flattening it and putting an edge on the blade until even to Menahem's unskilled eye it began to resemble the dagger it would become.

"As silver is melted in the middle of the furnace, so shall you be melted in the middle thereof; and you shall know that I, the Lord, have poured out my fury on you," Menahem breathed, the words of Ezekiel's ministry becoming a prayer on his lips as Eleazar folded the silver, heated it until it was malleable, then beat each fold flat. Each new layer of folds offered the blade more strength.

The sky through the temple window was dark. It could have been any time in the long night.

Eleazar worked on while Menahem watched, fascinated by his brother's skill. Finally, he was done. He wrapped the hilt with leather, and the dagger was finished.

Menahem took it from his hand.

The blade was curved slightly to resemble a serpent's tail. The rippled effect on the flat of the blade caught in the moon. It appeared almost as though it had been etched into the metal. There was a beautiful subtlety to it. More, he thought, examining it, there was a truth to it. The blade was strengthened by what appeared to be imperfections in its surface but were in fact the whisper-thin layers between the metal.

The dagger was much like the man wielding it.

Menahem was tempered by the heartbeats of happiness, those fleeting moments of joy and the agonies of disappointment hammered flat around his soul like protective armor.

"It's beautiful," he said, holding the dagger reverently.

"How could it be anything else?" bragged Eleazar. "It's forged from the coins that paid for an entire religion.

25

KILLING IN THE NAME OF
Now

As he reached the square Konstantin realized the extent of the crowd. It wasn't just people lining either side of the street anymore. More than two thousand people had crushed into the small square to witness the benediction. They were talking, excited. It took him a moment to realize what they were saying. The murmur ran through the crowd: "Papa is coming." He looked at his watch, then up at the huge clock above the door of St. Florin's church. It was a pointless gesture now. The clock on the church's facade and his watch said the same thing. Time had run out.

He looked around at the faces of the people. He knew what he was looking for. It was a curious truth that you could see people steeling themselves to kill. It wasn't just the perspiration; it was in the eyes. They tended to stare straight ahead, focusing on something directly in front of them, unable to look away from it. They didn't glance around the crowd, which was a natural thing. People's minds were curious; they were drawn to look at all of the different faces, but not someone about to commit murder. A killer's focus was absolute. It was understandable with a suicide bomber, not wanting to see the faces of the lives they were about to end, but with a killing like this, in front of the eyes of the world, it wasn't guilt and shame that kept him from looking, it was determination. A man driven to this kind of murder was almost assuredly driven by fanaticism. Be it the West Bank, Madrid, or the Twin Towers, religion was at the root. Religious extremists, knowing that they were about to die, would be offering a prayer to their chosen deity, squaring it away with them one last time before meeting face to face. So he was looking for someone staring straight ahead, lips moving as they mumbled their final prayer.

He looked up at the guards assembled on the stage. Every one of them stared eyes front. They didn't look left or right. They didn't glance down at their shoes.

He was too far away to see if any of them was perspiring unduly, but given the weight of their brightly colored uniforms and the weight of the halberds they held, and the fact that if the BKA had done their job and spread the warning to them that there was an assassin in the crowd, it was a safe bet they were all sweating more than usual.

It was a curious thing, how so many people put so much of their faith in an old man who couldn't speak their language and had no real way to relate to their lives. Every kind of person was out there in the crowd waiting for the cavalcade to go by.

Konstantin pushed his way into the crowd. There had to be agents in there. If Sir Charles had called in his favors, the entire congregation had to be crawling with BKA men. He saw bikers in their leathers, mothers in summer dresses stooped over their strollers, and boys in German soccer jerseys, and those few desperate enough to come looking for a miracle, hoping Papa's touch might help their children stand up out of their wheelchairs and walk. He didn't see anyone who was obviously police. He didn't see anyone overly anxious. He didn't see anyone moving sluggishly, either drunk or stoned. That was another thing, a man about to commit suicide, no matter how faithful he was to the cause, didn't want to be having second thoughts. So more often than not they would be under the influence of some narcotic stimulant in those final minutes. He looked back at the guards on and around the stage. For the life of him he couldn't see the difference between them. There was no one man who seemed more stressed or less alert than the others.

Konstantin pushed his way through the people, trying to work his way closer to the stage. He wanted to be right at the front when the gun fired its round into the tree. He looked up at the other trees in and around the square. Each one had been strung with the same bird feeders. They were full of birds. He didn't know if that meant there were more guns primed to fire into these other trees, or if they were relying upon the domino effect to carry the startled panic from one tree to the next.

Down the line he heard voices singing hymns. There was something about songs of praise that lifted the voices of even the worst singers and made them beautiful when they came together.

The murmurs of those closest to him intensified as a car came slowly down the middle of the road and turned into the square. It was a black BMW with its windows blacked out. It was the trailblazer. Konstantin watched it approach, trying to think of ways he could get close to the agents in the car to identify himself. It didn't slow and it didn't stop. He watched it pass him and then follow the curve of the railings to park behind the side of the church, out of sight.

Two more cars followed it a few minutes later.

A fourth car came. The sun glinted off the tinted wind-shields. Four agents walked beside this one, keeping pace with the black BMW. They scanned the crowd, never once allowing their gaze to settle. They were alert. They knew there was a threat. The old man had done his part. The warning had reached the BKA. That was all he could do from Nonesuch; the rest was up to Konstantin. The movement of the agents was synchronized. When one looked left, the other looked right so that together their field of vision was complete. There were no blind spots. They moved with an easy strength, but he could see the tension in their bodies. They were primed, ready for the slightest noise, the first sudden movement; anything that was out of place. They were trained to read the crowd and recognize the signs. More than just body language, this was about the split second between life and death.

A hundred yards after the car came the first of the foot patrol, Swiss Guard walking in their ceremonial uniforms like a marching band. They didn't look half as professional, aware or as imposing as the BKA men to Konstantin's trained eye. He knew that the Guard were professional soldiers, but there was something cartoonish about their appearance that made it easy to underestimate them—which made it the perfect cover for his assassin.

And then the crowd in front of him burst into cheers and applause as the Popemobile came around the corner. Konstantin's heart sank. He was still less than halfway to the stage. He felt the weight of people press up behind him and tried to go with it, hoping it would carry him through a few ranks closer to the front, like riding a crowd at a rock concert. He dropped his shoulder slightly, turning side on to the stage. He didn't want to start pushing people and making a scene, but he would if he had to.

The converted Mercedes Benz turned into the square.

Konstantin could see the white-haired old man in his seat waving slightly to the people as the car drove by. He looked serene, beatific. Even behind the glass there was a calm about him that touched the crowd. All of the crowd save Konstantin. His nearness only heightened his sense of desperation. He needed to get to the front. He needed to be there.

The car swept around the skirt of the crowd, already halfway to the stage.

Konstantin abandoned any pretense of calm and forced his way between the people in front of him. He knew what it would look like to the BKA agents. They'd see a desperate man forcing his way to the stage. They'd see his determined stare, his perspiration and his erratic breathing, and they would think he was their man. He lips weren't moving, but he had no way of knowing just how good the agents actually were, and whether they would see the difference between a man trying to do everything in his power to stop an assassination and an assassin fixated on the kill.

There were fifteen or sixteen rows of people between him and the stage.

"Excuse me, sorry, excuse me, danke," he said, pushing his way between a young family come to see the service, when he realized his lips were moving. They were moving all the time, his apologies like a mantra that from a distance would almost certainly look like a fanatic's prayer.

He shoved the back of the man in front of him, forcing his way between him and the woman at his side. The man stumbled forward, reaching out for support and shoving the man in front of him as he tried to catch his balance. The effect of the shove rippled throughout the crowd. Konstantin tried to duck away from the man as he turned to face him. He barked something at him in German. Konstantin ignored him. He only had eyes for the stage. He knew people were looking at him. He didn't care. He had maybe two minutes before the Pope walked onto the stage, six more until the gunshot was timed to go off and all hell broke loose.

He risked a backward glance, up in the direction of the window of number 13 with the sniper rifle, then stared straight ahead.

There were three television cameras, one set up on a crane, the other two on the left side of the square, looking out at the crowd. One of them seemed to be pointed directly at him. He realized that back in the mobile broadcast control trailer some very anxious people were staring at their screens, seeing him, and fearing the worst.

The Popemobile pulled up alongside the red carpet that led up to the stage steps. Two BKA men, bulky beneath their well-cut suits, moved quickly toward the back of the car and opened the door, stepping back so the Holy Father and the two Swiss Guards sitting inside with him could emerge. The guards were the first out. The second man turned and held out a hand for the Pope to take to steady himself as he walked down the short flight of steps, then stepped back as he turned and held his hand up to the crowd in blessing and welcome.

Konstantin's view was partially obscured. He could only see the Pope from the collar of his *Fanon*, the two superposed cloaks sewn together around his throat, and up. The precious miter, his conical headdress meant Konstantin could follow him as he walked through the crowd and climbed onto the stage. A papal throne had been set up in the center of the stage, and the Swiss Guard assembled at either side of it.

On the top step, the Pope turned to the people, again holding out his hand as they cheered and applauded. It struck the Russian as dreadfully wrong that a holy man should be accorded the same sort of frenzied welcome as a pop star.

He was six rows from the front.

He needed to be closer, but the people were packed in so tightly now he found himself having to move sideways along the line as he looked for a gap to squeeze himself through.

Up on the facade of St. Florin's church the huge iron minute hand of the clock juddered forward another minute, coming to hang over the Pope's head like some huge sword of Damocles. Konstantin was breathing hard, forcing himself to keep it regular: *in and out, hold, in and out. In and out, hold, in and out.*

He knew exactly what he looked like.

He didn't care.

In six minutes the Pope would be dead if he didn't stop it.

The Vicar of Christ walked to the center of the stage, coming up to the microphones. He leaned forward and, holding both hands up palms toward the congregation, said, "Thank you." He spoke in English, not German, not Latin, and not his native Italian. Up close Peter II, the man they called Peter the Roman, was older than he appeared in any of the photographs Konstantin had seen of the man. Indeed, he had aged since his election to office on the death of Benedict XVI a little over a year before.

Five minutes.

Peter II crossed himself then leaned on the lectern, supporting himself by grasping both sides of the stand. "Dear brothers and sisters," the Holy Father said, his voice carried by the microphones to the far reaches of the crowd. He offered them all a smile. Konstantin's eyes roved wildly from the Pope to the faces of the guards around him, looking for the traitor. "This evening we share between us is truly extraordinary, not for the sky beneath which we stand, nor for the friends at our sides, for both of which give thanks, but for the blazing light of the Risen Christ, which defeats the darkest power of evil and death and rekindles hope and joy in the hearts of believers. Look to the sky, see the failing sun and the rising moon, their light never fails us, for theirs is the light of the Risen Christ.

"Dear friends, let us pray together to the Lord Jesus so that the world may see and recognize that, thanks to his passion, death and resurrection, what was destroyed is rebuilt; what was aging is renewed and completely restored, more beautiful than ever, to its original wholeness." He lowered his head.

Everyone in the crowd did likewise, except for Konstantin, the BKA agents and the Swiss Guard on the stage.

Konstantin forced his way closer to the stage as the murmured prayers rose to exhort the heavens. Konstantin had a single prayer on his lips, but God wasn't listening, and the press of people mocked him. He risked a sideways glance and saw two of the black-suited BKA men pushing into the crowd behind him, and another running along the side toward the stage. They were hunting him. They hadn't drawn their guns. Yet.

He was two people from the stage.

The guards on either side of the Pope stared at him.

Konstantin stared back, trying to read murder in their faces. Any one of them could have been capable of the killing. That was the chilling realization he had as he got close enough to really see them. They were the same. Face by face there was nothing different in the way they looked at him. Any one of them, or all of them, could have been the assassin.

Or none of them.

He could be wrong.

No. The Sicarii made themselves invaluable to their targets. They stood at their side as best friends, then slipped their daggers into their "friends." This place, this crowd was perfect.

But that didn't mean he couldn't have been played by Devere, steered into another mistake—this one fatal. The man was playing a long game, and each move was thoughtful and well planned. The set-up here was perfect. It could have been a fake, luring him into the open, turning him into the "assassin" and allowing the BKA to take him out, allowing the Pope to die another day when their guard was down.

He glanced to the right and saw two more BKA agents running along the side of the crowd, following the route the cars had taken to the stage. The pair had their guns drawn and held low so as not to startle the crowd.

They were staring at him as they ran.

He pushed between another couple with their heads bowed in prayer. He didn't let them slow him. He couldn't afford to. He looked up at the big clock. He had a minute. Two. It was difficult to tell precisely. There would be a small disparity between the timer, his watch and the church clock, but he had no way of knowing precisely how big it would be until the gunshot came. And by then it would be academic.

There was less than a minute.

He reached the stage as the first of the BKA men reached the steps.

Four things happened at once. The gunshot cracked, followed a fraction of a second later by two more, and the trees exploded in feathers and fear, a hundred birds startled into flight. Peter II's head came up, his prayer broken. There was naked fear in his eyes. He knew the sound. Of course he knew it; it was hard-coded into the DNA of every man, woman and child under the sun. He stopped talking, so the speakers all around the square fell silent. There was a lull for a heartbeat as the shock registered, then people reacted, torn from their prayers by the unmistakable sound of the gunshot. At first there were screams of shock as the birds exploded from the trees, then the screams changed in nature and pitch from confused to frightened. On the stage the Swiss Guard reacted, lunging forward to protect the Holy Father. Konstantin saw the glint of silver in the nearest guard's hand.

He couldn't let the man reach the Pope—even though that meant throwing himself up onto the stage.

Konstantin shouted out a warning as he hit the red cloth of the stage.

He thought a second silent prayer then, gambling that the BKA agents wouldn't take a shot through the crowd for risk of hitting some innocent bystander. In their place he would have taken the shot, risking the collateral damage to protect the principal. He had to hope they were better men than he was. Because that was what it was going to come down to: How much did they value human life? Pope Peter II's, his, the crowd's? For this instant, this second, everything hung in the balance. Another shot would almost certainly cause a stampede as frightened people ran for their lives, and in such a tight enclosure more than a few of them would be hurt in the crush.

Konstantin hit the stage and rolled, coming up on his knees, hands pressed flat against the red cloth.

Two of the Swiss Guard reacted while the others seemed trapped in indecision. They came forward to stop him, halberds leveled at his chest. The only other guard moving reached the Pope and seemed to be protecting him from the madman that had rushed the stage. Konstantin saw the silver dagger clenched in his fist.

He didn't have a choice. He didn't even have time to reach around and pull his Glock. All he could do was launch himself toward the Pope and pray his momentum took the pair of them out of the range of the Judas dagger.

He threw himself at the pair of them full on, hitting the old man in the chest, both hands hard to the ribs and barreling him off his feet. The collision sent all three of them—Pope, assassin and savior—sprawling. Konstantin fell on top of the old man, his weight throwing him down hard. They landed on the red carpet together. All around them screams and shouts erupted. He couldn't hear any individual words. He didn't need to. There was no doubting what they were for.

It didn't matter.

He had done it. He had reached the Holy Father in time. He had beaten the clock, beaten the assassin. He had saved

Peter II's life. He closed his eyes, waiting for the hands to grab him and haul him off the white-haired Pontiff. He felt the man breathing beneath him. It wasn't a smooth regular rise and fall of the chest; it was erratic, desperate, like a man struggling desperately to draw his next breath.

Konstantin rolled away from the old man.

It wasn't his weight that had winded the priest.

There was blood on his hands when they came away from the Pope. He looked down at him. The old man lay sprawled across the red of the stage. It took Konstantin a second to see it. There was blood where the silver blade had pierced the Pope's white cassock. The hilt of the damned dagger jutted out through the purple tippet wrapped around Peter II's neck, driven in through the gold cross woven into the cloth. There was a lot of blood, too much. The gold and purple quickly stained red as the blood pumped out through the wound. The Holy Father clutched at the dagger's hilt. His lips moved. Konstantin heard the barest whisper of a prayer on his lips: *"Father, forgive . . . know not . . . what . . ."* It was the last prayer of Jesus as he hung dying on the cross, the prayer to his father to save the souls of his murderers.

Konstantin crawled toward him, unable to believe what he saw.

The entire front of his white cassock was stained red with holy blood.

The Vicar of Christ looked up at him without seeing him. His eyes already had the gloss of death stealing over them.

Konstantin was too late.

There was nothing he could do.

After everything, he had failed. He lifted his head to the sky and screamed one long terrible roar of guilt, agony and despair. He had come so close. Close enough to cradle the dying man in his arms as the BKA agents rushed the stage. "Please," Peter the Roman said. Konstantin didn't know what he meant, what he was asking for. The old man swallowed and the light in his eyes went out. He was dead.

Konstantin tried to pull his hand out of the way. The last thing he wanted to do was contaminate the evidence. But even as the Pope slumped into his arms and his blood soaked into his clothes, the knife clattered to the ground. The blood spatter fell like a handful of coins on the red carpet. He didn't need to count them. There would be thirty. Thirty splashes of red life to mark the betrayal.

The BKA men ran at him, guns aimed at his face and body, yelling, "Get down!"

"On your stomach!"

"Down!"

"Get your hands where we can see them!"

He saw their guns and the rage in their faces.

There was hate there. Burning. Blazing.

Outrage.

Each one of them wanted to pull the trigger.

And who could blame them?

Konstantin reverently lowered the dead man to the carpet. He didn't look at any of the others on the stage. He didn't hear the screams of the onlookers. He put his hands behind his head, interlacing his fingers.

The Judas dagger lay on the red carpet beside him, blood on its silver blade.

The Swiss Guard who had delivered the fatal blow looked at it, then at Konstantin, at the blood on his hands; and the ghost of a smile reached his lips as he cried, "Murder!"

Konstantin stared at the man, memorizing every inch of his face.

And then someone hit him from the behind, taking him down.

They pressed his face into the bloody carpet and stretched his arms out. Someone hissed in his ear, "Just give me an excuse to pull this trigger."

Konstantin closed his eyes and waited for the bullet.

He didn't realize it was happening until the man closed his hand around the dagger. Even with his weight pressing down on to his back he flinched instinctively, the blade lying inches from his face, smeared with bloody finger-prints.

26

SEVEN FOR A SECRET

Noah ran, head down, as he raced across the cobbled streets. He was gasping hard.

He had been chasing the joker for the best part of five minutes. It was a long time to run that hard. He knew every twist and every turn of the streets, which meant he was local, well enough acquainted with the city to know all of its byways and backstreets. Noah pushed between tourists looking at their street map and didn't slow down as they shouted at his back. The guy was fast. He wasn't just fast, he was lithe, agile, fit. He went over low walls as easily as a grease monkey up a pole and came down on the other side already running. Noah was out of shape. He hadn't realized just how badly until the clown led him a merry dance past the steps of the Castel San Angelo. They had run an entire circuit around the Vatican walls, the length of Via Vaticano and through Piazza Risorgimento, dodging traffic down Via Crescenzio and through the shadow of Archangel Michael's sword to the River Tiber.

As Noah chased the asshole, he ran all the bad names under the sun through his head, dickwad, dirtball, slimebag, scum bucket, prick, spitting them all like arrows at the guy's back.

He raced the length of Piazza Cavour and over the Cavour Bridge. Noah stumbled as he came to the steps that led the way down beside the bridge, looking left and right. Somehow he'd lost the son of a bitch. There were five roads he could have taken, three that fanned out into the heart of the old city and the labyrinth of close-pressed houses or two that ran along the river. Then he saw a bundle of clothing beside the foot of the bridge. He ran down the short flight of steps. It was the hoodie. He scanned left and right along the riverside, looking for a flash of gray from the bastard's tee-shirt. He was still running all of those names through his head, biting on them.

Then he saw him. He had slowed down and was walking as though he hadn't a care in the world. Had he not glanced back to see if Noah was still chasing him, he might have gotten away with it. Swallowing a deep breath, Noah set off after him.

Like Lot's wife, the asshat glanced back over his shoulder one time too many, saw Noah coming for him and bolted. The names were still coming thick and fast, and he was getting more and more inventive with them. The short walk had given the dick munch whatever rest he needed to gather his second wind. Noah raced, arms and legs blur, along the river bank past the first two bridges, then hurdled over the iron rail and took the steps up to the Vittorio two and three at a time.

If he hadn't wanted to take the guy alive, he would have pulled his gun and put a dozen slugs in his back out of spite. He really didn't appreciate the workout. As it was, he needed to get information.

It was all Noah could do to keep up.

It took him a moment to realize the tool was doubling back on himself to the broad street of Via de Conciliazoine, which in a few hundred yards opened back up into the elliptical ring of the Piazza di San Pietro, where the suicide bomber still lay in the street. He could see the tall obelisk of The Witness mocking him as every muscle in his body burned, and beyond it the ambulance and the crowd that had gathered. Gritting his teeth he tried to close the gap between them, forcing a burst of speed out of his legs. Every breath blazed in his lungs as he spat it out.

The cordon the Swiss Guard had set up to isolate the square had already begun to break up. The flock of tourists was already forty or fifty rows deep, and people were losing their patience. Disgruntled mutterings came in a dozen languages. The guards were doing all they could to keep the people back.

"I really want to shoot you!" he yelled at the douchebag's back as his legs tied up. Noah stopped running and bent over, hands braced on his knees. He muttered into the paving slabs, "And I've got no problem with putting that cap in your ass," but the threat had no power. He doubted the numbnuts even heard him.

The pole smoker slowed, almost skipping as he moved now, and turned to offer another mocking salute and disappeared into the crowd of people, one more tee-shirt-clad tourist among the press of tee-shirt-and-jeans-wearing pilgrims.

For a moment the crowd parted and Noah saw the way people melted away from the jerkoff. He couldn't hear what he was saying as he pushed through them, but whatever it was it was working. No one stayed in his way for more than a second.

Noah followed him into the crowd, shouting, "*Io sono con lui!*" in pigeon Italian as he tried to force his way through the press of people.

Suddenly the crowd opened up and he was confronted

by a brow-beaten Guard with his ceremonial halberd leveled squarely at Noah's chest. He didn't seem all that eager to let Noah through. Behind him, Noah saw the butt monkey jogging toward The Witness. Whatever he had said had been enough to get him through the security cordon, and the only thing Noah could think of that would do that wouldn't be words at all, or at least not alone. Words and a badge. The bonehead had pulled rank, making him either a really good liar, or the law.

Noah stared at the Guard and said simply, "I'm coming through, so you either stab me or you get the hell out of my way. One or the other," and he surged forward, dropping his shoulder as though to go right, wrong-footing the guard. It was a clumsy maneuver, but he executed it quickly and efficiently. As the guard rocked to go to his left to block Noah, Noah pushed off on his left and darted past him. He ran with the cheers of the crowd at his back, delighted in the fact one of their number had just humiliated the poe-faced guard in his motley. Noah didn't hesitate or risk a backward glance. He ran flat out for the center of the piazza.

The fudgepacker turned at the sudden surge of noise and saw Noah coming for him.

Noah reached for his gun, fully intending to make good on his threat. Then he saw Abandonato staring at him, and something in the Monsignor's face stopped him. Monkey boy followed the direction of his gaze. Noah wasn't watching him. He was focused on the cleric. If he hadn't been, he might have missed the flash of recognition that lit across his face. As it was, he saw it plain as day. He didn't know what it meant—or rather didn't want to know what it meant. He knew *exactly* what it meant. Abandonato knew the rug muncher. What that meant . . . well, that was what Noah didn't want to know.

Someone saw the gun and screamed.

He didn't care.

There was maybe thirty yards between him and the asswipe. He threw himself forward, running on pure adrenalin.

His feet slapped the concrete. He yelled, a primitive tribal roar, using the anger of it to spur him on.

He was running out of names to call the bozo.

It didn't matter.

The gap between them narrowed to twenty-five yards.

He ran straight through the middle of a flock of pigeons, startling the birds into flight. They exploded into the sky in a flurry of wings and feathers, beating frantically at the air as Noah charged through them. They changed direction slightly, toward the main portico. Noah chased him past the statue of St. Peter and up the steps and through the doors of the great cathedral into the nave. They weren't alone, but no one moved to stop them as they barreled down the central aisle toward the Papal Altar.

Noah felt like the guy behind the Pied Piper, the first rat suckered in by the sweet music. He didn't need to look back to know that they had quite the pack of rats chasing them, though in this case the rats had guns, swords and halberds instead of sharp teeth. He concentrated on reaching the man in front of him as he ran headlong toward the altar.

Before they reached it, the muppet skidded, arms pinwheeling as his momentum continued to carry him forward. He twisted, angling toward the gallery stairs that led up to the dome walkway. Cursing, Noah followed him up the stairs, taking them two and three at a time. His entire body screamed at the exertion. He felt his vision swimming and his heart hammering. Sweat stung his eyes. "Just give up, will you!" Noah yelled. His voice echoed all around the dome, startling loud in the silence.

The bastard started laughing manically, as though it were the funniest thing he had ever heard.

Noah heard others coming up the stairs behind him.

He stopped running and turned to face Noah. "You'll

never take me alive, you do know that, don't you?" he said, sounding hideously reasonable as he spoke, and barely out of breath, which was just insulting. Noah was surprised he spoke English.

"Give it up," Noah said, walking toward him. He aimed the gun at the center of the man's gray tee-shirt.

"Or what? You'll shoot me? In here?" His accent was curious, not Italian, but definitely not English, and not quite American, like he had learned it from watching MTV maybe.

"I'll shoot you anywhere, pal, I really don't give a damn. This isn't my church, and me and God are a long way from being pally."

"You can't stop us," he said. "It's too late for that. It's too late for all of you." He looked at his watch. It was a curious gesture, but seeing the time, he nodded as though the hours and minutes had proved him right, and that it really was too late.

"I already did," Noah said. "Look around you, where can you go? It's over."

The terrorist shook his head. "No, you've turned me into a martyr, the first saint of the new Messiah, the first angel of Judas. That's all you have done. You've lost. You've lost everything. And you've done it here, of all places. For that, I thank you." He turned on his heel, seemed almost to bounce, buoyed by new found purpose, took two steps and then launched himself up over the railing and into the nothing but air. For a heartbeat he seemed to hang there, suspended by the air itself, but without wings. And he fell.

Noah lurched forward, reaching out with the gun still in his hand.

It was a hopeless gesture.

The sound of impact, flesh on stone, echoed sickeningly throughout the entire inside of St. Peter's.

Noah leaned over the walkway railing and looked down, knowing exactly what he was going to see down there.

Blood puddled around the dead man, staining the consecrated ground.

The blood of the martyr was like a halo around his ruined head.

Noah had no other names left to call him.

He leaned on the railing, breathing hard, huge gulping breaths. His chest heaved. All he could hear in the silence was the ragged sound of his own breathing.

Priests and soldiers had begun to gather around the body. His arms and legs bent and broken into a whorish sprawl, but his head stared straight up at the vault of the ceiling, straight up at Noah. The dead man didn't look much like an angel or a saint. He looked like a dead terrorist.

Noah turned his back on the blind eyes and the blood.

He wanted answers, but everywhere he turned he found more questions.

All he had left was the look that had passed between the dead man and the priest. He looked up at the ceiling and said, "Give me this one, eh?"

Pushing through the rats that had swarmed up onto the gallery behind him, he went in search of Abandonato, and the truth.

He only found one of them.

27

NO SAFE PLACE LIKE HOME

Jude Lethe watched the world unravel in glorious Technicolor over and over again. The German television cameras had captured the assassination from three different angles. It didn't look good for Koni from any of them. Lethe froze the frame as the first glint of silver caught the low sun. It was too difficult to call where the knife had originated from. He wasn't a body language expert. He knew where it had come from—the Swiss Guard closest to the Holy Father had been concealing it within the folds of his clownish armor—but proving it was a different thing all together.

Suddenly they were two men down, and there was nothing the old man could do. His hands were tied by the very deniability that allowed them the freedom of movement their mandate granted them. He couldn't go to the Foreign Secretary and appeal, he couldn't contact the British ambassador in Germany. Ogmios didn't exist on any official charter. They had no right of recall. The embassy wasn't going to order an extradition for Konstantin, and for the same reason they weren't going to mount an assault to recover Orla. They were deniable. They screwed up for Queen and Country, but that didn't matter in the slightest. They screwed up. That was what it boiled down to.

Konstantin was on camera, prime suspect in the assassination of the Pope. The BKA would want a quick result, justice seen to be served. They wouldn't want an international incident. They wouldn't want him being extradited to the UK to stand trial. It had happened on German soil; it would be dealt with on German soil, with Germanic efficiency. In the eyes of the world Konstantin was already guilty—they'd seen it happen. Lethe needed to find proof that they hadn't, that their brains had connected the dots and filled in the blanks but got it all horribly wrong. And the damned cameras weren't helping.

Neither was the fact that when they started running their background checks the first thing they'd find out about Konstantin Khavin was that he was a defector from the old Soviet Republic. Two and two would make four, or an approximation of it, and they'd leap to the only logical conclusion: that you could take Konstantin Khavin out of Mother Russia, but you couldn't take Mother Russia and her black heart out of Konstantin Khavin. He was a spy—a deep plant—still at the beck and call of Moscow. Because no matter how enlightened everyone was now that the Wall had come down, it didn't take a lot to reignite all of the old fears and that deep-seated distrust. It was easier for people to believe that the old enemies were still enemies than it was to turn the blame around and point the finger at people like Miles Devere, capitalists driven by plain, simple, ugly greed.

When the first gunshots sounded the crane camera, the one that would otherwise have had the perfect angle to capture the entire thing, roved wildly away from the stage toward the explosion of black feathers as the birds burst out of the trees. By the time its lens was back on the stage the murder had already unfolded and the last moments of it were playing out. Konstantin knelt over the fallen Pope, blood on his hands and a sort of madness in his face. The silver dagger lay on the red carpet.

The second and third cameras were not much better. The right side of the stage stayed focused on the main players, but Konstantin's momentum as he came into the shot and the way he twisted his body, trying to get between the white-robed Pope and the assassin, only served to obscure the actual moment of murder. The initial angle wasn't wide enough to show the Swiss Guard drawing the Judas dagger moments before. The view from the left side was worse, focused as it was on the backs of the Pope and the guard and the light of anger-desperation-madness in Konstantin's face as he threw himself at the pair.

No matter how many times he studied the images, he couldn't find a single frame of the dagger before it was punched into the Pontiff's neck.

But of course these weren't the only cameras trained on the stage. Someone down there in that crowd had caught the truth on a cell phone or digital camera. Unfortunately there was no way of knowing who. If there were three thousand people packed into the square, perhaps three percent of them didn't turn and follow the sound of the gunshot or the resulting flurry of movement from the trees for whatever reason. Three percent meant ninety people. Of those ninety, it was safe to assume fifty percent were too far back or had partially obscured views of the stage for one reason or another, which meant forty-five people were not looking the wrong way and had a clear view of the stage. Of those forty-five, there would be a split between left and right side of the stage. It was statistically unlikely to be a fifty percent split. It just didn't work that way, but even if it was, then twenty-three and a half people were on the right side to see the dagger drawn.

Then it came down to wandering attention. How would people react? You hear a gunshot. Do you look immediately to the man in the center of the stage, fearing the worst? You bet your bottom dollar you do. Fifteen of those twenty-three and a half are going to look straight at the Pope as the gunshot reverberates through the square. That leaves eight and a half people who will be looking elsewhere, but in the right direction from the right side of the stage where they could conceivably see the blade going in, or at least see it in the murderer's hand before it went in. Of those eight and a half, how many would be drawn by the sudden movement of Konstantin erupting from the crowd, looking away from the real murderer at the last second? Two? Three? Four? Five was reasonable. Five was a good number—meaning that three and a half people would be looking the right way, with the right view and undistracted.

Then the question was, of those, how many would realize that what they were seeing was the actual assassination in progress? One, maybe, two. Would they come forward? Why would they when the entire world had already convicted Konstantin? After all it was there in far too many megapixels. So what good would one uncorroborated testimony that contradicted all the perceived evidence be?

Less than useless was the answer, and Lethe knew it, unless that one person had also been filming the blessing with his cell phone or digital camera and happened to catch the truth in megapixels.

Lethe wasn't a gambling man, but even he knew these weren't the kind of odds you wanted to stake your life on.

That was what Konstantin was up against, and all the favors in the world wouldn't change the evidence of two thousand eyes without something concrete.

So Lethe kept looking.

This time he blew up the image on the screen as large as it would go without pixilating too badly for him to make out the details and, instead of looking at the main players, turned his attention to the crowd, looking for that one cell phone or digital camera that might have actually recorded the truth. It was like looking for the needle in the proverbial haystack, but what else could he do?

Frost would be back soon. The ride back would probably take him two or three hours at most—closer to two given the hour and the relatively light traffic, and the way Frost flogged the Monster.

And he kept thinking about that third phone call Devere had made. The first to Geneva was obviously some routed warning to the dagger man; the second triggered the timer on the sniper rifle; but the third, back to the mother ship in London, made no sense.

He turned the music up because it helped him concentrate. The lead singer of the Gin Blossoms lamented that the past was gone and that he had blown his one chance with the hot chick years ago. Because of that, and because all he had been hearing for the last few hours was the screams of the crowd in Koblenz and the crack of the sniper rifle, Jude Lethe didn't hear the muffled sound of gunshots upstairs.

Sir Charles, however, did.

Even muffled nothing else sounds like a gunshot, not that a car would be backfiring this far out in the idyllic British countryside. The main road through to Ashmoor was far enough away that the sound wouldn't travel over the hedges and moorland, through the forested strips of field and then through the thick stone walls of Nonesuch. No, the two shots, even suppressed by whatever silencer the assassin used, were distinct and distinctly out of place in the quiet of the manor.

The old man came out of his bed, struggling to bring his legs around so they reached the floor. The wheelchair was beside the bed, but getting to it was agony. He reached out, trying to claw at the frame and drag it closer, and as it butted up against the bed frame he struggled to stand. Every muscle in his arms shivered as he labored, shifting his weight forward onto legs that wouldn't hold him. Then he twisted and came down hard, falling rather than sitting into the chair.

Sweat trickled down the side of the old man's face.

He looked around the room. His walking stick was on the window side of the bed.

His service revolver, a 1963 Webley Break-Top Revolver—one of the very last commissioned for the armed forces—was in the desk drawer on the far side of the room, under lock and key. It was a fragile lock, but he was an old man. And from the chair it was doubtful he could get the leverage he needed to yank the drawer out, breaking the brass tongue of the lock or the wood around it. There was a box of ammo in the drawer as well. He had hoarded them after the pistol was retired in '63. Two cartridges per man, per year, was the old joke. By the time the gun went out of service ammo for it was in short supply. The double-action revolver could pump out twenty to thirty rounds in a minute, more than the chamber could hold and more than the old man had. The box of ammunition contained twelve cartridges.

It was one or the other. The panic button was beside the walking stick, the phone on the desk.

He held his hands out in front of his face. They were shaking, and not just from the exertion of getting into the chair. Even if he broke the drawer open, his hands were so unsteady there was no guarantee he could load the revolver without spilling the shells all over the floor. Then again, he would only need one shot.

It wasn't much of a choice.

He made a decision.

He steered the wheelchair toward the desk. It bumped against the side of the bed and off the carved legs of the desk itself, rattling everything on the top. He pulled at the drawer, but it refused to budge. He pulled at it again, more desperately this time. The entire desk shook with the force of the movement, but still the drawer didn't budge. He couldn't get any better purchase on it, or exert any more pressure on any of the stress points.

He heard footsteps in the hall outside.

The old man pulled so hard on the drawer he nearly pulled the entire desk down on him. The lock held. He slammed his hand off it, spitting a curse, then stopped trying. He gripped the chair and tried to angle it back toward the window.

The door opened behind him.

He didn't turn. He didn't need to. He could see the intruder step into the room through the mirror above the desk. Wearing a black knitted balaclava with a ragged slash where the mouth had been cut out, and two narrow eye slits. Black curls slipped out from beneath the bottom of the balaclava. Even clothed head-to-toe in sexless black the woman's well-defined curves gave her gender away.

Her left arm was considerably thicker than her right, misshapen. The old man realized it was sheathed in a light cast. He remembered Frost's initial report from the house in Jesmond. This was the woman he had interrupted while she turned Sebastian Fisher's apartment over. He had broken her arm in the struggle. And here she was breaking in again. The old man reached for the phone. He knew he couldn't call, but knocking the handset out of the cradle would open a line, and an open line would blink on every telephone in the house. All he could do was hope that someone would see it. But who would see it? Max? Lethe? He had heard gunshots a moment before. She wouldn't have just fired at an offending umbrella stand. Max would have gone to investigate the noise. Max. The old man couldn't allow himself to regret or mourn. Max was dead or Max was alive; either way worrying about it now was pointless. He had his own sorry carcass to worry about.

"I wouldn't do that if I were you," the woman said. She had an accent. It wasn't distinct, but it was there even though she did her best to hide it. Middle Eastern, Israeli, or possibly Lebanese. Given the trail of breadcrumbs they'd been chasing back to Masada, Israel was the more likely of the two. The accent almost certainly meant it was the same woman who had got the jump on Frost in Jesmond, the old man realized.

"So Devere sent you to kill an old man in his chair?" Sir Charles asked, meeting her eyes in the backwards land through the looking glass. It made sense that Miles Devere would send one of his flunkies after him. It was all about power, showing Sir Charles that no matter how connected he was, no matter who he worked for or who he called friends, Devere could reach him. That was what the third call had been about. He had called London to arrange this little visit. "I'm flattered."

"You should be," the woman said, closing the door behind her.

"Perhaps we can make a deal?"

"I don't make deals."

"Everyone makes deals, my dear. There is a saying in my game, never send someone to kill a man with more money than you. I have a lot of money, believe me. Whatever Devere's paying you I'll double to send you back to his door. How does that sound?"

"Like a desperate man," she said.

She was right. That was exactly how he sounded.

But then, that was how he *wanted* to sound. Any man in his situation ought to sound desperate. Desperate or resigned; he wasn't resigned. He wasn't that kind of man. He made things happen. That only left him with the option of sounding desperate. A desperate man with money would look to strike a deal, so that was exactly what he had done. If she was as good as she no doubt thought she was, she would have been able to see it in his eyes, the shifting gears as one gambit was rejected, thinking quickly, looking for another alternative, anything other than the bullet in the back of the head. It was in-field thinking—reassess, redeploy, react.

He stopped himself from reaching for the phone.

The chair meant he looked up at her through the mirror. It added to the illusion of helplessness. All she saw was an old man in a wheelchair. It would have helped if he had managed to open the drawer, but guns weren't the only solution.

"Aren't you going to increase your offer? Isn't that what people like you do? Beg, plead, offer me riches beyond my wildest imagining?"

"No," the old man said. "Not today. Today I am going to ask you if you are fond of life?"

"What kind of question is that?"

"No matter how good you think you are, do you really believe you can walk in here, kill me and walk out again without consequences?"

"And here we are again, the dying man's twelve-step program. Denial, bargaining, and now we're into the threats. For some reason, the way my client described you, I thought you might be different. This is disappointing. He made you sound like some colossus. I hate to break it to you, but step twelve is always the same. You die."

"So it is pointless, my telling you about the security here, and what happens when my heart stops beating? My boy Lethe is a computer genius. Did Devere tell you that? Everything in this place is routed through the circuitry of my chair, dependent upon my heartbeat. My heart stops for some reason and Nonesuch goes into lockdown. There is no way out. When my team returns they will find you here. The good news is there is plenty of food, so you'll be well fed at least."

"You expect me to believe this is the Bat Cave and I just

killed Alfred? It's more creative than saying you've got the place surrounded by armed guards just waiting for your signal, I'll give you that. But correct me if I am wrong, I don't remember Bruce Wayne being a cripple?"

"Truth is stranger than fiction, isn't that what they say?"

"Some do, I am sure, probably the same ones who also say they booby trapped the entire house and have a remote detonating device in the arm of their wheelchair."

"That was the next thing I was going to try," the old man said. He smiled, doing his utmost to appear calm on the surface, but inside his heart was racing almost as quickly as his mind. The talk was all about buying time, but once bought it all came down to how he wanted to spend it.

"Enough talk," she said, as though she had been able to tap into his mind. "Do you want to die facing the end or with your back to it? Some people would rather not see it coming."

"Given the fact that I can see you whichever way I face, I am not sure it makes much difference, does it? It's like asking if I want a closed- or open-casket funeral. Back of the head, large exit wound in the face, or bullet between the eyes and the back of your head's blown out. It really doesn't matter because I'm going to be just as dead."

"That you are," she agreed.

"Let's do this, shall we? I think I'd rather like a pretty face to be the last thing I see, call me an old fool, but I always was weak for a certain kind of girl," Sir Charles said, reaching down for the rail on the wheel rims. He pulled back on one, and forward on the other, angling the chair around. The tight space between the bed and the desk made it impossible for him to turn properly. He knew that. That was precisely why he had twisted the chair into it.

Before he could start to back up, the phone on the desk started ringing.

"I don't suppose I can answer that?" the old man said, ruefully.

"No," she said. She didn't seem all that amused by the interruption.

"Then I suppose I can't say saved by the bell, either?"

"No," she said again. "No last minute reprieves. We've talked too much already. If you can't turn the chair around, I will."

"I can do it," the old man assured her, looking through the glass at the Rembrandt on the wall behind her. *Judas Repentant.*

The phone stopped ringing.

Ronan Frost killed the call.

It was the first time in all the years he had been with Ogmios that he had called Nonesuch and Lethe hadn't answered in a matter of seconds. There was nothing good about the silence. He looked up at the house at the far side of the long, winding drive. As always there were only a few lights on. The cars were all lined up on the gravel drive exactly where Orla and the guys had left them a few days ago. Instead of that being comforting it made the place look like an automotive graveyard, the place where sports cars come to die.

The reason he had made the call was parked, half-hidden in the bushes: an off-road dirt bike.

The drive would take him ten seconds to drive, gunning the Monster's engine and tearing up the gravel, or two minutes to run, silently. He chose silence over speed. If someone was inside the Manor, he didn't want to go in there all thud and blunder, even if a few seconds could make all the difference. Noise could just as easily get everyone killed. The old man was sharp. He'd go down swinging. And Lethe had probably turned the basement into his own personal panic room.

Frost kicked down the stand and killed the Ducati's idling engine. He stripped out of his leathers because they hampered his mobility. The time it spent getting out of them would be made up two-fold running across the lawn. He checked the dirt bike for any clue to the owner's identity, but there was nothing. Not that he had expected to find anything. It was difficult to be sure, because the mud was fairly hard after several days without rain, but he could only make out a single set of tracks. He pulled the Browning and set off at a sprint across the lawn. He kept his head up, looking frantically left and right for signs of the intruder. Frost knew that the unanswered phone meant they were already inside, but that didn't mean they weren't already done when he had called and on their way out. There was plenty of darkness to hide in. Too much of it. The spotlights were on, but they only illuminated the snake of the driveway as it came out of the darkness.

Halfway across the lawn he was breathing hard. His body hurt from the abuse it had taken over the last few days.

Through the portico he saw that the main door stood open.

There was something in the doorway, a dark shadow on the floor. As he got closer the shadow became a shape, and the shape became a body dressed in an immaculate black suit, white shirt, white gloves and bow tie. There was a single entry wound in the center of Maxwell's forehead, a cyclopean third eye. There wasn't a lot of blood and there was very little damage. Powder burns rimmed the wound. The gun had been pressed up close to the butler's head. He had that look of surprise on his face that robbed every dead man of his dignity. Even in death it didn't look as though Max had a hair out of place.

Frost knelt and closed his friend's eyes, then he stepped over the dead man and into the house.

Nonesuch had that eerie silence that accompanies a death house. It was as though the old stones were aware of the tragedy playing out within them. Frost crept into the hall, listening to the silence. He could hear the faintest hint of voices. The old grandfather clock across from the fireside chessboard told him how late it was. The old man would be in his room by now. The house might have been a warren of mezzanines, hidden servants' stairs and out of the way pantries, but the old man only used a fraction of the rooms. The chair kept him on the lower level; habit kept him in the same handful of rooms down here.

Frost crept across the hall.

The voices were quiet now.

He preferred it when he heard them. Dead men didn't talk. As long as they were talking all was almost well with the world. *Just keep them talking*, he prayed silently to whoever was listening. He ghosted toward the control room and tapped his personal code into the lock. The *beep* that acknowledged the right access code and opened the lock mechanism sounded sharp and too loud in the silence. He knew realistically it wouldn't have carried to any of the other rooms, but that didn't stop him from biting his lip and easing the door open painfully slow.

Frost slipped inside and eased the door closed behind him.

The room was empty. The array of screens either showed Konstantin Khavin in various frozen frames as he hurled himself at the Pope, or the shadow-wreathed shape of Orla Nyrén, naked and chained to the wall of a dank cell. Frost hadn't seen the images before. They took his breath away for a moment. He wanted to do something. Anything. Every instinct screamed at him. These were his people, his team, and they were in trouble. The only one who wasn't in trouble was Noah, which, given the usual series of events, was just plain wrong.

The staircase down to Lethe's den was still covered. It wasn't the only way down, but if he was going to go sneaking down there to stage a rescue, that was the way to go. He wished he'd paid more attention when Lethe gave them the briefing on the tabletop computer. He was pretty sure he could call up images from hidden cameras in all of the rooms, but he didn't have the slightest idea where to start and was more likely to set the sprinklers off than turn the security cameras on.

He had come in to the control room for a reason. Lethe had designed the room as a digital fortress. From here Frost could lock down the most vulnerable areas of Nonesuch, protecting the team's identity, and more importantly, their benefactor's. He could also isolate various parts of the house. He hit the panic button. There were no sirens, no flashing lights. Lethe's design didn't need it. In ten seconds flat the manor house became a steel trap, literally. He heard the rumble and felt the shiver of inch-thick steel sheets slamming into place. They were interspersed in various strategic points around the manor, isolating the wings, key rooms and the exits. There was no way in or out of Nonesuch. And this time the noise would have carried to every room in the house, but as long as the intruder didn't pry Max's eyes from his dead head, Frost had the only key: his bright blue eyes.

The set-up had appealed to Lethe's sense of the theatrical. The whole idea of a retina scan seemed far too *Blade Runner* for Frost, and the recessed steel doors like something out of the Death Star, but right now he couldn't argue with the genius of any of it. If the lad wanted to recreate his own movie sets, so be it. The one unarguable fact was that no one was leaving Nonesuch without the right eyes.

Lockdown established, Frost had a binary decision to make: down to Lethe or back to the old man. He had only seen one bike and one set of tracks, meaning one intruder. The fact that he had heard voices in the old man's room decided it.

He slipped out of the room.

He had been in there less than thirty seconds. The hand on the grandfather clock hadn't moved.

The main door out to the grounds was blocked by a thick metal plate. It had sliced through Max. The cut hadn't been clean. If it was the difference between his murderer escaping or not, he knew Max would forgive him.

Frost heard the voices, louder now. The old man and a woman. The old man was begging. Frost didn't hesitate.

He ran toward the old man's study.

"What the hell was that?" the woman barked at him. The echo of the steel sheets slamming into place reverberated through the floor.

Sir Charles smiled. Frost had arrived. There was a chance he might make it out of this alive, but if not, at least he had the consolation of knowing that his killer was not about to disappear into the night. It all depended upon the woman and whether her pity outweighed her killer instinct. It wasn't exactly a sure thing, but he was playing the only hand he had—the helpless old cripple card. With any luck she'd underestimate him, or his blathering would buy Frost enough time to find them. "The Bat Cave," the old man said.

He had wriggled the chair around so far he couldn't see her face in the mirror anymore. The benefit of that was that she couldn't see his, either. The old man twisted hard on the wheel with his left hand, wedged his foot beneath the edge of the bed and pulled down on the other wheel with his right, deliberately unbalancing the chair. He leaned forward and fell, sprawling across the rug. The chair came down on top of him.

He clawed his way out from under the chair, emerging on the window side of the bed. His walking stick was tantalizingly out of reach.

"You really are something," the woman said, dragging the chair out of the way. "It's a pity I have to kill you."

"It's a pity I have to die," Sir Charles said. He dragged

himself another six inches across the floor, toward the stick leaning against the wall. He willed her to keep on underestimating him. He twisted to look up at her, then deliberately, slowly, let his gaze drift back longingly toward his walking stick, knowing she would follow it, and knowing she wouldn't think for a minute what a devious old fool he was. The walking stick was more than just an old man's affectation, and he wasn't about to beat her over the head with a stick of wood. It was a sword cane. One twist of the elaborately carved handle and the brass coupling would break. There was an eighteen-inch blade secreted inside the wooden shaft. If he could get to it, and get her close enough, there was a chance. A slim one, but that was infinitely preferable to none.

He dragged himself to within touching distance of the stick.

"Well, no, there's no pity in it at all, is there?" she said, coming around the side of the bed to stand over him. "This feels like killing my own grandfather," she said, shaking her head. "I didn't enjoy that, either."

The old man was on his stomach, one leg twisted uncomfortably because it was still trapped beneath the bed frame, the other up by his side. He looked like a chalk outline waiting to be drawn around. The sword cane was six inches from his fingers. So close yet so far away. Everything around him developed a sense of hyper-reality. He saw the threads of the rug and smelled the rubber that had worn itself into them with all of those back-and-forths in the wheelchair. Even the grain in the wooden bed frame seemed so much starker, like seeing the truth of a treasure map for the first time.

He heard the study door burst open, but didn't waste time trying to turn. He knew it was Frost. He used that fraction of a second to push himself the last six inches to the sword cane. He reached out, barely grazing it with his fingers, then stretched, finding another inch in his reach. His hand closed around the thin wooden shaft. He pulled the sword cane to his chest and broke the shaft. It took less than a second, an entire second where he expected to hear the silenced gunshot and be swallowed by the nothing of death.

As soon as the blade was clear of the sheath he lunged upward with it. He didn't have the reach, but after years in the chair what he did have was incredible upper body strength. He thrust with all of his might, feeling it hit bone and scrape off it as it sank deeper into her side. He twisted savagely, opening her up. She screamed. The sound was cut brutally short. Her body twitched on the end of the blade, then stopped moving completely. For a long second she stood, held up only by the sword in her side and the strength of the old man's arm.

He heard a single shot but didn't feel anything.

A fountain of blood sprayed across his face and more poured down the blade and down his arm. Then gravity caught up with her corpse and pulled the woman down the length of the sword. He couldn't hold her dead weight. She carried on falling, landing awkwardly across his body and pinning him to the rug. He struggled, but he couldn't shift her.

He heard the floorboard creak beneath cautious footsteps.

A moment later the old man saw Frost looking down over her shoulder.

"You took your sweet time," he said. "Is Maxwell . . . ?"

Frost didn't say anything. Instead he hauled the dead assassin off the old man and dumped her on his bed. He pulled the sword from her side and dumped it on the bed beside her, then he peeled off her balaclava and grunted. It was a grunt of recognition. Next he righted the old man's chair and helped him up into it. All of this was done in silence.

The old man sat there soaked in his erstwhile killer's blood.

He looked at her lying there on the bed. There was no way anyone could confuse her death for sleep. She really was beautiful, or had been. He wondered what could have turned her into a gun for hire, but then realized the stupidity of that kind of thinking. It was like wondering what turned Frost into the man he was, a life of conflict in Derry and Belfast or the fields of blood in Kosovo, or some-thing else entirely, something coded on a genetic level.

"Lethe?" Sir Charles said, finally.

"As far as I can tell, she came alone, met Max at the door, then came looking for you. If Jude's got any common sense, he turned the basement into a panic room and is sitting down there waiting for the cavalry." He didn't voice the alternative—that Lethe had tried to be the cavalry himself and was lying somewhere inside the big old house with a bullet in his head. The second alternative explained why the phone rang off the hook when he called, the first didn't.

The old man wheeled his chair toward the doorway, then stopped, looking back toward the bed. "I will need fresh sheets," and in that horrible second where reality comes rushing in, he realized that without Maxwell no one was going to be changing his bed linen and that his world had just become a little smaller without his companion in it. He shook his head, clearing it. "All right, first things first," he said, all business. "What are we going to do with her?"

"I suggest we find a big mailing pouch and send her right back where she came from," Frost said.

"Appealing as that notion is, I was thinking something a little less problematic. One option would be burying her in the grounds. I doubt very much anyone save Devere knows she is here, and he's hardly likely to draw attention to his role in this. So given the circumstances, it shouldn't be too difficult to make like we never saw her. Another alternative is the incinerator."

"That works as well," Frost said, "but I'd still rather post her."

"I am sure you would, sealed with a kiss, no doubt."

"A line of C4 and a short fuse seems more fitting," Frost said. "Okay, better get this over with. Let's go find Lethe."

As it was, they didn't need to go far. Jude Lethe stood beside half of the butler's corpse looking down at it. He heard them approach and looked up. "The cameras," he said, as though that explained everything. It did in a way. The old man took it to mean he had seen the assassin shoot Maxwell on one of his many screens down there in the basement and he'd locked down the nerve center of Nonesuch. No second thoughts, no heroics. He'd followed the protocols to the letter, even if it meant leaving the old man in harm's reach. Sir Charles nodded.

He looked down at his friend.

"Mister Lethe, would you be so kind as to reset the shield doors. Frost, Maxwell was one of ours. I would count it a personal favor if you would take care of things."

Frost nodded. He seemed about to say something. It was rare that Ronan Frost didn't simply speak his mind.

"What is it?" the old man asked.

"I saw the screens in the control room," he licked his lips. "Konstantin, Orla. They're ours too. And has Noah checked in? This is a mess." The understatement of the year.

"There's nothing to be done," the old man said. It sounded harsh in his own ears even as he said it. Frost didn't so much as flinch. He accepted the judgment like the professional soldier he was.

"I'm not finished looking," Lethe said. "I found someone in the crowd who was filming the Pope's blessing on his cell phone. The angle's right, with a bit of luck he caught everything on film. The only problem is I've got no idea who he is and have only actually seen the back of his head."

"That's a bit of a problem," Frost said, but the possibility that someone had caught the truth of the assassination on their cell phone seemed to energize him. "But it's not insurmountable. Koblenz is a small enough city. Get the plod to go door to door with a photograph of the back of the guy's head. You know the deal: Is this you? Is this you? Is this you? It has to be someone."

There was nothing to say that that particular someone even came from Koblenz, but it was a straw worth clutching at. He could see that in Frost's face. No man left behind.

"The police won't go door to door. They took thousands of statements at the scene. If he had seen anything, the BKA will already know, and most likely, if they know he was filming, they will have confiscated his cell phone as potential evidence."

"They might not have looked at the film yet," Frost said.

"Or they might have seen it and deleted it already," Sir Charles said. He knew all too well how some of these profile investigations went. They had evidence, witnesses, and a prime suspect that the British Government would already have disowned. A Russian defector with paramilitary experience? They couldn't have asked for a better assassin. They wouldn't be looking for the knife in the hands of the supposedly most loyal guardsmen in the world. It didn't sit with their investigative mindset, and why would it? They all saw Konstantin do it. Or at least thought they did.

"It's worth a try. It has to be," Frost pushed. "What about the guardsmen themselves?" He looked at Lethe. "Any of them see what happened?"

"If they did, I'd expect another corpse to turn up any minute now, wouldn't you?" Lethe asked.

Frost nodded. "But will another dead body be enough to barter Koni's freedom?" Frost and the old man locked gazes. Sir Charles was the first to look away. "I want to go out there," Frost said. "I'm no use sitting on my hands here. Hell, if it comes right down to it, Noah and I can go in there and bust him out of that damned German prison cell. It'd only need the two of us to bring him home. Then the three of us can go get Orla."

He made it sound so simple.

It wasn't.

It was a geopolitical minefield.

The suits at Vauxhall Cross might deny Konstantin, but that didn't mean the Germans would necessarily believe their denials. It came down to whether they believed he was British or Russian, which side he was currently working for and which government they wanted to hang out to dry. Deals could be made, perhaps. The only fly in the ointment was the fact that the public needed to see someone suffer.

"That won't be necessary," Sir Charles told him. "You take care of Maxwell, I will make the call. If there is anything that can be done, it will be done. But I am making no promises. Understood?"

"This is becoming rather a bad habit, Charles," Control's reedy voice said over the telephone. "I don't suppose I need to remind you about the hour, or point out that civilized people are abed?"

"I'm not going to apologize," the old man said. "You know what is happening. Those are my people out there."

"And that's a damned shame, but there's nothing I can do about it. And even if there was, these midnight calls are hardly endearing, old boy."

"How long have we worked together?"

"Longer, I am sure, than either of us would like to admit."

"And how many times have I asked you for help, Quentin?"

"Oh, is that the card your playing? The 'I've been a good and faithful servant all these years and you owe me'? I thought better of you."

"You're the second person to say that to me tonight. The first one is dead. Regrettably, she killed Maxwell."

"Are you telling me Nonesuch was breeched?"

"That's exactly what I am telling you."

"Have you been compromised, Charles? Tell me the truth. There's nothing to be gained by protecting your pride." Quentin Carruther's tone shifted, his affected tones suddenly more urgent, all hint of playfulness stripped from his words.

"The situation was contained, this time."

"Are you sure?"

"I killed the intruder myself, Quentin. Her blood is still all over my clothes, and her corpse is in my bed. I couldn't be much surer."

"Well that's something, at least."

"I want him out of there, Quentin," the old man said, shifting the subject back to Konstantin Khavin.

"There's nothing I can do, Charles. I don't run you boys anymore, not that I ever did, really. You've had far too long a leash for too long a time. This is the new world order, my friend, and there's a new sheriff in town. Talk to him, talk to the Chief. If anyone can pull diplomatic strings it's him. My hands are decidedly stringless. But don't hold your breath. Your boy knew the risks when he signed up. Her Majesty is hardly about to claim responsibility for the papal assassin, now is she?"

"He didn't do it and you know full well that he didn't."

"Neither here nor there, though, is it? The camera never lies. If he was innocent, the picture proving it would have been all over the tabloids by now. As it is they're calling for his head as though he were John the Baptist."

"I want him out of there, Quentin."

"And I want Pretty Boy Floyd to come massage my aching feet. I suspect both of us are going to be disappointed, don't you?"

"Someone in the crowd filmed it," the old man said, trying a different tack.

"I am sure they did, but again, it doesn't help us. Your boy wasn't supposed to be there. He was operating without

347   SILVER

German consent. He assaulted the Israeli ambassador's men in Berlin. There is photographic evidence of him breaking and entering into a dead man's apartment, and enough to suggest he might be linked to the whole sorry affair. They want him, old boy, and there is sweet Fanny Anne that I can say or do that will change their minds. He was careless. He got caught."

"So you're saying he should have let the Pope die?"

"I don't know whether you noticed, but His Holiness died. So yes, as far as Her Majesty is concerned, Khavin's involvement in this debacle is nothing short of embarrassing. She could come out publicly and say, 'Yes, we sent an agent to try to protect the Holy Father, but that agent failed.' It doesn't look good for a monarch to admit fallibility. Then there are the questions of why we didn't turn everything over to the German authorities the moment he suspected something was going to happen on their soil. Things are fractious enough even sixty years on. To say that there is still bad blood between our countries is something of an understatement.

"We can't make him disappear; that will just make the Germans look foolish. We can't trade him one for one because it's been years since we've held a German citizen as a guest of Her Majesty's Displeasure. We can't bully them into giving him back; how would that make us look? Give us back the man who just killed the Pope! Can you imagine? Just be grateful they don't have the death penalty anymore. They'd have him hanging from a gibbet in the same town square, ironic given one of the purposes of the blessing, if you think about it." Control had the decency not to chuckle at his own joke. "No one is going to come out of this very well, Charles. Now it is all about damage limitation. The eyes of the world are on Koblenz. Give them Khavin. They have it all on film, they get to look good, a fast efficient clean up, justice served and everyone is happy. That's the long and the short of it."

"Not everyone," the old man said. "You don't want me to turn this into a war, Quentin. He's my boy. I lost one of mine today, and I refuse to lose another."

"Is that a threat, Charles?"

"You know it is, old boy," the old man said. "I suggest you make the call and don't try and fob me off with deniability. You've got a duty to Konstantin."

"I suppose you want me to mount an invasion? We could take Tel Aviv while we are at it, bring your girl home, a two-for-one special. Don't be so naive, Charles. Khavin is nothing more than an unfortunate incident. He doesn't even register as collateral damage. You need to understand, if you continue to push this, we'll cut you off. It's as simple as that. Ogmios will cease to be useful. You'll be closed down."

The old man breathed into the phone, letting his silence speak for him.

"In case the nuance was lost on you, that was a threat, dear boy," Quentin Carruthers said.

"Or I could just send Frost around to your house tonight. It's always tragic when an old man dies, but there's something natural about dying in your sleep, don't you think?"

"And to think I used to call you my friend."

"There is no such beast in this game, Quentin. There are those that can help us and those that stand against us. I want my boy back, and I will do anything to make it happen. So, I say again, make the call, bring him home."

"If I do this, and that's by no means a given, Charles, if I do this, you're through. I want everything you've got on this operation turned over to my people in the morning. I'll close you down. You understand just what it is you are asking?"

The old man didn't answer him.

He hung up.

28

IN CHAINS

Time lost all meaning in the dark of the dungeon. Occasionally Orla heard something. Sometimes it would be the skitter and scratch of rats scurrying along the edge of the cell wall; other times it would be a whimper in the blackness, a voice, a sob, a cry. And then there were the nightmares as her head went down and she thought she'd slipped into the dark for real, only to hear him whispering in her ear, goading her, "Tomorrow you die."

How could he not understand that tomorrow was all she wanted, because that tomorrow was an end and she was done with the fear and the fighting?

The cuffs dug into her wrists, cutting the balls of her palms bloody. She had hung herself, putting all of her weight onto them, only for the steel to bite deeper and the blood to run hotter, but it didn't matter how deep the cuffs sliced, she couldn't wriggle free of them. She twisted, pushing off the wall. The cold stone was damp against her back.

She had seen what had happened to the girl, how they had taken her head as a trophy and thrown it at the camera.

She knew that was her fate if she didn't get out of this dark country.

She was going to get out.

It was as simple as that.

She was going to get out.

She said it over and over, like a mantra.

Somehow she'd let herself be turned into a victim. It wasn't her. She was stronger than that. She'd been to hell and back and survived. She would survive again.

She was alone in the dark. She stood on her toes when she could no longer bear the agony of hanging, and hung from her wrists when she could no longer bear the torture of trying to stand.

Every ninth heartbeat a single drop of water dripped onto her skin from the damp ceiling. Sometimes it hit her shoulder and ran down through the valley between her breasts. Sometimes it her cheek and ran down her neck. And sometimes she tried to catch it with her tongue. It was never enough to slake her thirst.

She felt the rats brush up against her bare feet. They sniffed at her ankles. She knew they were drawn to the heat of her body, her blood and her bones, but they wouldn't feast while she was alive. Every inch of her skin crawled. Every ounce of her flesh burned. She shifted her weight and kicked out at the curious rat. The kick lacked any strength, but it was enough to send the rat scurrying away again.

There was a bucket in the corner. The rats liked to sniff around that, too. They made her wait for it, adding humiliation to the torture, bringing the bucket once a day, once every two days—it was hard to tell in the dark. They wanted her to degrade herself and then to have to hang in her own feces and urine. It was another step to robbing her of her humanity. She refused to give them the satisfaction. She didn't care if they made her crouch naked over a pot and laughed. She made them fight for every little victory they won, that way she didn't just give up and let those little victories become big victories. That bucket was her key to salvation. There as some leeway on the chain depending upon how her captors secured it against the wall. There was enough play for her to squat with her hands by her side for support, which meant, if the chain was played out to its longest, there was enough room for her to bring her hands down to her waist while standing, and almost all the way to the floor when she crouched.

Orla heard other sounds then. Footsteps in the darkness.

He was coming back.

She closed her eyes, steeling herself. Her first instinct was fear. Fear would get her killed. She needed to survive. That was the only thing she needed. Uzzi Sokol and his friends could rape and torture her, she would survive. Her body could take the abuse. So could her mind. They could try to break her, she was strong. They could demean her, beat her, spit at her, lash her, they could do all of that. She had suffered worse. There was nothing they could do to her that hadn't been done before. That was the truth of Israel. There was no torment the country could inflict upon her that it hadn't done already.

She heard the rattle of keys, and the door opened. The tiniest slither of light spilled into the cell. Her eyes had become so accustomed to the sensory deprivation of the dark that even that was enough to burn them. She twisted, trying to see her torturer. He was dressed head-to-toe in black, a hood over his face like an executioner. He had a pistol in his right hand, a Jericho 941. It was a standard issue Israeli security services handgun known as a Baby Eagle. She felt her breathing change, suddenly shallow and short. If she didn't get control of herself, she was going to hyperventilate. She struggled to slow the frantic rise and fall of her chest, to catch her breath.

He walked toward her, each footstep deliberately slow

and measured. They were deafening in the silence.

"I told you I'd come back," Sokol said. She felt his rancid breath against the nape of her neck. She knew it was him despite the hood. His voice was imprinted on her soul. She closed her eyes. She felt his hand touch her. She didn't flinch. Somehow his breath was worse than his touch. Orla stifled the urge to twist away as his hand cupped her breast and pulled her toward him. She knew better than to move. He would only hit her if she did. So she let him touch her despite the revulsion she felt at his hands. "I would never deny you your time in the spotlight. You're going to shine. I'm going to make you a movie star, like Marilyn, bigger even. By the end of today everyone will know your name. Would you like that, Orla? Would you like to be a star?"

He came in close, sloppily so, but he still had the sense to keep his gun hand away from her. She tasted his fetid breath in the back of her throat as she inhaled it. It stank of stale cigarettes. He let his fingers linger on the nape of her neck then caressed all the way down the ladder of her spine bone by bone to the soft swell of her buttocks. He hooked a foot around her ankle and forced her legs apart. There was nothing sexual about it. Sokol was showing her he had all of the power now.

Unbalanced, Orla stumbled slightly to the left, allowing his cold fingers to touch her. She winced despite herself.

"Did you miss me?"

She didn't say a word.

He stepped back and slapped her hard across the face.

"I asked you a question, woman. Didn't your mother teach you anything? When I ask you a question, you answer me. It isn't difficult. Let's try again. Did you miss me?"

She said nothing.

He backhanded her again, straight across the face. She turned her cheek with the blow. It made her eyes water.

"One more time. Did you miss me?"

Her mouth was painfully dry, but she managed to work

up enough saliva to spit in Sokol's face. The wad of phlegm hit the black hood. He didn't wipe it away.

"You disappoint me, Orla. Such a pointless thing to do." He leaned in again, close enough that the saliva smeared across her cheek. He was anything but gentle as he reached back between her legs. "Why should I care about a little bodily fluid when I can do this? It doesn't make any sense, Orla. I thought you were a smart girl."

It was a brutal invasion.

She arched her back and twisted her head, but there was nowhere she could go, nowhere she could hide from his vile touch. But she had no intention of hiding. She wanted him to come in closer. She needed his lust to rise. She needed him to forget about power. Her mind went cold, as though part of her soul detached itself and another creature, a harder one, took over to save her from the horror of what was happening. This other her waited for the single moment of sloppiness when his lust outweighed his sense.

It would come.

It had to.

Her life depended upon it.

She twisted around on the chains so she could look into his hooded face. His eyes were the only part of him she could see through the hood. They were wide. His breathing was shallow. She tried to hold his gaze, to draw him into hers, but couldn't bear the intensity of his eyes as they stared into her. She moved her lips as though to say something. He wanted to hear. She knew he would. That was why there were no words. She wanted him in closer.

He turned his back on her and walked away, taunting her. She counted his footsteps. Six. Eight was the magic number. Eight would take him to the brace on the wall where her chain was tied off. Eight would mean he thought he was in control.

He came back to her and slapped her hard across the face.

Her pain brought a smile from him.

"You don't want to make me angry, Orla," Sokol said. She hated the sound of his voice. She finished the line in her head: *You wouldn't like me when I am angry*. She didn't laugh. She didn't want him to think she was laughing at him. Sokol needed to think she was broken. She focused on that instead. She had survived before. She had survived worse. She would live through this.

Uzzi Sokol wouldn't.

She promised herself that much.

He turned his back on her. He walked away. Seven steps. She counted each of them, willing him to take the eighth, willing him to release the chain so it played out another four feet. Four feet meant she would live.

He didn't. He walked slowly back to her, tracing the muzzle of the Jericho from her cheek, slowly down her neck, following the artery that pulsed beneath the skin, over her collarbone and down around the swell of her breast. The metal was cold.

"Why are you doing this?" she said, barely a whisper.

Sokol's hand stopped moving. He looked at her as though he had forgotten she could speak. "Because I can," he said, and it was as simple as that. "Because in a few minutes the others are going to join us. They're going to drag you into the center of the room, and they are going to cut your head off with a sword while the world watches on the internet. Until then you are still beautiful. And if I can make your last few minutes pleasurable, then what is the crime in that?"

She wanted to claw his eyes out. Instead she said, "Thank you."

He hadn't expected that. He thought it was the ultimate act of submission. She was giving herself to him. He kissed her then, in the soft hollow at the nape where her throat met her body, and it was almost tender. She closed her eyes. She let herself seem to sag against the chains. He felt her move and touched her again, like lovers do. It was all she could do not to lunge forward and bite his throat out with her teeth. She couldn't do that. Not while her hands were still trussed above her head. She needed to be able to move her arms.

Uzzi Sokol touched her belly, pressing his palm flat against the taut muscle. It was a hideously intimate gesture, worse in some ways than all of the other invasions, because of the tenderness in it. She wanted the brutality because it made it easier to hate him. She waited out his touch. He had said the others were coming soon; that meant it was now or never, and never wasn't an option.

She arched her back, then came forward, pressing herself up against him. She leaned in, her lips tasting the salt of passion in his skin.

He backed away into the darkness of the cell.

He didn't like losing control. He didn't want her dictating their dance, even in chains. He wanted to orchestrate every twist and shudder. He was sick. He walked away from her, five, six, seven, eight steps. She felt the chain go slack. Her arms fell to her sides. Almost immediately she felt the rush of her blood beginning to circulate properly. It was like a drug. She closed her eyes. She had one chance. She needed to stay calm. If this went wrong—if he balked or she sent the gun spinning out of reach—she was dead.

He walked toward her, pulling the black hood off so she could see his face. He dropped it on the ground. His face was a mockery of handsome, twisted by lust. Whatever shred of decency had lived inside Uzzi Sokol was gone. All that remained was this creature driven by primal instincts.

Orla tensed every muscle in her lower body, ready to explode into motion.

She surrendered to her other senses, listening as he neared, listening as his breath sounded ragged and aroused in her ear, and as he came forward, losing control, Orla arched her back and drove her head forward into the middle of his face. She felt his nose explode in a spray of blood and blinding pain. Sokol staggered away from her, stunned. She heard the clatter as he dropped the Jericho and brought his hands up to his face. He screamed over and over, "You bitch! You miserable bitch!" as he stumbled backward, looking for the safety of the darkness. Orla dropped down into a crouch, praying the gun had fallen within reach. For one heart-stopping moment she couldn't see where it had fallen. She looked about frantically. Then she saw it. It had fallen right on the edge of the darkness, out of reach. She stretched out a foot, trying to hook it with her toes.

The barrel spun away from her.

Orla stretched, the steel cuffs cutting deep into her wrists. The blinding agony gave her another inch. She dragged the Jericho toward her.

Sokol came lurching out of the darkness, his ruined face like something out of a nightmare. He could barely stand. He staggered two steps sideways for every two forward. Orla reached down for the gun, the chain grating as it slid through the coupling. She gripped it with both hands and squeezed the trigger. The gunshot was deafening in the close confines of the cell. The bullet took Sokol in the shoulder, jerking him back a zombie-step. She fired again. The second shot took him in the other shoulder. He roared in agony. Blind rage drove him forward two more steps until he was close enough she could feel his erection die as the third slug pierced his skull. He collapsed at her feet.

Gasping, Orla leaned back and tried to put a bullet into the coupling in the ceiling. She missed with the fourth. The fifth split it.

The Jericho 941 shipped with different barrels, a 9x19mm parabellum and a .41 "hot cartridge." The difference was three shots. She either had ten shots left or seven, depending if Sokol had kept the gun fully loaded.

She prayed she wouldn't have to find out the hard way.

Orla put her left hand against the wall and blew out the cuff's coupling. She didn't bother wasting a bullet on the right cuff. Nine or six left. She kept a running count. She fed the loose chain through the cuff and padded over to the open door. The gunshots had made a lot of noise. Anyone inside the building would have heard them. She willed them on. She had a gun and a need to strike back. She wanted to hurt them for what they'd done to her. She wanted to kill them for what they had done to the girl before her, and for making her watch as they did it.

She ran the numbers. Schnur had claimed the Shrieks worked as blind cells, one person connected to two others, the guy below them and the guy above them in the chain. They would never risk having more than two operatives in the same place, as it exposed an extra link in the chain; and extra links weakened the chain. That was the whole point of blind cells. But Sokol had said the others would be here soon, and *others* was plural. The guy below Sokol in the chain, and Gavrel Schnur. Schnur had said Mabus liked to be a part of the beheadings when they filmed them. He had told her that in his office in the IDF HQ.

Schnur was Mabus. She was sure of that. It was the only explanation that made sense. He had fed her a bullshit story about Solomon being Mabus, but that is all it was, a bullshit story. Schnur was Mabus. And if Schnur was Mabus, he not only knew who Akim Caspi really was, he was the only person who did, because Caspi was the man above him in the chain. She had had time to think about it while they hung her up like a chicken waiting for the slaughter. Akim Caspi was the man who had recruited Schnur. He had to be. There was no other scenario that made sense. Mabus was only ever the herald, the piper at the gates of dawn. Solomon, though, Solomon was the Antichrist to Schnur's herald, the real evil—and Schnur had given them his name.

It was a mistake.

A slip.

He had said more than he should have.

And she was in the mood to make him pay for that.

She looked down the narrow passageway but didn't see anyone coming. There was a single naked bulb at the far end, and beneath it, the first stair leading up. She ran back to Uzzi Sokol's corpse and took the shirt from his back. He had no need for it, and she didn't want to step out into the middle of Tel Aviv buck naked with a gun if she didn't have to. She'd be drawing enough attention to herself even with the shirt.

She checked his pockets for a spare ammo clip. He didn't have one. She could have popped the magazine and counted out the bullets, but she didn't want to take the time—not here. She wasn't out of the woods yet, and any extra seconds were wasted seconds.

She buttoned the shirt up quickly and then ran down the narrow passage. There was a door at the bottom, just before the stairs, a rusty iron thing that appeared to have been welded shut. She checked it just in case. It didn't give. That was enough for her. She ran barefoot up the stairs, slowing just before she reached the top. She checked left and right. There was no one there. Sokol had come planning to play. He'd known he was alone and would be for a while.

She was on the ground floor now. To the right she could see the interior of a small grocery store. There were no groceries on the shelves. It had been bombed out during the hostilities. To the left was the store room. It was a perfect place to hide someone. The entire strip mall was probably deserted. She went for the door.

The shop floor was thick with dust and broken glass. The windows had been boarded up. It was convenient. It meant no one could see inside. She walked over the broken glass, cutting the souls of her feet. She barely felt the thin shards as they dug in deep. Behind her Orla left a trail of bloody footprints.

She looked back over her shoulder to be sure no one was following and that no one was lurking in the shelves to jump out at her. She reached the door. It was locked and chained. She didn't hesitate. She put a single shot into the center of the lock's hasp and unthreaded the chain as it splintered and the tongue came loose. The door itself was locked. She realized then the stupidity of shooting out the lock. The door being chained on the inside meant Sokol and the others had a different way of coming and going. Probably an old goods door around the back of the shop. She couldn't worry about it now. She had eight or five left. Another one into the lock would make it seven or four if the gun had been fully loaded when Sokol came to torment her. Less if not. The numbers were getting a little low for her liking.

Instead of shooting the final lock she tested the integrity of the boards on the windows. They were flimsy at best. She looked around the little grocery store for something she could use. Back by the till she found one of three old shopping carts. They were buckled and twisted where the heat from the mortar fire had warped them, but they'd be fine for what she had in mind. Orla wrestled one of the carts free of the others. The wheels were buckled and it didn't want to roll on them. It didn't matter. She dragged it back far enough to give her a run at the boarded-up window, then launched herself at it, running full-tilt forward with the cart out in front of her like a battering ram.

The cart hit the boards and kept on going through them as she ran.

She heard screaming.

It sounded like a mad banshee inside her head.

It took her a moment to realize it was her.

And then the boards tore free and daylight came flooding in.

Head down, Orla staggered out onto the street, tears streaming down her cheeks.

She breathed in the hot morning air.

She was alive.

Sokol was dead.

That was all that mattered to her.

She stumbled barefoot toward the side of the road. She needed to get as far away from this place as she could.

Cars passed her on the street. She held out her hand, trying to hitch a ride. A few slowed, then accelerated, seeing the gun and the mess she was in. Just when she was beginning to think there were no good Samaritans on the road to Tel Aviv a white SUV slowed. She tensed, expecting to see the toad behind the wheel. If it had been Gavrel Schnur driving she would have shot him through the windshield without a second thought. It wasn't. It was a middle-aged man with his wife in the seat beside him. Orla stumbled toward the passenger door as the car slowed to a stop at the side of the road.

The woman rolled down her window, took one look at Orla half-naked, battered and bruised and holding the Jericho 941 as though it were a snake, and seemed to understand. She was young, maybe twenty-five herself, but she had grown up in the conflicts of Palestine and Israel; and in Orla she saw a victim. It was as simple as that. Orla guessed the woman had made her husband pull over. The stranger didn't ask what happened, she simply said, "Get in." And when Orla was inside the SUV, she said, "Drive."

They peeled away from the curb and into the traffic.

There was a blonde-haired doll on the backseat. They had a daughter. She wasn't in the car with them. Orla's stomach tightened at the realization that the Barbie-ideal of womanhood transcended state and nation. In the passenger seat the woman turned to look at Orla in the back. Orla could see a dozen questions behind her eyes, not least of which was, what have we done? It was natural. People didn't want to interpose themselves into situations where trouble was rife. But thankfully, her first instinct had been maternal, to protect. Questions were fine now; they were out of there and getting further and further away from the abandoned grocery store by the minute.

"Thank you," Orla said, for the second time in a few short minutes. This time she really meant it.

"What happened to you?"

It was the biggest of all of the potential questions. Too big for her to answer in the back of the car. Orla shook her head. She knew it would look like she was in shock. She looked at the woman and told her, "I thought I was going to die. You saved my life." It wasn't much of an answer, but it seemed to appease the woman for the moment at least. She had more questions, practical ones: Where are you from? Where are you staying? Do you want us to take you to the police station?

That was the last thing she wanted. She fended the constant barrage of questions with one of her own. "Do you have a cell phone?" The woman nodded. Of course they did. Everyone in the world had cell phones these days. "Do you mind if I make a call? I need to tell people I am okay."

"Of course," the woman fumbled about in her purse and handed a small gold D&G Motorola. Orla took it and flipped it open. She dialed in the +44 for England and prayed the dial tone wouldn't cut off into the operator's voice telling her that her service plan didn't cover international calls. It didn't. She punched in the rest of the numbers for Nonsuch.

Lethe picked up on the second ring. He sounded like he was in the car beside her as he said, "Go for Lethe."

She breathed out a long shaky sigh. She hadn't realized just how good it would be to hear a familiar voice. She closed her eyes and smiled. "Hey Jude."

He answered her with the rest of the famous lyric, then said, "Are you okay? Ah, hell, stupid question, I know. I mean . . . are you . . . did they hurt you?"

"Yes," she said, meaning yes she was okay, yes she was out of there, and yes they had hurt her, but not as much as she was going to hurt them. "I want an address, Jude. Gavrel Schnur. It should be in the Ramat district, North Tel Aviv. He's with the IDF."

"I'm on it, gimme a sec. It's good to hear your voice, Orla. I thought I'd never . . ." He let the thought hang. He didn't need to finish it. She'd had the thought often enough from the other side while she was down there in the dark cellar.

"I know," she said. "Tell the old man I am coming home. I've just got one thing to clean up first."

"You know what he's going to say," Lethe told her.

"I know. That's why I am telling you, not him. Have you got that address for me?"

It was off the 481, close to the water. She knew the area. It wasn't an area a young politician could afford, even if he was a rising star in the Likud party and favored of Menachem Begin, Shamir and Netanyahu. It was old money. Lots and lots of filthy old money. That should have been her first clue all the way back when she had been looking at the photograph of Schnur and his wife, Dassah. Schnur had to have got his money somehow, and that offshore account in Hottinger & Cie and all of those Silverthorn deposits were making an awful lot of sense to her now. The money came from Caspi. That was the joke wasn't it? Made of Silver. And what was more Christian in terms of iconography than the crown of thorns? She stared out of the window, watching the streets go by.

"Who is he?"

"Mabus," she said, grateful that the conversation only made sense to the pair of them. She smiled at the woman. It was meant to assure her that everything was fine. She was sure she looked mad.

"Be careful, Orla. Promise me."

"I'll be home soon," she said. It wasn't the promise he'd wanted, but it was the only one she was prepared to give him. She wasn't about to be careful. The time for care had passed. She was hunting the man who had made her last few days a living hell. She hung up the phone on him and gave it back to the woman. "Thank you," she said again. "I can't pay for the call, I'm sorry. My money is all back at the hotel."

"That's okay, honey, don't worry. Where are you staying?"

She gave them Gavrel Schnur's address, the big house off the 481, down by the water.

She watched her good Samaritans drive off into the blue sky of the coast road.

Staying in Tel Aviv was counter-intuitive. They would expect her to run, to get as far away from them as she could. Schnur wouldn't expect her to go to his home and wait for him. It made no logical sense. But revenge wasn't about logic.

There was no security gate, and no cameras that she could see. That didn't mean they weren't there.

She had so many questions. She wanted to ask him to his face why he had done it. Why had he plotted with Solomon and Devere to cause so much pain. She wanted to hear him justify himself? Was he going to blame the murder of his wife? The death of his son? And did it even matter what he said? It could never be justification enough. Hearing it might humanize the toad, but it could never make him human. Nothing could ever do that again.

She walked toward the house.

It was odd that he had never moved, given what had happened to his wife in the driveway, but she reasoned, perhaps he needed the constant reminder to fuel his hatred?

It was the middle of the day, broad daylight, so most

likely the toad was at work, or heading to the grocery store basement to finish her. He wouldn't be home until later. Which would give her time to break in and cover her tracks so that when he finally came home she would be waiting for him.

There wouldn't be any questions, she decided.

She didn't want to hear his answers.

The toad didn't come home for three hours.

It gave her time.

She sat at his desk, breathing in his lingering smell. Everything in the place reeked of Gavrel Schnur. Orla sat back in his high-backed leather chair, wearing one of his wife's dresses. They were a similar size, if not exactly the same. Schnur had maintained her wardrobes as a shrine. Every garment still hung on its hanger, immaculately pressed. Her death really had affected him. She found a photograph of Dassah and styled her hair so that at first glance the toad might think there was an old ghost in his chair.

She went through his things, looking for the name Solomon. She wanted a surname. She wanted a place. Something. Anything. She wanted to link Schnur and Solomon and Devere and work out which one was the idealist, which one the fanatic and which one the opportunist. She assumed it was Solomon, Schnur and Devere, in that order, but she wasn't about to bet her life on it.

She rifled his drawers and searched the place for a safe. She couldn't find one, but that didn't mean the toad didn't have his hiding places. Everyone had their hiding places. She tried his computer, but it was password protected; and she wasn't remotely as tech-savvy as Lethe, so she simply pulled the hard drive out of the machine. She'd let Lethe play with it when she got home. She'd tell him it was a coming home present.

Orla swiveled the chair so it turned away from the door. He wouldn't see her as he came into the room. She sat there alone, waiting. She remembered something he had said in his office. He'd told her that Judas Iscariot wasn't mentioned anywhere in the Gospel of Peter and asked her what she thought of that. Now, thinking about it, she realized how odd that was. There was Peter, the rock on which the Church was founded, the first Apostle, and he didn't have a word for the betrayal of his Lord? According to John, Peter was the swordsman who cut off the ear of Malchus when they came to arrest Christ. How could he have not written about Judas, then, if Judas really had been the great betrayer?

Then it occurred to her that perhaps Judas and Peter had in fact been one and the same, that Judas had written the Gospel accredited to Peter. It was a passion, one of the most prominent in early Christianity but denounced as heretical because it blamed Herod Antipas and not Pilate for the crucifixion. The resurrection and the ascension weren't separate events, either. Where Matthew claimed Christ's cry from the cross was "Eli, Eli, lama sabachthani?" *My god, my god, why hast thou forsaken me?* Peter claimed Christ was not calling to God but asking, "My power, my power, why hast thou forsaken me?" and when he had said it he was taken up. There was no death. The other thing she recalled was that there was no disloyalty in Peter's story. The disciples were arrested for plotting to burn the temple. Could those have been Judas' thoughts? Judas' truths?

Peter was the rock the Church was founded upon. Judas' was the sacrifice the Church was founded upon. Could they be one and the same? Did it even matter, or was Schnur just playing with her, running theosophical rings around her?

The one thing she could understand was that if the Disciples of Judas didn't believe the words of Matthew, Mark, Luke and John, then there was no need for them to believe in redemption from man's sins by the suffering on the cross. It was all propaganda and lies, after all, wasn't it? Made up to sell this new ministry and create a faith in retrospect. What was it the toad had said? All of these random acts of violence, hate, war and death made him think we weren't redeemed at all, we were damned. She wondered if he actually believed the stuff he said, or if it was a convenient excuse to strike back at the people he believed had hurt him, the people behind his wife's murder? Attacking an entire system of faith seemed a little extreme for that.

No, surely in Acts, Peter, Prince of the Apostles, stood up and decried Judas as a traitor? In the same passage he described Judas' death in gory detail, his guts rupturing in the field of blood as he collapsed. Didn't the Apostles welcome Matthias in Judas' place? She could almost hear Schnur's counter argument in her head: the Gospel of Luke names Jude for Thaddeus; John doesn't name any of the twelve and adds his own Nathanael. All these testimonies and they can't keep their key players straight? Peter being described alongside Judas in these other texts and not in his own? Was it revisionist history, trying to erase the sinner from the course of history? Or was it a case of trying to hide something else?

These other gospels were the ones that promised the miracles, the healing of the sick, the driving out demons, even raising the dead. There was nothing like that in Peter's passion. The story of Akeldama was preposterous, Judas rupturing and exploding was like something out of a bad movie. It's not even a convincing lie. And of course there were the problems of language. In the original texts the vocabulary was quite limited, meaning that the translations could be very easily made more explicitly divine should the translator wish. For instance, the prepositions *on* and *by* were often the same word in Aramaic, which would completely change the whole walking on water thing. Walking by water was far less impressive a feat. So what was Peter hiding? What truth did he not want recorded? If he wasn't Judas, then perhaps he knew the truth about Judas?

It came back to the word messiah, didn't it?

And if a messiah really was no more divine or god-touched than the one who brings peace and restoration to Israel, well then it couldn't exactly be claimed that Judas' kiss brought peace. For almost a century after either Christ or Judas the Romans were still suppressing the names Judaea and Jerusalem. The Jews were still exiles.

Israel was in her blood. She knew its history and its pains as well as any Jew. She had studied the Diaspora and the destruction of the First Temple. She understood the effect the destruction of the Second Temple had on the people. And she understood the hope Simon bar Kokhba had represented. Bar Kokhba had reestablished a Jewish state of Israel seven centuries after the Diaspora began, a state which he ruled as Nasri for three years, bringing the scattered Jews home. Surely, by Schnur's definition this made Kokhba more effectively a messiah than either Judas or Jesus? For two of those years he fought tooth and nail against the Romans to maintain a free Israel, but for three years he gave his people a home, a place. He unified them. Of course after he failed history was unkind—the Jews were scattered, sold into slavery or driven out—and writers with little sympathy to his cause called him Simon bar Kozebah, or Simon, son of The Lie.

That was the way of the world though, was it not? History was written by the winners, not the valiant losers.

She didn't have the answer.

Two millennia on no one did.

She didn't think they were meant to.

It came down to faith. That was what all these contradictions came down to in the end. Some people needed to believe that Jesus suffered on the cross to redeem mankind's sins. They needed to believe that there was a point, that the sacrifice of his earthly body meant something.

These words that so many clung to, so many drew faith from and believed in, could be twisted to say almost anything, and there was no way of knowing one way or the other what the truth was.

In the end it didn't matter what she believed, what Schnur believed, what any of them believed. However improbable it was, Judas *could* be Peter, or he could be the Messiah, or a messiah; or he could be both or neither. It didn't matter. People would find a way to twist the truth into whatever they wanted it to be.

That was the only truth.

And then it hit her, all of the messages, the prophecy of the Popes, the quatrains of Nostradamus, the lectures on the meaning of the word messiah, all of it. It wasn't about Mabus ushering in the Antichrist, as Nostradamus had said, it was about a new messiah. Mabus was Caspi's herald. He had said Caspi's real name was Solomon. One sign of the Messiah was the restoration of Israel as a homeland for the Jews, and another was the rebuilding of the Temple. Who had built the First Temple?

Solomon.

It was Solomon's Temple.

That was it. Caspi didn't see himself as the Antichrist at all, he saw himself as the new Messiah. He was the man who was going to bring peace to Israel by creating a Jewish state. She didn't believe for a minute that his real name was Solomon any more than it was Caspi.

Suddenly it all made sense. She saw how Gavrel Schnur had been recruited by Solomon to his cause. Dassah. It really had all been about his wife. That explained the shrine in his office and the shrine upstairs. She still dominated his life. Dassah Schnur had been murdered because of his vocal support of the Jewish presence on the West Bank and Gaza. He had never changed that position. He lived his entire life to that one fundamental truth. He wanted a homeland for the Jewish settlers. The PLO had murdered his wife because of it, which only made him want it more.

She understood Schnur's role in her little triptych. He was the idealist who had been offered the one thing he always wanted.

Orla almost pitied him.

If Schnur was the idealist, the other roles were very easily defined. Miles Devere was the opportunist. There was money in death—there always had been—and he had started in Israel, in the very areas Schnur wanted to see a Jewish homeland. He understood the people and the politics and the needs of the region. Who better to help rebuild the infrastructure after the fallout? And, who better to be the grand architect and help build the new monument to Solomon's messiah? Was that what he had offered Devere, the Last Temple? Surely it would be the most iconographic building of modern times. That would appeal to a man like Devere, even if the money and power didn't.

The more she thought about it, the more she realized she was underestimating Miles Devere. There was a sinister undertone to his involvement. She recalled the payments into the Swiss bank made by Silverthorn and withdrawn by Caspi or Solomon or whatever his real name was. She remembered Humanity Capital and its modus operandi, how it stimulated unrest and promoted war for financial gain, and the final piece of the puzzle slotted into place. Devere wasn't some innocent attracted by Solomon, he was the money man. He was financing this war for a New Israel, pumping money into the Shrieks' coffers, knowing that every dollar spent would in time be reaped five, six, eight, tenfold. It was what he did, he traded in human suffering and disaster.

The irony that Judas' line was again being exploited for the gain of others didn't escape her. As far as Devere was concerned it wasn't about faith at all, it was about money.

His own thirty pieces of silver.

She sat back in the chair. It was all there to see.

That left Solomon as the fanatic, the one man who really did believe all of it—the broken faith, the false church, the defamation of Judas—and through it all, the truth of what being a messiah really meant. It was never about being the son of God.

Surely that made him the most dangerous animal of them all, because a man like that couldn't be reasoned with. Fanatics by definition weren't open to reason. They didn't want their eyes open to alternatives. And if they were persuasive, they could draw others closer to their flame of madness; but that wasn't reason, that was trading on their rigid insanity. And he was insane. Make no bones about it. He could act the part in public—he could be convincing—but underneath the skin he was gone. That made him all the more frightening. A man like that would stop at nothing to see his dream of a new Jerusalem, a new recognized Israeli state for people of the one faith, come to pass. A man like that wouldn't care if it meant stripping down the faiths of the Catholic Church and all of those other religions that didn't subscribe to the glory of man. The trappings of religion and heresy were meat and potatoes to a man like that. It played into his messianic complex.

It was like a trail of breadcrumbs had been left for her to follow, and all the way she'd been picking them up and not thinking about what they really meant. But now she'd got it. She knew who they were. She knew how their roles fitted together. Everything made sense.

She called Lethe on the toad's home phone and told him everything.

Then she waited for Mabus the Herald to come home.

And while she waited the sun went down.

Downstairs, she heard the front door slam.

The toad was home.

She waited.

She heard him breathing heavily as he labored up the large staircase. Gavrel Schnur was a grotesque man. He was gasping hard, seriously out of breath, before he was even halfway through the ascent. Orla was patient. She waited, looking at her ghostly reflection in the glass.

The toad came into his study. He paused momentarily, staring at the reflection of the devil in his wife's blue dress, and then he composed himself. "Did you think seeing you in my wife's dress, with your hair like that, would stop me from killing you?" he said. It was the last thing he ever said. Orla turned the chair around slowly. She looked at him. The arrogance faded when he saw the Jericho 941 she held low in her lap. She didn't see the man responsible for torturing her. She didn't see the man behind the terror attacks on Berlin and Rome and all of those other cities. She saw a fat, frightened man who had never recovered from losing his wife.

And right at that moment it didn't matter whether she had seven shots or four left.

She only needed one.

29

SCAPEGOAT

Konstantin Khavin didn't know where he was.

There was a glass of water on the table, a tape recorder and microphone, and two chairs on the other side of the table. He was alone in the room. They worked him in shifts, refusing to let him sleep. They had taken his prints and run him through the system. They knew who he was. Worse, they knew what he was. They wanted to know who he was working for, who else was with him in Germany, why he had killed the Pope. Then someone came in with a security photograph of him in Berlin on the day of the sarin gas attack.

They put it on the table in front of him and asked, "Is that you?" He couldn't deny it. It was a good picture. It caught all of his features in full frontal. Any half-decent facial recognition software would identify him. There was no point lying. "Yes." He said and suddenly they were looking at a two-for-one deal on a sociopathic killer.

Because they knew who he was, they knew all about his

training. They knew he was versed in interrogation techniques and torture. And they knew his experience wasn't just theoretical.

They came back in.

"I'm not going to lie to you," the woman said, taking the first seat on the other side of the table. "Things don't look good for you, Konstantin. You story does not check out."

Her partner, a straight-faced bodybuilder in a suit, sank into the seat beside her.

"That's her polite way of saying you're screwed. We've got hundreds of witness testimonies, video evidence, your prints on the weapon, all the physical evidence we could dream of, including the sworn testimony of the Swiss Guard who tried to stop you. That's what she means by 'things not looking good.' It gets substantially worse when we add your own story to the mix. A Russian defector, Konstantin? Do you have any conception of the word loyalty? Or is that it, you're some sort of sleeper agent? Did they plant you on this side of the Wall and wait for you to grow? Maybe this was always your mission? Is that it, Konstantin? Were you 'let go' so that you could do this all these years later? Did they think the humiliation of another defector was worth it in return for the death of the Holy Father? How did they sell the mission to you? Or are you programmed to obey?"

Konstantin stared straight ahead. He didn't so much as twitch. The words didn't register on his face. He gave them nothing, knowing it would frustrate them. People were behind the one-way glass watching the whole dance.

"In Moscow they would have brought a doctor in by now," he said, looking at the woman.

"Why?"

"To elicit a confession," Konstantin said.

"You mean soften you up with sodium pentothal to weaken your resolve? We have ways of making you talk and all that bullshit," the man said, full of scorn.

"I see you watch the movies," Konstantin said.

"I suppose they'd send the muscle in next to beat the confession out of you if the drugs didn't work?"

"Perhaps. Or perhaps they would let the doctor use the instruments of his trade. A lot of truths can be learned under a doctor's scalpel."

"That's barbaric," the woman said.

"It is one of the reasons I left Moscow. Not the only one. It was another world back then. Do not think you can intimidate me with threats like your colleague is trying. I come from a different world, one where violence is commonplace. I do not fear pain. I do not fear torture. But if you want to hear it, I will tell you the truth of torture, officer."

"Go on," she said.

"Everyone talks. That is the truth. Everyone talks even if they know it is going to kill them in the end. They just want the pain to end. The movies where the square-jawed hero doesn't break is just that, a movie. The reality is he will foul himself. He will cry snot and tears. He will piss down his legs and he will scream, and in the end, he will beg you not to hurt him anymore; he will tell you everything you want to know and more; he will offer secrets you didn't know he had, just to lessen the pain for a little while."

"Are you telling us to torture you?"

"Would you if you thought it would give you the truth?"

"We have the truth," the man cut across their little dance. "It's on bloody film for the entire world to see."

"That is not the truth," Konstantin said.

"You're insane. Do you know that? You're a freakin' sociopath! So what, you want us to waterboard you?" The man shook his head in disgust.

"There is no way I can convince you. Even if you open my stomach and reach in with your bare hands to pull at my guts, my truth will not change. I did not kill him."

"Easy to say," the man said. "We can all be brave when

it's only words."

"Then cut me," Konstantin said. "My people will not save me. I am alone here. I have nothing to gain by lying and nothing to lose by telling the truth."

"I don't believe you, Konstantin," the man said. "You're a liar. One way or the other. Either you lied to your people when you fled to the West, or you lied to us when we welcomed you? Which one is it?"

"Silence is not a lie."

"Why did you do it, Konstantin?" the woman asked, taking over the interrogation. Her voice was calm, honeyed. She smiled at him. It was a "we're all friends here" smile. It was the biggest lie of the day so far.

"I didn't do it."

"We know you did, Konstantin. What we don't know is why. We've got a lot of other questions as well, things we don't understand, like, how does killing the Pope link in with the Berlin subway attack? And how are you tied to Rome and the people who burned themselves alive in London and all of those other cities? We're only seeing part of the picture, Konstantin. Help us see all of it. Talk to us. If you help us, we can help you."

She wasn't particularly good. She wasn't one of the A team, Konstantin thought, listening to her. Neither was her partner. They were the breakers, the waves sent to crash against the shore just to wear him down. They were never meant to get the truth out of him. It was all about weakening his resolve. They were the sodium pentothal, figuratively speaking.

But they could ask all the questions they wanted, they could badger and push and probe; they were never going to catch him in lies, because he wasn't lying.

Or he could give them something.

"You want another truth?" he asked.

The woman nodded eagerly, like Pavlov's detective.

Konstantin's memory was good. It had to be. He remembered the zero plate from the car in Berlin.

He gave it to them. It was up to them what they did with it.

"Who does the car belong to? Your boss? Your contact?"

Konstantin shrugged. "How would I know? But the car is connected. It all is. Everything is connected."

"Very zen of you, Konstantin," the man said.

"Find the owner of the car, find the Berlin cell. Everything is connected."

The woman glanced toward the glass. Konstantin knew that behind the mirror people were frantically trying to connect the dots, work out who the car belonged to and if Konstantin was telling the truth. They had no reason to assume he wasn't, and every reason to believe he was selling one of his collaborators out. That was the way they broke terror cells, one small confession at a time. If Konstantin gave them the man behind Berlin, it would hardly prove his innocence, though. If anything, it would only serve to compound his guilt as far as they were concerned.

"Find Berlin and you will find Rome, or London or Madrid or Paris. Everything is connected. Information travels down channels; it isn't just plucked out of the air. Everything is connected. It has to be, because of the precision. The suicides had to know when to burn themselves. The poisoner in Rome had to know when to poison the water. He didn't want people dying early. He didn't want the deaths blending in with the deaths in Berlin. He didn't want the majority dying the same day the Pope was killed. Everything had to be separate. Forty days and forty nights of fear, see?"

Still, the clock was ticking on another day. Mabus had promised forty days and forty nights of terror, and nothing told Konstantin that had changed just because the Pope was dead. Now was the perfect time to increase the intensity of the attacks. So it didn't matter if they thought he was guilty or not. If he had something that could help save innocent lives, even something as simple as a registration number, he was always going to share it, even if it meant damning himself. That was his sacrifice.

The woman came back alone the next time. She brought him a warm cup of black coffee. It was a trade, he knew. She gave him warmth and sustenance—he gave her another truth, quid pro quo. It was straight out of the good cop/bad cop handbook.

He didn't complain. He warmed his hands on the cup, then sipped at it slowly.

"They found a body in the Moselle this morning."

Konstantin looked up at her. "And you think I killed him as well?"

She smiled that smile again. "Difficult. The coroner puts time of death almost a full day after we took you into custody, so I think you're safe on this one."

"Then why tell me about it? I assume you have a reason?"

"I do. His name was Emery Seifert. Does that name mean anything to you?"

Konstantin shook his head. "Should it?"

"He was a member of the Swiss Guard. More pertinently, he was one of the guards on the stage when you killed the Pope."

"I didn't kill the Pope," Konstantin said, reflexively.

She smiled at that. Again.

"Can you think why anyone would want to kill Seifert, Konstantin?"

Only one reason, Konstantin thought. He looked at the woman, trying to decide if she was deliberately trying to lead him into this line of reasoning. If she was, he couldn't see what she stood to gain from it. "Because he saw what really happened on the stage," Konstantin said, "or because he suspected."

"Either way we have all of this video evidence, so it's just one voice against the maddening crowd."

"And yet here you are telling me all about it."

"Maybe I want to believe you, Konstantin?"

"Maybe you do, maybe not. Either way won't change the truth."

"You're a strange man. You don't want legal representation. You don't want to confess. You aren't spouting any religious propaganda. You aren't trying to convince us that you had to strike for Lucifer to rise again. In fact you seem disturbingly rational. Yet you know things you clearly shouldn't know, such as the license plate of a diplomatic car that is registered in Berlin to the Israeli Ambassador's personal staff."

"Who? Who's it registered to?"

She looked at him, surprised by the sudden intensity of his question. For a fraction of a moment the implacable calm of Konstantin Khavin came down and she saw the real man beneath. It was like seeing the wizard behind the curtain.

"Lieutenant General Akim Caspi of the Israel Defense Force."

Konstantin closed his eyes. He had been that close.

"Caspi's dead," Konstantin told her.

"Did you kill him?"

He let out a slow breath, shaking his head. "No, the man in the car pretending to be him almost certainly did. Caspi died in June 2004."

"That doesn't mean you didn't kill him," she said reasonably. "One fact does not contradict the other."

"Check my service record with Ogmios."

"And again, you know we can't. As far as we can ascertain this Ogmios is a figment of your imagination."

"Do you believe that?"

"It doesn't matter what I believe, Konstantin."

"And yet here you are," he said again, "telling me about a

dead body in a river that could go some way to validating the truth of my story."

"Or, you could have had one of your people kill the guard for that selfsame purpose."

Konstantin nodded slowly. He couldn't help it, he rather liked this woman. She thought about things. She didn't leap to conclusions based upon what she could or could not see. He needed to find a way to get her to call the old man. He could give her all the truths she needed.

"You want me to give you names?"

She shrugged. "Rather depends whose names they are, doesn't it? You could start by telling me who you were working with in Berlin, and who helped you in Koblenz."

Konstantin slapped his forehead. He had thought for just a minute that she believed him, for what good it would have done him. She was just as blind as her partner.

"I work for Sir Charles Wyndham," he said. That was all she needed really. One name. If she was good at her job, she would ignore official channels and go to the old man directly. Of course, he didn't expect her to do that. Why would she? As she kept telling him, they had screeds of evidence against him. They could place him in Berlin at the time of the subway attack and on the stage with the silver dagger in his hand as the Pope died. They didn't need anything else. "Can I ask you a question?"

"You can ask," she said.

"How long have I been in here?"

"Four days," she said.

"They've taken the Pope back to Rome?"

She nodded. "It was on the news this morning. They are preparing Saint Paul's for over six million people to make the pilgrimage to see Pope Peter lying in state."

"Have there been any other attacks since the Pope? It's been three days. Forty days and forty nights of fear. That's what they promised."

"Nothing," she said. "Which rather supports the idea

that with you stuck in here there's no one out there to coordinate the attacks, doesn't it?"

"Or it means that Orla got Mabus."

She looked at him. She had obviously heard what he said but didn't know either of the two names, and because she didn't know them, that turned the simple sentence into something that made no sense to her.

He tried to think through the chain of events. They would have returned the Pope's body to the Vatican. The Cardinal Camerlengo would have officially declared him dead, calling out his real name three times. It was all ceremony, but that was part of believing, holding to the old rituals even as the world turned. Then the Camerlengo would have shattered the Papal seal of Peter II and split the Ring of the Fisherman, so that no one else might use it in the dead man's place to forge papal decrees. Then the Church would enter *Sede Vacante*, the Empty Seat. There were nine days of mourning between the death of the Pope and the conclave that would elect his successor. There were precedents for moving the conclave of the Cardinals forward in times when the Church and the faithful were at the greatest risk, but they would resist that at all costs. Moving the conclave forward would show the world they were frightened by Mabus and his terrors.

That meant there were five more days until the conclave would convene.

Five more days. And he was stuck in this interrogation room, helpless to do anything, while Mabus and Caspi and Devere moved into their endgame.

It disturbed him that there had been no more attacks since he had been taken. Terrorists needed to make good on their threats, otherwise the fear they instilled would be diluted. Cities would rally. Berlin and Rome would be stronger for their suffering, just like New York and London. There should have been something else, something more.

Five more days for the Disciples of Judas to strike the

most decisive blow of all.

They had promised to shatter the world's faith.

Killing one man would not do that.

He had no idea what would.

And then he realized what this was: the calm before the storm.

Everyone in the world would think this was it, that it couldn't get any worse. They'd seen cities ruined from within and without, and then the Father of the Catholic Church struck down.

He looked at the woman across the table from him. "Do you think this is over?"

She didn't answer him for a long moment. She genuinely seemed to be thinking about her answer rather than glibly saying yes. "We have no reason to suspect more attacks," she said finally, like she was parroting the official press release.

"Yes, you do," he said. "You have very good reason to expect more attacks, because they told you they were coming. Forty days and forty nights of terror in every city in the West. Wasn't that what they said? Something like that. Not just Berlin and Rome."

"But the threats in Rome and Berlin were different."

She was right. Lethe had pointed that out. They were. "So that's what you've decided? The threats were all about assassinating Peter II?"

"We have no reason to suspect otherwise."

"Until they give you a reason."

"They won't," she said, with surprising certainty.

"What about the promise to destroy the faith of the world? Are you just discounting that?"

"How do you destroy someone's faith?" she asked in all seriousness. "There are 1.3 billion Catholics in the world, 2.1 billion Christians. How could you possibly shatter the beliefs of a third of the world's population?"

"Not by killing one man," Konstantin said, trying to

force home the point.

"No, and every scientist who stands up to decry there is no god and has evidence to support his claim doesn't change the fact that these people believe. Evolutionary biologists can call them stupid for believing, they don't care. They still believe. So how do you do it?"

"You prove it wrong."

"But that's what the scientists are doing, isn't it?"

"Then how do you do it?"

"I don't know. That's why I am not worried about it. That's why I am much more interested in much more mundane questions like who you work for and who you are working with."

"I've told you, I work for Sir Charles Wyndham. The project is codenamed Ogmios. Ask him," he said again, willing her to just go and track down the old man herself.

The next time she came into the interrogation room she brought something for him. It wasn't a cup of coffee. She put the silver dagger on the table between them and said, "What's this?"

He looked at it. It was the first time he had seen it properly. It was obviously old. "You wouldn't believe me if I told you," he said.

"Try me."

He shrugged. "It's a dagger."

"I can see that, so that hardly counts as unbelievable. So tell me, what's so special about it?"

"It's two thousand years old for a start," Konstantin said. He didn't want to say more, saying more meant he knew more. Knowing more only implicated him further. He breathed deeply. What did it matter? He wasn't walking away from this. He might as well tell her what he knew, if for no other reason than talking to her kept her partner away. The man's constant badgering and boorishness was boring.

"Go on."

"It's silver."

"I can see that."

"Silver's not usually the stuff of weapons. Too soft. It'd break, maybe not the first time it's used, maybe not the second, but it would break. And no fighter wants to go to war knowing his weapon could fail him at any time."

"Makes sense."

"Because it is sense. Common sense.

"So it's ceremonial?"

"You'd think, but no. I think it is more accurate to say it is commemorative."

"That's an odd choice of words, don't you think? Are you saying the dagger used to murder the Pope was a com-memorative dagger? So what, it was made for a King's Jubilee? Something like that?"

He did like this woman. She was sharp. "Something exactly like that. A king two thousand years ago." If he said two thousand years often enough she'd make the intuitive leap. He knew she would. "That's one thing that makes this dagger special—it's silver, it's two thousand years old. What kings do you remember from two thousand years ago?"

She spread her arms wide.

"Think," Konstantin said. "King of the Jews, two thou-sand years ago?"

"Jesus? You're telling me this dagger was made to com-memorate the life of Jesus?" She didn't laugh, but he could see she wanted to.

"How does silver fit into the story?" he guided her. "Think."

"Silver?"

"Come on. You know this. Every one learns the story when they're kids. Thirty pieces of silver."

She shook her head. "No bloody way. Not possible. I don't believe you."

"You asked me. I told you you wouldn't believe me."

"You didn't say I wouldn't believe, because it was ludicrous though, did you? So, tell me, how did you get your hands on a dagger forged from Judas' silver? Hell, I can't even believe I am asking a question like that. Jesus, Judas, we just wandered off into criminally insane territory. Is that what this is? Are you fashioning your defense? Going to plead the Devil made you do it? That you heard the voice of Judas telling you to strike back? To punish the unfaithful for treating him so badly?"

"No," Konstantin said.

"Then what? Talk me through it, Konstantin. Help me understand, because right now I've got a murder weapon, a murderer, and a truckload of evidence, but something doesn't fit when I think about it. It's a niggle. The old cop instinct, if you like. I want to say I don't think you did it, but I've watched the footage a thousand times; you're as guilty as sin. So I don't know why I keep coming back to the fact that I *want* to believe you."

So Konstantin told her everything—Masada, Mabus, the two Akim Caspis, the prophecies and the threats, and his involvement in it. He told her about the gun in the apartment and the timer and the birdseed in the trees meant to cause a distraction. He told her about trying to fight his way through the crowd to save the Holy Father and being too late. He told her about the Swiss Guard and begged her to put his face out across the wire, to warn people. Because he was still out there, and the body in the Moselle proved someone else had witnessed the murder and he'd silenced them before they could talk. He told her about Humanity Capital trading on tragedy, about Miles Devere, about the hostages in England. He told her everything.

It felt good to confess it, to put the burden onto someone else, because it wasn't over yet. He knew that as surely as he knew the sun was going to rise on the ninth day and the College of the Cardinals would enter conclave to elect the next Pope. It wasn't over.

"What are you going to do with the dagger?" he asked her.

She looked at him. He couldn't read her face. He didn't know whether she believed a word he had said. What she couldn't argue with was how it all hung together. He couldn't have made up a story like that while they had him trapped in the interrogation room. "It's a murder weapon. It's evidence."

"When it's over?"

"Why?"

"Like you said, it's evidence, but not just of murder. In a weird kind of way it's proof, isn't it? Proof that Jesus and Judas existed, proof in the stuff they want us to believe. It's the kind of treasure the Vatican will want, no matter how tainted it might be."

He lost track of the time between visits. He was beyond tired. But they wouldn't let him sleep. Not properly. Only snatches here and there. That told him they had cameras on him and someone watching him at all times. Whenever he started to doze they returned, like clockwork.

They kept coming back, working away at him. Softly from the woman, great hammer blows from the guy. He kept trying to tell them they were wasting their time, that the real assassin was out there, still safe in his position inside the inner ring of the papal guard, but they refused to believe him.

He still didn't know their names. They were just the woman and the man. It kept it impersonal, stopped him from thinking of them as friends. If he had been running the interrogation, the first thing he would have done was make it personal. Sometimes he did not understand the logic of these people. If they wanted him to trust them, surely they should be using every trick at their disposal to convince him there were bonds between them. They couldn't bring in the torturer, so what else could they do?

This time when they came for him it was different.

They weren't alone.

There were six other men with them. Konstantin watched them file into the cell. It was like the tiled wall had been replaced with muscle. The muscle didn't talk. They didn't acknowledge his nod. It was as if he didn't exist to them. That suited Konstantin.

"Get up," the man said.

He didn't move.

"I said get up."

Konstantin placed his hands flat on the table and pushed the chair back, dragging the metal legs across the floor so they grated. He stood up slowly.

"What's going on?" he asked the woman.

She didn't answer him. She looked at the man.

"You're being moved."

He looked at the woman. "How many days has it been?"

This time she answered him. "Eight."

He had been out of touch with reality for eight days. Eight days. Anything could have happened in that time. Akim Caspi could be dead. Mabus could be dead. A third of the world's population could be dead. He wouldn't have known. All he did know was that tomorrow the *novem-diales* would be over.

If the Sicarii were going to strike tomorrow, it would be the perfect moment. For nine days the world would have mourned Peter II, and the victims of Rome and Berlin along with him, and each new dawn would be a day further away from the tragedies. Nine days was enough for the numbness to have receded. Nine days was enough for the world to think that final attack wasn't coming. Nine days was enough to make a fool out of everyone.

"Where are you taking me?"

"Russia, Italy, London? Does it matter? One cell looks

pretty much the same as another wherever it is," the man said.

"I'd like to know."

"Berlin," the man said. "The fun stuff's over. You're going to be held accountable for what you've done, and then we're going to bury you way down deep. And when the world has forgotten about you we'll whisper in the right ear and someone will find you in the showers or shiv you in the yard. It won't matter to us. But I am sure we'll find someone who really wants to hurt you; maybe an ex-countryman of yours? Or maybe someone who isn't enlightened enough to turn the other cheek. It doesn't matter one way or the other to me. Justice will have had its way, and the world will have its blood, so everyone is happy."

"Except for me," Konstantin said, as they came around the table and grabbed his arms. Two men forced them behind his back and cuffed him. They cuffed his ankles and ran a chain from one cuff to the other, meaning he could barely shuffle more than a foot at a time.

"And who the hell cares if you're happy?" the man asked.

The muscle bundled him into the back of an SUV and drove.

They left the man and the woman outside the BKA offices in Wiesbaden. They didn't talk until they were more than thirty minutes outside of the city, then the driver switched on his blinkers and followed the traffic off the next exit ramp, leaving the Autobahn. This wasn't the way to Berlin.

For a moment Konstantin thought that perhaps they had decided to do it the Russian way, drive him somewhere remote then finish him, cleaning up the problem he posed. He licked his lips.

The driver pulled over to the side of the road.

It was a remote spot, far enough away for his body not to

be found quickly. Remote enough the local wildlife might take care of that problem altogether.

There was little in the way of passing traffic. No one would accidentally see anything from the side of the road.

It was a good place to kill a man.

The driver leaned forward, opening the glove box.

Konstantin was suddenly aware of his breathing. It was hard. A regular push in, out, in, out. He looked at his options. There wasn't a lot he could do. He couldn't very well fight from the back seat of an SUV with six other slabs of solid muscle surrounding him. Well, he could, but he wouldn't win. He wasn't Superman. He couldn't run. The back doors would be child-locked to prevent him from opening them from the inside. So, he did the only thing he could do: nothing.

The driver pulled a padded envelope from the glove box. It didn't look bulky enough, or heavy enough in his hand, to contain a service revolver, and they wouldn't have risked a close-combat weapon like a Korshun knife or a SARO machete. He turned in his seat and looked straight at Konstantin. "We've got a message for the old man from Control," the driver said in a coarse Manchester accent. "This is it, all debts paid in full. He's kept up his end of the bargain, but this is the end of the road. You're cut off, as of now. You understand?"

He handed Konstantin the envelope.

It contained a passport with his picture on it in the name of John Smith, just about as English as names came, and a plane ticket from Frankfurt Main back to Heathrow, leaving in six hours. There was also a billfold with about 300 Euros in it.

"You get yourself caught, you're on your own."

"How are you going to explain this?" Konstantin said, meaning the plane ticket. "They're expecting me in Berlin."

"Yours is not to reason why, soldier. Yours is to get your ass home. End of story."

He nodded. He knew enough not to ask operational details. No doubt the real wall of muscle was arriving right about now at the BKA building and the man and woman were scratching their heads, wondering who the hell they'd just turned him over to if it wasn't the good guys. Or maybe only one of them was scratching his head. The woman had said she wanted to believe him. Maybe that had been enough to convince her to make the call? Had the simple act of telling the truth set this entire chain of events into action like the first domino going over?

One thing Six could do was paperwork. This crew would have presented every necessary piece of paper, with every i dotted and every t crossed. In and out, no one any the wiser until the real prisoner transport team arrived, hence the thirty minutes of driving rather than taking him straight to Frankfurt Main or the military airport at Wiesbaden. Six didn't want the Germans knowing it was Her Majesty who'd sprung their suspected papal assassin. It wasn't exactly good form for a monarch to be getting her royal hands dirty like that, even if she didn't know what was actually being done in her name.

Konstantin pocketed the passport and the ticket.

"Thank you," he said.

"Don't thank me, mate. I'm only doing what I'm told. Thank the old man for calling in every favor he had with every man, woman and child from here to Timbuktu. Without him you'd be rotting away in Berlin for the rest of your natural, pal."

He broke one of the smaller Euro notes at a kiosk, buying a phone card.

It took him the best part of an hour to find a working pay phone.

He called in to Nonesuch.

Lethe answered on the first ring. It took a moment for

the line to connect and then both of them were talking without the other hearing. Then the line opened. Konstantin started again, "I am on the evening flight from Frankfurt Main to Heathrow. When I land I am going to call again. By then I want you to have found Miles Devere for me."

He hung up before Lethe could get a word in.

It was an uneventful flight, both on the ground and in the air. A lot could happen in nine days it seemed, including people forgetting a face, or half-recognizing it and not being sure where from, even when it was a face they had seen day after day on the news reels and in the press. He wasn't a film star and he wasn't a pro ball player. What that meant was when they looked at him a few people did a weird sort of double-take, then shook their heads as though dismissing him. They had recognized him on some subliminal level, just like any other famous person, but they had filed him as just that, a famous person. Logic told them he had to be one, and who was he to argue with logic?

The fact of the matter was that the BKA were hardly about to announce to the world that they'd lost him. Airports, train stations and bus terminals would be swarming with agents on the ground looking for him—but they weren't looking for John Smith.

As it was, he landed in London refreshed from the flight and disembarked the plane. On the way along the metal passage back toward the gate, he asked one of the ground crew where the nearest pay phone was and made the call to Lethe.

"Welcome home, Koni," Lethe said, even before the phone had started to ring in his ear. "We were worried about you."

"Touching, I am sure. You have the address for me?"

"The old man told me to tell you he wants you here for a

debriefing first thing."

"Second thing. First thing I have a promise to keep."

"Whatever you say, man, I'm just passing on the message. Second thing it is."

"The address?"

"He's in England. He entered the country the day after the assassination."

"England isn't small. Where in England?"

"I just want you to appreciate my brilliance for a moment, Koni. I found him for you, just like you asked. But think about it, if I say he's in London, that means he's one of seven and a half million people spread over thirty-two different boroughs. That's a lot of people and a hell of a lot of streets. That's your needle in a haystack right there."

"Where is he?"

"Well, out of all those millions of buildings, I found the one he's in. That's how good I am at what I do, Koni. He has a place in the heart of London, Clippers Quay, off Taeping Street. You can take the DLR to Mudchute and walk from there in a couple of minutes. Most of the houses are built around the old Graving Dock. There are four apartments in the block. The penthouse is his. You can't miss it."

"A graving dock? Isn't that appropriate," Konstantin said.

"It doesn't mean they used to bury people there, Koni," Lethe said in his ear. The phone line started to beep, but he talked over them.

"Well it does now."

Konstantin hung up and went to keep a promise.

He left the train and walked quickly down the stairs that ran between the up and down escalator. He was the only person left on the train by the time it reached the Isle of Dogs. This part of the city was called Little Manhattan because of the mini-skyscrapers that had been built all along the riverside development of Canary Wharf. The Devere Holdings building was in there amid all of the merchant banks and import/export offices. Mudchute rather matched its name. Despite its nearness to the skyscrapers, it was like something out of the '50s and owed its curious name to the fact that when it was being built the country was suffering from football factories, and its hooligans were the fear of Europe; otherwise, it would have been called Millwall Park, after the football team.

He followed the road around. Twenty years ago this part of London would have been full of kids kicking tin cans and pretending to be Teddy Sheringham and Tony Cascarino. Tonight it was quiet.

There was more building going on on the other side of the tracks. The metal skeleton of the building was slowly being wrapped in bricks and mortar.

He didn't have a weapon. No doubt he could have climbed over the wall and dropped down onto the building site and found a decent sized rock. Or maybe a piece of steel pipe or rebar, a chisel, hammer or other tool. He decided against it, not for any ethical reasons—he had no problem with stealing from a construction site. No, he wanted to do this with his bare hands. He didn't want anything between him and Devere as he beat the life out of him.

Konstantin found the building. Lethe was right, he couldn't miss it. It was one of those carbuncles on the face of the city Prince Charles had been railing about for years while no one paid the slightest bit of notice to his royal raving.

He had lost his bump key when the BKA took him into custody, so getting past the security was going to be a little more complicated. He stepped back, standing just out of the puddle of light from the streetlight, and looked up at the facade. There was a fairly substantial drainage system on the outside of the house, with pipes running all the way down from the roof. He'd never understood why the British put their water pipes on the outside of their houses, when the cold came they were always going to crack, maybe not for ten years, but eventually they would. Freeze, thaw, and all of that. Pipes on the outside was asking for problems. Good metal pipes properly set into the mortar were asking for an entirely different set of problems.

Konstantin picked a path up to the first balcony. It was a long affair that actually ran around half of the frontage, then turned right to catch some of the lowering evening sun. The second story balcony repeated the pattern. It was the same for each of the four stories. The water pipes threaded through the narrowest of places, where the balconies didn't over lap. Once he got to the first one it would be relatively easy to climb to the next. Of course there was no guarantee that when he got there the balcony doors would be open—and if they weren't, hell would freeze over before Devere stopped playing Little Pig and let him in.

He could always try the buzzer trick again, but there were only three buzzers and no lights in any of the lower apartments. He didn't waste any more time. He shimmied up the drainpipe, scuffing his feet off the wall, and hooked his hand onto the first balcony so that he could pull himself up. Second to third was almost as easy. He stood on the balcony rail and reached up. The next level was six inches out of reach, so leaning out over the drop, he jumped.

Konstantin caught the concrete base of the balcony and hauled himself up as though he was doing chin-ups, then swung, hooking his leg up onto the balcony railing and climbed onto the third story balcony. He repeated the maneuver for the fourth story and stood there for a moment, looking in through the huge plate glass doors and dusting his hands off.

The television was on, casting shadow shapes across the contours of the lounge.

Miles Devere was slumped in a leather armchair. He had his eyes closed and rested in the posture of someone who'd slipped into sleep.

Konstantin wanted him awake for the fun.

He checked his watch. It wasn't quite midnight. There were chairs on the balcony, good cushioned chairs with high backs. Konstantin settled down into one of them. He was going to do this the Russian way. That meant coming late, four o'clock, coming in fast and hard and scaring the living crap out of Devere before he made him beg and plead and offer to pay anything, to give up his fortune, anything, and everything. Konstantin wasn't about to be bought. When Devere was through begging he would beat the man to death and leave him in his fancy skyscraper city apartment surrounded by all the fine things money could buy.

He had the patience of a saint when it came to keeping a promise.

He looked out over the river, watching the city at night. It was a curious beast. It never quietly slept. He couldn't understand the appeal of it. It was dirty, smelly, overcrowded, just like any other city in the world. He scanned the rooftops from The Tower to St. Paul's distinctive dome and over the rooftops to The London Eye and, almost on the edge of what could be seen, Big Ben. The night lights made it seem like a different place. Like a fairy tale city. They might soften the sharp edges of the architecture, but they couldn't hide the fact that right now murder was the only tale of the city worth telling.

He checked his watch again.

Two a.m.

Soon, he promised himself. The ambient light from the television went out.

Two hours passed slowly. Konstantin didn't mind. Some moments were worth savoring. This was one of them. The moon was full and bright.

He stood up and walked the length of the balcony, looking for a makeshift tool that would help him break the lock open if he needed it. Three out of ten burglaries in the city required no force at all because the occupants were too dumb to lock their own doors and windows, but Konstantin was working under the impression that Devere was security conscious. Rich men usually were—to the point of paranoia. Whatever he was, Devere wasn't a keen gardener. There was no ready supply of tools for turning the soil and planting bulbs in the window boxes.

He walked back slowly to the balcony doors. The basic locks that come with balcony doors are usually brittle and quite soft, meaning they will break under pressure. It didn't matter how tough the glass was if the lock was going to shatter under a decent amount of leverage. A broom handle was enough to break most of them, but thankfully, most of the people sleeping soundly out there under the soft lights in fairy tale city didn't know that. If they did, they wouldn't have been sleeping at all, never mind soundly.

The door was locked, but he couldn't see any additional locks or security—meaning Devere thought living four flights up made him safe. He wouldn't live to regret that mistake.

Konstantin found what he was looking for: a metal rod from the clothes hanger Devere used to dry his designer shirts.

He slipped it through the lock handle and applied a little pressure, testing it out. He felt the resistance, then pressed again, a little harder this time, working the lock. It split on the third try, with a crack like a gunshot.

He tossed the metal rod aside and slid the door open on its runner.

He went inside.

The apartment had that eerie four o'clock silence. He moved quickly through the place, walking from room to room. The decor was spartan, Scandinavian minimalist. It had absolutely no stamp of personality on it, and that wasn't just because of the dark. It wasn't actually that dark inside; the full moon painted everything silver.

Each white wall had a single piece of art on it. Konstantin couldn't tell if they were cheap prints or expensive originals. He wasn't much of an art lover. He recognized some pieces, especially by the old masters, but the new stuff, not so much. He liked his artists like he liked his enemies, dead.

Devere didn't look like a paranoid man. There were motion detectors in each room at strategic points, and the little red light blinked every time Konstantin moved, but no alarm sounded. Like most people, he obviously didn't set the alarm when he was in the apartment.

He found Devere's room.

He listened to the sleeping man's gentle snores through the door for a moment, checking his watch again. It was four o'clock sharp. It was time to raise some hell. Konstantin kicked the door open, yelling bloody murder as he charged into the room.

Miles Devere thrashed about in the starched white sheets of the bed. Brutally woken, he came up into the sitting position with his right hand across his heart.

Konstantin didn't give him a second to work out what was happening.

He flew at Devere, straight across the room and into his face like some sort of hellion out of his worst nightmare—and that was exactly what Devere would be thinking for those few seconds as the mad shrieking silhouette charged at him. He hit Devere once, a back-handed left across the side of his face, then grabbed his hair and dragged him out of the bed.

By then Devere had worked out what was happening.

It didn't help him.

Konstantin bundled Devere to the floor and laid into him with his booted feet, kicking him again and again until the naked man was crumpled up in a fetal ball trying to protect himself. He didn't say a word, he just stepped back, giving himself room to drive another kick into Devere's back.

He bent down and grabbed a handful of Devere's hair and dragged him through to the living room. Devere kicked, trying to get his feet under him, and grabbed and slapped at Konstantin's hand in between screams and howls of pain.

Konstantin threw him across the room and just stood there over him, watching Devere scramble around naked.

"I never break a promise," he said. "It is a Russian thing, all about honor."

"Please," Devere said, looking up and at the same time trying to draw his entire body in on itself to present the smallest target he could to the Russian.

"Please? Please what?" Konstantin mocked. "Please don't kill me?" Konstantin shook his head. "Not interested in that. Not interested in pleasing you at all. I was in Berlin. I saw what your money did. I saw them dragging the bodies out of the subway, all of those innocent people. Do you think they begged as they suffocated from the gas?"

"I didn't . . ." Devere pleaded.

"Yes you did. Have the balls to admit it. Maybe if you repent desperately enough in the next few minutes, God might forgive you, but I doubt it. I think there's a special place in hell reserved for scum like you."

"What do you want me to say?" Miles Devere looked pitiful, shivering, naked, clutching his legs under his chin, trying to hide his penis and his vulnerability, and utterly lacking any kind of spine or dignity. This was the real Devere stripped of all the power money could buy. This was the man stripped down to skin and bone and found wanting.

"I want you to do more than just 'say,' Miles. I want you to do what you do best. . . . I want you to buy me. I want you to buy your life from me."

Devere's eyes lit up, his face suddenly feral in the moonlight. "Name your price. Anything."

"Five thousand," Konstantin said. "No, make that ten. Ten thousand."

Devere almost laughed. "Ten thousand? Is that it? Not a million. Not a house in the Bahamas and a yacht? Ten thousand? Have you got no imagination?" Devere was in his element suddenly, bargaining, haggling, trying to fix a price, looking to capitalize on tragedy. "I can give you more. I can give you more than you can imagine. I can give you so much money it'll make your Russian dick hard just thinking about the numbers. Try again, name your price."

"Ten thousand," Konstantin said and sniffed. He started to undo the buttons of his shirt and peel it off.

Devere shook his head. "You don't get it. I can give you everything, all you want and more. Your wildest dreams. It's only money. I can always get more money."

Konstantin draped his shirt over the back of the leather armchair. "You haven't asked ten thousand what."

Devere shook his head, suddenly unsure as the ground shifted away beneath him. "Ten thousand what?" he asked, his voice quieter now, like he didn't want to hear the answer.

Konstantin kicked off his shoes one at a time.

"People. Ten thousand dead people. I want you to give them their lives back. You're to blame for their deaths—give them back their lives. You owe them. If you can't do that, then you've got nothing I am interested in."

Devere shook his head. "It's impossible. . . . You can't bring people back from the dead. You can't."

"Then I think our business here is done, don't you?" Konstantin asked.

"No. Please . . . please."

Konstantin didn't listen.

He undid his belt and stripped out of his trousers and boxers.

And naked he went to war.

He took his time, watching the clock slowly move around to five in the morning while he made Devere hurt. He beat him until he was bloody. He beat him until the flesh of his face caved in. He beat him until he couldn't breathe because his body was ruined. He beat him until he gave up begging and just wanted it over. He beat him until he was covered in his blood. Devere was right. No amount of beating would bring them back. No amount of pain could put right all of the hurt he had caused with his relentless pursuit of money. Konstantin didn't care. This was about making good on a promise.

He beat Miles Devere to death with his bare hands.

It was the Russian way. No distance between them. No advantage. It was man against man—naked, raw, like gladiators of old. He pretended it meant he had given Devere a chance. He hadn't. When he was done he went through to the bathroom and washed Devere's blood off his naked body, then dressed.

He left the apartment by the front door.

30

THE FORSAKEN

Noah was desperate. Time was merciless and Monsignor Gianni Abandonato was a ghost. The Vatican refused to open its doors to him. He had no legitimacy. That was the drawback of going off the books. When things were desperate, when the clock was ticking and all hell was waiting to break loose, there was no one he could turn to. Not that he was inclined to ask for help.

Noah was a lone wolf, an old-school warrior. Not one of those team players like Frost. He had spent his time as a professional soldier doing the job no one would officially admit existed but everyone knew did. Officially he had been classified as a marksman. That was a nice word for sniper, which in turn was a nice word for assassin. He killed people the government wanted dead. He didn't need to justify himself by saying he was only following orders. That might have been true, but Noah believed in what he did. He wondered how much pain the world would have been saved if he had been given bin Laden, back when he was called Usama, not Osama, and he wasn't the poster boy for global terrorism. Or Hussein. Of course it wasn't that simple.

Back then Usama had been our best friend against the bigger enemy, Russia. He'd been a rising star in the Mujahedeen, a local warlord who was making spectacular inroads against the Red Army. The West wanted Russia out of Afghanistan, and getting into bed with the likes of Usama was the cost of that. They called it The Greater Good. Noah believed in the Greater Good. The Greater Good would have been served if someone had fed bin Laden to his mountain goats tasty morsel by tasty morsel. The Greater Good would have been served by purging Iraq of the family Hussein after the first Gulf War when we started to hear the truth of his reign. The cold, hard truth was that the Greater Good was hardly ever served in the real world. People were too frightened, or their hands were too tied. That was where he had come in. That was where he still came in. He had a different uniform and didn't salute anymore, but the missions hadn't really changed all that much.

One bullet was all it would take, but to actually fire that bullet he had to find Abandonato.

Nine days ago, when he had walked out of the basilica of St. Peter's and gone looking for the priest, he had actually been worried for the man. His first thought was that he had been taken. That somehow one of Mabus' people had got to him while Noah chased his quarry in a merry dance across the streets of Rome all the way to suicide in St. Peter's.

It had taken him longer to realize the truth.

He should have worked it out sooner, but sometimes he wasn't the quickest thinker. It had never been a prerequisite for his chosen career. He did what he was told, which implied someone had to tell him what to do, and more often than not, what to think.

Then he started to think for himself. Nick Simmonds

couldn't have survived inside the Vatican alone. A simple volunteer wouldn't get access to the right parts of the archives and the right texts no matter how much help the holy librarians were in need of. There were too many secrets down there they wanted to protect. Abandonato had almost said as much. But like most people who didn't want to get caught into giving themselves away, he had checked himself. Simmonds would have needed someone to sign off on his assignments, someone to oversee his work.

There was no way a group of people so used to protecting some of the most precious and unique records of the written and printed word, the very thoughts of people thousands of years dead in some cases, would let just anyone get their hands on the irreplaceable texts and not make sure they were being treated carefully. The library was one thing, but the Vatican Archives? Noah hadn't seen them, but Neri had explained that some of texts were so frail they were stored in hermetically sealed chambers—low air content and pressure, moisture controlled environments. They weren't just books on a shelf, waiting to be piled into a box and stacked up in a corner while they waited for the refurbishments to be made.

That had set him to thinking even harder.

He had needed Neri to confirm his suspicions. Neri had checked with the head of the Vatican Police, but they both knew what the answers were going to be before it came back. Three questions, three answers: Abandonato hadn't returned to his apartment in nine days. He hadn't shown for work in the library since his meeting with Noah. And finally, Nick Simmonds' request to work in the library had been granted by Monsignor Gianni Abandonato.

They worked closely, mentor and student. He didn't know who had recruited whom, but during the course of that one morning Noah had spent in his company Abandonato had spoken enough heresy to last a good Catholic a lifetime.

He should have known. It was right there in front of him. The priest was too sympathetic. Sometimes guilt was as much about what someone didn't say as what they did. He tried to remember everything Abandonato had said, but couldn't. It had all blurred into one incoherent mess inside his head. There were lots of prophecies and lots of anti-christs, that seemed to be about the gist of it, and at least once a generation the world was supposed to be going to hell in a hand basket.

He had enlisted Neri's help again, trying to find the missing Monsignor the old fashioned way, on foot, knocking on doors. If he wasn't inside the Holy See, he had to be outside. But it was next to impossible. Rome was a big city, and it was filled with pilgrims in mourning, come to say farewell to Papa. Abandonato would have had to have been a six-foot-tall pink elephant in a tutu for people to notice him. A man in holy raiment was as good as invisible in Rome.

In return Noah gave Neri the photograph of the assass-ination Lethe had downloaded to his cell phone and told him to pass it on to the head of the Vatican's police force. There was a rat in the Swiss Guard, and his face was ringed in red so no one could mistake him. Neri trusted Noah. And Noah knew it. He might have seen the news footage everyone else had seen, but he was trained to see beyond the surface. He recognized the fact that the angles didn't allow for a single image of the dagger being driven home. So while everyone else was prepared to believe the evidence of their eyes, Neri was still willing to at least question.

Noah knew he had passed the photo on, but he had no idea whether the Gendarmerie ever acted on Neri's skepticism—if the walls of the Holy See were good at one thing, it was keeping secrets. It wasn't the *Gendarmerie's* job to provide protection for the Holy Father; that was the remit of the Swiss Guard. It was however very much in their remit to investigate criminal activity. He just had to trust that they would do their job, put aside their blind faith in the goodness of mankind and investigate. As long as they didn't the rat was free to wander the holy corridors.

Noah couldn't help but think it was a little bit like telling Adam there was a snake in Eden. He didn't know if it would change the final outcome, but he had to do it just the same. If they went and bit into the apple, at least he would know he had done his part.

Every day that nothing happened, the worse Noah feared what might happen the day something finally did. It was the basic rule of terrorism. He'd said it a hundred times: *you make a threat, you keep it*. The minute you broke those promises you diluted the fear every sub-sequent threat instilled in the public. It was like the boy who cried wolf, the boy who cried bomb. The suicides had promised forty days and forty nights of fear. They had all taken that to mean forty separate attacks across Europe, but after Berlin and Rome, then the murder of Peter II, what could they do? How could they escalate the horror? Because that was what terrorism was fundamentally about, escalating the horror. Blowing up an office block after something as insidious as poisoning the water of an entire city was de-escalation. It didn't work in the same way. It made the fear mundane.

Rome was actually breathing easy again, as though its time in the spotlight had passed. It had survived. There had been losses, horrible losses, but it had survived. Now it was another city's turn. They had suffered enough.

If he had been one of the unholy trinity—Mabus, Akim Caspi, or Miles Devere—he would have punished them for their presumption. He would have hit Rome again just to prove that no, they hadn't suffered enough. He would tell them when they had; they would not tell him.

Noah thought about the note he had found on the "suicide bomber": *We have tested your faith. Today we break it*. All of the messages had been enigmatic, laced with the vagueness of prophecy, but they had all come back to faith. The Church. The only two attacks to date, despite the promises of so much more, had come in Italy, home of the Catholic Church, and Germany, the country where the Pope happened to be on pilgrimage. The crowds outside St. Peter's were proof that killing one man would not break a world's faith. They had flocked to the square to show their love, and to show the terrorists their faith was not broken.

All of which meant something else was coming.

Something that would shake the very foundations of their unwavering faith.

Something that would make them all ask the same question their Messiah had: *My God, my God, why hast thou forsaken me?*

And Abandonato was the key.

That was the truth.

It had to be.

And he couldn't find the damned man anywhere.

Abandonato didn't want to die.

He didn't want to be a martyr to the truth.

At the outset he had believed fervently enough that he not only wanted to do it, he had volunteered to be the one to go out into the square and burn. But that had changed. It wasn't that he didn't believe anymore. It wasn't that he didn't question. Solomon had found him and bound him to his cause with the truth of the testimony. He had been the first to translate it. No one else knew what they had. The *Testimony of Menahem ben Jair*, grandson of Judas Iscariot, founder of the Sicarii assassins, the world's first fundamental terrorists. It was as close as anyone would ever get to a firsthand account of what happened in Gethsemane.

The Gospel of Matthew, written in Greek, not Hebrew or Aramaic, had to have been written after the fall of Jerusalem in AD70, possibly as late as AD100, and Mark, believed to be the oldest of the Gospels, also references the sacking of the Temple of Jerusalem, marking it as at least AD70; whereas Menahem's testimony of would have been written prior to the mass suicide of the Sicarii in AD73 and couldn't be any older. The Sicarii were at their height during the Jewish War, from the sacking of the Temple in AD70 to their suicide at Masada. That testimony was almost certainly Document Zero, the first account of the death of Judas. Unlike the Gospels, it showed a tragic hero, a man making the ultimate sacrifice. Of course the Gospels existed for a very different reason. They sought to deify the man Jesus, to prove him divine and elevate him above all others.

The Christ in ben Jair's testimony was far from divine. He was a man with all the flaws of a man. Ben Jair didn't claim that Judas was God's son, far from it. The Judas Iscariot in his story was another very normal man. The testimony spoke of love and friendship and of sacrifice. And it was Judas, ben Jair's grandfather, who had made the sacrifice, knowing what it would do to his family, but not really understanding how it would be warped and twisted through time. How could he have? How could ben Jair, really? They were living in that time. Reading it now, interpreting it, it was impossible not to read the document through the filter of our understanding, to apply our modern sensibilities to the reading.

The original Gospels didn't want any of that story. And not just because of its contradiction, but fundamentally to suggest Iscariot's death was murder over suicide would throw so much else into doubt. Judas would no longer be damned to eternity but elevated, and what of Matthew who had held the rope? Or Mark, Luke and the others who had cast the stones? What of their mortal souls if they went from enlightened beings carrying the teachings of Jesus Christ to the world and became murderers? What, then, was the truth of their ministry?

It undermined everything he had been taught to believe.

Solomon's words had been sympathetic. He had asked again and again what was the Messiah's destiny? Again and again, talking about the line of David and the reconstruction of Israel. It wasn't a message of war. It was all about peace. About a place in the world for people who had suffered for two and a half thousand years. And when he talked, he laid so much of that hardship at the door of Rome.

It was the Romans who had occupied his country for years, the Romans, who, following the bar Kokhba revolt, had killed more than half a million Jews, razed fifty fortified towns and nine hundred and eighty-five villages. It was slaughter, and all because Hadrian sought to root out Judaism; more atrocities in the name of religion. Hadrian prohibited the Torah, outlawed the Hebrew calendar, systematically hunted and killed Judaic scholars. And still he wasn't content. Hadrian sought to purge the name Judaea from public consciousness. His first step was to burn it off the map, naming the ancient country Syria Palaestina after the Philistines, the ancient enemy of the Jews. And since that time it had been known as Palestine, not Judaea, not Canaan, or Iudaea. It was the Romans who had created Palestine and took the holy city of Jerusalem away from them. Hadrian renamed it Aelia Capitolina and forbade Jews from entering it.

This was not a proud history.

How could he not be sympathetic to the horrors perpetrated against these people in their homeland? How could he not feel a historian's distant, diluted guilt? He would have to be a monster not to. In his head he heard the mocking cries and laughter of the Herodians and the Roman legionnaires calling Jesus King of the Jews.

It was a long time ago, he told himself, trying to make it less vile by adding the filter of time. It was difficult when

Rome itself was still full of reminders of Hadrian's rule, the Pantheon, even his mausoleum, Castel Sant'Angelo. His touch was everywhere in modern Rome.

Abandonato was a scholar.

He had dedicated his life to discovering the truth.

And then it had all started happening and the truth had stopped feeling so important. People started suffering. And it became real. It was different when it was academic, when it was conjecture, a puzzle, something to occupy his brain.

All of Solomon's talk of a messiah coalesced into murder on a grand and sickening scale.

He hadn't agreed to that. He hadn't sought to be a party to it.

And now all he could do was think, and all he could think was that some truths were better left hidden.

That was what he was supposed to do now. Remain hidden.

When Nick Simmonds had given him the small plastic sheath and bade him hide it amongst the coals in the fire grate of the Sistine Chapel two weeks ago he hadn't known what he was really being asked to do.

Now he did.

Now he understood.

He knew what he had to do, even if it meant surrendering his own life. It was a sacrifice he would have to make. He couldn't live, knowing more deaths were on his hands. He wasn't a murderer any more than the Apostles were. They had been saving their friends immortal soul. That was the only way the testimony of ben Jair made sense. They were angry, hurt, but they knew he could not live with his betrayal, and suicide would forever bar him from the kingdom of heaven. So they had saved him. Or so Abandonato believed.

But did Gianni Abandonato have it in him to save anyone?

He was a scholar. His world was paper. Words. Stories.

To step outside of that world would damn him as a

traitor, just as Judas himself had made the sacrifice that cast him forever as traitor. Abandonato had hidden that small plastic sheath in the fire pit, beneath the coals so no one would disturb it until they lit the coals. He hadn't known what was inside the sheath until the stories started to emerge from Berlin. Poison gas on the subway. He knew then what it was that he had hidden beneath the coals. And when the fire was lit to say the new Vicar of Christ had been chosen he would be responsible for the murder of the entire College.

He had been used.

He was a fool.

But stupidity was no excuse.

Abandonato knew himself.

He wouldn't be able to bear life if that fire was lit while the plastic sheath was still hidden inside it.

He was living—if it could be called living—in what had been Nick Simmonds' apartment down by the old ring of the Circus Maximus. That had always been the plan. It was a truth his masters had learned from years of fighting. The police didn't return to a place of interest once they had discounted it as abandoned. Simmonds' apartment offered him sanctuary. He had stocked up on bottled water and lived frugally without light or sound. He didn't want to reveal himself. It was ironic that he was hiding in the shadow of what had once been another Roman Emperor's playground. More than ironic, it was poetic, the scholar thought: of all the places in Rome, Circus Maximus was used to make decisions of life and death.

He knew what he had to do.

He couldn't stay hidden.

He had to get a message to the Cardinal Dean. They couldn't light the fire.

Noah Larkin begged Neri to get him inside. He had to

get inside the Vatican. That was all there was to it.

He was useless out here.

Nothing was going to happen in the square. That had been obvious from the start. It was always going to be inside the walls of the Holy See.

How did you break a man's faith?

You did something spectacular, that's how. You did something even God would take notice of.

"For all His omnipotence, what one place is God watching now?" Noah said, trying to reason with the man. "And even if God isn't, everyone else is?"

Neri looked at him. The grizzled Italian didn't like the way the conversation was going. "I don't know, you tell me."

He pointed right across the square from their table in the overpriced coffee shop at Maderno's facade. "The Vatican. Just like everyone else, God's looking at the chimney of the Sistine Chapel waiting for the white smoke to say His new best friend has been chosen."

"The Vatican is a fortress, my friend. There is no safer place on earth. No one is getting in, no one is getting out."

"That's called hubris, you know that? Forget the whole 'they aren't soldiers, they're following a divine calling' nonsense of the Swiss Guard. They're men! They aren't mythological heroes. They're fallible. End of discussion. One thing we've seen is, these guys we're up against are clever. They're patient, and they have pulled off the 'impossible' more than once in the last few days. They had already put the plan in motion to poison the water long before the first victim was found. So the Vatican's a fortress? So what? We don't know if they caught the real assassin, do we? We don't know if Abandonato's being sheltered by them. There's a snake in the garden, my friend—a bloody big one with poisonous fangs, just waiting to take a chunk out of some holy ass."

"I hear what you are saying, but the conclave is sealed.

No one can get in or out once it has begun. The doors were sealed at the end of the nine days of mourning. They will not be opened again until the bell rings and white smoke billows from the chimney. There's no way in and no way out. The chapel's even swept for bugs. This isn't the Middle Ages. The security is state of the art."

"This only reinforces my argument, Neri. There couldn't be a more shocking target, could there? Everyone thinks it is impenetrable. So what happens if it is penetrated? What happens in the worst case scenario? Can you imagine? Think like the other side for a minute. Does the difficulty outweigh the reward? If it does, it's got to be worth it, hasn't it? Hitting the Sistine Chapel during the election of the new Pope would send shockwaves around the world. You want to cause fear? This is how you cause fear! You want to break people's faith? This is how you do it! 'How could God let it happen?' You can hear all the questions can't you? You can see them in the square with their rosaries out, wailing and beseeching the heavens. With every Cardinal gone, hundreds of the most holy, the most faithful, wiped out.

"Let's extend the thought: What if it was never about the Pope as a person? What if it was always about the Pope as an office?"

Dominico Neri looked at Noah, hard. "Don't take this the wrong way, but we are way passed the point where I wished I'd never met you."

"You already said that. You know it makes sense."

"Unfortunately, it does. Not a good kind of sense, but sense."

"You have to get me inside that place."

"I can't. No one goes in or out during conclave."

"I don't give a crap about the rules, Neri. All I want to do is save lives. They can slap my hands about breaking the rules when they're all safe. Okay, I don't know the process. Tell me what's happening in there right now. Talk me through it. I need to get a handle on how Abandonato's going to do it."

Neri took his cigarette tin from his pocket and took his time fixing a smoke. He lit it and breathed deeply before he answered. "The College of the Cardinals is meeting inside the Sistine Chapel. It is one of the most isolated parts of the entire Vatican, one of the hardest to get to. And you can't get to it from the outside. You have to be inside the Holy See. Like I said, it is a fortress. The Cardinals will choose one of their number best suited to lead the Church into the future, and until they make their decision, the doors will stay locked."

"Right, that's pretty much what I thought," Noah said, following the thought to its natural conclusion. "So every Cardinal in the world is in that one room, yes? The holiest of the holy men all in the same place?"

The Roman sucked on his thin cigarette. "Not quite. The eldest, the cardinals over 80, lose their right to participate in conclave. Around 120 of the 186 Cardinals will be inside the chapel."

"Okay, so let's rephrase it, assuming the worst: the only ones left will either have Alzheimer's or one foot and a couple of toes in the grave. That's just about as bad."

"I don't like the way your mind works."

"Try living with it every day," Noah said. "You have to get me in there. You have to. Whatever it takes. If you have to beg your man, beg."

"He isn't my man, as you put it. There's no love between the *Corpo della Gendarmeria* and the Carabinieri. It's jurisdictional. It's like cats pissing on their territory. They don't want us in there. We've got no right to be there. And liaising to make it happen? It's a nightmare."

"You've got a badge, you've got a gun, get me in there."

"It really isn't that simple. This is Rome, my friend, home of bureaucracy. Take your worst nightmare, multiply it a thousandfold and you've got a jurisdictional fiasco.

Throw in God's faithful not wanting to admit crimes could actually happen on their patch and you've got the definition of a Vatican jurisdictional fiasco. It's always that one step beyond the usual pain in the ass. What can I say? Once you walk across that line into Vatican City, all logic goes out the window."

"I hear that's what happens when God gets involved," Noah said. "But there's a time for paperwork, Neri, and there's a time for a swift kick in the ass. We're well past filling in requisitions. I'll let you in on a little secret: sometimes it is a lot easier to beg forgiveness that it was to ask permission to do it in the first place."

Neri looked at him with that world-weary face that seemed to say, *Are you serious?* And when he realized he was, he went very quiet.

Noah could almost read his mind: *You get to go home tomorrow, I don't. All the crap we cause today is mine to swim in for the rest of my natural life.* That's what Noah would have been thinking if he was in his place.

Gianni Abandonato was desperate. He almost ran every third step he was hurrying so quickly. Traffic was not in his favor. There wasn't a cab to be found on the streets. He ended up running the entire length of Via Del Circo Massimo with his cassock lifted to his knees. There was nothing gracious or glorious about his race. He stared straight ahead, sweat streaming down his face as he ran. His breathing was out of control. He wasn't a fit man. He lived in the stacks. His exercise was lifting a book down, turning a page. By the time he hit the Ponte Palatino he was on his knees, gasping and panting and struggling to push himself back to his feet and keep running.

Fear drove him.

He could have phoned the Corpo della Gendarmeria offices, but what was he going to say? I have poisoned the entire College of Cardinals? You have to stop the conclave? You have to get them out of the chapel? They wouldn't believe him, and he wouldn't have been able to convince them over the phone. He needed to be there. He needed them to see his face. Then they would understand.

But they still wouldn't interrupt the conclave.

He was on a fool's mission.

He knew that, but knowing it didn't stop him from trying.

He had to. If not to save them, to save himself.

"Confiteor Deo omnipotenti et vobis," he mumbled, the prayer comfortable on his lips. *"Fratres, quia peccavi nimis, cogitatione, verbo, opere, et omissióne: mea culpa, mea culpa, mea maxima culpa. Ideo precor beatam Mariam semper Vírginem, omnes Angelos et Sanctos, et vos, fratres, orare pro me ad Dominum Deum nostrum."* I confess to almighty God, and to you, my brothers and sisters, that I have sinned through my own fault, in my thoughts and in my words, in what I have done, and in what I have failed to do; and ask blessed Mary, ever virgin, all the angels and saints, and you, my brothers and sisters, to pray for me to the Lord our God.

No confession would ever be enough if he couldn't stop them lighting the fire.

He couldn't think. Keeping his legs moving, staying on his feet, took all of his strength. By the time he reached Della Farnesina he was spent. Every new step came on trembling legs. His muscles burned. His lungs were on fire. He reached out to steady himself, stumbling against the walls of the houses set back off the street, and pushed himself on. And he was still so far from Bernini's piazza. He regretted running, but he couldn't stop. He knew what he must have looked like to passersby. He wasn't a hero running to save the day.

He stumbled on.

Dominico Neri walked up to the Swiss Guard's station and held out the badge that identified his as Carabinieri as though it would mysteriously lift the barrier for him. It didn't. The guard barely looked at it and shrugged as though to say, *So what? That doesn't impress me.*

There were four guards at the station.

None of them seemed particularly enamored with the combination of hot weather and their heavy uniforms.

It wasn't one of the main entrances. There was no point trying to get anywhere near the front of St. Peter's with the crowd. It would be a fight they wouldn't win. Neri wasn't big on fights he couldn't win. He led Noah to a side entrance. There was a sentry box, stern-faced boy-guards and a road beyond the barrier that opened up into a fore-court and beyond that splintered into a dozen paths between the cramped buildings.

"Get me the Inspector General," Neri demanded, staring straight at the youngest guard. It was simple bully-boy tactics and he knew it. But Noah was right; there was plenty of time to apologize later. Right now it was enough that the young guard snapped to attention.

"Your identification," one of the guards beside him demanded, a little older, a little less willing to be intim-idated. He didn't just want a little flash of the badge, he held out his hand. Neri handed over his ID. The guard looked pointedly at Noah.

"I don't have any," he said. "I'm still going inside though, so why don't you just open up the barrier and save us all a lot of wasted time and energy."

His almost flippant attitude didn't amuse the soldier.

The guard who had taken Neri's ID disappeared into the guardhouse. No doubt he was going to call the Carabinieri offices to confirm he was who he said he was, then call his superiors and ask for a reason to turn them away. A few minutes later he emerged with a wireless phone in his hand and an expression on his face that said, *You lose.* He handed the phone across to Neri and moved to block his way.

They weren't getting in, Neri knew, even as he raised the phone to his ear.

Before he could begin to argue their case with the policeman on the other end of the line, Noah ducked under the barrier and sprinted off across the forecourt.

One of the guards drew his pistol and started to aim it at Noah's back as though he intended to shoot him dead in his tracks.

"Don't you dare, soldier!" Neri barked, slapping the man's arm aside. "That man's with the British Secret Service!" He had no idea what effect his words would have.

What he didn't expect was for the youngest soldier to look at him and say, "Like James Bond 007 Licensed to Kill?" all in one rushed breath, as he took off after Noah Larkin as though someone had just lit a fire under his ass.

For a moment Neri thought he was trying to stop him, and then he realized the young soldier intended to help any way he could. He shook his head. Sometimes there was no accounting for the stupidity of youth.

Noah didn't know where he was going.

He just ran.

The place was a warren of little paths, overhung alleys and twisting side streets that wove a labyrinthine course through the chapels and apartments in this oddest of cities. He needed to get inside, which meant finding a door. As far as he was concerned any door would do. He knew it wasn't true, but he didn't know what else to do.

He tried to see over the rooftops to get a fix on the chimney above the Sistine Chapel and orientate himself. It was pointless.

He heard the heavy slap of running feet behind him and glanced over his shoulder. The young guard from the barrier was running with his Beretta held out in front of him as though it might bite. For a moment Noah thought he was going to try and stop him, and he started to turn back, figuring the soldier's training wouldn't be enough to stay his hand if it came down to shooting him in the back or letting him get away. Then the young soldier surprised him and shouted in terrible fractured English, "I help you, James Bond!"

It took Noah a moment to realize what the hell he meant, and that he wasn't about to get himself shot in the back. "The Sistine Chapel? Where is it?"

"I help you, James Bond!" the guard repeated. "Follow me!"

He didn't exactly have a lot of choice. He could have run around like a blind mouse in the maze for a month of Sundays without getting any closer to the chapel if he was left to his own devices.

Abandonato closed his eyes. His entire face was flushed, his hair was plastered down across his scalp. He was shaking. He was walking awkwardly, favoring his right side because a stitch burned there. He was panting.

The guard looked at him as he approached. He felt sure the guard was going to stop him, to challenge him to prove his right to be there. He had every right, of course, his apartment was beyond the wall. This was where he lived. There were only one hundred and ten guards sworn in the service of the Holy See. He knew them all by sight. Likewise they knew him by sight. If they were looking for him, now was when he would find out. They didn't stop him. The guard nodded slightly, then stepped back, allowing Abandonato through. It was ludicrously simple. Even after the assassination, they trusted the outfit. It was a costume, clothes, the familiarity of his face. He wanted to scream in the man's face. It didn't make him good! He might have had the olive-white complexion of the Mediterranean, but he was every bit as vile a terrorist as any Middle Eastern suicide bomber. The only difference was he was too much of a coward. His "bomb" was already in place, just waiting for the flame that would shrivel the plastic and release the toxic gas.

He shuffled along quickly, heading for the Sistine Chapel.

He didn't know how he was going to stop the conclave.

He hadn't thought that far ahead.

The washed-out colors of the murals and the corridors seemed so much more alive to Abandonato. It was almost as though knowing it was all going to end heightened his senses and made everything so much brighter and more vivid. He saw the paintings of Michelangelo's apprentices and Bernini's journeymen as though looking at them through new eyes. Every brush stroke was rendered exquisitely. He wanted to linger, to run his fingers over the colors as though he might soak up their brilliance and absorb it into his skin. But that was the Devil talking, trying to delay him while his evil work was done.

He cursed himself and hurried on, following the path his feet knew so well, praying the Lord still believed in him. Give me the strength, he thought, coming around the final corner.

He had made it. A surge of relief broke over him. He thought he was going to collapse under it. He stumbled into the antechamber. He was consumed by a single thought: get inside the chapel before they lit the coals.

Six guards stood at the door of the Pope Sixtus' chapel, the same six who had stood on the stage with Peter the Roman in Germany, the inner ring, the six most loyal. Five stared eyes front. The sixth looked at Abandonato as he buckled. For a moment he thought he was going collapse and go sprawling across the floor. He didn't. The only collapse was internal, hope caving in to despair. It is always the most loyal, Abandonato thought, locking eyes with the man whose silver blade had slain the Holy Father. That had always been the Sicarii way.

He was so close.

One door away.

But that door wasn't merely chained and guarded, it was chained and guarded by Peter's murderer, the last Sicarii assassin. The assassin had one final task: to see that the conclave's seal would not be broken until the new Vicar of Christ had been chosen—by which time the College of Cardinal's would be dead, murdered not by the assassin, but by Abandonato's hand.

He knew it was useless.

He knew he had failed.

Still he had to try.

"I have to speak with the Cardinal Dean," he demanded, breathless. There was no conviction behind his words, as though he expected to be denied. He barely had the air in his lungs to fuel the words. He was a broken man.

"The conclave is sealed, Monsignor," the assassin said. "It cannot be broken. That is the law of the conclave. What-ever your message, it must wait."

"No," Abandonato pleaded. "It cannot. I must speak with the Cardinal Dean." He stepped forward, reaching out to grab the guard's uniform and shake him to make him understand—but of course he understood. He had engi-neered it. The man was Solomon's left hand. Abandonato hesitated at the thought of "most loyal." It seemed foul when he applied it to the murderer's cause. The priest didn't even know what his real name was. He wasn't Swiss; his entire identity was a lie, though he did bare a passing resemblance to the young man whose life he had stolen. When the fire was lit he would leave the Holy See and return to his master, his job here done. Abandonato stopped himself from clutching the man's doublet. His hand just hung there between them, reaching out, while the guard stared at him. Abandonato could see the black hatred smoldering in his eyes.

"Control yourself, Monsignor. Conclave will not be broken."

"You don't understand," he said. "You have to open the doors. You have to let me in. Please," Abandonato begged. He didn't know what else to say. All the way here he had thought about nothing more than reaching the doors, as though God would see them break open before him, like the waves of the Red Sea for Moses. He hadn't expected the assassin to bar his way. He had thought he would simply throw himself on their mercy. He was so close. One door was all that stood between him and redemption. He couldn't bear it. He reached out for the chains, but two of the guards beside him closed ranks and took hold of his arms, restraining him physically. They weren't gentle. "There is a traitor," he said, barely able to say the words. "The conclave is breached. . . ."

"Impossible," the assassin said, reasonably. His black eyes burned into Abandonato. "We have been on duty since the doors were sealed. No one has entered. No one has left. That is the law of conclave. You are mistaken. There is no traitor here. If you insist on trying to force your way in to the chapel, we will have no choice but to think you are the one with treachery in your heart, and we would have to stop you. I take no pleasure in this, Monsignor, but the law is the law."

Abandonato felt every ounce of strength drain out of him. "Have mercy," he pleaded. But there was no mercy here, and no redemption. His sins would find him out.

The assassin stepped in close, his lips no more than a few inches away from Abandonato's ear and said, "Return to your chambers, Monsignor. Let God's will be done. I will come to look in on you when my duty is done. I will see you are taken care of. I understand your grief and pain, but you must abide by the will of Our Father, just as we all must."

Abandonato slumped.

"Go with God, Monsignor," the assassin said, and from his tone Abandonato knew he was mocking him.

He wanted to scream, but all he could do was turn his back. He wasn't a fighter. He didn't have a gun and even if he had, he would not have been able to wield it. Force went against everything he believed in. But there was so little left for him to believe. He wanted to believe he had been seduced, like Eve, tempted into the path of evil. He had chosen his path. He had set his foot on it. It was his choice. There was a serpent, but the choice was his. The Lord had given him free will and he used it to betray Him.

There was nothing Abandonato could do to force them to break the seal and pull back the chains. This was his punishment. He had brought death into the House of the Lord, and death would not be appeased by begging, prayers or guilt. Its hunger was rapacious. It would only be sated by the inevitable. More than one hundred souls would find the glory of God ahead of their time. *That is my doing*, he told himself.

The two guards who held his arms escorted him to the end of the passageway, then crossed their halberds across the entry, barring any possible return.

He looked at them each in turn. "You have to break the conclave," he pleaded. "They can't be allowed to vote. They will all die." He knew he sounded like a crazed man. He was desperate. That stripped him of his reason.

Their gazes didn't waver. It was as though he had already become a ghost.

Finally he had no choice but to walk away. There was no second way into the chamber. The assassin was right when he said it was a fortress. If he couldn't get past them, there was no way he could stop the vote. And if he couldn't stop the vote, he couldn't stop the fire.

He was damned.

He had failed the living.

He would inevitably fail the dead.

Names had power. He was named true. Gianni Abandonato, Gianni the Forsaken.

There would be no place at the Lord's side for him. Not with their blood still fresh on his hands. How apt that he had fallen for the silver tongue of Solomon and the so-called truth of Judas. He laughed bitterly. The sound chased him through the Holy See.

He knew then how Iscariot must have felt, trapped into the only possible course of action left to him at the end.

Abandonato shuffled through the corridors, lost in grief, his head down, hands clutched together in prayer, but those prayers failed to reach his lips. He resolved to kill himself, not that his one death would sate the beast he had loosed within the Holy See.

"Father, forgive me," he said, doubting that even the Almighty's capacity for forgiveness could be so vast as to accommodate his crime.

And then someone shouted his name.

He looked up.

Noah couldn't believe his eyes.

It took him a moment and a double-take to recognize that the man shuffling quickly towards them down the narrow passage was Gianni Abandonato. He had walked out of one of the smaller passageways that fed into this one. Abandonato had his head down, his fingers laced in front of him as though in prayer, but when Noah called out his name his head snapped up and he stopped dead in his tracks. There was no mistaking the man.

"Abandonato!" His voice swelled to fill the hand-painted chamber. The Monsignor looked like a startled rabbit, trapped, and he backed up a step. Noah saw the sweat, the nervous twitches, the almost robotic walk—they were all classic signs of a suicide bomber. He had a split second to think. His hands were hidden in his cassock. They could be holding a detonator; they could be empty. He didn't have the luxury of being able to make a mistake.

Abandonato's robes were bulky enough to hide a vest under. A bomb didn't have to be a complex thing. If he got into the chapel, even the least sophisticated ball bearings and nails sewn into a stockade of dynamite would take out everyone in the blast radius. And it would be messy. There was no way for Noah to tell whether the priest was wired to blow. He was walking unevenly. He seemed to be favoring one side, his right over his left. That could mean he was packing something heavy, something that changed his walk. He had a split second to weigh it all up.

"On your knees! Now!" he yelled. When Abandonato didn't go down, he didn't yell again. He couldn't risk what would happen if he insisted on taking the martyr's way out.

Abandonato seemed trapped in indecision for a moment, then turned and bolted.

That one desperate action told Noah all he needed to know.

He drew and fired in a single smooth motion.

Beside him, the man who wanted to be best friends with James Bond put three shots into the Monsignor as his body jerked and jived and fell. He put another one in him as he hit the floor. Abandonato twitched once, a violent spasm, then lay utterly still.

Noah approached the body cautiously, his gun aimed at the man. Anything, the slightest movement, and he would put another bullet into him. Noah felt the adrenalin flood his system. That was always the way, the sudden kick, too late to do any good, the rush of the chemical in his blood. He felt good. He'd done his job. He'd succeeded where Konstantin had failed. He'd saved the Cardinals. He knew then and there he was going to gloat. Just once. Just to see the Russian's face. He smiled to himself, imagining the look his wisecrack would earn him. He had the entire journey from Rome back to Nonesuch to come up with a killer line.

He stood over Abandonato and looked down at him. The priest wasn't quite gone. He held on for dear life. Noah crouched down beside him, pulling his hands out from the folds of his cassock. There was no detonator. The holy man's last breaths made a curious whistling noise as they leaked between his teeth.

Abandonato was trying to say something.

"No last rites, Father," Noah said, kneeling down beside him. "It's too late for that. You're going to hell."

"Please," Abandonato managed. It was barely a breath. Noah leaned in closer until he could feel the dying breath on his cheek. Words came out with it like ghosts. "Fire."

"That's right, pal. That's where you're going. You're going to burn in hellfire."

Abandonato didn't hear him.

He was already dead.

Noah checked for a pulse at his throat. Barring resurrection, Abandonato wasn't getting up again.

He didn't close his eyes.

He patted the dead man down. He wasn't wearing a bomb belt or anything else. He checked his pockets. There was no detonator. If he was a suicide bomber, he wasn't a particularly good one. He'd only managed fifty percent of the job.

Noah pushed himself back up to his feet.

"You better get someone to clean this mess up," he told the young soldier beside him.

He had done it.

Had he been a religious man, he would have given thanks to God.

He wasn't.

Instead he took the cell phone from his pocket and dialed home. "It's over," he told Lethe. "The priest's dead. I got to him before he could finish it."

"Then I'd say today's a good day, wouldn't you?" Lethe said.

"One of the better ones," he agreed. "Sometimes it's nice to be on the side of the angels."

"Amen to that, brother man, time to come on home."

Noah hung up the phone.

"Humor me," he said to the soldier. "I want to go check out the chapel, make sure everything is okay. You stay here. If that guy moves, shoot him again."

The young guard nodded earnestly.

Noah followed the passageway all the way to the doors of the Sistine Chapel. There were only five guards standing sentry. One of the guards came toward him. He recognized the man vaguely, but horribly, he had already begun to think that one joker looked pretty much the same as the other.

He saw the ceremonial chain looped through the silver door handles. From where he was he couldn't see whether the seal had been broken.

"Has anyone entered the chapel since the conclave began?" Noah asked.

"No one is permitted to break the conclave, sir," the guard said, his English slightly accented. The man's smile was just as slight.

"I know. But just because no one is allowed to go in doesn't mean no one has gone in. I mean, I'm not allowed to be here, and here I am," Noah said.

"The seal has not been broken, sir."

It wasn't until he was on the steps of St. Peter's and walking down in the piazza that it hit him: the priest was coming the wrong way. He wasn't going to the chapel at all. He couldn't have been. He had to have been coming back from it. Otherwise Noah would have come up behind him. There was only one way in and one way out of the Sistine Chapel.

He had checked Abandonato's corpse. He had been clean. No bomb. No detonator. No gun. Nothing.

It didn't make sense.

The guard had sworn no one had been inside the chapel after it had been sealed. Neri had assured him about all of the security measures the Vatican Police took before the Cardinals were locked away, sweeping for bugs and other devices. The place was a fortress. People had been telling him that all day. There was only one way in and one way out, and that was through the guards. The place couldn't have been much safer if it was lined with lead and buried sixty feet under.

He twisted around to look back at the Basilica.

Black smoke billowed out of the chimney.

All around him disappointment murmured through the faithful.

There wouldn't be a new Pope today.

And Noah relaxed because the smoke meant they were safe.

Behind him news crews began reporting the black smoke to the waiting world. The message was clear. The Cardinals had failed to reach agreement. There would be another election in three days.

Until then the faithful would be without a spiritual leader.

He walked away through the crowds.

All he wanted to do now was go home. He didn't feel like being alone. He never felt like being alone. He didn't like the dark hours. He didn't like the silence. That was the dark country where his ghosts lived. That was why he drank. That was why he paid women to share his bed. He would face his dead when he joined them down in the fiery pits of hell. Until then he wanted to hear breathing beside him, as if the shallow rise and fall of someone else's chest could stop the dead from finding him.

Blessed is the silence.

Noah was with Neri in the same café, drinking the same thick, strong coffees when the TV feed switched from the news anchor to one of the many on-the-spot reporters covering the conclave. Their conversation veered from Juventus to supermodels and fast cars. It was the easy chat of two men whose friendship had been forged in hell and had come out on the other side of the pit together. He checked his watch. He had four hours until Sir Charles' G5 would be ready for takeoff, which meant plenty of time to look at the stunning beauty of the city or the stunning beauties of the city as they walked by. He opted for the less energetic option. There really was something about the twenty-something Roman women he watched laughing and joking and utterly self-absorbed as only twenty-somethings can be. It was as if the world around them didn't exist. He appreciated the view. "Very easy on the eye," he said to Neri.

"This is Rome, my friend," Dominico Neri agreed. "Even the buildings have the good grace to look hot."

Noah grinned. "I need to come back one day when there isn't a crisis, take some time to appreciate the natural beauty of the city on the seven hills."

"There is a couch with your name on it."

There was the flicker of movement on the screen over Neri's shoulder. It caught Noah's eye. The face on the screen held it. It was Akim Caspi. Solomon. He was holding an RTL microphone and talking.

"Turn it up!" Noah shouted, dragging his chair back from the table and standing up.

Neri turned around trying to see what Noah was shouting about.

"Carabinieri! Turn the damned TV up!" Noah yelled at the barista behind the counter. She didn't seem to know what to do. "Just give me the bloody remote!"

Noah dodged between the tables to stand beneath the television set. He could barely hear Solomon's speech. He would hear it again and again over the coming days, but at that moment it was barely a whisper until the barista found the volume.

Neri came up beside him.

"You don't know my name," Solomon said to him through the TV speaker, "but you will. It will be on your lips every day now for the rest of your lives. I will tell you this, your church is built on lies and death. Its very foundation is not the rock of Peter; it is the glorification of a false messiah. Today I bring the death back to the door of Rome. For five hundred years Rome tortured my people. For five centuries and more it turned them into slaves. It drove them out of their own homeland. It tried to purge the name of them and their home from the earth, so deep and unreasoning was its hatred. Today that changes. It was my blade that killed Peter Romanus. That blade forged from the silver pieces of Judas Iscariot. The coins that bought the death of your Messiah spend just as well today. They have bought another death—this time the Roman Pontiff— and with his death the world is ready for the new Messiah." He stared out through the screen. His beautiful face was made for Hollywood.

Behind him the picture broke into a grainy image from a pinhole spy camera hidden within the Sistine Chapel.

It took Noah a moment to realize what he was seeing.

The Cardinals were dead.

Some had died on their knees in prayer, staring down into the pits of hell itself. Others on their backs, staring blindly up at the beauty of Michelangelo's ceiling, out of reach like heaven itself.

Solomon's face came back onto the screen.

"I am Solomon. Remember my name."

Then he was gone, and the camera was focused on

Maderno's facade. A moment later the live feed broke and the grainy image of the dead in the chapel returned to fill the television screen.

Noah pushed out through the glass doors of the café into the rising heat of the afternoon. There were thousands of people still packed into the square. He could see the RTL mobile broadcast trailer. He started pushing through the people to get to it.

But by the time he reached it Solomon was long gone.

Noah slammed his fist off the side of the trailer.

He had been there.

He had stood right in the middle of them and as good as said your God is dead.

He opened the trailer door and climbed up and inside.

The female anchor lay dead and bloody in one of the chairs, her cameraman lifeless on the floor at her feet. The screens all showed the grainy live feed from inside the chapel itself. He had no idea how to kill the transmission, so he went down the banks of switches and dials, tripping them all until the picture died.

Neri came into the trailer behind him.

He looked like a living dead man. He was talking into his cell phone in rapid Italian, shaking his head and gesticulating.

Noah wasn't listening to him.

He had found the gift Solomon had left for him.

The woman clutched a battered leather drawstring purse in her hands. Noah pried it from her lifeless fingers and emptied it out. Thirty pieces of silver spilled out across the bank of displays. There was a note. He unfolded it. The message was written in blood.

All debts paid in full.

"Not even close," Noah said.

The truth of just how badly he had failed was only beginning to sink in.

Beside him, Dominico Neri made the sign of the cross.

Steven Savile's Ogmios Team will return in 2011 with

GOLD

From Variance Publishing

AUTHOR'S NOTE

Silver is a work of fiction, which, by necessity, means I have taken liberties with the facts to suit the purpose of my story—that is, to entertain, to thrill, to shock, to scare, to keep you turning pages, in other words; and every now and then, to make you think. However, where possible, I haven't told any "lies." Even so, where I have taken liberties, like the very best of lies, I have done everything I could to keep the story's basis in what could well be the "truth." Or, at the very least, aspects of it. That's not to say that Menahem and Eleazar did inherit the thirty pieces of silver, nor to suggest that in the final days of Masada that they forged them into a silver dagger and hid it away. That's a bit of creative license. The truth is that there are many conflicting explanations of what happened to those Tyrian shekels. But the one enduring impression is that, try as he might, Judas Iscariot could not rid himself of the damned things.

That set me to thinking.

This is how I work. Something gets under my skin and won't leave me alone. Right around the same time as this started niggling at me, I read The Gospel of Judas, published by The National Geographic Society, and was, like a lot of the rest of the world, fascinated by the idea that the Great Betrayal could, in fact, have been the Ultimate Sacrifice.

I knew immediately that I wanted to tell the story from the other side.

Actually we need to go back a little further in time. It was the middle of the night, 3 or 4 am, September 1996, Counting Crows' August and Everything After was on the CD player, and the yellow-faced Simpsons were flickering away on the small portable TV in the corner. I lay on a bed in a seedy student apartment in Newcastle (just around the corner from the place Ronan breaks into in the opening chapters, actually) with my then two best friends, Gary and Dene, when Gary flicked through the channels on the TV, bored, and stumbled across Henry Lincoln telling his fabulous story about Rennes-le-Château and Bérenger Saunière (check out Holy Blood, Holy Grail by Baigent, Lincoln and Leigh if you haven't already). I was hooked. I kept thinking 'this would make an awesome novel,' but I knew I was a long way from accomplished enough to tackle something like that, so I filed it away, always intending to come back to it.

Move on the best part of a decade . . . move from the seedy apartment in Newcastle to a baking beach in Egypt . . . and dripping with sweat, I am finishing the last few pages of Angels and Demons by Dan Brown, and instead of closing the book on the final scene, I skimmed the ads in the back (don't tell me I am the only one who does this, I won't believe you) and saw the write up for his next novel, The Da Vinci Code, which, while being nothing like the story I had spent ten years imagining (being as I wanted to do it as an historical, from the perspective of the Templar Knights guarding the road to Jerusalem and holing themselves up in the temple before emerging with both mother and child they must smuggle out of the Holy Land), pretty much killed the idea stone dead. My wife tells me I actually threw my paperback into the sea. I do admit to feeling a huge amount of frustration. And of course, The Da Vinci Code had been out for several years by this point, but somehow I had managed to avoid hearing what it was all about.

Apparently I am very good at avoiding spoilers.

So, flash forward to London as 2005 became 2006 . . . I walked into Waterstones on Oxford Street, determined to find research material to write a thriller about Antarctica being the foundation for the lost civilization of Atlantis, and found hundreds upon hundreds of copies of Stel Pavlou's Decipher everywhere. A quick glance at the back and my heart sank. Yet again, a great idea torpedoed by arriving late to the party. I think this is every writer's nightmare. We could literally stop ourselves from writing a word if we discounted every idea that has been done before. On the shelf beside Decipher, however, was the very striking hardcover of the Gospel of Judas. I bought both books and had finished the Gospel before I went to bed that night. The beginnings of Silver were with me when I awoke the next day.

I didn't talk about it with anyone, but decided I needed to do some research. Like most people, I had a passing familiarity with the biblical Gospels, and thanks to the millennial fear that had gripped the world around 1999, was au fait with a lot of end-of-the-world prophecies, the Gnostic gospels, the Dead Sea

Scrolls and such.

Having decided I wanted to tell the story of Judas in some way, my mind went back to the shekels. It was a short step from 'he can't get rid of them' to turning them into a cursed inheritance his children couldn't get rid of, but I am getting ahead of myself here. One of my very first research days was spent looking at the name Iscariot and its etymology. It was one of those days when, as a writer, you start to think not only does your story make sense, you've stumbled onto the truth . . .

The most likely explanation derives from the Hebrew איש-קריות (Îš-Qrîyôth) or 'Man of Kerioth,' Kerioth being the name of not one, but two Judean towns.

The second theory, and the one that I chose to exploit in Silver, is that Iscariot identifies Judas as descending from the line of Sicarii assassins, who were almost certainly the world's first terrorist group. Historians argue that the Sicarii did not come into being until the fifth or sixth decades of the first century, which would mean Judas himself could not have been a member. . . but this is where fiction and reality blur so well.

Very few reliable histories exist from the day, obviously, but a lot of what we take as truth comes from the writings of Jospehus, i.e., The Jewish War and Antiquities of the Jews. The Jewish War is an account of the Jewish revolt against Rome (AD 66-70), and whilst reading this, I came across one reference to Menahem ben Jair, the grandson of Judas Iscariot. Until that point I had never considered the idea that Judas would have had children. It was as alien a concept as the idea that Jesus' bloodline might have been smuggled out of the Holy Land. Menahem, grandson of Judas, leader of the Sicarii assassins.

Suddenly things began to formulate, threads of a story pulled together, and the idea of the cursed coins becoming a 'family inheritance' was born. But of course, with the revelations of the Gospel of Judas fresh in my mind, how cursed would these coins truly have been? Wouldn't they have been more like a treasured reminder of just how much their grandfather had sacrificed? And how better to remember that sacrifice and honor the man 'of the sicarii' than to forge them into a silver dagger?

Of course silver makes a very impractical weapon because it

is so soft, but as a ceremonial piece it makes perfect sense.

The next moment of synchronicity came in discovering that there had been an earthquake in the Masada region a few years earlier, and with that I knew not only how I would lose the dagger for two thousand years, but how I would recover it.

It was one of those beautiful moments where research gives us an answer every bit as good as any our creative subconscious could dream up. Give me a truth to lay down as a foundation for the building blocks of story every day of the week.

But, of course, *Silver* as a novel demands many more foundations.

Another moment of wonderful synchronicity came about on the 24th of February 2009, right in the heart of the writing. The green comet, Lulin, an astrological phenomenon that many had taken to calling Nostradamus' comet, blazed across the night sky. Actually, it was a wonderful collision of The Book of Revelation and just about every end-of-the-world prophecy out there. The Four Horsemen of the Apocalypse are traditionally said to be riding a white horse, a red, a black and a pale horse. Now, considering white has already been taken by the first horse, the Fourth Horseman's (Death) mount is written χλωρός (khlôros) in the original Koine Greek, which translates as pale, ashen, pale green or yellowish green. The color is indicative of a corpse's pallor. Now, given the biblical links of astrological phenomena (the Wise men's star, for instance), it is unsurprising that many consider the Four Horsemen to actually be astrological events; so, a green comet, like Lulin, could be interpreted as Death riding straight out of Revelation upon his pale horse.

That they were calling it Nostradamus' comet dove-tailed beautifully with another dimension of the story I was developing—the idea of the Thirteen Martyrs that opens the book. Michel de Nostradame's prophecies provided the basis for two important factions in Silver: Mabus and Ogmios. Nostradamus' Mabus is the herald of the antichrist who must die for the Third Antichrist to rise.

Mythologically, Ogmios was a deity frequently depicted as a bald old man leading a band of prisoners with chains running from his tongue to their ears. The Gauls associated him with Hercules, whereas the Eastern Celtic tradition tied him to Hermes. The Irish equivalent would be the Dagda, brother of

Ogma. Unlike Hercules, the chain linking the followers to the silver-tongued deity suggests a certain gift of gab, or as his Irish heritage would suggest, blarney. Ogmios appears in the quatrains of Nostradamus, although not once is it spelled with an s. Instead it always appears with an n—Ogmion or l'ogmion. In The Centuries, Ogmios counters the Antichrist, as it is prophesied that he is the only one who can stand in his way. So it seemed fitting that Sir Charles' band of brothers take their name from him.

Of course, having inverted the story once by taking direction from the Gospel of Judas, it seemed just as fitting to invert it again, and instead of looking for a 'Third Antichrist' I turned to the meaning of the word messiah. I wasn't surprised to learn that different faiths had different definitions and made different demands upon their messiah, or more accurately, messiahs. I was most taken with the Judaic definition—one who is anointed. Considering it was the Jewish faith that invented the term, I thought it fascinating that the Jewish meaning had become all but lost outside of their faith; but in story terms, it offered a wonderful avenue of exploration. Obviously the main aspects of the definition have been covered by The Disciples of Judas in the story, but it is worth mentioning them again here, as well as aspects I didn't bring up. According to Rabbinical Law, the Messiah is born of two human parents, is able to trace his lineage through his father—back to King David—through the line of King Solomon and not through the lines of Jehoiakim, Jeconiah, or Shealtiel, because this particular royal line was cursed.

These are four major reasons that the Jewish faith doesn't view Jesus as the real Messiah. Indeed, according to the Jewish definition of the term, the real Messiah will make substantive and quantifiable changes in the real world, including re-establishing the Davidic dynasty through his own children; bringing an eternal peace between all nations, between all peoples, and people; bringing about the universal conversion of all peoples to Judaism, or at least to Ethical Monotheism; gathering to Israel, all of the Twelve Tribes; rebuilding The Temple; restoring each tribe of Israel to their lands of inheritance; and causing the nations of the earth to recognize that they have been wrong, that the Jews have been right, and that the sins of the Gentile nations—their persecutions and the murders they committed—have been borne by the Jewish people.

Together, these become the backbone of the beliefs of the Disciples of Judas in the book, and in a world where fear has become a commonplace negotiating tool (this isn't new; think of the Templars, Holy Crusades and other attempts to influence faith with force), it made sense to turn my disciples militant.

During the course of researching Silver I came across over 250 End of Days prophecies ranging over 2000 years. Every one of the prophecies Abandonato cites Noah during his visit to the Vatican library is genuine. As a species, we've been obsessed with predicting the end of the line and, more often than not, these prophecies have been linked to 'portentous' dates, say, for instance, the end of a century, the turning of a millennium, the devil's number, and so on. It's fascinating, really.

But, back to Nostradamus and prophecies for a moment . . . Mabus the herald. I came across hundreds of intriguing discussions as to the nature of Mabus, from it being Sadam in mirror writing (misspelling aside, as Nostradmus had a habit of misspelling those he was predicting, like Hister); the Obama-Bush transition period (which mated wonderfully with the Lulin comet, for instance); Mahmoud Abbas, the Palestinian leader; and so on and so forth. Like Archduke Ferdinand, Mabus, according to Nostradmus, is only important because he dies. Ferdinand's assassination started World War I and paved the way for the rise of the Second Antichrist, Adolf Hitler.

The death of Mabus precipitates the End of Days. An event such as the assassination of Abbas would make a lot of sense, given that the ramifications of such an act would almost certainly provoke vengeance, but again, from a writer's perspective, I was looking to tell a different story—one that linked back in with the notion of the Messiah, not the Antichrist. Rather than a political figure, it had to be a spiritual one, and of course, Nostradamus had also predicted the assassination of the Pope. Quite independently, we have the Prophecy of the Popes, attributed to Saint Malachy, which details, supposedly, every Pope from first to last. And as of writing, it appears that we have reached the penultimate name on that list—Gloria olivae—the Glory of the Olive, Joseph

Cardinal Ratzinger.

The last name on that list is Petrus Romanus, whose death will lead us into the Time of Tribulation.

"In persecutione extrema S.R.E. sedebit.
Petrus Romanus, qui pascet oves in multis tribulationibus:
quibus transactis civitas septicollis diruetur,
et Iudex tremendus iudicabit populum suum.
Finis."

"During the final persecution of the Holy Roman Church, the seat will be occupied by
Peter the Roman, who will feed his sheep in many tribulations:
and when these things are finished, the seven-hilled city will be destroyed,
and the formidable Judge will judge his people.
The End."

Like the term messiah, it is possible to interpret the Tribulation not as the End of Days, but rather, in a Judaic manner, going all the way back to the fall of Masada beginning in the 70s AD and continuing for centuries, covering the same time span, as "the times of the Gentiles" during which "Jerusalem shall be trodden down by the Gentiles" (Luke 21:24). By choosing this interpretation instead of the notion of Armageddon, trumpets, seals and the end of the world, we encompass not only the death of a million Jews at the hands of Roman legions, but also the death of six million Jews in the Holocaust.

The seven-hilled city, founded by Romulus and Remus of legend, is of course, Rome.

So, according to the Prophecy of the Popes, Rome will fall with the death of Peter Romanus, the next and final Pope. According to the Jewish definition of the real Messiah, we will see monotheism, which would explain no more Popes in Saint Malachy's prophecy. According to Nostradamus, we're destined for a 27-year war precipitated by the pale rider in the sky, quite possibly Lulin the green comet, as well as, of course, the assassination of Peter Romanus in the city where two rivers water (traditionally this would have been the Tigris and Euphrates, but for the demands of my story I was drawn to Germany, again for its links to another of Nostradamus' Antichrist prophecies).

Even if you didn't choose Lulin as your pale rider, you could just as easily go back to the Space Shuttle Columbia disaster which left a trail of 'fire and sparks' much like a comet in 2003, the same year as the Iraq invasion. That's the joy of prophecy, the more you want it, the easier it is to find what you are looking for—or at least to force your own interpretations onto it and make world events conform to what you need. It's a writer's dream, really. That interpretation could potentially make Nostradamus' 27-year war the War on Terror, for instance. But, again, that's not the only interpretation out there.

Another of Nostradamus' comets was the McNaught Comet of 2007, which reached perihelion (it's brightest phase) during the same period of days that one Senator Barack Hussein Obama announced his candidacy as President of the United States. Given the Obama-Bush transition theory and the fact that a little literary symmetry (taking the first letter of Barack, the second and third letters of Hussein and the fourth and fifth letters of Obama) provides us with an anagram of, yes, you guessed it, Mabus, it all becomes wonderful grist to the writer's mill. Even tonight, as of writing, the news channels are filled with film of a spiral phenomenon in the sky above Norway on the eve of President Obama's visit to Oslo to collect his Nobel Peace Prize. The spiral has been explained away as the halo of missile fuel, the result of a failed Bulava missile test in the White Sea.

If you ask me, it's no surprise that the Disciples of Judas chose now to reveal themselves.

You can almost hear the sound of trumpets, can't you?

Steven Savile
Stockholm
December 10th 2009